WINDS
OF
REDEMPTION

WINDS
OF
REDEMPTION

HARVEY GOODMAN

JUPITER SKY PUBLISHING
WESTCLIFFE

Jupiter Sky Publishing, LLC
2689 County Road 318
Suite 100
Westcliffe, Colorado, 81252

ISBN - 978-1-617507-29-8
ISBN - 1-617507-29-8
LCCN - 2009939650

Cover Photo by Harvey Goodman and Sean Goodman

To our United States Military and all
who have ever served in defense of life and liberty.
Home of the free because of the brave

1

At the edge of town, Lucius Hammond slowed his horse to a walk and felt his adrenaline begin to rise. Even in the cool of the early evening, he felt the heat swell on his neck and spread up around his ears, involuntarily signaling like a hammer that the time had come. He was here to kill a man.

His horse walked easy, but with each step of its left hind leg, his saddle creaked like a rhythmic dirge, portending in Lucius's mind the possible coming doom, though not casting heavily enough to shake his confidence to a change of heart. Why should it. He was Lucius Hammond, and the money was too good. Still, the feeling of momentary doubt was something new and unexpected, and blew through him like a cold wind across an empty plain. He pulled his hat lower and remembered his skills; his blazing speed on the draw and the number of men he had killed without so much as a scratch. This time would be no different.

Lucius had scoffed at his employer's suggestion that he simply bushwhack the man. Raised in the South, such a thought was repulsive to his sense of honor, even if he was nothing more than a hired killer. Face to face was the only way he'd ever taken someone's life, and Lucius thought of any other fashion as cowardly. His employer had agreed to Lucius's plan, knowing that suspicion and questions would be infinitely greater with a bushwhacking than a public showdown that appeared to be a spontaneous fight. But if something went wrong and Lucius was jailed, there was always the chance that Lucius would talk. His employer had a plan for that, too.

The night sky was choked with stars that sparkled above the Palace Hotel. Lucius passed and turned up the main street of Dumas, a small town that sat in the high country of northern New Mexico Territory. Several towering cottonwoods loomed on either side of the street, their branches clustered with unfurling leaves of the spring bloom. A stagecoach with a team of four horses stood idle in front of the territorial bank, its outboard lanterns dimly illuminating two men with shotguns that sat on the driver's bench. No passengers were present, but another man with a shotgun stood guard at the door to the bank, which was slightly ajar and casting a wedge of light across the boardwalk. The men atop the stage looked at Lucius as he rode by, offering nothing more than hard stares in the darkness. Lucius kept his gaze forward. He didn't care to draw any appraisal or speculation beyond being a plain man riding up Main Street on a Saturday night. Even his clothes were modest. He looked like any commoner or laborer, which was just what he wanted.

The sounds of the tin-pan piano and female singing drifted on the night air as Lucius continued up the street toward the Little Bear Saloon. As he reined up in front, the sour notes of both the piano and the singer became more evident, momentarily taking his mind back to his home in Alabama where, as a child, he had regularly witnessed and marveled in the angelic vocal perfection of the Foothills Baptist Church choir. But that memory quickly vanished and was replaced by the scars of the Civil War, now seven years gone. It had left a swath of destruction that had taken his loved ones and his soul.

He'd marched off naively and romantically like all the others, defending his homeland with a sense of honor and bravado that was to be scorched to ashes with the ensuing slaughter of all that he'd known. The final battle at Selma just weeks before the war's end had produced another twenty-five hundred Confederate casualties as a last statement to the futility of the cause. Lucius had been one of the lucky ones to escape with his life, but nothing more.

After the war, northern carpetbaggers descended on the South like scavengers arriving to pick at the corpse. There were more than a few Southerners who wanted to see the profiteering vermin dead, and some had the funds to pay for the privilege. Lucius hired out as a killer and spent most of his time perfecting his quick-draw and devising his methods. His natural ability was astonishing, and his continuous practice turned him into sheer lightning and thunder. Talent and bitterness forged his temperament into that of a cold-blooded killer. The real evil in him revealed itself in how he baited his prey with inflammatory comments that intentionally lacked confidence and intelligence, as if he were a no-account fool who'd just talked himself into a corner with nothing to back it up. Most fell for it. Then he would strike like the reaper of death.

He'd killed twenty men since the war, sixteen of whom had been deviously baited into drawing on him. The other four he'd caught alone, each time simply announcing his intention to kill the man, and each time giving his victim the chance to draw first. They had, and saw the flash of Lucius's hand and the flame from the barrel as their last earthly moment.

His exploits eventually brought scrutiny and infamy beyond repair, and he fled west where a man could blend in like a tumbleweed on the prairie. For several years, he drifted, spending his savings and becoming an expert with cards. He did well and made a fair living just from his nights at the gaming tables. But there was no retreat from his ruin; the road to hell was branded on his soul, and he eventually sought out more opportunity to ply his brilliance for killing.

Lucius had been in Mexico, Texas, California, Arizona Territory, and, finally, New Mexico Territory, where he came to feel he'd stumbled on to a good thing. His new employer, Rupert Crowder, paid the best money Lucius had ever seen. Rupert was guarded, offering no information beyond whatever facts would help Lucius to complete the job. That, however, suited Lucius just fine. He didn't know much about Rupert and preferred to know less about whoever the intended target was. Tonight's job was only the third one that Crowder had contracted for in their six-month association. The money was so good from each deal that Lucius didn't mind the infrequency of his work.

A dust-devil suddenly materialized and danced errantly up the street as Lucius dismounted. He watched it for a moment as it spun its mystery then veered toward a storefront and vanished when it hit the boardwalk in front of the door, leaving behind a settling cloud of dust as if a spirit had entered the building. Lucius tied his horse amongst the others and headed for the entrance of the saloon.

The girl on the tiny stage at the back of the room wore a red bustier with a pink frilly mid-calf skirt that she held up to mid-thigh, revealing black lace stockings as she danced and kicked her legs and sang raucously: *"Come on boooys and pull out your money, I'll call ya honey, let's have a real good time."* She extended her leg and rubbed it seductively across the back of the piano player's head as she winked at the small gallery of men who sat in a row of chairs close to the action. A few of the men whooped and cheered.

Lucius let his eyes nonchalantly scan the saloon as he entered and headed for the bar. The bartender was talking to two men at the bar, but broke off his conversation and headed for Lucius when he arrived a few feet away. "What'll you have?"

Lucius looked him in the eye. "Whiskey," he said in a flat tone, and looked to the stage where the randy singer had twirled and was shaking her derriere in the faces of the men who responded with some more whoops. The bartender put the glass on the bar and poured from a new bottle. Lucius immediately picked it up and drained it. "Another," he said, as the bartender was turning to return the bottle to its place.

The bartender wheeled back to Lucius and poured again. "Ten cents a shot, or twelve bits for the bottle."

A brunette, dressed much like her counterpart on the stage, arrived next to Lucius just as the bartender was presenting the options. "Why don't you buy the bottle, mister, and I'll help you drink it," she cooed.

He looked at her and considered it for a moment. She was painted and pretty. "All right, leave the bottle and bring her a glass," he said to the barkeep, digging out silver and placing it on the bar.

She pushed up close to him. "Thanks, sweet pea. That's a nice accent you got. Southern ain't it? Where you from?"

"Why don't you guess?"

She picked up the glass the bartender had just poured for her and drank it. "Okay, I'm guessin' the South," she said, and laughed. "I don't know what's in the South anyway. I heard of Mississippi and Louisiana and some others. They're in the South, ain't they?"

Lucius gave her a half smile.

She placed her hands on his waist and brought all she had. "Well, I'll tell you what, sweet pea, we can take that bottle to my room upstairs, and I'll show you more fun than you ever had in the South."

Lucius's eyes were passive. "That surely is inviting, buttercup. Maybe later. I'm gonna go win some money," he said, looking to the card table along the opposite wall that had a game going and two open chairs. He poured her another drink. "You come pour yourself some more anytime you want...I'll be right yonder."

She put her hand on his side and gave it a soft squeeze. "Don't be too long."

"Long as it takes," Lucius replied then recognized the opening. "Tomorrow I'll be trailin' west to Arizona with the wagon train I'm workin' for. Tonight, I'm livin' easy for as long as it takes." He took the bottle and headed for the table, knowing that if things went as planned, he'd be forty miles east tomorrow afternoon.

Lucius stood to the side of the table, holding his bottle and glass, waiting for the hand to finish. At five feet six inches tall and one hundred forty pounds, Lucius did not present an imposing figure. He diminished himself more with meek posture and common clothes. That he had a tie-down holster seemed slightly out of place with the rest of his look but went unnoticed by the men at the table. They all wore holsters with revolvers.

The four men finishing out the hand of draw poker ranged in age from twenty-five to fifty. Lucius figured the two youngest to be cowboys. Another had the appearance of a town merchant, while the last one was duded up like a prosperous rancher or farmer. The cowboys were drinking beer. The other two had empty shot glasses in front of them. From the money on the table, it looked like the duded-up one was getting the best of the others, and the current pot was sizeable.

They laid their cards down and the duded-up one proclaimed, "Three tens...winner!" His hand bested the three eights of one man, and the high two-pair hands of the others. The winner leaned forward and raked in the pot.

"You want in, mister?" one of the cowboys asked.

"If you don't mind another player," Lucius replied.

"That's what them open chairs is for," replied the cowboy.

"Yeah, just get your money out, and I'll see if I can add it to my pile," the duded-up one added.

"I hope not," Lucius replied, taking his seat. Lucius poured himself another drink then held the bottle out. "Anyone want some?"

One of the cowboys took the bottle and poured some in his beer. "Much obliged, mister," he said, then passed it around the table. The other cowboy did likewise with his beer, and the other two filled their shot glasses.

They all bid their thanks, and the merchant slapped the deck on the table in front of Lucius. "New player...it's your deal. We're playing five card draw."

"All right," Lucius said, and began shuffling the cards like a man who hadn't done much of it.

Lucius threw the first several hands, playing like an amateur. Then he began to steadily win. And he offered more of his bottle around the table, which all of them partook in at different times as it made its way around the table. Neither of the cowboys was losing much, each electing to fold if the initial deal didn't offer strong cards. But the merchant and the duded-up one were bolder, and consequently were losing at a good clip.

"This is workin' out pretty good," Lucius mildly said, raking in the winnings from a hand he'd just won.

7

"Almost too good, mister," the duded-up one accusingly replied.

Lucius let the statement go by and calmly replied, "Yeah, it beats losing."

Clint Smith, the duded-up one, sensed it didn't quite add up, but he was a little drunk and there was nothing he could put his finger on. Maybe this man with the Southern accent that sat across from him was just on a legitimate lucky streak, Smith considered. Dumb luck. Or maybe he was a cheat, a cardsharp. There was certainly no cockiness to him. Most men he knew would have taken issue with the tone of his statement. Both cowboys had perked up and looked at each other when he'd said it. *Maybe the man was yellow,* Clint thought. Or, maybe the man wouldn't rile as long as he was winning.

The cowboy to Clint Smith's left dealt the next hand. Clint Smith ended up holding three aces and had the opening bid. He didn't care about trying to keep anyone in, preferring instead to scare them out and pick up the two-bit ante of each man. Or, if they wanted to stay and play, they had to pay. Clint bid the table limit, which hadn't been bid once during the evening. "Five dollars!" he announced like a man who owned the world. He slid his money to the center.

The merchant was next up. "No, I don't think so," he said, folding his hand.

"There ain't no thinkin' needed for me," the cowboy to his right said, dropping his cards face down on the table.

Clint looked at Lucius who feigned ever so slightly as if he might fold, but then almost imperceptibly stopped. "I'll see it," Lucius said in a tone that revealed nothing. He pushed his money to the center.

"Adios," the dealer said, folding his cards.

"Two here," Clint said as he discarded. He picked up the two new cards dealt from the cowboy with a stern look. Clint waited on Lucius, keenly interested in how many cards he would want. Lucius took his time and looked at his cards like a man considering a choice between pie or cake.

"Give me two," Lucius finally said as he discarded. Clint watched closely as Lucius picked up his new cards, looking for anything to read. There was nothing.

Clint figured that at best, Lucius had drawn to improve on three of a kind. Clint hadn't improved on his three aces and was betting that Lucius hadn't pulled a full house or four of a kind. "Five dollars," Clint confidently announced.

Eyes widened around the table. Lucius looked down at his hand again as if reappraising his prospects. After a moment, he looked up and said, "I'll see you and raise five."

Clint straightened in his chair and frowned, then slowly slid his money forward. "Call," he said, throwing his cards on the table without hesitation. "Can you beat three bullets?" he asked like he knew damn well that Lucius couldn't.

Lucius put his cards down, revealing a jack-high flush in hearts. "Yes, I believe I just did."

Clint's eyes bulged. "What the hell is that? You mean to tell me you drew two cards to a flush? You didn't even have a pair! What in the hell were you betting on?"

"I was betting on winning," Lucius replied mildly as he began to rake the pot to him.

Clint glared at him, at Lucius's light-blue eyes and curly black hair that sprouted out from under his low-dome farmer's hat like matted, oily vine clumps. Lucius began to sing softly while he stacked his silver:

"I wish I was in the land of cotton, old times there are not forgotten

Look away, look away, look away, Dixie land."

9

Clint's face tightened and his hands clenched. "Don't you sing that Dixieland shit here. You're not in the South now, Reb."

"Let's get us a beer," the one cowboy said to the other, and they promptly collected their money from the table then headed for the bar. The merchant stayed put.

Lucius looked at Clint with a mild face. "I didn't mean nothin' by it...it's just my home is all."

"Well, your home ain't worth spit now. We whipped your asses good...all you yellow-dog Rebs."

Lucius remained calm. "Not around here, you didn't. I know an ole boy that fought at Valverde, south of here. He said the Yankee boys skedaddled like scared rabbits, pissin' their britches all the way."

The words cut Clint Smith like a whip on soft flesh. He'd fought at the Battle of Valverde ten years earlier, and the memory of it was still vividly fresh. It had been a humiliating defeat in which Union troops had fled from the battlefield in the face of a blistering Confederate attack. But Clint didn't care about those facts now. He was in the mood to kill the man sitting across the table, never imagining that the stranger knew he'd been at Valverde. Clint spoke with venom in his voice, "I was at Valverde and killed some Johnny Rebs...low-down yellow mule-shit like you!"

Lucius sat still for a moment then answered dispassionately as if he were reading from a newspaper. "Well, if you were at Valverde, I guess that makes you one of those britches-pissin', backside-showin', tit-suckin' babies...screamin' as you ran for your mammy."

Clint Smith jumped up from his chair and yelled as his hand hung poised at his holster. "Get up, Reb, or die sitting there!" The merchant got up and backed away from the action like a wall of fire was bearing down on him. The music stopped and people scrambled to get out of the line of fire.

Lucius looked Clint dead in the eye. He stood up slowly, coming completely erect and parting his feet slightly while he gently flexed his gun hand several times. "I'm up now. If you got killin' me in mind, go ahead and draw first…boot licker."

Clint Smith's hand flashed for his gun as a glimpse of doubt burst in his mind. Maybe he'd been had. Maybe he'd been led to this very instant like a sheep led to slaughter, one step at a time with gentle guiding and prodding that defied realization until it was too late. It hit him like lightning in his last moment of life and breath and thought. The man before him was too unaffected, too deliberate, too calculating—diabolical. Clint Smith's hand filled with his gun and he was bringing it out, clearing the leather of his holster, and the other man hadn't moved yet. He had him! His gun came level and cocked, and he was beginning to squeeze the trigger when he saw the flame from Lucius's gun and felt the two shots rip into his chest like cannon balls. Clint Smith staggered back several steps. His feet came to a stop, and he fell backwards, hitting the floor dead.

The room was silent. Nobody moved. All eyes were on Lucius. Lucius kept his eyes on the room while he quickly collected his money with his free hand. "You folks saw what happened!" he yelled. "He drew on me! I had no choice!" Lucius pocketed his money then holstered his pistol and began backing toward the door as the stunned onlookers watched. "You saw it! He drew on me!" Lucius yelled again as he backed out the door and onto the street. A moment later, he was riding out of town at a lope. Then he turned east and vanished into the night.

2

T he tall, green grass of spring flexed down in a rolling
        wave as the rushing wind pressed it and swirled over it,
        creating a pulse of color and movement like that above
of the fast-moving clouds, swollen with shades from gray to
black. A storm loomed on the flank of the men and the herd,
over the foothills to the southwest of them. They moved
steadily along the expansive plain, heading north with patches
of blue overhead and the wind pushing across their face to the
direction of the squall.

Bill Lohmeyer raced his Palomino alongside the line of
cattle as they trailed forward, still calm. He reined to a trot as
he came up next to Sammy Winds. "Whadaya think about
that?" he asked Sammy, who was presently staring hard at the
storm that appeared to be about five miles away.

"I think we could get lucky the way this wind is blowin'.
Might stay on the fringe of it."

"Yeah, or it could just loop around behind us and give us
the ole lasso," Bill replied.

"Sure could. Ground wind and sky wind can be doin' two
different things...end up conspirin' against us. I got a hunch
that's not the story this time, though."

Bill raised his eyebrows. "Hope you're right."

"Yeah, well, we're not gonna outrun it whatever the story. I figure we've made twenty miles today. This is good grass and there's water just ahead. Swing back and tell Roasty we're makin' camp a mile up."

Sammy knew this stretch of the drive well. They were halfway between Albuquerque and his spread, the Sky W Ranch. Three more days would see them home. He'd made the same drive many times before as a hand for the Twin T, driving herds to Albuquerque. This time, he was driving four-hundred heifers and eight prime bulls back to his own ranch to start his own cow-calf operation. He'd bought them in Albuquerque, along with two heavy wagons and supplies and implements not readily available in the smaller towns close to his spread. Now, he was ready to make a go of it on his own land with his own crew and herd. And Jenny would be waiting for him.

Things had moved fast after Sammy returned from Denver. His journey there, just a year earlier, had changed everything. He'd collected the reward for killing an outlaw with a price on his head then returned home with enough money to do whatever he wanted. So he bought the good ranch land that Homer and Reuben Taylor had offered him, then hired some of the Twin T crew and built a ranch house, bunkhouse, barn, corrals, and privies. He and the boys had also dug several wells. There was more to do and build, and they would do it and build it in time. But now, it was time to move the stock in and get the operation running. Sammy was happy and proud to live close to the Twin T and the Taylor brothers, the men who'd taken him in after being orphaned at the age of seven. The Twin T had been his home for fifteen years, but now he headed for his own home.

The storm had kept to the south of them and the wind calmed as the day faded with streaks of red across the western sky. Sitting around the fire close to the chuck wagon, the boys drank coffee and waited for word from the cook, Roasty, that supper was ready. Knuckles Kopine was getting impatient. "How we lookin', Roasty?"

Roasty was stirring a pot of pintos and venison stew and gauging the time remaining on the biscuits in the Dutch oven. He glanced over at Knuckles. "You're lookin' like hell, but the rest of us look pretty good."

"Yeah, well, I look like hell 'cause I'm a starving man."

"No, I don't reckon that's it," Roasty said, then paused and offered nothing more.

Knuckles waited for the retort. When it never came, he couldn't resist. "Well, why is it then?"

Roasty seemed distracted as he cracked the lid and peeked in on the biscuits. He dropped the lid back in place and acted like he'd just become aware of the inquiry. "Why's what?"

"Why do I look like hell?"

"See...you said it yourself," Roasty replied as if the revelation was now clear for all.

"I said I look like hell 'cause I'm a starving man!"

"Then come eat. Supper's ready!"

Porter Loomis was instantly on his feet and bounding to the chuck like a running antelope. Jasper Dunleavy, Bill Lohmeyer, and Ben Kettle were right on his heels while Knuckles was still struggling to get up from the nearly full recline he'd settled into.

"Damn it to hell," Knuckles said with disgust, arriving at his feet but realizing even Sammy was going to hit the line before him, making him last. "You tell these boys there's some hot grub ready and they stampede like wild animals...trample a man to death who didn't have the presence of mind to get out of the way."

Porter and Jasper immediately whooped and snorted and made with a few cattle noises. "Careful you don't trample the fat man," Bill cracked.

"He'd take a whole lotta trampling," Porter replied.

Knuckles Kopine was anything but fat, though there was no mistaking his substantial girth. At five foot nine inches and two hundred ten pounds, he resembled a prize hog, rotund and freakishly strong and dangerous if provoked. But the men working for Sammy were all well-acquainted and mostly good friends, having become so during their time working together as hands for the Twin T Ranch.

Knuckles finally got his plate and joined the rest of the boys, who were all making short work of the fixings as the fire crackled and the evening lived. "Don't you reckon the first to eat should be the first to go take up for Matt so he can come get some supper?" Knuckles casually asked Sammy.

Porter looked up from his plate. "Well, if it's the first to finish, that'll be you, Knuckles. But you just sit there. I'll go take up watch directly. Just let me get the rest of this down my throat with a little chewin' of it on the way."

"I'll take the shift after you, Porter," Ben Kettle offered.

"I'll go after you," Knuckles said.

"Follow you up, Knuckles," Bill Lohmeyer chimed.

"Just leaves us two…which shift you want?" Jasper asked Sammy.

All the boys looked to Sammy with the half realization that he was the one to decide the shifts. Knuckles knew his comment about Porter relieving Matt to come have supper had brought the chain of declarations for watch shifts. Sammy was nearly the youngest of them all, but he was the boss. They all knew it and had respect for him. He could cowboy better than any of them, even though they were mostly top hands. And Sammy had a level of education and intellect uncommon to most men of the West. Homer Taylor had largely seen to that, educating the young boy in the classics and mathematics, science, history, philosophy, and ethics as Sammy grew up on the Twin T. But Sammy never made a show of any of it. He was plain spoken and good natured. When needed, he could be all business, but usually showed humility beyond his natural and undeniable confidence. And the boys all knew they didn't come any tougher than Sammy Winds. He could be ruthless and brutal. Sammy had proved it against the outlaw, and had proved it several more times on his trip to Denver to collect the reward. Most of all, he lived every day as an example of hard work and character. It was easy to call him boss.

"Take your pick, Jasper," Sammy nonchalantly replied, sensing the slight discomfort of his men but not caring to give any weight to the way things had played out. This was the first drive with his own cattle and crew. As a young boss, things would naturally be a little different from an older trail boss where age brought additional consideration and respect. Sammy was most concerned about men doing their jobs well, and if they didn't, he'd let them know about it.

"Well, I guess I'll take up for Bill," Jasper said.

"Then I'll be last watch. Suits me just right tonight," Sammy said. He preferred sleeping the night uninterrupted until his watch. Then he would rise early and begin his day with his shift. The previous two nights of the drive, Sammy had assigned shifts and taken the midnight slot for himself, wanting the midway point to best gauge the routine and how his herd was doing. Now, he was happy to sleep a full night.

The boys ate in silence for the next several minutes, their hunger directing all their attention to the food on their plates after a long day in the saddle. Knuckles popped the question first. "Anymore grub, Roasty?" he asked, staring at his empty plate like it was his death certificate.

Roasty was working hard at his plate. "Yep...always is. Nuff for ya all if you're reasonable. Make sure you leave enough for Matt to get his fill."

Knuckles was up first and took a modest amount. The other boys followed moments later and usually ended up with more because Knuckles had already been there, and they could better see how much they could take while still leaving plenty for whoever was on perimeter watch during supper.

After they all had finished eating, Porter left to relieve Matt, who quickly made his way to the chuck and loaded up his plate. The rest of the boys broke out the tobacco and commenced with smoking or chewing. Most of them engaged in both from time to time, preferring to smoke after a meal, and mostly preferring chewing tobacco while in the saddle.

Sammy had a smoke then stood up. "You boys don't howl at the moon too much," he said as he left to find a spot and lay out his bedroll. A chorus of evening farewells followed him.

Laid out under the stars with his head on his saddle, he had a final smoke and listened to the harmonica tune that Bill played from the campfire a hundred feet away. He thought of Jenny. They'd become engaged to marry just before he'd left for Denver a year earlier. When he'd returned and bought the land for his own ranch, they'd decided to wait until the ranch was built before marrying, until they could live as man and wife in their own home. Many of the nights of the last year, he and the boys had spent camping under a lean-to on his land while the construction took place. The ranch house was ready now and he and Jenny had planned the wedding for mid-May, less than a month away. He loved her and had seen too little of her during the last year. Now, he couldn't wait to be with her.

His mind returned to the task at hand. He had a lot at stake seeing this drive safely through to his land. It was the start-up stock for his operation and had taken a lot of time and inquiries to buy four hundred heifers. If there was no trouble, they'd be home in three days. The rest of the drive would start tomorrow. Sammy snuffed out his smoke and closed his eyes. Sleep came almost instantly.

3

The small stand of pines stood oddly alone on top of the bluff, a vantage point that offered a panoramic view of anything approaching from the south and east. Lucius watched from the edge of the trees as the moving dot on the landscape below grew enough in size to be identified as a rider. He took a long pull off his flask, savoring the burn as the whiskey went down. Then he unhitched his canteen from his saddle and took a short pull of water. It would be another fifteen minutes before the rider arrived. Lucius returned the canteen then pulled the small cigar from his shirt pocket and fired the match, lighting the cigar and taking a long drag, inhaling deeply and finally exhaling the smoke mostly out his nose. He pulled out his pocket watch and checked it again for the third time in the last hour. Rupert Crowder was an hour late, and Lucius had grown moody with the delay. It was another two hours to a hot meal and soft bed. Lucius intended to partake in both tonight. Last night had been cold with no fire, and the ground had been hard.

Rupert Crowder finally reined up and dismounted stiffly. "This will be the last time we meet out here," he said with a tone that revealed his displeasure at coming so far for a clandestine meeting.

"You picked it. Why don't you pick something closer to wherever the hell you're coming from."

"Most the time this is closer. Just not this time."

"Must be why you're late. Give me my money…the job's done," Lucius said, dispensing with any formalities.

"I know it. Went off just like you said it would."

Lucius looked at Rupert, squinting slightly. "How do you know that?" he asked, not really caring about the answer. He knew Rupert had ways of knowing.

"It's my business to know. I don't pay the second half of a job until I know it's done." Rupert pulled out the leather pouch of gold coins and handed it to Lucius. "Two-hundred dollars."

Lucius shook out the coins and quickly counted them, then returned them to the pouch. He wondered again why the man he'd killed in the bar was worth four hundred dollars. He didn't bother asking. They'd covered that ground early in their association. No questions ever about why someone had become the assignment, the target. That was the agreement.

"You sure know how to get it done," Rupert said. "The best I've seen."

"I don't recall you seein' anything…but you're right about me being the best. Your knowing about him bein' at that Valverde battle was helpful, though. You got any more work for me anytime soon?"

"Yeah…there's some things coming up. You know where Cuerno Verde is?"

"No."

"Where you headed from here?"

"Over to Reeger for a few days, and then on to a place I like."

Rupert didn't ask what that might be. He knew the rules, too. "Cuerno Verde's about ten miles due north of Reeger. It's just a little village. There's a cantina there—the Blue Cactus.

They post mail there…hold messages, too. There'll be word there for you in about three weeks…under your usual name."

"Okay," Lucius said, then mounted up.

Rupert watched as Lucius loped away. He *was* the best he'd ever seen. Rupert had heard tale of Lucius before they met, and their first meeting was not happenstance, at least not on Rupert's part. It was Rupert's job to use good people and insulate his employer from ever being known. For the few jobs that Rupert had used him, Lucius had proven his worth as a specialist. No suspicion would accompany Clint Smith's sudden demise by way of a barroom fight. Rupert had received the report from his eyewitness. It had been perfectly played by Lucius. Everybody present had given pretty much the same story. Clint Smith had told Lucius to get up or die sitting in his chair. And Clint Smith had drawn first.

Rupert had a gang working for him, too. The other six men that Rupert oversaw didn't know of Lucius, and Lucius didn't know of them. They were less skilled and cunning than Lucius, but were equally effective in producing results. Recruited from Kansas, none of them were known in the territory. They operated as Rupert's private posse at his discretion and direction. They were killers and thugs who were currently living and operating from a secluded location in the northern part of the territory. Rupert saw to it that they had what they needed. There were three small cabins at the location, along with beef, hogs, chickens, liquor, and other stores of food stuffs. Rupert even had several women living there who cooked and saw to the gang's every need.

Boothe Haney was the leader of the gang, and Rupert counted heavily on Boothe to keep order. Boothe was up to it. At thirty-seven years old and two hundred pounds, Boothe was bigger and stronger than any of the others, and he was also meaner than a rattlesnake and the worst of the lot. Boothe had killed many men, having perpetrated savage attacks on those who'd crossed him in the most trivial ways. He'd bitten off noses and ears and fingers, and he'd gouged out several eyes. He used a gun occasionally but was not particularly good with it, being slow on the draw and anything but a crack shot. Boothe preferred instead to walk up to the intended and would either pull his knife and begin carving, or set upon him like a starved wolf.

It hadn't always worked out for Boothe, but he had survived. He'd lost his left ear to a man who took particular offense to Boothe's carnivorous methods, and so returned the favor. And Boothe had been shot twice and had a knife scar that ran diagonally across his face. Starting above his left eye, it ran across his nose and down across his right cheek. Between his natural surliness and his daunting physical appearance, even his own men knew he was not to be trifled with.

Rupert dealt only with Boothe. Unbeknownst to the other men, he paid Boothe three times the money any of them got, explicitly for making sure that rules were followed, the most important being that no one got drunk in some town and ran their mouth about the gang or their location or their work. Boothe said that he'd slow-kill any man who compromised or betrayed the gang. They had heeded his warning. The operation would only last twelve to eighteen months, with the promise of a sizeable bonus to all the men who were still there at the end. Boothe wanted all the money there was to be made from the job before leaving the territory for good.

4

T he chatter of robins, sparrows, finches, and warblers filled the morning air as they flew about in the stream of morning sun, its radiance seeping like tendrils through the branches and boughs of Gambel oak, juniper, birch, and aspen, stirring the birds in a flurry of instinct to build their nests and carry forth their rites of renewal.

The padre read the Bible passage to the children who sat on arranged logs amidst the trees. Sunlight had already warmed the April morning and glistened upon their heads like frosting upon different colored cakes. The eyes of the children moved about, their attention swept away with the birds that darted and dived and swooped and spiraled close by. Undeterred by the competition for attention, Padre Tomas read on: "The plants and the flowers grow not by their own care or anxiety or effort, but by receiving that which God has furnished to minister to their life. The child cannot, by any anxiety or power of its own, add to its stature. No more can you, by anxiety or effort of yourself, secure spiritual growth. The plant, the child, grows by receiving from its surroundings that which ministers to its life—air, sunshine, and food. What these gifts of nature are to animal and plant, such is Christ to those who trust in Him."

Jing Lu was overwhelmed with curiosity that ebbed simply from what the padre had just read. "Where do birds go in winter?" she innocently asked. "I do not hear them or see them in the coldest times. Where do they go?"

The other children suddenly looked more alert, Jing Lu's question having brought to mind what each had wondered subconsciously or otherwise. The padre considered it for a moment. "Some fly to other places...to the south where it is warmer. Or..." He paused a moment. "The birds might say that they do not see you in the winter and ask where you have gone. Where did you go Jing Lu?"

The other children looked inquisitively at her. Jing Lu smiled, her nine-year-old face beaming forth. "I am inside by the fire to stay warm."

The padre smiled back at her. "So, too, are the birds."

Jing Lu frowned. "But they do not have a cabin and a fire inside."

"No, not as we have or think of it, but they have all of this...the trees, the earth, the sky," the padre said, sweeping his arms in a movement to show the grandeur of it all. "They, too, receive that which God has furnished to minister to their lives."

"And they got feathers all over to keep 'em warm," Rory added. Jing Lu looked at Rory with the sunlight sprinkled on his hair, making it redder than it usually looked. "They got what they need," Rory continued. "Some of 'em live in holes in the ground during winter, or caves, or holes in the trees. And they make those nice nests for their youngins, so they might make blankets and coats and socks for their little bird feet outta the same stuff. Thinkin' on it, I wouldn't want to be a bird during winter...but it sure would be somethin' to fly around in the warm sunshine like they're doin' this morning. They're goin' crazy!"

The children laughed, and the padre did not attempt to contain himself. He laughed too. As their laughter began to fade, the padre thought he heard the distant sound of pounding hoofs. His hand went up in a gesture to quiet the children. They fell silent and listened as they looked at the padre. He was moving to a spot where he could see through the trees to where he thought the sound was coming from. The padre and children were on a gentle hillside in an elevated position to the flat below where two cabins and a barn stood in a clearing of meadow.

The padre could see six men on horseback galloping toward the cabins. They began to slow to a trot as they got close. Two of them broke away from the pack and continued at a gallop. They looked to be headed for the shack another half mile beyond the main cabins, toward the shack where the padre and five children had lived through the winter.

The padre turned back to the children. "Be quiet now and stay still," he said.

"Who is it, Padre?" Rory asked.

"I don't know…be still now."

Padre Tomas didn't like the look of any of it. He moved to the best position to see what was happening but stayed hidden amongst the trees. Four riders had pulled up in front of the larger of the cabins, while the other two riders continued on across the meadow toward the shack. Then one of the riders suddenly broke off and began doubling back.

Boothe Haney and his men stopped in front of the cabin and sat abreast on their horses, with the man on each end half a horse length back. "Anybody in there?" Boothe yelled. Smoke was drifting from the stove pipe that came out of the roof. The door opened, and an Indian woman in a long buckskin dress appeared in the doorway holding a rifle with the barrel pointed slightly down. She did not step out. Her face was round and passive, framed by long, black hair braided into two ropes that hung from each side of her face, down her front to her waist. Her black eyes did not blink and focused intensely on the four men before her.

"He's got hisself a squaw woman," one of Boothe's men said.

"Shut up!" Boothe ordered without turning to look at his man. "Where's Clint Smith?" Boothe asked, watching the woman carefully. She didn't answer. "Anybody else here? In that other cabin?" Boothe asked, loudly.

The door to the smaller, adjacent cabin that sat to the left about fifty feet away opened. A man stepped out holding a rifle in the crook of his arm, its barrel hanging down. He had on wool trousers with suspenders but no shirt. The lace-up work boots he wore were not tied, and he stood with his thumbs hooked inside the top of his pants "Mister Smith ain't here," he said, with authority.

Boothe already knew that Clint Smith wasn't there. "Anybody livin' in that shed across the meadow?" he asked, like he wanted an answer.

"Just an old padre and some orphans. Why do you care?"

"I don't. Whose cattle are those?" Booth asked, nodding off to the side.

The man glanced in the direction of Boothe's nod. Boothe and his men all drew at once and the shots rang out rapid fire. The two riders on Boothe's left shot at the man. He never got his rifle up before his shirtless torso jerked violently and burst to crimson. Boothe and the rider on his right had drawn on the Indian woman. Her eyes had never left Boothe when he made his false comment about the cattle. Her rifle came up as they drew, and she fired. The rider next to Booth was falling from his horse, while Boothe was pulling the trigger again and again before she could jack another shell into the Winchester. She fell back into the cabin and lay motionless. Suddenly, a shot came from a small window of the other cabin where the shirtless man lay dead. Another of Boothe's men toppled from his horse. Boothe and the remaining man both fired at the window as each desperately pulled their reins hard to the right, kicking their bobbing horses to get out of the way of being sitting targets. Their horses leapt to the right in a burst and then were pulled hard left to get behind the end of the cabin. Just before they were out of sight, Boothe heard two more shots. He knew he wasn't hit and looked at Del once they were safe. Del looked all right

"Come on!" Boothe yelled. The two men raced their horses around the next corner to the backside of the cabin then reined to a stop.

"I got him, Boothe!" came the yell from behind the smaller cabin.

Boothe suddenly stared hard across the meadow to the shed that was tiny in the distance. He saw only one horse there, standing in front of the open door. There should have been two. "Is that you Andy?" Boothe yelled toward the back of the adjacent cabin, realizing that one of his riders must have doubled back.

"Yeah!"

Boothe and Del rode forward and saw Andy at the back window of the other cabin, looking in. Suddenly, Andy fired two more shots into the cabin. "He ain't movin' now!" Andy yelled.

"Where's Crom?" Boothe asked, perplexed.

"Across the way. I doubled back when I saw that smoke," Andy replied, nodding to the stovepipe coming through the wall at his chest level. It had a small stream of smoke coming from it. "Didn't figure you could see that from the front. I pulled up in back here just as the shootin' started."

"That was good figurin'. I don't think it helped Baker, though. Duncan's hit too. Check this cabin and make sure that squaw's dead."

Boothe and the two men returned to the front of the cabin, and Andy went in, stepping around the body of the Indian woman. Boothe and Del surveyed the scene outside. One of Boothe's men lay dead and the other, Duncan, was getting to his feet. He was shot through the shoulder. "That damn squaw shot me!" he said with worry in his voice as he looked at his wound. It was bleeding badly.

Andy came back out of the cabin. "She's dead. The rest is empty."

The other rider suddenly returned at a gallop from across the meadow and reined to a stop. "There's nobody around, but somebody's livin' there...looked like five or six spots for bedding down...packed in. The place is tiny... stove in there is still warm. I seen a buckboard and a dun around the backside."

Boothe looked around, scanning the area and the treed hills within a half mile. "That dude said there's a padre and some orphans livin' there. They must be close by. Hell, they might be watchin' us right now. Spread out and find 'em!

"Ain't one of you gonna help me get this bleedin' stopped first?" Duncan asked.

Del, Crom, and Andy looked at Boothe who didn't think about his response for more than an instant. "Plug it yourself. You should of never let that squaw get the drop on you. If I hadn't shot her, she'd a put some more holes in you." Boothe turned his attention back to the other men. You boys split out on that hillside...I'll swing down to this other end. Let's go!"

5

When the shots pierced the air, the padre gasped as the killings occurred. The children could not see what was happening from the logs where the padre had told them to sit and be still. Gunshots were nothing unusual, but the padre's gasp and sudden tensing of the body told the children that something bad was taking place.

"Who's shooting?" Rory blurted out.

"What are they shooting at?" Jing Lu quickly followed.

The padre immediately turned to the children, his old face lined with worry and his leathery hands shaking slightly as they grasped the Good Book. His voice became steady and calm as his immediate sense of panic transformed into purpose, with the mission now at hand. "Quiet now, children. We must go right away and find a place to hide."

Jing Lu spoke softly and hurriedly, her voice at a higher pitch than normal. "Why? Did you see Chapawee? Is she all right? Did you see Mister Smith?"

"He said to be quiet, so be quiet," Rory sternly reminded her, as if his words were the final command. At twelve years old, Rory was the eldest, but didn't usually assert his position in the pecking order with direct commands. That was for the padre. Rory usually just lent advice and freely dispensed with his twelve year old wisdom as if he were the natural big brother of the others. But he understood the weight of the moment and stepped forward to help the padre any way he could.

"I know where we can hide," eight-year-old Tobias whispered loudly, his face registering the conviction of his declaration.

Rory instantly knew what Tobias spoke of. "The rock castle?" he asked for confirmation.

"Uh-huh," Tobias answered. He had shown it to Rory just a few weeks earlier, and the two of them had played there several times, being the imaginary knights from a story the padre had read to the children.

"It's a really good hiding spot, Padre. It goes underground, and it's a really secret way in," Rory said, confidently in a hushed tone.

"Where is it?" the padre asked.

"Up over there...not too far," Rory replied, pointing a direction that was slightly uphill and farther south from the cabins and the men below.

"All right...show us the way. We must stay out of sight while we move there. Can we do that, Rory?"

"Yes, Padre, we can be hidden all the way I reckon."

"Good...let's go. Stay together and be silent," the padre said. He stuffed the Bible in the back waist of his heavy cotton pants.

Rory and Tobias took the lead, with Jing Lu, Payat, and Camille bunched together close behind. The padre took the rear position and continually looked back to see if they ever came into a full line of sight of the cabins. They didn't.

Rory did well in keeping a line toward the destination while avoiding open patches of hillside to stay in the thickest line of trees. They hiked diagonally up the hillside for several hundred yards until Rory said, "There it is." He pointed to a cluster of granite rocks just ahead, embedded in the hillside in many irregular sizes and shapes like the shards of a redoubt, standing boldly amongst the thick of the pinion pine that enveloped them.

The padre surveyed it, worrying immediately that when the men came looking, they would most certainly consider the rocks as a hiding place if they happened by. He knew they would be searching soon. "Go, Rory, show me...go with him children."

Rory strode forward in large steps, with Tobias on his heels and the rest scrambling quickly behind. The padre walked forward with them another twenty feet then stopped and watched, wanting to consider where Rory would go and what sort of obvious inspection it might draw. He watched as Rory led the children farther ahead, where upon reaching the rocks they weaved to and fro as they navigated amongst the granite formations. The padre could make out nothing notable about where Rory might stop, but suddenly he did. Rory turned back to the padre, waving for him to come.

Padre Tomas motioned intensely for Rory to continue. The boy stared for a moment before turning and falling onto his stomach upon a large, flat piece of granite that lay like a plate upon the gentle angle of the hillside. Then Rory swung his feet up to the right, so that he was still on his stomach but now laying horizontal to the hill. He immediately began to scoot backwards, feet first, toward another plate of rock that rested at a slim angle against the plate Rory was on, cantilevering above it just slightly.

The padre could not imagine where Rory was going. From where he stood, it appeared there was nowhere to go. The two plates rested together at an edge, appearing to be a dead end. But as Rory scooted backwards under the cantilever into the space that looked like it would go no farther, he kept going, his legs disappearing with each push of his arms.

The padre's eyes widened. He began moving quickly toward the children as Rory disappeared completely. And then, like Rory had done, Jing Lu lay down and began to vanish as she scooted backwards. Camille got down on her stomach to go next as the padre arrived on the plate of granite, immediately falling to his knees and staring hard under the cantilever to see where Jing Lu was disappearing into. Only her head and shoulders remained, but she quickly vanished through a small notch at the back of the plate.

When she was gone, the padre gazed at the notch. It didn't look large enough from where he was, but Rory had already gone in and he was a good-sized boy. The padre concluded that the hole couldn't be seen at all unless someone stooped way down to look under the cantilever. And even then, it did not look like a person could possibly fit. He was very encouraged. "Good! Good! Go now, Camille. You go next, Payat. Then you, Tobias." A thought suddenly invaded the padre's mind. "Tobias, you have been in there before?"

"Yes, Padre."

"Is there room enough for us all?"

The boy considered the question a moment, well aware of the seriousness etched on the padre's face. "Yes, Padre, there is room enough."

"Good. Good. Get ready now."

Camille, Payat, and Tobias disappeared one by one, and then the padre did as they had done before him: getting down on his stomach with his feet toward the cantilever. Using his open palms against the sun-warmed granite, the padre began to push and scoot backwards. He saw the flash of movement through the trees just as he heard the hooves, soft on the earth in the cadence of an easy lope. In moving glimpses, splintered in reveal by the branches of trees, the rider appeared. The padre caught full sight of him for an instant and realized that the rider was looking his way. Had he seen him? Or were his eyes merely taking in the rocks for that instant of view? The rider flashed from sight, and the padre desperately pushed and scooted backwards, going fully under the cantilever and feeling his feet hit the openness of the hole. As fast as he could manage, he pushed and wiggled, disappearing into the void like a varmint escaping a predator. Back and down, the padre slid through the hole, into a tunnel that was tight to his body. A few feet farther down, he felt a hand grab his foot, and then heard Rory's voice as the tunnel gave way into a larger void of darkness. "Here, Padre…we're here."

The padre was able to roll to his back and sit up. He could see nothing out in front of him, but only the bit of light that descended the tunnel and ended at his side. "You must be silent now," he whispered into the darkness. "There is a bad man near." He scooted a bit farther into the chamber and instinctively felt about in the darkness, his hands touching knees and arms and faces. They were huddled together in this underground chamber, which, the padre quickly guessed, had served as a den for a hibernating bear, and perhaps some cubs as well. It seemed to be about four foot high and six feet long, with a width of five feet or so. They were packed in. The air was stale and carried the scent of recent animal habitation. His eyes adjusted enough to make out the shapes of the children.

A muffled voice came from above. It was close, but the padre couldn't make out what was being said. Then there was a second voice from just outside. "Yeah, found some logs back there, set up for like a meetin' place…and footprints that trailed from there up this ways. But I lost 'em up by these rocks. Could be hiding here somewhere."

The breath caught in each of their chests as they sat silently, terrified they would be discovered any second. But the padre now knew that he hadn't been seen, and he was certain that the notch through which they had crawled was only visible if a rider dismounted and stooped very low, or got down on his hands and knees to look under the cantilever. And the padre was confident that it looked like a dead end from above.

All was quiet. They sat in the blackness, hearing only the sounds of each other's breathing as the seconds lingered interminably. He whispered into the darkness to put the children at ease. "God is watching over us...He is with us." The padre bowed his head and began to pray, a prayer that was quickly interrupted by the sound of hooves clicking on the rock of the granite plate as the horse walked just above. Then it stopped and the padre prayed that the rider would not dismount to examine things more closely.

"I don't see nothin'!" the voice shouted from above. They heard the sound of another voice in reply but could not make out the words.

"Let's go! They ain't here!" came the first voice again. The padre listened to the sound of the retreating horse as it faded away, suspicious though that it could be a ploy to lure them out. He would keep the children hidden until nightfall.

It was half an hour later when Boothe Haney arrived back at the front of the cabin where his men had returned minutes before. "You didn't find anything?" he asked, his tone clearly irritated.

"Nope. We gave that hillside a good goin' over, one end to the other. Found a meeting place with some footprints leadin' away...small prints, like kids, but they just petered out."

"What do you mean a meeting place?" Boothe fired back.

"Well, just some logs fixed in a kind of circle for settin'. Had a fire pit, too, but nothin' burned lately."

Boothe didn't like it. Loose ends could mean a big problem, and Rupert Crowder didn't want any loose ends. The warm stove in the shed meant that somebody had been there this morning. Boothe looked at Duncan who was sitting on the porch with a wad of cloth pushed against his shoulder. He looked pale. "All right, Andy and Crom, stay here with Duncan and get this place cleaned up. Haul them bodies to those north woods there and bury 'em. When you're done, see if you can get him patched up and then set up watch. We gotta find that bunch. I don't figure they're ridin', so they can't be too far. They might be headed for Dumas. Me and Del will head that way. Might be morning before we're back. If they show up here before then, bury 'em with the others.

"I didn't sign on with this outfit to kill kids," Duncan stated, pushing the wadded cotton harder against his shoulder.

Boothe looked at him with contempt. "You signed on for killing."

"Men and squaws, yeah...not women or children."

"I didn't hear you claim any such thing when you joined up."

"Maybe not...but I'm sayin' it now. I'll help bury 'em but I won't do the killin'."

Boothe took a deep breath. "You won't have to do nothin'," he said maliciously, then drew his gun and shot Duncan three times. He looked at the other men. "More money for the rest of us. Any of you other boys against killing?" he asked, holding his gun at the ready with hate in his eyes. None of the others replied.

35

6

The surroundings were cramped and black and grew more uncomfortable as the air became stuffier and the minutes hung on like hours. Camille began to sob quietly, overwhelmed by it all, but fighting to keep control and not be the one to break down in the face of their predicament. She was seven years old and the youngest of the group. The padre's insistence that they pray in this dark hole had summoned up all the bad that had befallen her in her short life. Her sobbing was unnatural to the other children. They had only known her to be like a small rock, her stoic demeanor and ability to work hard was beyond her years, as if her survival had depended on the shell of will she had erected. Now, in her fright, she wept, but even this outpouring had restraint and composure. It unnerved Jing Lu who began to shake. Rory and Payat sat silently aware, while Tobias began to fidget.

The padre continued on for a few more moments with his whispered prayer, his deep concentration not broken by the soft sobs. Then he heard it and stopped, listening for a moment. "It is all right, Camille," he said, leaning forward and placing his hand gently on her head.

"I'm scared," she said, her voice quaking.

"Me too," Jing Lu added.

"I have to go, Padre," Rory quickly followed.

"We cannot go yet. We must wait longer. All will be well. Do not be afraid," the padre replied, understanding that they could not remain in this hole until evening.

"No, I mean I have to piss," Rory replied.

"Yes," Payat said, indicating he also had the need.

The padre paused for a moment. "I do not think it is safe yet," he said, knowing that it would never again be safe for them on Clint Smith's property. The men had seen the shed where he and the children lived. They would search until they found them, and, if the men had left, they would come back very soon, he thought.

"I gotta go, Padre. They're not out there anymore...I'll be fast. I'm not gonna go here. Please don't tell me I have to go here with everybody," Rory pleaded.

"All right, but look to see that no one is near before you climb all the way out."

"Yes, Padre."

"I go too," Payat said, and quickly followed Rory up the hole.

"Be quick boys," the padre whispered loudly behind them. He knew he had to stay with Camille, Jing Lu, and Tobias.

The padre turned back to the children and extended his hands, touching them on their heads and faces. "God is with us...all will be well." But he wondered if his words were true. Sitting in the darkness all seemed so perilous. His life had taken a road of thorns that tested his faith and invaded his mind with thoughts of punishment.

A decade earlier, he had been a priest at the small mission in Ranchos de Taos until an overpowering desire for a woman of the Pueblo led to a secret love affair. Before his violation of church doctrine became known, he left the mission and married his love, Estella. With their combined money, they moved to a smaller area of the territory and bought half a hectare of good farmland, upon which they built a modest adobe home and a small barn. He farmed and she made pottery and clothes, selling her wares in the small settlement nearby. They lived happily if not prosperously.

Estella was in her early thirties and had been infertile to the padre who was already in his late forties. She desperately wanted a child but her prayers were not answered with pregnancy. When Estella learned of an eight-year-old boy whose father had been sent to prison and whose mother had left the boy at the local chapel before simply vanishing, Estella beseeched her husband to take the boy into their home. The padre gladly agreed, and the chapel's pastor was delighted to turn the boy over to such a grounded and religious couple. Young Rory quickly took to the loving and disciplined home, something quite foreign to the beatings and neglect that had defined his upbringing to that point.

Brutally tough circumstances of the continuing westward expansion mortally tested many, leaving countless orphaned children to be absorbed by a land short of formal institutions, and so they were scattered like seeds to the winds of fate. Many ended up at the doors of churches and missions, who in turn acted as clearinghouses for placing the children in homes or securing travel to the closest orphanage, if possible. But most were already full. The padre and Estella let it be known that they would take other children who had no place to go. They took in the young Indian boy, Payat, a year after Rory. No story accompanied the five-year-old, and he could speak no English. They guessed from his dialect that he was Navajo, but had no certainty of it. The little Chinese girl, Jing Lu, came next and was followed a few months later by Tobias.

The padre built an additional room onto the house and fashioned bunk beds so each child had their own bed. The children worked at assigned tasks. Rory, Payat, and Tobias helped with the farming, harvesting, milking, and woodcutting and splitting. And Rory proved to be a particularly good shot and naturally skilled at hunting with the old musket that the padre let him use. Payat and Tobias became good fishermen, and also built snares and traps to catch smaller animals. Jing Lu learned pottery making, sewing, and cooking from Estella, and diligently helped with household chores. In the evenings, the padre and Estella taught the children reading, writing, and basic mathematics; in the mornings before breakfast, they conducted Bible study. For the next few years, it was a happy and formative time for the children, and a deeply fulfilling mission for the padre and Estella who felt the Lord's calling and blessing.

Two months after Camille had arrived and become Jing Lu's little sister, the cholera epidemic broke out, sweeping the land and leaving a wake of death that took nine of the local townspeople and another fifteen of the rural community, including Estella. The padre was devastated and cursed himself, thinking his sins had taken her. He struggled mightily to maintain a semblance of order within the house, understanding the children's grief and bewilderment, and doing his best to stay strong through his faith. But he was tortured and doubted God's love and mercy, even as it became stronger in him. He wanted to collapse and die, but his passion yielded a stronger bond and sense of purpose to the children, as if his resentment and bitterness would be the ultimate proving grounds. He would fight back. He would see these children through until he himself was struck down.

A fortnight after Estella's death, the padre drank down a bottle of wine late at night as the children slept, his own sleeplessness rendering an agony that knew no bounds. The wine finally sedated him to sleep. He had not blown out his bedside candle and hit it with his arm in his turbulent slumber, knocking it to the floor where it caught his clothes afire and the chair from which they hung. The fire spread quickly.

Payat was awakened by the strong smell of smoke. He sat straight up and yelled the warning: "Fire! Fire!"

Rory was instantly awakened and smelled the danger. He leapt from his bed yelling, "Wake up you all! Padre, there's fire!" But he heard no response from the other room where the padre slept. The other children were awake and yelling questions that Rory didn't bother answering as he lit the lantern. "Stay low! The smoke is high up!" he yelled. He could hear the flames roaring from the other side of the house as the glow permeated the doorway. He knew the safest way out. "Take your clothes! Grab your stuff and get out the window!"

"What about Padre?" Jing Lu frantically shouted.

"I'm going for him now," Rory yelled back as he threw open their bedroom window and tossed his clothes and some of his immediate belongings out the window. "Get going...now!" he commanded then headed to the door where he crouched low and disappeared into the house.

Payat grabbed his clothes and his few possessions and threw them out the window before turning back. "You go! I help Rory!" he proclaimed, then crouched down and went through the doorway in search of Rory and the padre.

Camille, Jing Lu, and Tobias climbed out the window and stood a ways from the house, clutching their things and watching, as the flames and smoke poured from the roof, lighting the night. Suddenly, Payat was emerging from the window, high on the padre's bedroom wall, as if he were being pushed. He fell to the ground outside and jumped to his feet, ready to help as Rory appeared and was immediately followed by the padre, who fell to the ground then stood and stumbled with the boys to safety.

All was lost to the fire, even the barn, which was close enough to the house that burning embers carried on the wind to set the barn roof ablaze. The padre acted in time to turn out the animals and push the wagon from the flames. But all else was consumed. His grief and shame that he had caused their predicament was almost more than he could bear. There was no money to rebuild, and he no longer wanted to remain where he had lost his beloved Estella, and now everything else. Rory and Payat had saved his life, but in his despair, the padre wished that he had died with the rest of it.

Once again, the children cast thought to him beyond himself, and the clarity lifted his heart as they spoke of God and prayed and uttered the same assurances to him that he had spoken to them so many times. As if their prayers were answered, a good offer for the land came only days after the fire. The padre accepted, knowing it was enough to build again somewhere else. He knew that the whispers of him and Estella's past had circulated through the town over the years and had grown to common speculation, with a recent cruel nature by some who said that his sin of the church had caused the epidemic, and that the fire had proved it.

So, he sold the land and his ox, and traded the cow and chickens for a Winchester rifle, a forty-four revolver, and a good store of ammunition for both. He talked to the children about how he loved them and wanted to remain a family, but that he would understand if any of them did not want to leave with him, and that the chapel pastor would take any who wished to stay. "You are our father...our Padre," Jing Lu had cried. "We have lost our mother. Please do not make us go away. I will be good. I love you, Padre."

Rory had looked hurt that such an option was even talked about. "I go wherever you go, Padre."

41

Camille, Tobias, and Payat all had confirmed Rory's sentiment, shaking their heads in agreement and offering short verbal affirmations that they had no interest in anything other than staying with the padre.

They had left in the fall in a buckboard wagon pulled by an old dun horse, the padre having learned of homestead opportunities that had recently become available farther south in the territory. Ten days into their sluggish journey, an early storm dropped two feet of snow and was followed by days of frigid weather that paralyzed their progress and forced them to seek shelter for survival. The storm had come as they happened to pass Clint Smith's land. Mister Smith had offered them the old miner's shack. It was tiny but had a stove and a good creek close by. Smith also gave them a store of firewood and some provisions for which the padre paid him.

Camille and Tobias had come down with pneumonia from the initial exposure to the storm and were deathly ill for the better part of a month. The padre knew the foolishness of trying to move on before spring and asked Mister Smith if they could remain through the winter, offering him a modest sum for the use of the shed.

"Hell no, Padre, I don't want money for the use of that. It's just been sitting empty since I built these cabins six years ago. I'm doing well. Keep your money and stay till spring," Clint Smith had told him. So the padre made one trip to town and bought dry goods and other provisions, and Rory shot several elk which were bountiful in the area. They lived out the winter and were preparing to resume their journey in another week or so. Then this beautiful Sunday morning had arrived and turned to a nightmare.

In a sliding scramble, Payat came down the hole, returning to the small, dark chamber. The padre recognized him when his long, black hair was revealed for an instant as he moved clear of the end of the hole where the dim shaft of light came from above. "Where is Rory?" the padre asked, realizing that no one else was following.

"He come soon."

"What do you mean? Where is he?"

"He look to see if men still here."

The padre was suddenly angry and worried. "He was not supposed to do that! Where did he go?"

"He climb a tree."

"Climb a tree? Oh, no!" the padre worriedly said. "Is the tree far?"

"No...close."

"Did you see any men when you were outside?"

"No. No men."

"Go and get him, Payat...and come right back!"

"Yes, Padre," Payat replied, and then he moved quickly to climb out of the hole. But before he entered the shaft, the light from it vanished as Rory swiftly emerged into the blackness with them.

His voice rang out high-pitched and slightly quaking. "Padre, I saw two men leaving in Mister Smith's wagon...headed toward the woods where the beaver pond is. Padre...there was bodies piled in the back of the wagon. I think Chapawee was one of 'em...and, maybe Johnny, too."

Jing Lu gasped loudly.

"And they had some shovels," Rory said, in a tone that conveyed his understanding of what the purpose was.

"Did you see any other men? There were six before," the padre said as his mind worked to make sense of it.

"No, nobody else."

"Did you see horses by the cabins or back by our casita?"

Rory thought for a moment. "Nope, just Roca in the pen. Scooter and Dandy were pulling the wagon, with two saddled horses tied to the back. Must be those men's horses."

"And you are sure you saw no other horses?"

"I'm sure."

"Good. Be quiet for a moment now and let me think."

All fell silent in the darkness as each of them understood that what they would do next was being contemplated by Padre. The contemplation was swift, and the words came abruptly. "We are leaving now, children. Rory, you go first, then the girls, then the boys. Wait for me right on top. Do not move until I am with you. Understand?"

"Yes, Padre," Rory, Jing Lu, and Camille answered almost simultaneously.

"All right, let's hurry along now."

They left the tiny chamber, crawling up and out and into the bright sunshine. The padre led them straight down the slope to the edge of the trees and the beginning of the flat, open meadow. Their shed was a quarter mile away. The woods and beaver pond, where Rory said the men were headed, was at least a mile north and partly obscured by Clint Smith's cabins, which sat halfway between.

The padre turned and faced the children. "We must hitch Roca and get the guns and ammunition and whatever we can collect very quickly. Then we will head south toward Zapata Falls. Wait here now. I will go first and then will wave you across."

"Shouldn't we all go together, Padre?" Rory asked.

"No. If they see me, they will not see you...and I can get to the rifle before they come."

"Let me go first, Padre. I can get to the casita a lot faster than you...and I can shoot a whole lot better than you, too...no offense."

The padre considered Rory's idea and looked into the boy's eyes, amazed at his courage and resolve. He knew that the boy was right. It would be the best chance for all of them. "All right, Rory. Run as fast as you can and get the rifle and the pistola and load them up."

"They're already loaded, Padre," Rory confirmed instantly.

"Yes, yes. Good. Get all the ammunition, too. Then take aim to the north where you saw the men in the wagon. If you see them coming for us, wait until they are in range and then shoot them. Can you do that, Rory? It is not a sin in this case."

"Yes, Padre, if they come, I'll shoot 'em dead."

The padre turned to Tobias and Payat. "You boys run with him. When you get there, hitch Roca to the wagon right away. You know how to do that, yes?"

"I know how," Payat said. Tobias shook his head affirmatively, his eyes wide with concentration.

The padre then turned to the girls. "Jing Lu, you and Camille run together. Collect blankets and clothes and food and pots, and load them in the wagon. If we have time, we'll get other personals, too. All right?"

"Yes, Padre," they both answered.

The padre looked at each of them. "I love you all. God be with us." He glanced to the north one more time and saw nothing. "Now, run children, run!"

Rory took off as if he'd been shot from a sling. The others burst after him, knowing it might be a race for their lives. Jing Lu forgot about running with Camille and passed Tobias and Payat, running second to Rory whose long legs turned over and over, putting more distance between them with each second. The padre's old legs had not run since his youth, but he moved along fairly well and stayed with Camille.

Across the open meadow they ran, strung out in a line under the white sun, adrenaline pushing each of them as the distance took its toll and their breath came in heaves. No one saw them.

45

7

J enny pulled the linens from the clothesline behind Watson's Boarding House as a warm, afternoon breeze played through her hair, carrying the scent of the honeysuckle blooms that grew along the edge of the yard. She folded the last linen and stood for a moment, wistfully looking to the west as great, billowing, snow-white clouds drifted in formation above the distant range like vessels upon the sea of blue. She thought about Sammy, wondering how much longer before his return. They would be married soon, and she would leave the employ of the boarding house. Missus Watson had been good to her over the last several years, but she was anxious to go now and make her own home with the man she loved.

She returned inside and sang softly as she shelved the laundry in the linen closet on the back porch. The bell on the front door jingled from someone entering, and then she heard the boots on the hardwood floor of the main parlor. The footsteps crossed the room toward the kitchen. She saw the kitchen door swing inward, but it blocked her view of who it was, and no one entered. "Jenny," the quiet but anxious voice called. She knew it instantly and ran to it, coming around the edge of the door and into his arms.

"Sam...oh Sam," she joyfully whispered as they embraced. She looked beyond him to see that no one else was in view, and then kissed him passionately.

"That's the kind of homecoming I like," he said when their lips finally came apart. "I missed you so much," he said, looking deep into her eyes.

"You should have. You've been gone nearly a month!"

"Well, I'm here now."

He kissed her again in a long and heated exchange, their mouths sublimely melding as their bodies instinctively crushed together.

Jenny looked into the parlor again when they eventually came apart, the flush of her body surprising her. She knew Missus Watson or one of the boarders would appear at any moment. "Let's go out front...I want to hear about your trip."

"You sure you don't want to go to your room?"

She slapped him playfully on the chest. "I'm sure I *do*, but we'd make too much noise."

"I can be the silent stallion on a quiet quest," he whispered, leaning in and kissing her neck."

She closed her eyes and enjoyed it for a moment, then pushed him away. "Not me," she seductively replied.

Sammy smiled. "All right, let's go out front. I'm ripe of the range anyway."

They sat on the front porch, and he told her of the journey's good fortune with weather and absence of mishaps, and about the quality of the heifers and bulls that he'd bought. "The boys'll be getting 'em settled in at the ranch about now. I broke off when we got close...had to see you."

"I'm so glad you did. Three weeks till the wedding!" she said, excitedly. For the last month it had been the only thing on her mind besides Sammy's safe return. Now, with him here beside her, she could be completely absorbed by it. "Mother and Joe will be arriving two days before…on the twelfth. They can help with the final preparations."

"I look forward to finally meeting your brother. And it'll be good to see Miss Yolanda again. But I don't think they'll have to help with any preparations. Jacqueline said she'd ramrod the whole thing…and she's got plenty of help. She pretty much runs the Twin T on matters like this."

"Oh, Sammy, they will want to help…at least mother will. After all, they will be guests."

"Yep, that's the point. Jacqueline won't warm up to guests workin'. That's just the way she is. Homer and Reuben wouldn't have it either."

Jenny knew Sammy was right. The wedding was at the Twin T, the biggest and most famous ranch in New Mexico Territory, where Sammy had grown up. Jacqueline ran the kitchen at the T, and had been there all of Sammy's years. She had been as a mother to him, and this wedding would be like her own son getting married. It would be a show of Twin T hospitality and a feast that she and her crew would take pride in hosting.

Jenny smiled. "I guess mother and Jacqueline will work that out between them. It's so nice of the Taylor's to host our wedding."

Sammy laughed. "I don't think they had a choice where Jacqueline was concerned. Besides, the church is tiny. Ain't near big enough for all the folks that are invited." Sammy looked at her seriously. "You said you didn't mind about not being married in the church. Do you still feel that way? Tell me true, Jenny…there's still time if you feel different now."

She looked into his hazel eyes and ran her fingers through his thick, light brown hair. "Pastor Riddering is marrying us, and God will be watching wherever we take our vows. I'd marry you on the back of a galloping horse. I love you, Sammy."

Her violet-blue eyes settled on him like a sunset, sweeping his soul. "I love you, too," he said and kissed her again, then looked at her with a sly smile. "Any chance of stayin' in the cottage tonight?"

The cottage was a small, one-room cabin at the back of the yard. Missus Watson used it for occasional overflow. Jenny returned a knowing smile. "It's not taken right now. I can get it for us, but what will people think?"

"Whatever they want to. But nobody will know. I'll be careful in my arrival. Are you off right after supper?"

"Yes…I can be, right after cleanup."

"You know you don't have to work here another minute," he said, with the tone of a decree.

"I know. I told her May seventh is my last day. Missus Watson has been good to me. I would never leave her in a pinch."

"Of course you wouldn't. That was just the selfishness in me talkin'. Well, how 'bout I go get a bath at the Buckskin and collect you for a late supper."

"That would be fine, Mister Winds. I'll be ready at six-thirty."

"I'll be here, Missus Winds." He tilted his head with the recognition of his words. "I sure like the sound of that."

"May fourteenth, I will be Missus Winds."

The moonlight flooded through the window, sliding across the hardwood floor and adjacent wall like silver paint. They lay together contentedly, her head on his chest, her black hair spread across him as his hand caressed her locks that felt as silk string. "I want to tell you something," he said easily. "I haven't told anybody…didn't want it gettin' around. I thought it would be better for you not to know until we were married. Hope you're not mad about it."

Jenny lifted her head from his chest and looked at him, unsure if she wanted to hear what it was. "You don't have to tell me now. It doesn't matter."

"No, it's nothing bad."

"It isn't?"

"No…it's good, really."

"All right, what is it?"

"The reward I collected wasn't ten thousand…it was fifty thousand."

Jenny straightened up onto an elbow. "Fifty thousand! How did that happen?"

"I'm not exactly sure. The railroad owner, Mister Westerfeld, just said he was upping it—said it was worth it to him. He knew about the gals and the cave. Said I deserved it for that alone, but then said that that wasn't why he raised it. Strange thing it was. I didn't figure turning it down was the right thing to do."

"I should say not."

"Well, it's more than a lifetime of money. We could just lie around and get fat."

Jenny laughed. "I don't believe that is in your nature, Mister Winds."

"No, I guess not. Your's neither. Makes a man think, though."

"About what?"

"Oh, I suppose about what's important in life. Chasin' that brass ring is always in the back of a man's mind, but when you have it in the blink of an eye for killing someone, it doesn't exactly come with much sense of accomplishment."

"You've accomplished so much, and you're just getting started."

"*We're* just getting started," he said, pulling her to him.

"Why did you want to tell me now, Sammy? The money doesn't matter to me."

"You need to know about it, in the event something ever happened to me. After we're married, I'll file a will and leave instructions for you."

"You're frightening me now. I don't want to hear anymore about it."

"That's fine 'cause I don't really want to talk anymore."

She caressed his chest playfully. "I'll have to be in early to make breakfast."

"I'll be headed to the ranch at first light. Time's wastin'."

The night sweetened with their passion as they fell together again.

8

The heifer bawled as the red-hot iron sizzled against its hide, burning away the hair and leaving the blackened Sky W brand. A plume of smoke lifted and quickly vanished into the breeze, leaving behind the pungent stink. Knuckles had never gotten used to the smell. "God awful that is!" he proclaimed, as the breeze blew the worst of the cloud right into his face just as he and Ben turned the heifer loose.

"Just the perfume of the prairie," Ben said. "Downright sweet next to some women I knowed."

"Well, if you got a sister anything like you, I see the truth in it."

Ben raised an eyebrow. "I ain't got a sister."

"Lucky for her."

Matt tossed the iron down. "That's the last one of this bunch. Let's go see if Roasty's got that noon chuck set up."

"Yes, sir, I'm for that," Knuckles heartily agreed.

"Think one of us oughta go pull them boys off that fence building?" Ben asked.

Knuckles looked at Ben with wonderment of his logic. "Sure, Ben, why don't you go get 'em. Might be workin' so hard, they'll just plum forget about eatin'."

"Ain't you the apple cider," Ben said with mild sarcasm. "Don't eat it all 'fore we get there." He walked to his horse and swung up to the saddle

"I ain't seen a meal yet where Roasty didn't make enough to choke a herd a grizzlies," Knuckles retorted as Ben galloped away.

"Rider comin'," Matt said, his eyes cast to the south.

Knuckles looked hard for a moment. "That's Sammy."

"You can tell from here? It's half a mile."

"I can see that tan vest and brown hat."

Matt stared hard. "You got better eyes'n me."

Knuckles pulled out his plug tobacco and bit off a hunk. Ben drew his makings and began rolling a cigarette. "You know, this is the damn prettiest country I ever saw. The Taylors sold him the best of their land. Water everywhere, trees, hills, grass.... If I was a bull, here's where I'd wanna be," Matt said, then lit his smoke and took a drag as he looked south down the long row of cottonwoods and birch that flanked a creek.

Knuckles let loose with a stream of tobacco juice. "This country don't look much different'n where the Twin T's sittin'."

"Well, yeah...but the surrounding area of the T ain't as nice. Whole spread here is like this...leastways from what I seen."

Knuckles contemplated. "It's farther to town from here."

"To La Jara, yeah. Five miles maybe. But closer to Two Rock."

"Two Rock ain't got half of what La Jara's got."

Matt looked incredulous. "Snakebite Saloon? That's a fine one...and that ole boy's got a couple nice lookin' whores now. Leastways had 'em just before we went to Albuquerque."

Knuckles was suddenly more interested. "Nice lookin', huh?"

"Oh man...there's one called Monique that'll grab your attention. You'll wanna see how much you can spend." Matt took a long drag and exhaled slowly like he was reliving a moment of paradise.

"I never saw anything like that there. Course, one time's all I been," Knuckles said as he looked at Matt's face that had a faraway expression plastered on it. "Monique, huh? Might have to go take a look."

"Yep, Monique."

Sammy loped up and reined to a stop, surveying the scene of the freshly branded cattle. He flashed a smile. "Hello boys. Got these all branded, eh?"

"Just finished up," Knuckles replied. "Work the next bunch this afternoon. Ben went to fetch Jasper and Porter for noon chuck. They're workin' fence on the west pasture."

"Any difficulties?"

"Nope...smooth and stinky here. Can't say them boys didn't fence themselves in though."

"Well, let's get to that noon chuck. I could eat my saddle."

Matt exhaled a last drag and tossed the butt. "Jenny didn't feed you this mornin'?"

"She offered, but she's got enough to do there without doin' for me, too."

Matt smiled. "Not for much longer I reckon."

"That's a fact...just like you gettin' your grub after me is about to be a fact." Sammy gave Dobe light heels and a flick of the reins. The appaloosa broke to a gallop toward the bunkhouse.

Unlike the setup at the Twin T, Sammy had built his crew's bunkhouse a good half-mile from the ranch house where he and Jenny would soon be living together. Privacy was what he wanted for Jenny and himself. She wouldn't be cooking for his crew. That was Roasty's job. The hands would take their meals at the bunkhouse. At the Twin T, where he'd grown up, the bunkhouse was only a hundred feet from the ranch house. He and the other hands took meals in the ranch house dining room, along with the Taylor brothers. But neither of them had ever been married, so concerns of privacy for a wife had never been an issue.

Sammy walked into the bunkhouse where the aroma of fry bread, pintos, and coffee mingled in the air. "Hello, Roasty. Smells good and I'm ready!" Sammy said, as he retrieved a plate and headed straight for it.

Roasty was sitting in a chair reading, *A Journey to the Centre of the Earth.* "Howdy, Sammy. Didn't expect you'd be the first through the door."

"Me neither. The rest of 'em will be here directly," Sammy said as he loaded his plate then headed to the table. "How's the adventure tale?"

Roasty gave a look of thought. "Well, these three ole boys went down a volcano to the center of the earth without getting burned up, but now they might get eaten by the dinosaurs that's down there. It is a tall tale. Sure has pulled me in."

Sammy swallowed a bite. "Nothin' like a tall tale to spark you along."

"Well, I'm gettin' toward the end now, so this Verne fella is gonna have to come up with something good to get these boys out alive. You were right...I sure am enjoyin' it. I never worked anywhere before with books for the choosing. Usually just old newspapers or catalogues, or maybe a dime novel."

Sammy had stocked the bunkhouse with some of the books he'd collected and read over the years, figuring the boys would enjoy them. They all could read with some proficiency, and most of them were warming up to it. Roasty and Ben had even ordered a few titles of their own from the catalogue at Agapito's Mercantile, and had been told they could expect a late summer delivery. Ben had thought about the money he'd save being entertained by something other than cards, drink, and women. But most of the boys didn't care about those kinds of savings.

Knuckles had become partial to Grimm's Fairy Tales, delighting in the darkness and lessons of the stories. Nobody else had read any of it because Knuckles kept the book stashed by his bed and occasionally enjoyed launching into his own rendition of a story he'd read, only to be told to shut the hell up. Porter had clearly expressed his sentiments on the matter. "I ain't read it yet, and I'm damn sure you won't tell it near as good as them boys that wrote it."

The door opened, and Jasper, Porter, and Bill came in with a short-haired black and white dog. It was of medium size but painfully thin. "Hey, boys," Jasper said, "look what followed us back."

Sammy looked at the dog. His ribs were showing badly, and he was wagging his whole back end. "Where'd he come from?"

"Don't know," Porter replied, reaching down to pat the dog on the head. The dog cowered slightly, but then accepted the affection as if someone was feeding him steak. "We were settin' a post, looked up, and there he was."

Sammy broke off a piece of his fry bread and held it out. "Hey, boy, you want some of Roasty's cookin'?" The dog cautiously moved to Sammy. "Come on, boy...get it." The dog gingerly took the fry bread then devoured it.

"Now, you've gone and done it," Roasty proclaimed with mock disgust. "That dog just signed on to the Sky W. Could be he'll work harder than some of the loafers we got around here."

Porter and Jasper got their plates and began dishing up when Jasper remembered. "Oh, yeah, we saw two men passin' through this morning. Looked like prospectors. Stringin' along two mules with picks and shovels and some packs. One of 'em was a Chinaman I reckon. Had one a those pointy hats and a funny lookin' shirt."

"Did you have a conversation with them?" Sammy asked.

"No. They was headin' east along the flute row...near a mile from where we was working. I had my glass on 'em."

Sammy thought about it for a moment. He'd seen folks in that area before. The northwest end of his land had a natural cutoff trail through it that connected larger north-south and east-west trails beyond his land. Sammy had given thought to posting signs that it was Sky W land, but there were so few people that happened along on it, he hadn't bothered. Prospectors were something new, though. He considered it, knowing some of the formations and creeks in that area might look promising to prospectors. Tomorrow he'd take a ride up and see if the two men were anywhere in the area.

Knuckles and Matt walked in. Knuckles headed straight for the chow. Matt looked at Jasper and Porter. "Did you see Ben? He rode over to get you."

Porter's garbled reply came through a mouthful of beans. "We came back through the Red Creek...didn't see him."

Knuckles laughed. "Well, don't that smoke the hog. I told that boy you'd know when to eat. Now, *he's* going to be last." Knuckles finished loading his plate and was headed to the table when he finally noticed the dog. "Who's poochie?" he asked with delighted surprise.

"Whoever feeds him," Sammy replied, breaking off another piece of fry bread for the dog.

"Well, that'll be everyone," Roasty dryly quipped. "Better give 'im a name so he ain't confused with dog and poochie and whatever other harebrained notion of names this outfit comes up with from day to day." Roasty looked at the dog. "How 'bout Skinny or Sack a Bones?"

"Hell, Roasty...he ain't gonna be neither of those after a month around here," Matt replied. "He looks like a Chester to me."

"Chester? Well...yeah...okay. Got a nice ring to it. I like it. Anybody against it?" Roasty asked.

The boys kept eating without response, which Roasty took as confirmation of Matt's suggestion. "Chester it is."

The boys all broke off chunks of their fry bread and began feeding Chester at will. Sammy noted the enthusiasm of it. "Yep, Chester won't be showin' those ribs for long."

9

The gray of first light swept in like a ghost, a presence unknown until it was upon in a blink. Sammy stood on the front porch of his new home, letting his eyes scan the meadow and the tree line beyond. He sipped the strong, hot coffee and watched as a group of white-tailed deer appeared from the trees and began feeding on the lush grass. As the light became more, he looked across the half mile to the east where the bunkhouse stood silhouetted against the hills beyond. Smoke rose from the stovepipe.

Thick with dew, the air was still and offered the sounds of dove cooing in the distance. The staccato fire of a woodpecker's beak rang out from one of the nearby stands of ponderosa pine, mixing with the ever present soothing song of moving water from the creek behind his cabin. Sammy reveled it all in and prayed to be worthy of his blessings. His land was magnificent.

He saddled Dobe and stopped in at the bunkhouse, in time for the fresh biscuits and gravy. None of the other boys were out yet. "You sure are good with these," he commented to Roasty.

"Glad you think so. My mama made 'em better'n that."

Roasty was the newest member of the crew, having signed on when Sammy started construction at the Sky W a year earlier. He hailed from Kansas and had cooked for several different outfits. At age thirty-two, he was the eldest of the outfit and seven years older than Knuckles who was the next oldest. The premature gray in his hair and his quick wit made him something of a sage to the boys. But mostly, they just revered his cooking. He had happily given up his given name of Bartholomew Pinkton in favor of Roasty, which he'd been dubbed by an earlier outfit for his perfection at cutting and roasting enormous T-bone steaks. The two-word nickname of Roast T had quickly become simply Roasty. Roasty oversaw all things related to cooking. He tended the chickens, hogs, and cows, and butchered the beef and other game and fish that the boys brought. And he was a master at smoking any meat using different woods, spices, and berries. It was the best smoked meat that any of the boys had ever tasted before, even better than Jacqueline's, the legendary cook at the Twin T Ranch.

Sammy finished his meal and rolled a smoke to have with his coffee. All the boys were up and out over the next few minutes, and Sammy spoke of the day's work with them. Knuckles went right to negotiating. "Hey, Porter, you want to switch out today? I'd rather build fence than whiff on more branding smoke."

"Suits me. But watch that wind today...yer dress might blow up."

The boys all laughed.

Knuckles knew he had to take it with humor. "Yeah, I know. My nose is just too perceptive."

"I'll see you on the fence later on," Sammy announced as he got up to leave. "I'm goin' to ride the north end...see if those prospectors are poking around." He walked out the front door and pitched the half biscuit he was holding. It landed directly in front of Chester, who was lying by a rocker on the front porch. The dog quickly ate it and got to all fours, wagging with happiness and wondering if any more was to follow. "Don't worry, Chester, there'll be more comin' when those boys finish breakfast."

Sammy mounted up and headed northwest at a lope. Chester fell in beside him at a run. "No! Go on back!" Sammy yelled when he noticed Chester alongside. The dog stopped for a moment and watched as the horse and rider continued on. Then Chester ran after them. "Okay, give it the hot iron," Sammy declared upon seeing Chester alongside again.

He rode at a good pace across meadow and plain, winding through pinion and juniper, and across creeks that fed vast stands of aspen, birch, and cottonwoods, and on over rolling hills dotted with orange paintbrush amidst the sage and scrub oak. Chester ran right along beside, occasionally stopping to sniff something out or drink from the stream crossings. But then he'd run and catch up just as quickly as he'd fallen behind. "You're starved but you ain't weak," Sammy said, amazed at the energy and stamina the dog had.

Sammy arrived at the canyon, still inside his land. He rode east along the ridge of it as the sun climbed the sky. The canyon fell away in an easy slope through Scottish pines and over patches of granite and sandstone to the creek below. A little farther along, he caught sight of two men down at the creek. Sammy watched them for several minutes, expecting to see them panning. But instead, it looked like the white man was working at the direction of the Chinaman, digging samples of soil and presenting them to the man with the pointy hat and long, braided pigtail down his back. The Chinaman sifted through the soil given to him and drew some of it, adding it to a jar with a solution in it, then swirling it and examining the contents closely.

Sammy began working his way down the slope toward the men. Halfway down, the white man caught sight of him and immediately talked to the Chinaman who did not look up but moved quickly to one of the mules and put the jar in a pack bag. The white man moved to his horse and stood by the rifle scabbard that showed the stock protruding. He rested his hands on his gun belt. Sammy watched them carefully as he closed the final distance.

"Howdy, stranger, what brings you down here?" the white man asked in a tone that conveyed anything but sincere greetings. He looked to be in his early forties and wore work clothes and a derby hat. Sammy glanced at the Chinaman who gave a slight nod forward of his head but said nothing.

"I like to ride about on my land, so I am not the stranger here. What is it that brings you down here?"

"Your land?" the man retorted, ignoring Sammy's question. "I don't see how that's possible."

"It's more than possible, it's a fact."

"I checked land records over at Two Rock. Didn't see any ownership listed for this area."

"Well, mister, they don't keep land records in Two Rock for this area. But if you care to ride to La Jara, you'll find this land is owned...by me. Now, I can see you're prospecting, and I don't allow that. So you'll have to move on...today."

"You don't allow it?" the man chuckled with slight contempt.

"That's right."

"Then maybe I'll just go check in La Jara. How much land do you own here?

"You can find that out in La Jara."

"Well, what's your name, mister?"

"I'm Sammy Winds, and this is the Sky W Ranch."

"You look awful young to own much more than your horse and that dog."

Sammy didn't bother responding. He pulled out his makings and began to roll a smoke, keeping his eyes glued firmly on the two men.

The white man watched him, trying to measure him and the truthfulness of what Sammy had said. He seemed confident and that troubled the man. "You say so. I suppose I'll have to take you at your word for now. I hope you're not mistaken."

Sammy lit his smoke and took a drag, watching them, saying nothing.

The man paused for a moment, and then looked at the Chinaman who gave a soft nod of his head. The man looked back at Sammy. "All right then, we'll move on."

"Everything south and east of here is my land for about four miles. After that, you'll be on the Twin T Ranch. They don't want prospecting on their place either. If you're headin' southeast to Santa Fe or Albuquerque, you'll have to get back north two miles and trail east till you get to the Fantana Trail. You'll see the traces."

"No, we'll be riding north," the man said, as he considered what Sammy had just told him.

"Good travels to you then," said Sammy, as he started his horse moving.

The man was irritated with what had just transpired and couldn't resist the comment. "Make sure your dog gets gone with you, or I'll have to shoot him for my friend here. He thinks them a delicacy for eating."

Sammy reined to a stop and turned back to face the two men. "You better mount up and be headin' north in the next half minute," he said, then took a last drag of his cigarette and flicked it to the ground.

"Or what?" the man asked.

"Or defend your life," Sammy said then let his hand hang loosely by his holster.

Beneath his derby hat, the man's face turned red, but he thought better of saying anything more. The Chinaman muttered a few words to the man who then immediately began securing their gear and collecting their animals.

Sammy watched as they mounted up and began moving north. "If I see you on my land again, I won't bother with talk."

10

The knock at the door came as the spectacled man was drinking brandy and surveying a topographical map spread before him on a large cherrywood desk. Shadows loomed in the corners and on the far walls, cast by the room's only light, a six-headed serpent lamp made of copper that sat upon the great desk, each of the heads rising forth with open mouths holding lime-colored opaque glass into which the flames licked upward. The hour was late. Sheldon Lambmorton sat in his black leather high back chair, wearing his suit with his vest buttoned. It helped to contain his rotund figure.

Momentarily ignoring the knock, he casually put the snifter down and retrieved a cigar from the box upon the desk. He snipped the end and lit it, appreciating its fine palate as he drew from it repeatedly then blew some out before inhaling the final bit. There was no hurry to his response. The meeting had been scheduled earlier that day and he knew that the visitor would humbly wait without knocking again. After another sip of brandy and a long pull from the cigar, Lambmorton was ready to receive the visitor. "Come," he said with the tone of a curt command.

The Chinaman opened the door slowly and entered. He closed the door softly then shuffled over to the desk and stood before it.

"Sit down, Mister Han."

"Thank you, Mister Lambmorton," the Chinaman replied. He was more than happy to sit. It had been two hard days of travel back from the land where the unexpected cowboy had run him and his assistant off. But they had already been in the area for five days before being discovered, more than adequate time for the Chinaman to do his analysis. Mister Lambmorton would be interested in his report.

Lambmorton offered him nothing and got right to the point. "What have your travels revealed? You have encouraging news perhaps?" They were the same two questions that Lambmorton always led off with after Han had been on assignment. Aside from Clint Smith's land and a few other marginal finds, there hadn't been much good to report in the last half year. But tonight would be different.

"Yes...encouraging, good. Not all, but good in places...very good," Han replied.

"Lambmorton's chin came up, giving the folds of his neck a momentary reprieve from compression as air found creases that were normally buried. "Very good?"

"Yes, very, very good."

Lambmorton suckled his cigar as if it were the tit of prosperity. Mister Han had proven to be a geologist of note, primarily because he was seldom mistaken and had never been wrong about places he showed enthusiasm about. His abilities seemed mystical, like the man himself. He was in his mid-fifties but looked ageless. His round face was smooth with clear eyes, and his black hair, braided to a long pigtail, showed only the faintest traces of gray. Unscarred or wrinkled were his fleshy hands, soft and malleable, devoid of calluses of labor.

Lambmorton considered Han for a moment. He knew what kind of money the Chinaman was being paid because he was tasked with paying him. It was a lot of money. But Han's successful discoveries meant more money for Lambmorton who sat forward now. "Show me where and tell me," Lambmorton said, with piqued interest brought by Han's words and the good brandy.

Mister Han leaned forward and studied the map then slowly began to trace his finger over an area. "All of this very good for gold and silver. Also emerald, garnet, opal, turquoise. Much water, too, and other resources."

"Such as?"

"Coal, copper, iron." Han paused for a moment then included the other pertinent information. "A man come and say this whole area belong to him. He a very young man...look like a cowboy. He say his name is Sammy Winds. We see him here." Han put his finger to a spot on the map. "He say four miles east and south of here all belong to him...Sky W Ranch."

Lambmorton had pulled the ink pen from its well and was making notes. He didn't comment about the cowboy. Mister Han knew nothing of acquisition methods or the true nature of the organization he was working for.

Lambmorton would soon know all there was to know about this land and who owned it. He would put Rupert Crowder on it immediately.

"Mister Lambmorton," Han said, in a suddenly more reserved tone.

"Yes."

"Assistant Stanley too stupid in way he talk to cowboy. Cowboy become angry...say he shoot us if we not leave right away. He get me killed with stupid talk. You have new man?"

Lambmorton raised an eyebrow at the unexpected declaration and request. Han had never complained about anything, and Lambmorton understood Han was an asset he had to protect. "Do not worry Mister Han. I will have it taken care of it."

"Thank you, thank you."

Rupert Crowder filed the abandoned homestead claim at the courthouse in Dumas. It was for Clint Smith's property. The recently deceased Mister Smith was the only name on the filed claim, and the sheriff's visit to the property to inform Smith's help that Smith had taken up residence in the afterlife turned up no one. The place was vacant. Everything was gone except for a few valueless personal things, some furniture, and several chickens scouring the bare yard where they had always found their portion of grain.

At the end of the Civil War, Clint Smith had filed a homestead claim on one hundred and sixty acres and bought an additional two hundred acres that adjoined his claim. He devoted the first few years to farming but shifted to full-time prospecting for gold after stumbling across a few nuggets in the stream running through his place. So he dammed it up and began panning with fair success. He reaped enough to live comfortably and eventually added two helpers to dig the higher ground of the stream in hopes of hitting a vein. But their methods were crude and yielded only enough to keep the fever alive of hitting it big.

Han had scouted the area and quickly deduced that Smith and his help were working nowhere near where Han believed the real gold was. And Han thought there was likely a fortune to be harvested from the Smith property.

After Smith declined the less than enticing offer made by Rupert Crowder, the deadly methods of Lucius Hammond and Boothe Haney were employed. Now, all that was left was to claim the land.

Claims on abandoned homestead property were not normally considered before the ninety days of owner absence had passed. After that, barring no will or last testament that named a beneficiary, the land could be claimed by any other known resident of the property. But none were present now, at least, not above ground. Rupert Crowder had filed for expedited consideration based on the fact that the owner was known to be dead and the premises appeared abandoned. "You sure didn't waste any time," the clerk had said when Crowder submitted the claim.

"Westgate Railroad doesn't care to waste time, sir," Crowder had replied. Westgate Railroad was the company that Crowder had listed himself an agent for on the submitted claim. And he had listed a New York address for the company.

A territorial circuit judge would soon be through Dumas and would rule on the request for an expedited claim. Crowder was confident about the outcome.

11

The morning was warm and humid from rain that had fallen the night before. The heavily laden wagon rumbled slowly along over mostly firm ground, just miles from the Sky W Ranch. Sammy was returning from town with needed supplies, but the trip had been equally spurred by his want of seeing Jenny. Her black hair and blue-violet eyes ran through his mind once more as the scent of pine and wildflowers hung on the moist air. He smiled as he thought of their evening together and the home ahead that they would soon share as man and wife. Sammy lifted his eyes to the squawking above as two hawks glided noisily past as if they were carrying on a conversation.

His mind turned to the two men he had run off the morning before. He would never say "no" to folks passing through, but prospectors could be a dangerous thing that could bring hordes, with a few careless words passed in a saloon. And the man with the derby hat had conducted himself rudely, running his mouth in a manner that had rubbed Sammy the wrong way. Sammy wondered about the second man, the Chinaman. What had he been doing with those jars? Had he discovered anything? He had remained silent and kept his eyes down during the encounter. Sammy suspected that he was the brains of the outfit, if nothing more.

Through a stand of ponderosa pine and into a meadow, the wagon rolled on with Sammy's mind rolling through all that consumed his young life. He came alert when he spotted a wagon on the far side of the meadow. It was headed his way at a crawl, pulled by a single horse with two men atop the driver's bench. He caught the glint of the rifle barrel in the late morning sun. The man riding shotgun held it. Sammy reached back and pulled the Winchester from its scabbard, then cocked it and laid it across his lap. His gun belt was coiled on the floorboard.

As the distance closed, Sammy thought he saw movement in the back of their wagon, though the two men up front blocked the view. Then he saw a head pop up, and another, and another. They looked like children. Then he could see that the man who held the rifle riding shotgun had a very young face, that of a boy. The only man aboard was the driver. They all stared intently at Sammy as the last of the distance yielded and the wagons came side by side.

"Whoa," Sammy said as he pulled on the reins and brought his team to a stop. The driver of the other wagon reined the limping horse to a stop. "Good morning," Sammy cheerfully said, surveying the occupants of the wagon. They looked ragged and wary, like that of a hard and dangerous journey endured.

"Good morning," the children all chimed in response. There were two girls and three boys, the oldest of which was the boy with the rifle. Sammy guessed him at no more than twelve or thirteen, and he held the rifle loosely and pointed up, but at the ready.

"Good morning to you...though it may be noon by now," the man replied. He had a pleasant but fatigued expression. He removed his hat and wiped his brow. His hair was all gray and

71

his face showed the lines of a man of years. His eyes looked kind and wise but hollow and slightly gaunt. Sammy noticed it on the children as well. There seemed a pall of hunger and worry in their faces.

"Yes, it might be noon by now and warm it is," Sammy replied. "Are you lost? The traces here are just a ranch trail."

"Why, yes, I suppose we are. I have not a compass but have tried to stay on a southern course. Forgive us if we have trespassed onto someone's land."

"It's my land, and you're welcome to be here. I'm Sammy Winds, and this is the Sky W Ranch."

"Thank you, Mister Winds. I am Tomas Cordero and these are my children, Rory, Jing Lu, Payat, Tobias, and Camille." Each of the children nodded or smiled as the padre said their name. "We are traveling to the Madras Country...near Albuquerque."

"Well, I'm pleased to make your acquaintance," Sammy said, his tone trying to conceal his intrigue at the old man's pronouncement that the children were his. The oldest boy was white with blazing red hair, and the one named Tobias was also white with brown hair. But the other three all had black hair, with one being Chinese, one being Indian, and one being Mexican. And the man was old enough to be their grandfather, perhaps great-grandfather. There was only one explanation. But it wasn't Sammy's business. He spoke to the issue at hand. "That would be farther south, all right...but as much east, too, another hundred and twenty-five miles or so. Your horse looks to be lame. My ranch is just another mile on up. You're welcome to stay and rest him...or I could fix you up with another horse. We have plenty of food, too, if you need provisions."

The children's faces lit up at the invitation and the mention of food. Even the padre's eyes widened a bit. "That is a very kind offer, Mister Winds. But I have little money, which I must save for our journey's end."

Jing Lu blurted out what the other children were thinking. "Oh, could not we stay, Padre? Just for a little while?"

"Jing Lu, hush," the padre said.

Rory took up Jing Lu's defense. "Roca could sure use a few days of rest, Padre. He's been gettin' worse every day since he took that stumble."

"Padre? You're a priest?" Sammy asked, his curiosity getting the better of him.

The padre had a slight look of consternation upon his face that quickly faded. "Years ago, I was a priest at the mission in Ranchos de Taos, but I left the church to marry." The padre paused for a moment then decided to continue with what he knew this stranger was wondering about, sensing the goodwill and honesty of the young man before him. "My wife and I took these children in. They were all orphans. She died last spring of the cholera." The words stung him as he said them, and the children's faces all suddenly registered the remembrance and loss. "We are going to Madras for land and a new start."

"I am sorry for your loss, Padre," Sammy said. "Is it all right if I call you Padre?"

"Yes, of course, Mister Winds."

"I would like all of you to call me Sammy."

"Yes, Sammy!" Camille nearly shouted with a broad smile. The children laughed at the suddenness of it. The padre smiled at the ease of the moment. It had been a while since a laugh had taken hold.

"Why don't you come along to the ranch, and we'll get a good look at your horse. I don't think he's making it to Madras anytime soon," Sammy said. The padre looked into Sammy's eyes with an expression of reluctance that wanted to yield.

"I'm not trying to sell you anything, Padre. You don't need to spend any money."

"Thank you, Mister Winds...and our horse Roca thanks you, too."

"Are you going to tell him, Padre?...about the men?" Jing Lu asked.

"This is not the time or place, child."

Roasty had the look of a bewildered man when Sammy walked in followed by the padre and five children. "Hello, Roasty. The boys already had noon and gone?" Sammy asked.

"About half an hour ago. Hello to you folks."

"Roasty, this is Padre Tomas and...and his children," Sammy said, knowing he wouldn't get all the names right.

"Tell Mister Roasty your names, children," the padre said.

Rory led off and the others followed by order of age, the way they had always done it when the padre asked them to introduce themselves. Camille was last. "My name is Camille...and I like your name, Mister Roasty."

Roasty laughed. "It's just Roasty...no 'Mister' in front of it. I'm pleased to meet you all. Say, are you folks hungry? 'Cause I got a pot of beef stew that ain't seen the bottom yet. And you know what else I got?" Roasty let his eyes drift from child to child, taking in the looks of curiosity.

Rory took a step forward like he was volunteering for duty. "What else you got, Roasty, sir?

"I got four fresh apple pies. Made six of 'em this mornin' and our ranch crew only ate two of 'em with noon dinner. You think you could help me whittle these down some?"

"I help," Payat instantly said.

"Me too," Tobias followed.

"I love pie...any kind," Jing Lu added.

"Me too!" Camille said.

"Well, sit on down at the table and let's get after some stew and pie!" Roasty said with delight.

When they all had their food before them, Camille spoke up. "May I say grace, Padre?"

"Yes, Camille. We would all like that."

She glanced at Sammy and Roasty who were caught unaware for a moment, but quickly bowed their heads with the others. "Heavenly Father, thank you for this food and bless our family...and please bless Sammy and Roasty, too. Oh, and please bless Chester, too. He's the nice dog we met outside...and that's where he is right now. And please heal Roca's leg, but not too fast. I like it here. Amen."

The children all laughed and Roasty slapped his leg. "That was a good one," he said. "Much obliged for the blessing."

The padre ate with some restraint, even though he was starving, but the children stuffed their faces. "Children!" he exclaimed upon seeing the food being shoveled into their mouths with astonishing speed and lack of regard for choking. "Do not forget your manners. We are guests."

Roasty chuckled. "Looks downright mannerful next to the outfit that just rolled through here."

The children slowed their pace at the padre's admonishment. The padre smiled at Sammy and Roasty. "Forgive us. We have had little food since we started our journey...and nothing yesterday."

"Where did you start from?" Roasty asked.

The padre hesitated for a moment. "About ten miles east of Dumas. We began this way a week ago."

"I know of Dumas," Sammy said. "Never been through there. It's nigh to a hundred miles north or so...up by the Saguatch Range?"

"Yes, I suppose that would be about the right distance. We have been traveling very slowly. Our horse stumbled in a stream as we were crossing. It was the first day and he has limped a little more each day after. Much of the trip, the children have walked to lighten the wagon."

"Well, we'll get him in a stall with some liniment and good feed," Sammy said. "I'm guessing it's just a sprain. He'll need some rest, though."

After they ate, Sammy took them to his ranch house and put their injured horse in the barn. Then he showed them around. "You boys can stay in here, and Jing Lu and Camille can stay in this room," Sammy said, as he led them through the house with its three bedrooms, den, kitchen, and great room.

"It is so big!" Jing Lu exclaimed. "Where is your family?"

The padre winced. "Jing Lu, you are a guest. You should not ask of private matters that do not concern you."

She looked at Sammy sheepishly, realizing that her question could bring an answer of pain with a story of tragedy. She had already known as much herself. "I am sorry, Mister Sammy."

Sammy smiled and touched her on the head. "No harm, Jing Lu. I don't have a family of my own yet, but I'm getting married in a few weeks. I'm sure my wife and I will be having one soon enough."

12

From the gift came the sound of laughter as dusk settled upon the long sky, serenaded by the last color and hue in magnificence to the day's end. The children ran in the meadow, playing the game that all partook in, even Rory, who, as oldest, sometimes abstained, feeling instinctually that he should be beyond such things. But he laughed and played, the joy of the game momentarily erasing the danger and hardships so fresh on their lives.

The padre and Sammy watched from the porch of the house as they drank coffee and rocked in their chairs. Sammy wanted to know more. "I don't mean to press, Padre, but the contents of your wagon look scant for starting new. Not much more there than some clothes and a few personals."

"We did not have much to begin with. And we left hurriedly."

"Would that have anything to do with the men Jing Lu mentioned?"

The padre sipped his coffee and cast his eyes to Sammy's. "Yes," he said. The padre slowly began to tell the story of how their journey had stalled in the big fall storm, how Clint Smith had given them use of the old shed on his property, and how they had wintered there. Then he spoke of what had happened.

"A week ago, on Sunday morning, the children and I were worshipping on the hillside when a group of men rode to Mister Smith's cabin in the meadow below. They shot Chapawee, the Indian woman he lived with, and also Jimmy and Luke, two young men who worked for Mister Smith. I saw it all from where I watched in the trees. The children did not."

"What about Smith?"

"I do not know. I never saw him. He must have been away. The men also looked in the casita where we stayed. We hid in the hills as they searched for us. Then later, two of the men drove a wagon with the bodies toward the north woods. The other men were gone. I knew they would come back for us. Men such as that do not rest until they rid all evidence of their deeds. While they were gone, we went to the casita and quickly gathered a few things and our horse and wagon. But my fear of their return brought too much haste in the packing, and we ended up leaving with little food, or much else. Rory is skilled with the rifle and pistol, though we have seen no game close enough for the taking during our journey. Now, God has answered our prayers with your hospitality, Mister Winds."

"I'm glad to be of help, Padre. Do you have any idea who the men were or why they shot those people?"

"No."

"Do you know what Mister Smith did for a living? Cattle? Farming?"

"I believe he did some farming. He had horses and a plow and good land and water. But most of our time there was in winter, and we knew them little. Several times, Mister Smith gave us deer and elk meat. He was a private man, and they kept to themselves. The children knew Chapawee best. She was kind to them."

The padre was about to speak of how Smith and his men had been heading off each morning with the wagon, picks, and shovels since the winter had turned to spring, when the yell of Tobias broke his thought. "Oooooowww! You broke my leg, Payat!" Tobias shouted. Payat had tackled Tobias with a crunching shoulder through the thigh. The game had gotten more competitive than Tobias was ready for, at least for the moment. The children huddled around Tobias, wanting to discover the extent of the injury.

Rory ran his hand over the leg in question, feeling and squeezing. "Where's it hurt?"

"Ooooww! Right there," Tobias hollered, as Rory squeezed his thigh.

"Your leg ain't broke...get up! All you got is a corky."

"A corky? That must be a broke leg 'cause that's what it feels like. Ooowww!"

"I told you...it ain't broke. You just got a bruised muscle, so get up!"

"Children, come inside and prepare for night time," the padre called out to them.

"You tore it now," Rory said to Tobias in a whispered voice. "I'm gonna try and get us some more time, and you better not make another peep about your leg. Just get up and shut up. Got it?"

Tobias nodded at Rory and the others with a pained look of agreement.

"Aaahhh, just a few more minutes, Padre? Can we go stick our feet in the creek for a little bit?" Rory pleaded.

"Is Tobias all right? I heard him yell out about his leg being hurt."

"He's fine!" Camille replied loudly.

Rory looked at Tobias with a commanding expression that the boy understood.

"Yes, Padre. I am fine!" Tobias yelled out.

"All right then...a few more minutes. Do not go too far."

"You've got yourself quite a family there, Padre," Sammy said as he pulled out the makings and began to roll a smoke.

"Yes," the padre replied, slowly nodding his head.

"I know it's none of my business, but why do you want to go to Madras?"

"I was told that there is still land available for homesteading…good land. And now we must get far away from those men also. I am certain they would have killed us if they had found us. They may search for us now. I will send a letter to the sheriff of Dumas and tell him of all that I saw. I do not know if it will help catch those men, but the truth about what happened to Chapawee and Luke and Jimmy must be known."

"I understand. How many men were there?"

"There were six, but I think two of them were shot."

"Dead?"

"I do not know. I saw them fall from their horses, and then we immediately left to hide."

"You were wise, Padre. Can you recollect anything about them or their horses?"

"Not so much of the men. It was a good distance. But one man rode a pure black horse…big, a stallion I would think. There was also a brown and white paint…and a gray." The padre looked off to the side, his eyes tightening in deep concentration as he tried to remember. "I don't remember more. It happened very fast."

"Well, if more comes to you, you can include it all in the letter you post to the sheriff."

"Yes, yes…I will try to remember more."

"Padre, I didn't want to tell you before in front of your children, but I don't believe there's any more homestead land to be had in Madras."

The padre's face tightened. "Why do you say this?"

"I was just recently in Albuquerque. Drove cattle back past that Madras area. Talked to an hombre there who said the whole place filled up when the government made that land available for homesteading two years back. He said he didn't think the land was worth spit for farming, but the folks flocked in anyway."

"I see," the padre stoically said. The news was crushing to hear.

Sammy lit his cigarette and took a sip of his coffee. "Now, I don't know it to be a fact that the land's all taken. It could be that ole boy was trying to send a discouraging word up the trail...tryin' to keep people out. But I reckon he was probably right about it not being particularly suitable for farming. It looked awful arid out that way."

"I see," the padre said again, his eyes cast down.

"I've got a better idea for you anyway."

The padre's eyes slowly lifted and settled intently on Sammy's. "And what would that be young Mister Winds?"

"Stay here, Padre. I own twenty thousand acres of good land. I'll give you a hundred acres over on Red Creek. Good soil and plenty of water. We'll get a place built...big enough for all of you, and then some."

The padre's eyes widened and bore into Sammy's with a gaze of perplexity. He leaned forward as if he had not heard. "Why would you do this thing? I have told you there is little money."

Sammy took a long, slow drag off his cigarette, the smoke filling his lungs as his memories crystallized. He exhaled the smoke into the darkening sky. "When I was seven years old, I was the only survivor of an Indian attack on the wagon train my family was traveling with. I lost my mother and father and brother. Some men found me a few days later...men that worked for the Twin T Ranch. They took me there. The ranch owners, Homer and Reuben Taylor, took me in and gave me a good home...taught me and provided for me. I lived there all my life. Then about a year and a half ago, things got turned upside down. I was in town one day and got in a fight with an outlaw who was passin' through. He was itchin' for trouble. I had to kill him. He nearly killed me. Turned out there was a reward on his head. I collected that reward, and now I'm startin' my own ranch...and getting married to a wonderful, beautiful woman. My blessings have been more than I ever deserved. But to come into money over killin' a man..." Sammy paused and took another drag from his cigarette, slightly shaking his head over the irony of it. "I've had it in mind that the Lord had a purpose for such a thing. Didn't rightly understand what it might be, but I don't see how running into you could be anything but part of that purpose. I was an orphan, Padre. Now, I have the chance to help like I was helped...to give like I was given to. You don't need money, Padre. You don't need to go any farther either. But if you do want to go, I'll give you horses and enough money to make a good start. I'd be honored to have you stay here...to make a life with your kids here."

The padre leaned back again; stunned at the words Sammy had spoken. "You are a good man...a generous man, Mister Winds. Your offer is enchanting, but I must wonder if it is too hasty, perhaps premature. We have just met, and your regard for our circumstances may bring words that you would think better of upon reflection. I would advise that you consider such a matter for more time. Pray on it."

"Bullshit, Padre." The words came calmly from Sammy with matter-of-fact conviction.

"Bullshit?" The padre repeated curiously. "I do not believe I ever heard such a retort in a confessional."

"I didn't mean to give offense, Padre… merely stark weight to my position, glib though it might have been."

The padre looked at Sammy, realizing he was no run-of-the-mill cowboy. "But you said you are to be married soon. You have not consulted with your intended about this matter. There are many things to consider."

'Look, Padre, perhaps you need more time to reflect, to consider and pray about what to do. That's fine. Take all the time you need. The offer stands. I'm not one to speak lightly, particularly on matters where a divine calling is as certain to me as the breath I take. I don't always do what's right, but I know what's right because I know God. I know this is right."

The padre took a deep breath, letting the sweet air of the meadow and pines fill his lungs and soul with tranquility. His senses stirred and his tired muscles relaxed in the revelation that the young man was right. It was meant to be. "Yes, Mister Winds, we humbly accept your most gracious offer to live here. God bless you, Mister Winds."

"He already has, Padre. And the name is Sammy."

13

T he next morning, Sammy was making coffee when Jing Lu appeared by his side so quietly that he was not aware of her until she spoke. "Good morning, Mister Winds," she said softly.

"Good morning, Jing Lu. You're up early...before the light, and anybody else."

"Not before you," she replied matter-of-factly. Then she smiled. "I would like to make the breakfast. Would that be all right?"

"Well, sure. I'm not real well stocked yet. I usually eat with the boys at the bunkhouse...for a few more weeks, anyway. But I've got a few things here. What do you know how to make?"

"I make very good biscuits. What food things do you have?"

"I've got flour over here, and sugar, and beans...and some smoked pork and potatoes and onions right down in here," he said, lifting a trap door in the floor that revealed stairs into a cellar. Sammy grabbed the lamp off the table. "Come to think of it, I've got some eggs down here, too."

"Can I come, too?" Jing Lu asked as Sammy began descending the stairs with the lamp.

"Come on down."

Jing Lu quickly descended the stairs and felt the noticeable temperature change at the bottom. "It is very cool down here," she said, looking around the eight-by-eight room that was completely paneled with pine boards. There were shelves for storing things, and hooks for hanging things.

A large smoked ham hung in a cheesecloth. Sammy took the knife that was stuck in it, and began cutting off a sizeable hunk. "The coolness helps keep the food fresh," he said, as he whittled away. "This cellar is built along the north wall on the east end. That's where the earth will stay the coolest."

"Because the sun passes to the south?"

"That's right...more so in the winter than the summer. The north wall of the house casts shadow on the ground just beyond it. Here, hold this." Sammy handed the hunk of meat to her then knelt to the floor and opened a small trap door to a two-foot-by-two-foot cube below, lined with mortared granite rock. "This is the coldest spot...good for eggs and such. Only have about eight right now...you want 'em for your makings?"

"Oh, yes, please," she replied. "I can make a good scrambled egg hash with the things you have. It will be delicious."

"I'm gettin' hungry just hearing about it."

When they got back into the kitchen, Sammy showed her the pots and plates and cooking utensils, then refilled his coffee cup and headed for the porch. "It's all yours, Jing Lu. Give a holler if you need any help. I'll be right out front here."

"I will help her," Camille said, as she came into the kitchen rubbing the sleep from her eyes.

"Yes, you will," Jing Lu happily replied.

The padre stood on the porch, gazing out as first light crept on the land. "Mornin', Padre," came Sammy's greeting.

"Yes, indeed, a good morning it is. And a good night it was. I slept very deep and restful…the first good night's sleep I have had in many nights. The children, too, I am sure."

Sammy nodded. "Yep, nothin' like a good night's sleep to put the world back in order."

The padre let his eyes drift over the vista. "Your land is so very beautiful…and the air is cool."

"Yeah, mountain land's cooler in the summer. More snow in the winter, though. Speaking of land, how 'bout after breakfast we go on over to Red Creek, and I'll show you the piece I've got in mind for you…pick a building site."

"That would be very exciting. Is it far?"

"Just the other side of that hill over there…about a mile."

"The children can go, yes?"

"Of course. And your boys can help when we start building."

"Jing Lu and Camille will help, too, Mister Winds. They are good workers. All the children are good workers."

"Well, Jing Lu and Camille are workin' on breakfast right now."

"They are good cooks. You will be surprised."

Jing Lu and Camille served up a feast that everyone ate heartily of, and then the padre told them, "Children, I have something to tell you. Mister Winds has made us a most generous offer."

"It's Sammy, Padre," Sammy reminded him again.

"Yes, Sammy has offered us some of his land right here on his ranch…and also offered to help us build our own home on the land. Would you all like that?"

"Yeaaaaahh!" the collective roar went up.

The padre smiled broadly. "Good! Then our journey to find a new home is over."

"Where will we build? When can we start building?" Rory asked, excitedly.

"We're going to look at the land right now, and we'll start building just as soon as you pick a site and we figure a house plan," Sammy replied.

"Yeaaaah!" the children cheered again.

"All right then. Let's go look. It's about a mile away. You all want to walk or ride? I can hitch up the wagon in a snap."

"Let's walk...okay?" Rory said nodding his head.

"Okay," Payat replied.

"Yes, it will be good to stretch our legs over the beautiful land," the padre agreed.

They walked as the early morning sun rose in the blue, cloudless sky, quickly blanching the remaining shadows on the land and stealing the chill from the air. Over the soft undulation of hill, they hiked, coming into a long valley rich with meadow. It was bordered on the far side by aspen and cottonwood that stood thick in a meandering course along the Red Creek. Sammy led them to the wooden bridge wide enough for a wagon. They crossed over the creek below that was fifteen feet wide and nearly three feet deep, with clear, cold water, a rocky bottom, and mossy banks that had a distinctly red hue. On the other side, they stood amidst the aspen and cottonwood as Sammy pointed to more meadow beyond. "This is it, Padre. All of this meadow and land along the creek, roughly back to those boulders and up to that stand of ponderosa north and the hollow with the pinion to the south."

"It is beyond words," the padre finally mumbled as he took it all in.

"I'm glad you like it. There are a lot of good building sites here. You could be back in the open meadow or over to the rise by the pines...or right up close on the creek here in the trees.

There's a real pretty natural clearing just a little bit up the bank. Walk around a while and see if a spot strikes you."

"Yes, yes, Sammy. First, we must pray," the padre said, clearly overwhelmed by the majesty of the moment and the desire to clear his head in communion with God. He carefully knelt to his knees, his body beyond the agility of youth. "Come children, kneel and let us pray. Please pray with us, Sammy, if you would like."

Sammy backed up slowly, feeling a bit awkward about breaching the intimacy of the group. "I'm with you in prayer, Padre. Go ahead now," he said, as he moved farther away to the bank of the creek and stood with his head bowed, the music of the running water filling his ears and muting most of the padre's words. Sammy heard his name early on in the prayer and was embarrassed.

Rory had been patiently waiting for the right time since he'd spotted them as he crossed the bridge. But he said nothing because they had come, after all, to see the land that Sammy was giving them. When the "Amen" was said at the conclusion of the prayer, Rory's desire was fully ripe. "Padre, I saw some huge rainbows in that stream. I got my line and hook and could rig a pole in no time. Can I go give it a try? Uh, that is if you don't need me to figure where we should build. It all looks good to me!"

The padre shot him a wry look then smiled. "I suppose you had better before the sun is too high."

"Can we go with him?" Jing Lu immediately blurted out.

"Yes, yes. Go and enjoy God's creation."

The children broke to an instant stampede toward the creek. Rory pulled his pocketknife and began yanking and cutting at a suitable aspen branch. When he had it loose, he began fashioning his pole.

"Yeah, there's some big ole fish in that water," Sammy said. "Caught some good ones here myself years ago when the Twin T crew was building that bridge. I was about Rory's age come to think of it. He oughta do well if his peanut gallery doesn't scare 'em all off."

The padre smiled. "They have been very good together, these children. Bickering has been very rare, and they have had reason to bicker or complain. Instead, they have pulled for each other, recognizing God's blessings and their chance to be part of a family together."

"Well, Padre, let's walk a bit and pick a spot to build 'em a home."

"Do you think there is a most suitable spot to build? We would not need a well if we build close to the river."

"No, you don't want to haul water if you don't need to. We'll dig a well wherever you build. The water's not deep anywhere around here. But if you'd like to be closer to the creek, there's a high spot in a clearing up here that's plum beautiful. C'mon, I'll show you."

They walked north along the creek through the trees for several minutes, and then up a gentle grade that ended at a flat clearing some hundred feet back from the creek, slightly elevated to it. The clearing was flanked by spruce and aspen and offered beautiful views east and west. Stunned, as he slowly turned and looked, the padre was transfixed at all there was to admire. His judgment came quickly. "This is a most beautiful spot. I do not imagine there is need for looking any further." Then he looked to the meadow behind him. "And the earth looks rich for planting...yes?"

"You bet. It's good soil. We'll fence it off, too...so when my herd gets built up, they won't be stompin' around anywhere near it." Sammy pulled out the makings and began rolling a cigarette as the padre walked a hundred feet into the meadow and got to his hands and knees then began digging his fingers through the soil, marveling at the deep, nutrient-rich color of it.

Sammy lit his smoke and walked over to the padre who was rising with his hand full of dirt. "It is very good soil, ripe for tilling and seed and bounty," he said as he grated the soft black dirt through his fingers, letting it fall back to the earth.

"Well, I never farmed it, but I'm sure it'll grow whatever you're of a mind to plant. It sure turns out good grass all by itself." Sammy took a drag and let the smoke slowly drift out as if he were thinking. "Now, about that house, Padre. What do you think about a two-story, with the upstairs havin' a big room as a sleepin' area for the boys, and another big room for the girls."

The padre looked puzzled, but understood the possible thinking behind Sammy's statement. He sought to validate his hunch. "There are few of us. Why do we need big rooms?"

"The West is a tough land...tough life. There might be more comin' sometime."

"More what?" the padre asked, innocently.

"Orphans!"

"You would allow me to take in more if God presents them to us?"

"This will be your land, Padre...lawfully deeded. You do whatever you want to here."

The padre reached out and took Sammy's hand, holding it with both of his own, his eyes taking in Sammy's face and soul. "Your gift is heaven sent. My heart trembles at your humility and generosity, son."

Sammy was a bit discomfited. "You're a good man, Padre. *That*, I believe, is a truth by God. I'm blessed for the chance to help. We don't need to make anymore about it now other than goin' on with it."

The padre knowingly patted his hand. "Yes, yes... all right, my son."

14

Lucius stared at the ceiling, his head resting on a pillow upon the bed that he laid. He took a drag of his cigarette then reached for the tequila bottle on the bed stand. *This tequila was a treat,* he thought. He never drank it growing up in the South, and his years in the West had proved it mostly unavailable. There was always mescal, but he liked whiskey better. That was until he happened on the pure agave, expertly distilled to tequila. The bottle he drank from now was the best he'd had in some time. It was smooth on the throat, with an essence like the shade of a tree on a hot day. He took a long pull from the bottle and felt the light breeze from the window blow across his body, cooling the sheen of sweat on him. The slight throb in his head began to fade with the coursing of the spirit through his body, its radiance dissolving unwanted sensation like fresh paint over moldy walls.

He stood up from the bed and saw her chamber pot. Thinking himself chivalrous, he pissed instead into the spittoon in the corner. The reverberant pinging of the urine that was mostly finding its mark woke her. "Why don't you take me out for a big, fancy steak...I'm hungry," she said sleepily, "Unless you need to work up more appetite first."

Lucius walked naked to his clothes and began to dress as he looked out the window. The sun was high. He guessed it to be noon already. He'd won almost forty dollars at the poker table the night before, and then had turned his sporting attention to the prettiest whore in the saloon, making a marathon of it with her and the tequila until an hour before dawn.

"Well?" she queried with a tone of excited impatience. He'd been so sweet with her the night before.

Lucius turned and looked at her. "I got business," he said flatly. He pulled the ten-dollar gold piece from his pocket and flipped it onto the bed. "Get yourself a steak and pretty yourself up for tonight. Maybe we'll do it again."

After his trip to the bath house and a meal of biscuits and gravy with a side of bacon, Lucius mounted up and left town, deciding he'd meander through some of the other northern settlements before making his way to Cuerno Verde where word of his next assignment would come from Rupert Crowder.

The large parlor off the lobby of the Palace Hotel served as the Dumas Courtroom when the territorial judge made his twice monthly rounds. It was late afternoon and the courtroom was empty of all but the judge, a court reporter, the sheriff, and Rupert Crowder.

The morning's proceedings had been busy and included a trial for a man who'd held a gun to a traveling tonic salesman's head, forcing him to eat some pig shit that he'd brought along for the occasion. The accused man's wife, who had been ill for some time, died shortly after beginning regular doses of the tonic that the salesman guaranteed as a miracle cure for virtually any ailment. The accused had put it succinctly. "He sold worthless shit, so I reckoned he should eat some."

After the salesman had eaten the pig shit at gunpoint, he was forced to drink a bottle of his miracle cure, which he did and promptly threw up, along with his latest meal. The accused made him drink another entire bottle, which was later determined to contain mostly alcohol and kerosene. The salesman lapsed into a coma and died two days later. The local justice of the peace, who presided over smaller infractions, wanted no part of it and remanded the defendant to jail until the territorial judge came through.

Several witnesses who'd bought the tonic testified that it had made them ill with gastrointestinal affliction, although one local man, known for his drunkenness, testified that it made him feel like "Blue sky!" and added that the tonic was also particularly good at removing rust from his tools.

The trial had worn on into the afternoon before the judge convicted the man of "manslaughter" and imposed a two-hundred-dollar fine, saying that the man had suffered enough with the death of his wife, and that the dead salesman was nothing more than a charlatan who sold dangerous goods.

Then, with the fireworks over and a nearly vacant courtroom before him, the judge heard the request for an expedited claim on the deceased Clint Smith's property. The sheriff gave brief testimony about Clint Smith being killed in a gunfight of his own volition, and that the Smith homestead was now deserted.

The judge, himself a crook, who would receive a handsome payment from Sheldon Lambmorton for his forthcoming ruling, listened intently, tapping his finger to his chin as if weighing the facts with deep thought and judicial wisdom that might bring something other than the prearranged outcome. But once the facts had been laid out, Judge Capuano quickly rapped his gavel, dispensing with anymore proclivity toward further consideration of the matter. "The request for the claim on said property is granted to Westgate Railroad of New York for a sum of five hundred dollars, with a new deed recorded to reflect such! Is that it for today, Lawrence?"

The court clerk, Lawrence, looked like he'd been caught flat-footed at the speed of the ruling. "Uhh… yes, Judge, that's all there is."

"Good. See you all next time."

Lambmorton wired his encrypted message to his employer in Washington, detailing the Chinaman's recent findings and the progress that had taken place on other acquisition efforts. The specific areas and locations that his employer picked for acquisition were curious to Lambmorton. Lambmorton knew Westgate Railroad was just a front, although the acquisitions did seem to form a route from north to south. Lambmorton had assumed it was all about gold and silver. Northern New Mexico Territory had produced some good strikes. Still, his employer had demanded acquisition of land that the Chinaman didn't consider to hold precious metal. And with the exception of a few gaps, the acquisitions formed a nearly contiguous stretch.

In addition to his lucrative salary, Lambmorton was also to receive a fractional percentage of gold and silver strikes, so he was naturally most interested in securing the land that held that potential. He didn't know what his employer's other angle was, but knew it wouldn't be very much longer before the territory became a state, and those who held the best land and mineral rights would profit greatly.

Some of the acquisitions had come easy and without violence. The landowners accepted the lowball offers and con talk that Rupert Crowder was so good at. But those who wouldn't sell met up with the likes of Lucius Hammond or Boothe Haney and his band of killers.

Lambmorton wondered if the cowboy who owned the Sky W Ranch would be a problem—this man named Sammy

Winds, who had run Han and Stanley off with the threat of killing. It was only a passing curiosity, though, and nothing of concern to him. They would take his land in any event, one way or another.

15

"She's close!"

"Yeah, get ready to move, quick! This one might fool us!" Sammy yelled back to Knuckles, from the other end of the seven-foot crosscut saw. His shoulder and arm muscles were on fire as he and Knuckles pulled and pushed back and forth, the saw cutting through the last of the eighty-foot tall pine. A loud cracking and tearing accompanied the movement of the trunk as gravity took over and the tree slowly tipped, gaining speed with each instant of its unstoppable course.

"Timmmberrrr!" Knuckles yelled. He and Sammy quickly abandoned each end of the saw, backpedaling to safety and watching as the tree reached its full arc of fall, its limbs parting the air with a *woosh* until the trunk crashed to the ground.

Bill Lohmeyer looked half disgusted as he watched from several hundred feet away where he and Porter Loomis manned another saw. "They're kickin' our ass…two up on us now."

"Ain't much for possible keeping up with Knuckles. He's strong as a bear," Porter opined.

"Yeah, well, if it ain't close, he'll make a show about it."

"So? He can't cowboy near close to you."

Bill considered the accuracy of Porter's words and suddenly seemed a little relieved. "Yeah, that's a fact. All right…let's heat this saw up."

Matt, Jasper, and Ben, along with the padre, Rory, Payat, and Tobias descended on the fallen trees and went to work, removing the limbs. The project was in full swing three days after the padre and Sammy had decided on the building site. Sammy figured he could use all the hands for a week during the log felling. Then half would go back to ranch business and half would stay on building the home. Knuckles had already expressed his desire to stay on with the construction. It was more to his talents.

The logs piled up quickly at the building site. Two crosscut saw crews toppled the pine trees that were selected for uniformity and trunk diameters of about sixteen inches. Then after the limbs had been removed, the logs were hitched to the team of horses that pulled each log a half mile back to the site.

Roasty made trips back and forth to town with a freight wagon, picking up plank lumber and other building materials and things for the home. He had pulled the chuck wagon out to the building site on the first day of work and shown Jing Lu and Camille all its secrets. The two girls had been put in charge of the noon chuck and took to it as a sacred mission, serving up fare that was eaten well and was much appreciated by all.

The last day of log felling had come. Warm was the afternoon that waned with the sweetness of work and accomplishment. Sammy had swapped jobs with Roasty this last day. Roasty enjoyed the change of pace and kept Knuckles entertained with a retelling of *A Journey to the Centre of the Earth*, which he'd recently finished reading. Roasty initially tried telling the story while they were sawing, but quickly found that his breathing and talking could not coincide when his body yearned for more oxygen. So he talked nonstop during short periods of rest, which were quite frequent, and allowed the other team of Bill and Porter to easily be the tree felling champions of the day.

Knuckles was mostly oblivious to the slowed pace, marveling in Roasty's magical storytelling. By the end of Roasty's recounting of it, Knuckles was hooked. "I'm going to have to read that one! Going down a volcano all the way to the middle of the earth!"

Roasty switched subjects. "I believe I like the things that's above ground most. I saw the Pacific Ocean once…swam in it…got pounded into the sand by waves that never stopped coming. Why, it was as blue and vast as all the sky…no end to it. And the whales that swim in it are as big as hotels."

"I gotta see such a thing one day," Knuckles said, his eyes wide with imagination as he stood daydreaming with the thought of it. His trance finally broke. "It ain't gonna be today, though," he said, grabbing his end of the saw. "Let's get to it."

Sammy and Jenny sat upon the bench of the freight wagon, its wheels rolling over the bridge of Red Creek. In the bed of the wagon sat the new wellhead pump handle and sections of well piping. There was also a cook stove and flue pipe for it. He'd gone for the materials this time, wanting to collect Jenny and tell her about the padre and the children who had happened by.

On the way back from town, he had told her of their story and of all that had befallen them, and likewise his offer of land and help to the padre. He was momentarily unsure of her reaction as she sat spellbound, listening to the story with a blank expression that did not betray one way or the other what she might have felt or thought. The padre's admonition that he should consult with her before making such an offer fleetingly passed through his mind as he studied her face and wondered if he had misjudged. But her expression turned to wonderment at the beauty of what she had been told, the revelation of its majesty flowing over her like a wave of goodness. "What do you think, Jenny?" he finally asked.

"I think it is inspired and beautiful, Sammy. I am so proud of you. You are a wonderful man whose heart is pure and full of love."

Sammy frowned slightly. "I'm glad you like the idea, but don't think me too pure. There's some pure hate somewhere in there, too. I've killed men, and I can't say I won't kill again if I have to. This is a tough land...a man does what he has to do."

"Yes, Sammy, I know that of you. But you didn't have to do this...and yet you did. Your love is much stronger than your hate."

"I wish that were true. I believe they're both equally powerful when they take hold. The lovin' part sure is the best part of livin', though." Then he held her.

The wagon rolled up to the building site. Sammy pulled on the brake and jumped to the ground from the high seat, not bothering with the side steps. "Hello, Padre! Kids!" he bellowed as he hurried around the wagon to help Jenny down.

They had all stopped their work on the logs and said their "hellos" back, but mostly they just stared as Sammy helped the dark-haired, beautiful woman down. Jing Lu and Camille were enthralled by the vision. Jing Lu began running over to the wagon, with Camille hot on her heels.

"Hello, girls," Jenny said to Jing Lu and Camille who stood before her with eyes wide in stunned admiration. Jing Lu was quite certain this was the most beautiful woman she had ever seen. She was overwhelmed in her presence and did not blink as the woman smiled at her. "I'm Jenny Simpson, and I am so very happy to meet you."

Jing Lu and Camille stood speechless, something the padre and the boys had never seen before. Sammy put his hand to

Jing Lu's shoulder. "Jenny, this is Jing Lu." He moved his hand to the top of Camille's head. "And this is Camille."

"Camille smiled with big, happy eyes. "Hello, Jenny Simpson!" she proclaimed.

The padre and the boys arrived and stepped in close beside the girls. "Jenny, this is Tobias, Payat, and Rory," Sammy announced, waving a hand to each one as he said their name.

Jenny stepped to them and shook each of their hands. "Hello, ma'am," Tobias and Rory each said.

Payat gave a slight bow of his head as he shook her hand, "Hello."

"Hello, boys, I am very pleased to meet you."

Rory grinned, embarrassed. Payat and Tobias fidgeted.

The padre was standing behind the boys who now parted, allowing him to step forward for the introduction they knew was coming. Sammy spoke with admiration in his voice, "And this is their father, Padre Tomas Cordero. Padre, I'm pleased to introduce to you my fiancée, Miss Jenny Simpson."

"It is my great pleasure to make your acquaintance, Miss Simpson."

"And I, yours, Padre. Please call me Jenny. May I call you Padre?"

"I will be most pleased, Jenny."

"We are so happy to have all of you here, as friends and neighbors."

"And we are eternally blessed to be such," the padre warmly replied with a slight nod forward.

Sammy's crew came from the forest and across the open grass that revealed its multicolored hues of green, gold, red, and yellow in the late afternoon sun. They carried the crosscut saws and led the horses pulling the final two logs. Knuckles, Roasty, Matt, Jasper, Bill, Porter, and Ben looked worn but lively as they walked up to the site where Sammy, Jenny, Padre, and the children were visiting.

The hellos and other greetings rang out, and then Bill Lohmeyer came right to the point. "Tomorrow's Sunday...figured we'd camp right here tonight. Good weather and stars a plenty. Porter shot our supper a little earlier...nice white tail...and Ben's got his guitar in the chuck wagon. Get a little hootenanny goin'. Proud to have ya all join us if you like."

Sammy knew his men were ready to blow off a little steam. They could be good at it, too. He looked at Jenny and could tell she liked the idea. She'd worked her last day at Watson Boarding House and had a glow of liberation to her. "We'll stay for supper and the floor show," Sammy said.

The padre looked a little uncertain of the circumstance, but there was no mistaking what the children thought about it. Their faces registered a sort of awe. The word "hootenanny" had excited all their senses, though Rory and Tobias were the only children who had ever heard the term before, and neither of them was very sure about what it was. But everyone had a notion that it was some kind of good time.

Sammy was about to prod the padre to at least stay for supper when Roasty spoke up. "We have lots of food, Padre...biscuits, potatoes, and more venison than all of us could eat in three days. You won't want to miss the singing either. It's a Sky W treat when all these mouths commence to song. Scare off any varmints that might be livin' nearby. We have plenty of bedding in the wagon, too."

"Me and Camille will help with the cooking," Jing Lu excitedly said, her eyes imploring the padre to say "yes."

"Well, I suppose we could stay for supper and some hootenanny," the padre replied.

"Good!" Knuckles chimed in. "Uh, you little gals and Miss Jenny may want to stay clear of the creek on the other side of those trees for a bit. Us boys are going to clean up some…it's been a hot day."

At the area Knuckles referred to, the creek hit a naturally wide hollow that formed a wide and deep pool. Other than the water being very cold, it was perfect for bathing. One by one the outfit stripped down and took a good pull off the bottle of whiskey Jasper had brought. Then in they jumped, one after another with showmanship and loud hoots for good measure. There were cannonballs and belly flops and some twisted half flips, each man trying to outdo the previous. Knuckles got the splash award with an artfully executed cannonball. Then the hollering continued as the two bars of soap that were present got tossed around. The men quickly washed before being driven from the bone-chilling water that even the whiskey could not overcome.

In the heat of the waning afternoon, they sat on the grassy bank and smoked or chewed tobacco as the bottle got passed around and the sun dried them. They returned to camp clean and invigorated. Bill Lohmeyer walked over to where Rory, Tobias, and Payat were finishing up a large campfire pit that was nicely ringed with rocks, complete with sitting stumps and enough firewood to blaze the night sky till dawn. "Any of you boys done any roping before?" he asked.

"No, I reckon not," Rory replied, half embarrassed that he hadn't.

"We just had a milk cow. Never had to lasso her or Roca…just threw a lead on 'em," Tobias added. Payat remained silent.

"Well, you wanna have a go at it? Boss Sammy might need you on a roundup someday."

The boys' eyes widened. "Sure!" Rory said.

"All right! We'll get Porter in on this, too. He's the best of us with a rope, save for the boss."

Minutes later, they had some stumps set to create a raised target. Then Bill and Porter began showing the boys the basics of the lariat and honda knot. Porter quickly talked them through lassoing on the ground versus throwing from a saddle. "There's not much more to it than some good swing and release…comes from a lot of practice," he said. Then, fifty feet from the target, Porter began the whirl of his lariat over his head, achieving an easy rhythm with the circular motion at his elbow and wrist. In an instant, he flicked forward, extending his arm toward the target and causing the rope to sail flawlessly until the noose dropped precisely over the elevated stump.

"Wow!" Tobias exclaimed.

Payat shook his head. "No can throw rope that far."

"Aw, he's just showin' fancy," Bill said. "Come on up here close."

From twenty feet away, the boys took turns as Bill and Porter coached them on the technique. All of them eventually roped the stump, pulling the noose tight and smiling broadly with the feat.

In the twilight of the day, they sat with their plates full and ate and talked about all manner of things. Rory, Tobias, and Payat drove the conversation among the men. In their innocent curiosity, they asked about everything, from the construction of the cabin to hunting and fishing, cattle drives, horses, and bronc busting, and Indians, bears, and legends.

Jenny and the girls sat a little removed from the men, with Jenny in the middle and Jing Lu and Camille up close on each side of her. They had hijacked her. Their conversation was markedly different from the men's. The young girls, having been starved of female mentoring, wanted to know all about Jenny and womanly things, and, of course, the upcoming wedding. Jenny was patient and kind, enduring every question as if it were the most meaningful one yet. She told them all there was to tell about her and Sammy's upcoming wedding day. It was only a week away now. Then, in turn, she asked the girls about their likes and dreams and all that interested them. Jing Lu and Camille were enchanted to have this beautiful woman, who was so kind, engaging them on topics they wanted to talk about or know about. The bond was immediate and deeply shared.

As darkness came, all helped with the cleanup and evening's preparation, then wood was heaped in the boys' new fire pit and the blaze commenced. Matt played his guitar and was accompanied by Bill playing a lively harmonica. Their music pierced the darkness like the clarion call of spirited souls. Occasionally, one of Sammy's crew would make their way to the other side of the wagon to take a quick snort of the bottle. They thought better of doing so in front of the young ones, but it was Saturday night, so do it they would.

Under a full moon rising and a cloudless sky riddled with stars glistening of the never-ending, they sang songs and danced, compelled by their shared season and place in creation.

16

Reuben Taylor spotted them on the veranda as he approached at a lope. He didn't bother taking his mount to the barn but instead rode to the front of his sprawling ranch house and dismounted, then tied his horse to the hitching rail. "Hello, Sammy," he said, as he walked up the several steps to the long, covered porch where the two men sat, shaded from the noon sun. "Thought we'd be seeing you anytime now."

"Yes, sir, I brought Jenny over. Her mother and brother might arrive here today…if not, tomorrow for sure."

"Where is that delightful beauty? Wouldn't you rather be sitting with her than my brother?"

Sammy smiled. "She's in catching up with Jacqueline."

Reuben pulled the olla and gourd dipper from the beam where they hung. He dipped the gourd and took a long drink of the cool water, then rehung them and sat down in one of the many rockers. "Are you getting nervous yet? Only a few more days of the single life."

"I don't feel nervous. Can't say what I'll feel like come Saturday…but if my knees start knockin', it won't be about any second thoughts of givin' up the single life."

Homer Taylor chuckled, "Well, hell no. You're marrying an angel."

Reuben nodded. "That's a fact. She's a fine girl...fine as they come. It's going to be quite a show here on Saturday...lots of folks."

"There'll be a few more now," Homer said, as if he were an informant. "Sammy just confirmed all that we'd heard about the padre and children."

Reuben's eyes widened. "Oh? Just like we heard? Ole boy used to be a priest ...took in orphaned kids. His wife died?"

"Yeah...quite a bit more to it than that," Homer replied. "I'll fill you in on the rest later."

"I'm givin' him some land over on Red Creek and setting them up," Sammy happily said. "Started a cabin. Logs are all cut and were digging the well and workin' the foundation."

Reuben smiled with amazement. "That's a good thing you're doing. You need some more help? We're a little slow here at the moment...right, Homer? We could spare four or five hands for a couple of weeks. They'll stay on our payroll."

"Must be why we're brothers," Homer shrugged. "I was just getting ready to make the same offer when you showed up."

Sammy was stunned. "Well...sure. I don't want to put anybody out, though."

"You're not," Homer replied dryly. "Besides, from about Thursday on, you'll be spending time with your bride-to-be and her family. And then you sure as hell better spend some honeymoon days alone after the wedding. No, there won't be any work for you for a bit. We'll send over JP and a few of the boys. JP really knows building. I'm sure this padre would like a barn, coral, couple of privies..."

"Where they staying now?" Reuben asked.

"They were in my place with me for a few days, but moved into my work shed. Padre said it wouldn't be right for them to stay in the house with Jenny movin' in after the wedding. He insisted."

Homer flashed a look of agreement. "The padre's right on that score...but that work shed is awful small isn't it?"

"Padre said it's bigger than where they spent all last winter. It's got a cook stove."

"Sounds like they've been up against it," Reuben said with a tone of respect.

Homer shifted in his chair. "That ain't the half of it. Sammy said the padre witnessed some men killing the folks who lived in the main house on the spread where they were staying...but he didn't think the owner was there when the killings took place." Homer looked at Sammy for confirmation that he'd recounted it correctly. "Right?"

"Yeah, that's what he said."

Reuben looked half perplexed and half angry. "Well, what in hell do you suppose that was all about? Did the padre have any ideas on that?"

Sammy shook his head. "Not the foggiest notion. He said about six men rode up to the house and just started shootin'. Killed an Indian woman and two men...but they shot back and dropped two themselves."

"I take it these men never saw the padre."

"No, he and the kids were on a hillside nearby...in the trees. He said the men searched for them like they knew other folks were livin' there, too. They hid."

"Where was this?"

"Just east of Dumas."

"What was the landowner's business?"

"He said he knew they farmed. Wasn't sure of much beyond that. Padre and the kids were just holed up there for the winter."

"Well, that's a hell of a thing."

Sammy nodded his head. "Sure is."

Reuben slapped his thigh. "They won't have to spend too much time in your work shed. We'll get enough men on that job to have the roof on lickety cut."

17

Against the beauty of all that was before him, the dark shadows of his past retreated slowly like the fading of something exposed to the sun, or as rocks eventually erode to sand from wind and rain. Sammy entertained remembrance of the men he'd killed out of necessity to let such thoughts run their course. He didn't regret the killings, only that he'd had to do it. He feared ever having to kill again over some circumstance beyond his control. The West was a place that could demand such acts for survival. Still, he knew it was a thing that could prey on a man's soul, his soul. But tomorrow he would marry Jenny, the woman he loved, and their union would take him another step beyond such recollections.

Franklin saw the detached, faraway expression on Sammy's face. "You look like a man who's mind just galloped south on a runaway horse...Mexico maybe. Is your brown eye puckerin' about the halter you're puttin' on tomorrow?"

Sammy's eyes became alert again. "Halter?"

"Yeah, you know...ball and chain, iron saddle, nut corset."

Sammy smiled. "I pucker at the thought of losing her. No, I'm ready for this."

"Well, good. All the boys is ready, too. Anything that brings a party."

"I'm glad Jenny and I could oblige."

Sammy and Franklin continued setting up the rest of the chairs and tables that would accommodate all the guests and food for the wedding and celebration to follow. They were just finishing up when Sammy spotted the buckboard wagon throwing a light wake of dust. He stared hard for a moment. "Man and a woman comin'."

"They're a might early for the festivities."

"Yeah," Sammy agreed as recognition started to form. The hat looked familiar, a tall, Silverbelly with a wide brim. He'd come to know its owner very well during his journey to Denver to collect the reward money for killing the outlaw. Sammy and Blaine Corker had both worked on the Twin T Ranch and had ridden north together. Along the way, they had ended up saving each other's lives and those of three women who'd been kidnapped by a band of renegade Apaches. It had happened when the two cowboys had sought shelter in a blinding snowstorm, finding a cave that of pure chance was where the women were being held. They'd gunned the Apaches down in a bloody shootout, having been lucky with the element of surprise and good positioning. Nevertheless, the fight had left Blaine badly injured and unable to continue the journey to Denver with Sammy. He had recuperated in Santa Fe at Claire's house while Sammy had continued on north to Denver. They had not seen each other in the year that had passed.

As the buckboard rolled closer, Sammy thought he recognized the girl. It was Margaret, the youngest of the women he and Blaine had saved, only sixteen at the time. He could see she was cradling a baby in her arms wrapped in a small, blue blanket. His mind paced through the possibilities, wondering whose baby it could be. Another of the women they'd saved, Claire Studdard, had been in early pregnancy and unsure if her dead husband or one of the renegades was the father. Her husband had been murdered by the Apaches when she was abducted. Margaret had moved in with Claire in Santa Fe after Sammy and Blaine had returned them to safety. Sammy wondered where Claire might be now.

Franklin squinted. "That looks like Ole Blaine Corker."

"Sure does," Sammy agreed.

"Hey, amigo!" Blaine called out from the wagon. "Did we make it in time? You didn't jump the gun and get hitched already did ya? It's a long way from Santa Fe to come up empty and miss the show...and we sure wouldn't miss it!"

Blaine reined the two-horse team to a stop as Sammy and Franklin walked up. "How'd you know?" Sammy asked with an ear to ear grin.

"We found out, no thanks to you Sammy Winds," Margaret said.

Sammy walked to Margaret's side of the wagon as Franklin and Blaine greeted each other and began talking. Sammy helped her down, gazing upon her and marveling at how wonderful she looked—another year older and every bit a woman. "Hello, Margaret. It sure is good to see you," he said, hugging her lightly with the baby between them. She used her free arm to hug him back.

"Oh, Sammy, it's good to see you, too...so good."

"You're beautiful, Margaret. Old age is very becoming to you."

She laughed the light laugh of youth, and Sammy was glad to hear it. The horrors she had endured during her captivity would hang on her and require all of her resiliency and spirit to overcome, but he knew she was up to it. She looked down at the child she held and pulled back the blanket, revealing the sleeping infant with long, blond hair. It appeared to be about six months old. Sammy felt some trepidation about asking of the child, unsure of what any question might evoke. "This is

Robert...Claire's son," Margaret quickly offered with a soft, subdued voice.

Sammy felt the anxiety. "Claire...how is she? Where is she?"

Margaret's eyes continued to gaze upon the child. "I wrote to you, Sammy...when little Robert was born. Did you receive my letter?"

"No."

Margaret's eyes lifted from the child's to meet Sammy's. They welled with tears and her bottom lip trembled. He feared what he was about to hear. "She died, Sammy...during childbirth. The doctor told us later that she had hemorrhaged and that there was nothing we could have done. Just Blaine and I were there when it happened. I could not stop the bleeding. I did not know how."

"Oh, Lord," Sammy uttered.

Margaret took a slow, deep breath then continued. "Claire saw her son before she passed. She held him and kissed him. She was so happy he was not Indian. She said to name him Robert, after her husband. She knew she was dying, Sammy, but she was calm, like she had an inner peace. She said she would tell Robert about their son, and they would watch him from heaven, and that they would all be together again someday." Tears streamed down Margaret's face but her composure held. "She asked me to be his mother and love him and raise him. I told her I would...and that is what I am going to do."

Sammy stood dazed by the telling of it. "Jesus...I'm sorry, Margaret. It sure is good you were there with her...Blaine too."

A faint smile came to her face. "Blaine has been so good with little Robert... helping the best he knows how. He and Claire fell in love not long after you left. I think they were planning on marrying."

Sammy nodded knowingly. "I thought I saw the spark in their eyes when they looked at each other. Are you still living at Claire's house?"

"Yes, but we will have to move soon. It has been almost six months...then the court will auction it because it is within the town's claimed territory. We are not any kind of legal heirs. Her kin is in Texas...I don't even know where. She had a bad split with them is all I know. We could try to buy it, but..." She looked over at Blaine who was deep in conversation with Franklin and seemed very happy to be back at the ranch where he had once worked. She leaned in close to Sammy and spoke in a whispered tone. "I can't hold Blaine down. We are friends...but that is all...at least that is all it has ever been. He has stayed to help me and little Robert, but I am sure he wants to move on."

"You could go back home, couldn't you?"

"Yes, but there is nothing there for me. I am past it now." Her face suddenly brightened a bit. "Besides, I am studying to be a teacher...at a teacher preparatory school in Santa Fe. There is great need of teachers in the West."

"Well, that's grand, Margaret. And a fine teacher you'll be."

"I hope so. I have another year to go before I graduate. Thank you for your confidence. And you can thank Jenny for letting us know about the wedding. She wrote to us."

"I'm glad she did," he replied, then suddenly looked thoughtful as if he'd forgotten something relevant to their conversation. "You know, baby Robert here is a rightful heir to Claire's property. If you're his mother now, it seems to me you're a rightful heir, too...as his representative, or some such thing...I reckon. I think a good lawyer would have some thoughts about it."

Margaret's expression became thoughtful. "Just before she died, she said she wanted us to have her place. But nothing was ever written down. It all happened so fast...and then she was gone. Besides, I don't know any lawyers, and I do not have the money to pursue something I cannot prove true."

"I know a great lawyer. We'll get it sorted out later. Come inside now and meet Jenny and the others. Would you like me to hold Robert? He looks bigger'n a Christmas ham. Your arms must be tired."

"Why, thank you, Sammy. Yes, that would be a nice break." She lifted him into Sammy's cradled arms. Baby Robert stayed fast asleep.

18

The wagons and buggies and folks on horseback began arriving in the late morning that swelled of blue sky and a shimmering sun. The owners of the Twin T Ranch, Homer and Reuben Taylor, were first in line to greet the arriving wedding guests, followed by Sammy and several of the ranch's longtime employees, including the house manager, Jacqueline, and her cooks Raquel and Lucilla, and the crew bosses, Lundy, J.P., and Franklin, all of whom had been with the T for twenty years or more.

Bouquets of wild spring flowers adorned the tops of temporary posts, creating the perimeter of the wedding area, which had seating for a hundred and an aisle that led to a ten-foot braided aspen branch altar, laced with peach globe mallows, red angel fires, and white daisies. A separate area for the feasting was close by and presently had a makeshift bar of soft refreshments that would include more spirited choices after the ceremony. Beyond was an area for games that included horseshoes and targets for hatchet and knife-throwing. Some of the hands had a trick riding exhibition planned for later in the day, and the local renowned musical group, The Miller Boys, were on hand to provide the music for the celebration. The scent of roasting beef drifted from the back of the ranch house where slabs cooked over a large pit, basted with a molasses, mustard, herb, pepper, and wine sauce that seeded the breeze with anticipation.

Children ran from one thing to another in separate packs of boys and girls, curious and thrilled to be at such an event that enlivened every sense. But upon eventual discovery of it, they quickly migrated to a nearby old pine that had been sawed off at about sixty feet high. All the branches below had been removed, giving it the appearance of a giant, barren pole, poking up into the sky. A thick rope was affixed to the top and hung to the bottom where it was knotted several times for a makeshift seat. To one side of the tree, forty feet out from the base of it, an elevated area of hill provided a runway from where a rider could run with the rope until the elevated area gave way. Then the rider would jump, wrapping the legs around the rope and securing the seat upon the knot, swinging in a long, circular path about eight feet off the ground until the long revolution was completed, delivering the rider back to the takeoff area where the others stood, anxiously waiting for their turn. The girls stood off to the side in their dresses and watched as the boys tried to outdo each other for speed and height.

Rory's ride was particularly impressive. Towards the end, just before he was back to the takeoff area, he pulled up with his hands and swung his feet up hard, letting go of the rope and catapulting himself acrobatically high into the air, sailing for twenty feet before landing cat-like, and then running several steps to keep from tumbling.

"Wow!" a few of the children exclaimed.

The next rider was the oldest boy, about two years older than Rory. He sprinted with the rope in hand and then jumped to the seat and sailed high above the ground in a giant revolution around the tree. At the end, he imitated what Rory had done and flung himself into the air for the big finale, though his path through the air never brought his body vertical and he landed on his back with a brutal thud. He lay still for a moment as the children looked on. Finally, he got to his feet with a red face, his pride more injured than his body. "Hey, that was pretty close, Horace," one of the older boys yelled. "Give it another try...maybe you can land on your head!" All of the children laughed.

"Shut up!" Horace yelled, as he moved gingerly away from the landing area.

Jing Lu noted when each boy had had a turn. "I would like to swing on the rope," she formally announced. The other girls immediately looked at her. She stood with her hands clasped against her modest, brown dress.

"Girls don't get to ride," Horace declared authoritatively.

"She can have a turn," Rory said.

"Who are you to say?" Horace asked toughly.

"I'm her brother."

"I am brother, too," Payat declared.

"Me too," Tobias said.

"She's my sister...and I want to ride, too," Camille said.

Horace looked at each of them, his face registering confusion. "She's a China girl. He looks like an Indian, and she's a Mexican. How can you be brothers and sisters?"

"Don't you fret about it," Rory replied.

"You no fret," Payat added."

"I reckon they let anybody in this place," Horace said. "Well, *my* sister's not riding."

"Can't I ride if they get a turn?" the pretty girl in a yellow dress asked.

"No," Horace replied.

Rory looked from the girl to Horace. "Is that your sister?"

"Yeah, that's right. So what?"

117

Rory had a confused look. "Just hard to figure is all. She looks so nice, and you look like an idiot." The children broke into riotous laughter.

Horace clenched his fists. "I'll pound your face in."

"Yeah? Well, you talkin' about it ain't gonna get it done."

Horace started at Rory just as the padre called out. "Rory, you come now...the wedding will start soon. Bring your brothers and sisters."

Rory looked to the padre. "All right...comin'!" He nodded to Payat, Tobias, Jing Lu, and Camille. "Let's go. You two can get a ride later," he said to Jing Lu and Camille. They all fell in beside him and walked proudly away with their big brother.

Horace did not say anything but looked at the strange group of siblings as they walked away. The other children watched and wondered, too.

Harmonic chords from a guitar and fiddle wove together in the soft, ethereal melody of Scottish Highlands' music. The tune "Greensleeves" was followed by "The Favourite Dram," and the "Aran Boat Song." Then, after a short pause, the air filled with "O' Carolan's Concerto." The guests stood and turned to see Jenny coming forth up the aisle, dressed in the beautiful white, silk gown her mother had worn on her wedding day. Jenny's mother wept at the sight of her angelically beautiful daughter donned in her dress, her younger brother escorting her slowly and looking stoic in his responsibility to fulfill what would have fallen to his father had he not been killed in the Civil War. The crowd was silent and watched with awe as the stunning bride and her handsome younger brother moved elegantly forward.

Sammy's eyes locked with Jenny's as she approached. He knew she was beautiful, but he had never been as entranced by her beauty and grace as he was at this moment. His breath held in his chest. "My word," he said in a whisper to himself. She arrived and took his hand. "I love you," she said softly.

"I love you, too."

They turned to face Pastor Riddering, who smiled warmly and commenced into his sermon on the sanctity of their union and all that it meant. His words were true and straight and stirred many in the crowd with his inspired message that went on for twenty minutes. Then he led Sammy and Jenny through their vows and exchange of rings before God and the assembled witnesses. The pastor was joyful in making it official: "By the authority of God invested in me, I now pronounce you man and wife! You may kiss your bride."

Sammy gazed into Jenny's eyes, seemingly oblivious to the pastor's final direction, leaving the crowd wondering what was taking so long.

"I'll kiss that beautiful woman for ya if can't do it yourself!" Blaine Corker finally shouted out.

Sammy laughed with everyone else. "I can do it myself," he professed. Then he took Jenny into his arms and kissed her as the guests cheered and applauded.

The celebration commenced and wore on late into the afternoon with the feasting, dancing and singing, and games and trick riding exhibitions. Then, with the crowd giving them a cheering sendoff, Sammy and Jenny took their leave and left for their new home in Homer Taylor's finest black buggy. Not long after, most of the guests said their good-byes and headed for their homes, miles away. Some of those with the farthest to travel accepted the Taylor brothers' invitation to camp and rallied on into the evening.

The five guest bedrooms of the sprawling ranch house were occupied by Jenny's mother and brother, with the padre and the boys in another room, Jing Lu, Camille, Margaret, and baby Robert in another room, and a few of the Taylors' closest friends in the other rooms. Blaine opted to stay in the bunkhouse where he'd previously lived two years during his employ at the Twin T. He was more than happy to partake in the reunion with old friends who saw that the whiskey and stories last long into the night.

In their bedroom, Margaret talked with Jing Lu and Camille late into the night. Jing Lu and Camille told Margaret of their lives and how they came to be orphaned, and of eventually coming into Padre and Estella's wonderful home. And they told of how Estella had died, and of the fire that took their home, prompting their journey in search of another home. And then they told her of the mysterious killers at Clint Smith's place, and of how they hid and eventually escaped, traveling for days until they met Sammy Winds who took them in and gave Padre land and was helping to build them a home.

Margaret listened raptly to Jing Lu telling most of it, with Camille occasionally reminding Jing Lu about some particular part of the story that she thought should be included. "Oh, yes," Jing Lu would say to Camille's prompts, and then she would continue on, weaving in that which Camille had thought relevant.

When Jing Lu had exhausted their story, she asked Margaret about her baby and how she had come to know Sammy. It was Jing Lu and Camille's turn to sit wide eyed and listen as Margaret told them of being kidnapped by Indians, and of how she and two other kidnapped women had spent several months of winter in a cave as prisoners of renegade Apaches until Sammy Winds and Blaine Corker had come and saved them. She told of the other women, Claire and Emily, and that baby Robert was Claire's baby. She narrated how Claire had died during childbirth and how, just before she died, she had asked Margaret to take Robert and be his mother. Jing Lu and Camille looked with awe at the sleeping baby.

"It seems we have some things in common," Margaret finally said.

"What does that mean…in common? Jing Lu asked.

"It means we have shared the same kinds of experiences. We have had pain and grief and fear…and loss."

Jing Lu looked thoughtful for a moment. "And we have Mister Sammy Winds in common?"

"That's right, dear. He saved my life, and he is certainly helping you all, too."

"He sure is," Camille said.

The next morning after breakfast, the padre led the children in a worship ceremony next to a stand of cottonwoods that shaded the ground from the warm sun. Margaret and Jenny's mother also joined the worship. Afterwards, the padre and his children gave their thanks and said their good-byes to the all at the ranch, then loaded into their wagon and headed home. The day was beautiful; the trip was quiet and serene.

"Miss Margaret is so nice," Jing Lu said to the padre as the wagon rolled slowly along.

"Yes, she is," the padre agreed.

"Padre, did you know that her baby boy was born to another woman who died, but that before she died, she asked Miss Margaret to be his mother?"

"Yes, Jing Lu. Mister Winds told me about it."

"Did you know that Mister Sammy and his friend saved her and baby Robert's mother and another woman from Indians?"

"Yes, child, I know of that, too."

Jing Lu frowned with sadness. "They were saved and then baby Robert's mother died anyway. It is terrible, Padre. Why does God let bad things happen? Why does he not let bad things happen just to bad people?"

The padre was driving the wagon with Rory on the bench next to him. He turned and looked back at Jing Lu, whose dark eyes searched the padre's face for understanding. The rest of the children were looking and listening intently, too. Their interest captured by Jing Lu's question. The padre paused, summoning his thoughts and praying for wisdom. "Let bad things happen to bad people? Remember, Jing Lu...'We all like sheep have gone astray. Each of us has turned to his own way. But the Lord has laid on Him the iniquities of us all.'"

Jing Lu recognized the verse and knew its meaning but pressed on. "I know, Padre, but why does He let bad things happen to good people?"

"Would you turn to God, would you seek him if everything was always good and comfortable, if nothing bad ever happened in our lives, in your life?"

"I would thank Him for keeping me safe and providing for me."

"Yes, but why would you thank Him for keeping you safe? How would you know you were safe if there were not such a thing as danger? We understand joy because there is sorrow. We know love because there is hate, good because there is evil, comfort because there is discomfort. Would you know day if there were no night? Ecclesiastes teaches us that to all things there is a season, and a time to every purpose under the heaven. He has made everything appropriate in its time. He has also set eternity in the heart of man, yet so that man will not find out the work which God has done from the beginning even to the end."

"Sometimes it's hard to figure what the purpose is when bad things happen," Rory said.

"Yes, Padre, it is," Jing Lu agreed.

"Faith will be shaken and tested by trying to understand what purpose there is in bad things happening. 'Trust in the Lord with all your heart and do not lean on your own understanding. In all your ways acknowledge Him and He will direct your steps. And we know that for those who love God all things work together for good, for those who are called according to his purpose.' You see, children, such a verse does not say that all things are good. Some things and events are bad or terribly evil and beyond our understanding, but God in His eternal providence is able to work them *together for good, for those who are called according to his purpose*. Such work we cannot understand any more than we can look to the sky and comprehend no end to it."

"Yes, Padre," Jing Lu said halfheartedly. Rory said nothing.

The padre knew that his words had not fully found the mark. He tried again. "When you play a game, why do you play?"

"To have fun," Jing Lu replied.

"To win," Rory said.

"Well, yes...to have fun and to try to win. But would you prefer just to be told that you had fun, and you were the winner without playing the game?"

"No," came the simultaneous reply.

"Why not?"

"'Cause the fun's in playin'," Rory instantly proclaimed.

The padre smiled. "Yes, but is it fun if you lose...if you are beaten badly?"

"Not as much, I reckon."

"Would you want the chance to play again, perhaps in some other kind of game or challenge?"

"Sure, yes, uh-huh," came the replies from the children, except for Jing Lu who was confused by the question.

"I do not understand, Padre. What do you mean?"

He reached back with one hand and gently touched her head. "I mean that we are not potted plants, existing merely with water and sun. We are in this game, this life, as human beings. Life is God's gift to us, and we are God's gifts to each other. He has made us in His image and He has given us His Word...but He has made us free to choose what we will do and believe. And because we are free by Him, all things must be possible to us, which means that bad things can and will happen to good people. But as one might be badly beaten in a game, those who seek Him when badly beaten in life will be lifted up, for He is the safe harbor from the storms that will come. He is the light from our darkest despair. He alone is the path to true peace and contentment through His grace, mercy, and salvation. He is the Giver and Redeemer. So think not that He lets bad things happen. Think instead that if you seek Him and know Him, He will be there as your eternal protector and provider Who can overcome anything bad, and give you the strength to do so, too."

Jing Lu absorbed his words, thinking for a moment. "Yes, Padre, I think I understand."

"Always put your trust in the Lord, child."

Payat nodded his head. "God is biggest...best chief."

19

"Hurry up with that grub!"

"All right, all right. Keep your shirt on."

Boothe Haney was drunk. He'd been that way for the better part of a week. After collecting his money from Rupert Crowder for his murderous escapade at Clint Smith's place, he and his remaining men returned to their remote cabins. Rupert had told him that more work would be forthcoming and that he would send word within a month. It had been that long already, and the boredom had become intolerable sober. So he drank steadily.

"Don't you smart-mouth me woman, or I'll cut your tongue out!" Boothe yelled.

She knew the danger and said nothing more, hurrying to get the food on the table and placate the beast.

Boothe shoveled the hot stew in his mouth without testing it, scorching his tongue before he could spit it out, which he did with haste. "Goddamn it! Why didn't you tell me it's hot!"

She couldn't hold back. "Seein' as how I was cookin' it on a stove, and that steam was coming off it, I thought you could figure it out yourself."

"Arrggghhh!" Boothe grunted loudly as he jumped from his chair, but she was a step ahead of him. She had grabbed the

125

large kitchen knife and was already at the door. She flung it open and ran, figuring she wouldn't try her luck with the knife unless she had to. "You better run, you devil woman!" The pistol shots rang out. She kept running into the woods, realizing she wasn't hit. Boothe returned to the table and blew on the hot food before gingerly testing it, then stuffing his mouth as quickly as his cooling technique would permit.

Boothe and his men had been unable to find the padre and the orphans but knew they'd sneaked back to their shack and then cleared out with the horse and wagon, while Boothe searched toward town and his men buried bodies. He didn't even know what this padre looked like or anything about the kids. The inescapable conclusion for Boothe was that the runaways likely saw the killings and could maybe identify Boothe and his men. For all he knew, the sheriff of Dumas might have descriptions of Boothe and his men right now. He had no way to contact Rupert Crowder and couldn't be certain of anything until he received word. So they had stayed holed up, avoiding towns and waiting. But he was sick of it now. If he didn't hear something soon, he'd pull out and get clear of this northern country, the money be damned.

He ate the stew and was surly and foul. Some of each bite dribbled from his mouth and caked in his beard, which was thoroughly unkempt and greasy like his hair. He hadn't washed himself or his clothes for some time and gave off a putrid aroma. His continual drunkenness erased any regard of it. When he finished eating, he drank some more whiskey and then slept.

The loud knocking at the door quickly turned to banging, but it was not heard by Boothe who had fallen into a sort of sleep coma. He was not happy to be awakened when the door finally opened and Crom began shouting his name, finally permeating Boothe's drunken slumber. Boothe's eyes opened in shock, like a man who'd dreamt he'd fallen off a cliff. The acid in his throat sizzled throughout his chest and his head pounded in time with the rapid beat of his heart. "What!" he yelled, realizing he might vomit any second.

"There's some dude here to see you."

"Who? Who the hell is it? Son of a bitch! I was sleepin'!"

Boothe came quickly off the bed as he felt the rising bile in his throat. He just made the open window when the contraction hit full force and his vomit shot out like a volcanic eruption. The contractions continued with the briefest of moments between, allowing him only an instant to gasp for air before the next was upon him. On and on they went, emptying all that was within him and persisting even then, as if the spasms would not be quenched until his stomach and guts came forth, too.

"Damn, I didn't know you were sick," Crom said apologetically.

Boothe gasped for air as the rate of contractions finally began to slow. He worked at steadying his breathing, his arms quivering from holding his weight above the window sill. He took a few deep breaths. "All right, where is this son of a bitch?"

"Out to the hitchin' rail. Hey...another thing. Gina's back from Dumas. Got the whiskey and all...but she overheard talk at the mercantile 'bout the sheriff gettin' a letter sayin' them folks we hit was murdered. Must of been witnesses...that padre and orphans I'm thinking."

Boothe's expression was a mix of worry and anger. "Hell! If that don't tear it! I knew they was around there somewhere. Shit!" He paused for a moment, considering it. "Had to be from a distance. Couldn't a seen our faces...just the horses," he said, then thought hard again, trying to remember if they'd yelled each other's names that day, knowing that their voices could have carried enough to be heard. "We got to get clear of this country," he declared with certainty.

Boothe walked into the late afternoon sun, sweating and looking pale. The man spoke first with a tone reeking of his displeasure at having to wait. "Are you Boothe?"

Boothe didn't care for the question or the tone. "Who the hell are you?"

"Your boss sent me."

Boothe squinted. "Well?"

The man retrieved an envelope from his pocket. "This is for you."

Boothe grabbed it and tore it open, blinking his eyes several times to gain focus. There was cash and a note. The man turned and started to leave. "Hold on," Boothe commanded.

"Well, hurry it up. It took me a long time to find this place. I'm ready to get shut of it."

Boothe looked at the man with a hard stare but said nothing. He was a big man, as big as Boothe. Boothe looked back down at the paper. The message was brief: "Head south to Two Rock—two or three days ride—check post office under your usual name—RC."

Boothe looked up again. "Where's Crowder now?"

"Who's Crowder?"

Boothe didn't bother with an answer. "You know where Two Rock is?"

"No, but I know where I'm headed," the man replied as he turned to leave.

"You're not goin' anywhere till I say so!"

The man turned back to Boothe, taking the measure of him. Boothe looked haggard and wasn't wearing a gun. No one else was around. Boothe's man had gone back to another cabin. "I leave when I want to…and that's now. I'm downwind…you smell like a shithouse, mister."

The man turned to walk to his horse. Boothe pulled the knife from the sheath on the backside of his right hip and stepped quickly, his arm swinging in an overhead downward arc that viciously brought the blade through the brim of the man's hat, sweeping the side of the man's head and nearly severing his right ear.

"Ahhhhh!" the man screamed, bringing his hand up to where his ear hung by a tendril of skin. Blood ran like a river down his neck and onto his shirt.

"That might improve your hearing some," Boothe cracked.

The man spun around, his hand moving from his ear to his gun. Before he could draw clear of his holster, Boothe's knife plunged into his abdomen, then came out and was driven in again and again. The man pulled the trigger but Boothe's other hand had clamped on his gun wrist and held it firmly from coming level. Two shots went into the dirt while the knife burrowed deep another time. The man's grasp on his gun loosened as his knees buckled. He collapsed.

A few of Boothe's men had drifted out when the man had screamed, witnessing the finale of Boothe's onslaught. They weren't surprised. Boothe stood over him, his knife and hand covered in the dying man's blood.

"The horse, saddle, and gun are mine. Nice lookin' boots and gun belt for whoever claims them first." A couple of the boys hustled over to see what they might salvage from the man who was now dead. Boothe leaned down and wiped his knife clean on the dead man's pants. "We're leavin' in the morning…riding south."

20

The ground broke easily as the padre chopped at it with the hoe. He stopped and wiped the sweat from his brow as he watched Jing Lu and Camille on their knees, carefully planting seeds in the newly created rows. The quarter-acre vegetable garden would yield wonderful delights to accompany the corn and wheat planted farther out on several acres.

The girls paused when Chester came to them wagging his tail, seeking their affection, which they happily offered. In the month since Chester had mysteriously showed up at the Sky W, the dog had put on needed weight and no longer looked emaciated. He made the rounds between the bunkhouse, the ranch house, and the construction site looking for food or company. Nobody knew where he might show up and when it might be. Chester licked Jing Lu's face and then Camille's as if he were being mindful to give equal attention. The girls giggled, and then Jing Lu looked very serious and animated as she spoke. "Chester! It will be your job to keep the rabbits and moles from eating our vegetables while they are growing, understand?" Chester put his paw forward on her leg.

"What if *he* eats the vegetables?" Camille asked.

"Dogs do not like vegetables."

"How do you know?"

Jing Lu thought for a moment. She looked at the dog. "You do not like vegetables, do you, Chester?" The dog licked her face again. "Do not eat the vegetables," she said, wagging a finger emphatically in the dog's face.

The padre smiled at the scene then looked to their new home where an army of ten men were working. Six of them were on the roof, nailing on the last of the roof boards that would finally enclose the home from the weather. Rory, Payat, and Tobias worked a mud pit, mixing earth, grass, and hog bristles to make the chinking for sealing the gaps of the log walls. Four windows and a door had been set, and a few of the crew were finishing the plank floor inside. There was still much to do, but the large cabin already had a root cellar, well pump, cook stove, and privies close by. With so many men from the Twin T and Sky W working on the house, its exterior completion had been a feat of speed and a sight to watch. The padre and children would move in permanently this day. They would sleep on bedrolls on the floor for now.

Knuckles and Matt were building beds for them that would soon be done. The padre had told them he would build the beds and furniture. Knuckles wouldn't hear of it. "You got more to do than you know...what with the chicken coop and corral and barn. You *are* going to build a barn, ain't you?

"Yes, we will in time," the padre replied.

"Good...got to have a barn...get you a cow or two...maybe some goats... and you'll have butter and milk...and cheese if you know how. Roasty could show you. He's good at all those makin's from cows. And you'll need some shelves in your cabin. And you could build you a porch on the front of the cabin with some rocking chairs and such."

The padre had frowned and locked eyes with Knuckles. "Is there anything else you can think of?"

"Oh, I could think of all sorts of things…" He was about to rattle off some more ideas when he realized there had been the slightest hint of sarcasm in the padre's question. Knuckles smiled. "Okay, Padre, I reckon you can figure out what needs doing without my help. But don't you worry about the beds. Me and Matt are good with the woodworkin'. They'll be nice and sturdy."

From a half mile away, Sammy and Blaine approached the site, their horses at a slow walk after a morning of checking cattle and assisting with some calving that the season had brought. They saw the men working on the roof, and the boys at the mud pit, and the padre and the girls working the field. "Busier'n a beehive around here," Blaine said, astonished at all the progress that had taken place in the ten days since the wedding.

"Yeah, flat gettin' with it," Sammy agreed.

"Glad I got to stay for a bit and help out. I know Margaret's enjoyed it, too. I'll be regretting leavin' tomorrow. Forgot I liked cowboyin' so much."

Sammy nodded knowingly. "Gets in your blood. You could get back on with the Twin T right now. My herd'll swell fast. I'll need an extra hand or two in time."

"Sounds awful good. I got to see Margaret through for a while more, though. I'll tell ya Sammy, I feel like I been flipped on my head and hogtied with love twine. I don't rightly know what to do…what with making promises to Claire right when she was dying. I loved her. Now, it's lookin' like her place will get sold right out from under us. Don't matter about me, but Margaret's mule stubborn about goin' home."

Sammy reined to a stop and pulled his makings out. He began to roll a cigarette and spoke as he worked at it. "Reuben talked to his lawyer, Buck Thornton, about that yesterday. Buck is of the opinion Margaret is a rightful heir to Claire's property, being that Claire's dying wish was to have Margaret be baby Robert's mother. Buck is going to petition to the court on Margaret's behalf. He said he would need you as a witness, seeing as you were there when Claire died."

"Sure. Boy, that'd be great if she gets the place. My mind would rest easier about movin' on. She's good friends with some of them gals in that teacher school. Some that ain't married. Maybe they'd band together. They all know baby Robert. She takes 'im with her when she goes to the school."

"Yeah? Well, that would be good. She shouldn't live alone out of town. Maybe one of those gals could move in with her, or she could sell the place and live in town."

"I 'spect she'll have to move on at some point anyway. Go where the teachin' job is...unless it's right there in Santa Fe. I wouldn't know about that. I know there ain't work I'm interested in there. I appreciate gettin' hired on at that wagon buildin' shop this past year. Not bad wages, but it ain't for me.

Sammy lit his smoke. "Yeah, last I remember you were going to hunt buffalo or open a whore house."

Blaine smiled. "Yep, those were big plans...just before we rode up on that cave as I recall. I also recall rollin' you a smoke whenever I did for myself. Strange how plans and ways change with time."

Sammy winced with humor. "She's already lit for you," he said, handing his cigarette to Blaine and retrieving his makings again to roll one for himself.

21

A strong gust of wind blew a cloud of dirt down the small, main street of Cuerno Verde. Lucius tucked his chin down and watched to the side as his horse continued into the blowing dirt. He spotted the Blue Cactus Cantina and reined up to the hitching rail.

Inside, a nearly toothless barkeep was playing checkers with an old Mexican who was the only one occupying a bar stool. The barkeep was chuckling over having made a double jump. "Snuck up on you that time," he proudly said. He had rarely beaten the old man.

The old Mexican had long white hair and dark brown, leathery skin, speckled with age spots. "Si...you are sneaky like the wolf." He squinted in thought as if bedeviled. Deep lines on his face cast a portrait of a long, hard life, and acquired wisdom. His shriveled, bony hand moved to one of his pieces on the board. "Si, sneaky like the wolf...and also dumb like the ox." His old hand steadily and slowly moved the piece forward, jumping four of the barkeep's pieces and arriving at the back row to be kinged.

"You are the devil himself...El Diablo!" the barkeep said in disgust.

The old Mexican looked up with no expression on his face, but humor in his clear, brown eyes. "No, no. I will only take the victory. The devil will take your soul. If you make a deal with him now, perhaps he will let you win. I won't."

The barkeep looked to Lucius who stood just inside the door, beating the dust from his shirt and pants with his hat. "Can I get you something, mister?"

Lucius looked up. "Maybe"

The old Mexican turned his head and looked at Lucius's eyes. They were lifeless, soulless, a killer's eyes. The old Mexican's body shuddered as if all the heat had been sucked from the room. He turned his eyes quickly back to the checkerboard.

Lucius walked to the bar. "You post mail here?"

"Yep...about once a week...usually Fridays."

"You have a letter here for Steve Peterman?"

The barkeep turned to a box in amongst the bottles and began looking quickly through what he had. "Yep, Steve Peterman...here it is."

"Obliged," Lucius said, taking the letter from him. "Tequila?"

"Mescal."

"I'll have whiskey. How about food?"

"Not till five...another hour."

"Why not right now?"

"Cook's not here yet. The wait is worth it, that's for sure. Fried chicken tonight. She can really cook."

"Any night flowers around here?"

"What?"

"Whores."

"Two. They'll be around a little later."

"Rooms?

"Yep, six bits a night."

"I need my horse put up…watered and fed."

"Some stalls in back. I have a boy that can see to it. That dark bay out front?"

"That's him," Lucius said and put silver on the bar. The barkeep poured the whiskey.

"Might as well leave the bottle. Only thing goin' on in this town right now is dirt blowin' down the street. You want a drink old timer?" Lucius asked, directing his question to the old man who sat upon the bar stool.

The old Mexican had not moved his eyes from the checkerboard since Lucius had arrived at the bar next to him. He felt the hair on the back of his neck stand up as if the devil were standing next to him. "Yes, that is kind of you, señor," the old Mexican said nervously, not wanting to offend the stranger by declining the offer.

The barkeep put a shot glass down in front of the old Mexican, and Lucius poured him a drink.

"Thank you, señor."

Lucius didn't respond. He took his bottle and walked to a table at the back. After sitting down and pouring himself another drink, he opened the letter from Rupert Crowder. The message was short: "Get to the town called La Jara—pick up posting at Buckskin Hotel." There was one hundred dollars of paper money folded into the note and a crudely drawn map that showed La Jara to be southwest of where he was now. The map also showed some landmarks and La Jara's position relative to Two Rock and Stratford. Lucius had been through Stratford once. From the map, he figured La Jara to be two or three days of hard riding. He also figured he'd get there in his own time.

When the cook arrived, Lucius had the fried chicken, biscuits, and a pitcher of water, then continued to nurse the bottle while waiting for the whores to show up, or a card game to materialize. The prospect for cards seemed thin; the barkeep, the old Mexican, and two poor looking men eating at another table were the only people in the place.

Lucius had just lit a smoke when a whore stuck her head in the door, giving the place the once over for prospective clients. She pulled back as if she were leaving.

"Hey, girl! Where you goin'!" Lucius yelled. She pushed through the batwing doors and stopped her grand largeness just inside. "That's right double buttercup, I'm right over here," he said, and took a drag of his smoke.

She sashayed over in her frilly, burgundy dress that stressed at the seams and revealed a buxom cleavage promising of fun. "Why, you're just a scrawny southern boy. You think you can handle me?" she asked in a teasing tone.

"You'll find out soon enough. Sit down and have a drink. Bring this gal a glass!"

The barkeep brought the glass and Lucius poured.

She looked him over and thought him very plain, his clothes and hat not bespeaking a man of any means. "Say, you got any money, honey? I don't make your willie dance just for drinks."

Lucius looked her in the eye as he pulled out his money and put five dollars in front of her.

Her eyes widened. "Oh, honey, for that much, I'll make willie dance all night long."

The doors pushed open and a slender girl in her mid-twenties entered. She wore a long, blue checkered dress that looked worn, giving her the appearance of a farmer's wife. But her cowboy boots, sombrero, and beautiful face dispelled any notion of her being anything other than a true oddity of the frontier. She let go with a stream of tobacco juice that found the spittoon. Her eyes drifted over the room, settling on Lucius and his big mama at the back table.

"You know that thing?" Lucius asked his new companion.

"That's Quinny."

"Quinny?"

"Yeah, Quinny."

"What is she?"

"She's working, too."

"She's a whore?"

"Well, she ain't the preacher's daughter." The big girl leaned in close to Lucius. "Don't look at her, honey. You already made a deal for me, and I'm gonna drain you down like a month of hard plowin'."

Lucius smiled. "Don't you worry pork butt...that money's yours, and you'll earn it. I feel like a real party is all." He looked again to where the girl stood, more taken this time by how beautiful she was, even with the puffed cheek where the wad of tobacco resided. "Quinny girl, come on over here and have a drink," he called.

Quinny clomped across the room, more like a bull on the prod than the beauty she was. She stopped at the table and placed her hands on her hips. "Hey, Molly," she said to the big girl.

"Hey, Quinny," Molly replied

"Whadaya want, mister? Looks like yer already saddled up."

"I wanna rodeo."

"Rodeo?"

"That's right. Some bull ridin'...bronc bustin', sheep shearin'...whatever else comes to mind."

"Quinny leaned to the side and let go with some more juice to the spittoon by the table. "How about nut cuttin'?" she asked.

Lucius laughed. "Only as a manner of speaking. How 'bout it? You wanna rodeo?" Lucius pushed another five dollars across the table to where Quinny was standing.

Quinny looked at the money, then at Molly, then at Lucius. "You, me, and Molly? All in one big heap?"

Lucius exhaled a drag of his cigarette. "Sounds fun, don't it?"

Quinny looked back at Molly. "What about it, Mol...you game for that?"

"Sure. Let's rodeo this boy right down to a dried up sack."

Quinny leaned over to the spittoon and spit out the wad of chew. She sat down and poured herself a drink, then drained it. "I guess we'll see just how sportin' you are. What's yer name, mister?"

"You can call me Peterman."

"Boasting already! We'll find out soon enough," Molly said. And she and Quinny laughed rowdily.

The old Mexican had finished his meal and had beaten the barkeep in checkers enough for one day. He climbed carefully off the bar stool. Evening was upon the land and the wind had died. It was time for him to return to his shanty. He would come back the next day to sweep and clean for his evening meal, and to beat the barkeep in checkers once more. Just as he arrived at the doorway, two men burst in, their force knocking the old Mexican to the floor where he slammed his head and lay motionless.

The two men, who were dirty and drunk, laughed at the sight of it. "Looky there, Len, we just took out General Santa Anna."

"Who?" Len asked. They looked around the room with hard stares, sizing up their right to run roughshod any way they wanted to, their gun rigs hitched and tied like that of gunfighters. Nothing they saw concerned them. They strode to the bar just as the barkeep was coming out to aid his old friend, who was now beginning to move and moan.

"Leave 'im!...get us some whiskey!" one of them commanded.

"He is hurt...and old," the barkeep replied.

The taller one kicked the old Mexican in the ribs. The old man gasped. "Now, he's hurt some more. You'll be young and dead if you don't fetch that whiskey."

At the back of the room, Lucius stood up slowly. "You boys help that old man up," he said, coolly and deadly serious.

They turned and faced Lucius, both of them frowning at the no-account look of him and the order he'd just issued. "Did you just get lippy with us sodbuster?" Len asked incredulously. Then they saw his tie-down rig, and they looked in Lucius's eyes—dead like windows down a wormhole to hell.

"We'll wait right over here, honey," Molly said as she and Quinny vacated the table and moved to the side of the room.

"Lippy? Yessum, I just got lippy. I didn't care about killin' anyone tonight, but I'll kill you both if you don't help that old man up. That lippy enough for you?"

"You hear that, Coots?" Len said to his partner. "This ole boy's sounds like a Johnny Reb. Whatcha gonna do, Reb? Pull on us both?"

"Looks like it."

Out of the corner of his eye, Coots saw his partner on the draw, so he drew, too. Neither one of them had cleared their holsters when Lucius put a slug through each of their hearts. They both collapsed, falling dead nearly instantly, just feet from where the old Mexican was still lying on the floor.

Lucius holstered his gun and walked briskly over to where they lay. He grabbed the first man's feet and quickly pulled him out the door onto the street, then pulled the other one out a moment later. He went through their pockets and took their money, then walked back inside and lifted the old Mexican to his feet. "They wanted you to have this for your get-well time,"

Lucius said, pushing the money into the old Mexican's hand. The old man looked at Lucius, shaken and afraid. Lucius leaned in close to him and whispered to his ear, "It's all right, old timer. You knew I was a killer when you saw me. Vaya con Dios."

Lucius walked to his table and grabbed the bottle. Then he went to Quinny and Molly who looked at him with wide eyes. He gave the bottle to Molly and took them each by a hand. With the girls in tow, he headed for the rooms. "I'm ready to rodeo."

22

Rory's eyes opened and fixed for a moment on the rough-hewn plank ceiling above as his whereabouts came to him. The roof had been finished the day before, and the hands from the Twin T and Sky W had returned to their ranches, their work finished, and much they had done. The rest would be up to Padre and the children to finish.

He looked to the window on the gable end-wall and saw daylight, still the faint gray of early morning before sunrise. His excitement was immediate. It was all new; the first morning waking up in the new house—their home—not the string of places they'd lived or camped since Estella had died and the fire had taken the rest. This was really theirs. It seemed enormous. He turned his head and saw them all around him. Payat, Tobias, Jing Lu, and Camille were still heavy in slumber upon thin mattresses on the floor. They had all slept in the same room upstairs, except for Padre, who had his own room downstairs. There were two rooms upstairs, one for the boys and one for the girls. But it had seemed awkward to split up at the end of the evening, the last of which was spent with Rory reading Aesop's to the others by lamplight in the room they now shared. Perhaps when the beds were ready, they would split up, boys and girls, but they'd always slept in the same room, and any adjustment to that was not going to happen on their first night.

Chester's head rested on Payat's leg. His eyes were open and looking at Rory. When Rory made eye contact, the dog's tail began to thump on the bedding. "Shhhh!" Rory quietly implored as he quickly got up and tapped his leg for Chester to follow him. They made their way downstairs where Rory let Chester outside. "I'll be there in a minute," Rory said, before closing the door and heading to the stove. It was still warm from cooking the night before. Rory opened the firebox and strategically loaded the wood, then lit the match and blew gently, coaxing the fire to life. He grabbed his fishing rig and some bread and had reached the front door when Padre emerged from his room.

"Good morning, Rory," came his quiet greeting.

"Good morning, Padre. I fired the stove. Can I go fish for a little while?"

"Yes, son, but do not be too long. And Rory…"

"Yes, Padre?"

"Be skillful enough for tonight's supper. I am sure we would all enjoy some fish."

Rory's eyes brightened. "I found a spot where they must have fish meetings…'cause they're all there. Yes, sir, I'll catch plenty for supper, Lord willing.

"Go then, we have much work to do today."

Rory opened the door and was halfway out when he suddenly stopped. "Isn't this the best, Padre?"

The padre looked at Rory, taken with the exuberant joy in the tone of his question. His old eyes softened with his love for the boy. "Yes, son, it is the best."

Rory closed the door and bounded forward, running toward the creek and his new favorite spot. Down through the tall grass and then in amongst the trees, he ran with Chester right alongside him. The sun would soon rise, and so would the fish. The boy and the dog moved quickly along the bank, leaping over rocks and deadfall till they came to the place Rory knew. He pulled a thick crust of bread from his pocket and tossed it to Chester. "Breakfast, boy. Now set back and don't scare my fish." Chester took the crust and moved back from the bank where he lay down and chewed contentedly.

The sun pierced the horizon like a rising globe of peach ice cream, its light stretching through the trees and flicking upon the water in the dance of daybreak. Rory looked closely at the pool and saw them thick. He rigged his fly and cast with a deft wrist, making the fly light just where he was aiming. A strike came almost instantly, the force of it jolting his pole with all the fight the eighteen-inch fish could bring to bear before the struggle was consummated. Within an hour, he had five more that looked nearly identical. He cleaned them and stung them. "Let's go, boy. We got all we need, and then some."

When he got close to the cabin, he staked his stringer to the creek bank, letting the fish float in the cold water. "Stay put till I come for you," he said, to his catch. He ran up the hill and saw Sammy and Padre standing in front of the cabin, drinking coffee. There were two new horses in the corral with Roca.

"Mornin', Rory."

"Good morning, Mister Winds. I didn't see you get here."

"I saw *you*...fishing. Had your back to me."

"But I didn't hear you, neither."

"I didn't care to be heard. I wasn't that close. Besides, it appeared you had all your wits fixed on those fish. It's good to save a few wits for what may be goin' on around you, though."

"Yes, sir."

"Did you do any good? All I see is your rig."

Rory smiled broadly. "Sure did...plenty for supper. I got 'em cached in the creek."

"Good." Sammy let his eyes drift to the corral. Rory's eyes followed.

"Are those your horses, Mister Winds?"

"They were. That mustang's yours now. The roan can pull your wagon or anyone can ride 'im. He's broke gentle as a spring day. The mustang's just rough broke. You'll have to work him awhile before he's suitable."

Rory was unsure of what he had just heard, with the talk of the roan and "anyone" mixed into heap. "I'm sorry, Mister Winds. I don't think I heard what you said. Whose horse is the mustang?"

"Yours!"

"Mine?" Rory stood speechless.

"You should thank, Mister Winds," the padre said after a long pause.

Rory dropped his fishing rig and quickly stepped toward Sammy, extending his right hand to him. "Thank you, sir! I will take good care of him...I surely will!"

"Fine," Sammy said, shaking the boy's hand. "We've got more horses than we know what to do with lately. Wild herds staked a claim on my ranch. I'll bring a few more when we've had time to break 'em...and you get some more corrals built or a barn."

"Yes, sir!"

"Now pull that extra saddle off Dobe. That's for you, too."

"Yes, sir! Much obliged, Mister Winds!" Rory exclaimed elatedly, as he ran to Sammy's horse and untied the extra saddle.

"Thanks for the coffee, Padre. Have to go get some work done," Sammy announced.

"As do we. Thank you for the horses, Sammy. It is most generous of you...once again."

Sammy shook his head, as if embarrassed once again. He mounted up and looked down at Rory, who stood holding the saddle. "First time up, hold tight and don't get thrown on your head. Work 'im good for a while and spend time on him. He'll be a good horse."

"I will, Mister Winds."

The afternoon was warm and still, with a sky that had loosed a collage of high clouds, the farthest of which were dark and pregnant. Rain was coming.

"That looks good," the padre said as he stood and considered the last of the shelving he and Rory had built in the kitchen area. "Go and help Payat and Tobias with the chicken house now. We will need a high fence around it with a gate, lest the coyotes and wolves will take them before we have enjoyed many eggs. This certainly looks like country for such animals."

"Bears, too," Rory added as he headed for the door.

Jing Lu was planting more seed in the vegetable garden, and Camille was toting a bucket of water toward her, having come from the stream. Rory ran over to Camille who was struggling with the weight of the water. "Here, give me that," he said, taking the bucket from her.

She looked at him as if her task had been interrupted. "I can do it."

"Well, whadaya want with the water anyways? And why didn't you just come inside and pump it? It's a whole lot closer."

"I like to go down to the stream. The pump handle is hard for me. Can't you see we are planting seed? We need to water them in."

"I can see rain is comin' in an hour or two. Look at that sky yonder."

146

Camille looked in the direction Rory was looking. She saw the lone rider. "Who's that?"

Rory looked hard, conscious she'd spotted him before he had, and that it was the second time that day he'd missed a rider. The rider was nearly a mile away. "Can't say. Comin' from the town cutoff looks like. We'll know soon enough. He's comin' this way...and he's coverin' ground."

Rory carried the water over to where Jing Lu was planting. He placed the bucket next to her. "There you go...but looks like rain later."

"Yes, but there is no wind. The rain clouds may not reach here."

Camille kneeled down next to Jing Lu and began helping her.

Rory looked doubtful. "They'll get here tonight for sure, I reckon." He watched the girls for a minute as they continued on: Jing Lu planting, and Camille carefully scooping water over the area already planted.

"You do not have to stand here and watch us," Jing Lu finally said.

"Uh-huh, we know how to do it," Camille added.

"I'm just waitin' to see who's comin'."

A minute later, the well-dressed man arrived on a chestnut Rocky Mountain that was well lathered. He reined to a stop at the edge of the garden, taking care not to disturb the ground. "Hello, there," he said in a genial tone, not making any move to dismount. Chester lay still on the ground but began a low growl.

"Hello, mister," Rory replied. Jing Lu and Camille stopped their work and looked up at the man who was some thirty feet away. They said nothing. He looked important; middle-aged with a finely manicured grayish beard beneath dark eyes that held more serious intent than the lightness of his greeting. It

147

was an expensive wool suit and hat he wore, with a fresh, white cotton blouse, adorned by a turquoise bola attached to finely braided, black leather cord with silver tips on the ends.

"Is this the Sky W Ranch...the ranch of Mister Sam Winds?

"Well...yeah, all around us."

"Is Mister Winds here?"

"May I help you?" came the call from the front door of the house where the padre had just come out." Tobias and Payat had stopped their work and were watching, too.

"He's looking for Mister Winds, Padre," Rory called back.

"Do not interrupt, son."

The man rode around the garden and over to the front of the house where the padre stood. He did not dismount. "Padre, is it?

"That is what my children call me."

"Your children?"

"Yes."

The man waited a moment to see if the padre would add anything. He didn't. "Your son said the Sky W Ranch is all around us. This isn't Sky W land I'm on?"

"No, it is not. If you seek Mister Winds, his ranch is just over that rise...about a mile," the padre replied as he pointed the way.

"Where does his land border yours?"

"Why do you ask, sir? If you have business with me concerning this land, please state it. If your business is with Mister Winds, I suggest you direct your questions to him."

"I didn't mean to be presumptuous, mister."

"Then perhaps you should not sit atop your horse and ask personal questions of me before you have introduced yourself and stated your reason for being here."

Rupert Crowder was irritated. "Well, I might just end up having business with you, mister," he shot back in a tone absent of any pleasantness. "We'll see." He spurred his horse to a lope in the direction the padre had indicated.

"Who was that man?" Jing Lu asked loudly.

"I do not know. He never offered his name. But none of you are to answer any of his questions if you see him again. Just direct him to me. Do you understand?"

"Yes, Padre," came the chorus of replies.

"He sure was a fancy lookin' one," Rory said.

"Yes, fancy as the devil," the padre mumbled under his breath as he turned to go back into the house.

23

J enny mixed the flour, shortening, and water in a bowl, kneading it with her hands until the mixture reached the consistency she wanted. Then she rolled out the dough with the rolling pin and cut out the two pieces for top and bottom. She molded a piece into the greased pan and added the sliced apple and rhubarb, sprinkling sugar and cinnamon generously over it before covering with the top dough and crimping the edges. Into the hot oven she placed it, noting the time on the cuckoo clock that she wound each morning.

She was retrieving her knitting from the basket by the front window when the suddenness of his presence startled her. The man sat there on his horse in front of the house, just looking at it, his eyes moving slowly over it and then to all that was in close proximity. She backed away from the window into the darker interior of the room as his eyes came to rest on the glass. It was not something she was accustomed to, living out of town and being alone for hours.

He was well dressed and rode a fine mount, but his behavior was curious to her. Though not frightened, she wished Sammy was home. The man peered at the glass a moment more then slowly dismounted and tied his horse to the rail. Sammy's words were still fresh in her mind from the short time ago when he'd spoken them as a commandment: "Don't you ever open this door to a stranger without a gun in your hand...preferably the scatter gun."

Jenny moved over to where the shotgun and several other rifles rested in a rack, but instead took the .44-caliber revolver from the mantle and pulled the hammer back to the first position. A knock came at the door. She walked to it and stopped, with the gun at her side. "Yes, who is it?" she called loudly enough to be heard, still wondering why the stranger had not called out from outside before ever coming up on the porch.

"I see from the sign out front, this is the Sky W Ranch. I have business with Mister Winds. Is he here?"

"Please back down off the porch."

Rupert turned and walked down the steps to the ground, continuing on for another twenty feet before turning and facing the house again. Jenny opened the door and stepped out onto the porch. "My husband is not here at the moment. He may be back any moment, or it may be an hour or two."

"You're Missus Winds?"

"I am...and who are you?"

Rupert saw the pistol in her right hand, partly obscured by the folds of her dress against which she held it. But there was no hiding the beauty of the woman before him. His concentration was momentarily glazed. "My name is Lionel Doan. I have business with Mister Winds."

"Yes, you mentioned that, Mister Doan. What is the nature of your business?"

"I'm sorry, ma'am. I can only discuss that with Mister Winds."

"Very well, then. He's working cattle today, to the south I think, although he could be anywhere. You're welcome to look."

Rupert turned and looked at the countryside as if considering if he wanted to strike out in search of Sam Winds. "I'll wait for him here…if that's all right, ma'am."

"Yes, that's fine. You can water your horse at the trough by the barn and wait there."

"Thank you, ma'am." Rupert moved to his horse and untied it, then looked to Jenny again. "Oh, by the way, coming here I passed by a cabin over that hill. There were five youngsters and an older man…"

Jenny nodded. "Yes…Padre and his children."

"I thought this was all Sky W land around here. Where does the Sky W border their land?"

"All around it. It was a piece of Sky W land that my husband deeded to them."

"How big a piece?"

She considered the question for a moment. "When you see my husband, you can explain why such a question may be any of your business."

Rupert said nothing and led his horse toward the trough by the barn. Jenny returned inside and bolted the door, then sat by the window continuing her work on a quilt she had begun days earlier. An aroma of the baking pie filled the house. The gun remained in her lap, and she had a good view of the man.

Rupert sat on a bench beside the barn and smoked a cigar. That Missus Winds had not invited him to wait on the porch in one of the nice rockers was not lost on him. *She was a smart woman*, he thought. He wondered what he would encounter with Mister Winds. No matter. He would remain polite and try to be persuasive, but in the end, all that would be determined, for his conversation was the means by which they would take his land. A simple buyout was preferred, but not necessary.

The sky transformed slowly, with darker clouds massing to the northwest like a gathering army in preparation of a march to battle with the blue sky directly above. As he rode from the trees into the open meadow across which his ranch house sat, Sammy saw the man sitting at the barn. He spurred Dobe to a gallop, wanting the wind in his face and curious about who it might be. The horse was happy to run. Soft sod flew as they raced in a full stretch for home. It was already customary.

The quarter mile over open ground faded quickly, and then he was there at the barn, swinging down from his horse with the grace and ease of a trick rider before Dobe had ever stopped. He tipped his hat to Jenny who had stepped out on the porch. She did a slight curtsey and returned inside. "Hello, mister, what can I do for you?" Sammy asked, with the satisfaction of a good day's work in his voice.

"You must be Mister Winds...Mister Sam Winds."

"The one and only, around here anyways," Sammy replied, as he loosened his saddle cinch. Seconds later, he headed for the barn, saddle in hand. Rupert followed him into the barn where Sammy chunked his rig onto a tack rail, then turned to Rupert and extended his hand. "Nice to make your acquaintance, Mister...?"

"I'm Lionel Doan. I represent the Westgate Railroad Company," Rupert said as he shook hands and was taken with the power in the cowboy's grip.

"Railroad?" Sammy replied inquisitively, as he strode out of the barn and headed to the corral. Rupert followed him again. Sammy gave a clipped, sharp whistle and opened the corral gate. Dobe trotted in.

"Yes, Mister Winds, Westgate Railroad. Let me come right to the point of this call. We want to buy your land."

"Buy my land? I own twenty thousand acres."

"Yes, we know."

"I suppose that doesn't surprise me. Why in creation would a railroad have an interest my land?"

"Spur lines, Mister Winds. Now that a transcontinental rail line is complete, there's need for spur lines to provide for areas north and south of it. Westgate is procuring land for those routes."

Sammy pulled out his makings and began to roll a smoke as he thought about what the man had just told him. It didn't make sense to Sammy. "Well, we ain't exactly sittin' near any major trails or between any big cities or towns. Spur lines from where to where? I don't see where tracks through this country would be goin' to, or comin' from." Sammy fired his smoke and took a long drag, savoring the tobacco.

"The West is growing faster than you or I can imagine. This country is filling up, and Westgate wants to be ready."

"I guess so, but the fact is my land's not for sale."

"Mister Winds, Westgate is prepared to offer you twelve thousand dollars for your land," Rupert declared, as if he'd just offered the king's jewels. He knew the offer was three times what Sammy had paid for it less than a year before. But he didn't know that Sammy was independently wealthy, and like a son to the Taylor Brothers of the Twin T. Rupert figured that the young cowboy was likely to be heavily leveraged with such a new operation. He threw out the final enticement: "And we'll buy your herd at twice the market price to help you out."

"Help me out?" Sammy smiled.

"Yes, Mister Winds, Westgate wants to be more than fair. The cattle business is tough. You can go broke a lot of ways. Why not walk now with a stake that would take you years to come by, if ever. You have a pretty young wife. Do right for her and yourself."

Sammy looked at him. "I guess my pretty, young wife sent you down here to wait, huh?"

"Well, yes. I believe she was uncomfortable with a stranger here while you weren't around."

"Did you talk to her about this?"

"No, sir!"

"Well, it wouldn't have mattered if you had. My land's not for sale."

Rupert paused, his eyes squinting with curiosity. "What price would you sell for?"

"There is no price, Mister Doan."

"I must tell you, the government is backing railroads in land procurement. If you don't sell, the government may seize it under eminent domain, and they'll pay you a lot less than I just offered you. You know what that means, boy…eminent domain?"

"Yeah, if recollection serves me, I believe that would fall under the fifth amendment of the Constitution."

Rupert's eyes widened with trepidation from the quick response, having expected to catch the young cowboy flat-footed. "Yes…yes, I believe that may be correct," he awkwardly agreed, bluffing all the way. "It's all for the greater good, you know."

"Whose greater good? Yours? 'Cause it sure as hell won't be for the greater good of anyone showin' up here tryin' to take my land against my will."

"No need to get riled. I just wanted to make you aware of the possible consequences."

"I'll take it under advisement," Sammy said flatly, signaling he'd heard enough. "I'm ready for supper now. You're welcome to eat with us and bunk in with the boys across the way there. Looks like a storm comin'."

"Is that your final word on this matter, Mister Winds?" Rupert queried, astonished at the speed of Sammy's dismissal.

"Sure is."

"Well, then, I'll be on my way."

Sammy stood and watched as Rupert quickly mounted and rode from the yard at a lope.

"Good evening, Mister Winds," Jenny said to him when he walked through the door. She came to him, and they embraced and kissed.

"I smell that pie, Missus Winds," he said when their lips came apart. "Apple?"

"And rhubarb," she added.

"My favorite."

"I know. Can you smell the pot roast, too?"

"Sure can. It smells almost as good as you are beautiful." She kissed him again. "You know what else I smell?" he asked, sniffing with his nose in the air like a hound catching scent. "My own pitiful self. I'll go wash up."

"It doesn't bother me."

"Well, it bothers me if I'm around you."

Her expression turned serious. "Who was that man...Mister Doan?"

"No tellin' exactly. Said he was representing Westgate Railroad."

"Railroad?"

"Yeah, that's what I said, too. They want to buy our land...lock, stock, and barrel."

"What did you tell him?"

He frowned at her. "I told him 'no,' 'no,' and 'no' again."

Jenny smiled, and then looked thoughtful. "There was something about him I didn't like or trust."

"Ahh! He was a blowhard charlatan. Offered twelve thousand dollars like it was big bearskin. He knew the size of our spread, so I'm sure he knows what I paid for it, too...public records. This is prime country, Jenny. There's not better water and grass, and Lord knows what else, anywhere in the territory. It's worth five times what he offered, and he knows it. Just thought I didn't, or that I'd jump at the chance to triple my money. No, you're right, sweetness. Nothin' to trust about that one."

24

The thunderheads stayed to the north and slowly drifted east, leaving a few light sprinkles of rain over the Sky W that came from the last wisps of stray, dark clouds streaking along as if trying to catch the mother beast. The day's work done and the supper finished, Rory was itching to have a go at the mustang Sammy had given him that morning.

"What name will you give him?" Jing Lu asked, as Rory stroked the side of the horse's head. They were all there watching. The padre leaned against the top rail of the corral as the other children sat upon it and intently watched Rory's every move with the mustang at the center of the ring. Roca and the other horse Sammy had brought were hobbled nearby, eating of the late-spring grass and paying no attention to what was happening at the corral. "Well?" Jing Lu asked, just as Rory slipped on the bridle and reins.

"Don't know yet. I ain't even been on 'im."

The horse stood easy as Rory fetched his saddle then hoisted it up and on. As he worked the cinch straps, the horse turned its head and peered back at the boy, its great black eye watching as the ritual to which it was yet unaccustomed was performed. The mustang's body was peppered gray and black, with full black ears, mane, and tail, white socks, and a large, white diamond between its eyes.

The padre guessed what the response would be, but spoke anyway. "I can hold him while you mount."

"No, I reckon he'll be all right. Mister Winds said he was rough broke...and he ain't gone squirrelly yet. If he does, no sense in both of us gettin' whomped. Just open the gate if I ask. He might wanna run after a little work in here."

Payat jumped down from the top rail. "We open when you say."

"Well, here goes nothin'," Rory said as he hitched his foot in the stirrup and pulled himself up quick and light. The horse stood still. Rory sat easy without moving.

"He doesn't even know you're on him," Tobias said.

"Yes, he does," Camille opined shaking her head up and down with a wide-eyed expression like all hell was going to break loose.

"All right, boy." Rory reined the horse's head left as he gave the slightest heels to it. The horse began walking to his left, then to its right when Rory reined over.

"See, he's no trouble," Tobias said confidently. Just then, as if a lit fuse had finally reached the powder, the horse blasted straight up in the air, all four hooves equally high, and its chin tucked down towards its chest.

"Whoa!" Rory blurted out reflexively, as the padre and children watched in awe at the height the horse had achieved. Its great body returned to earth and instantly leaped forward, then bucked and whipped side to side and up and down with Rory clamped on tight, fighting to stay aboard. Three more seconds of fury was unleashed before the horse sprinted across the small corral then dug in its hooves, sliding several feet and slamming the top rail, sending Rory flying high over the horse's head, his body somersaulting through the air and turning a complete forward flip before he landed on his feet and pitched forward face-first into the dirt some twenty feet beyond the corral. The horse stood easy again, looking passively at the boy, its victory complete.

Rory was already on his feet by the time the padre and children arrived at his side. He spit the blood from his mouth and wiped the dirt from his eyes.

"Are you all right, my son!?"

"Rory smiled, his teeth red with the blood that continued to flow. "Aw, sure. Don't feel like nothin's broke. My teeth's all here." He pulled his lower lip down to reveal the small puncture in it. "How's it look?" he mumbled proudly. The padre inspected his mouth as Camille and Jing Lu stood on their tiptoes to gawk at it.

"Good ride! Good ride!" Payat offered as he hopped from foot to foot in his excitement.

"Yep. It was a hoot and a holler right up till the landing," Rory replied, then pulled back from the padre and spit again.

"It looks to be just a small cut on your lip. Are any of your teeth loose?" the padre asked.

Rory tested each of his teeth with his fingers, then he spit again. "Nope. I'm ready for another go at 'im."

"Tomorrow, son. It is getting dark now."

Rory suddenly looked more hurt than anything the horse had inflicted on him. "Please, Padre! If I don't get back on 'im now, he'll think he won. Then it will really be hard next time. It won't be dark for a half hour. Please, Padre."

The padre fully understood the boy's spirit and toughness, and he saw the logic in his words. "All right, son. Until dark or you cannot ride anymore…whichever comes first."

Rory spit again. "Thank you, Padre," he said, and promptly stomped back to the corral like he was going to a fight. They continued to watch as he was thrown several more times, managing to stay aboard a bit longer with each attempt, and at least landing inside the corral when he was bucked off. Then, with the evening star present in the twilight, the horse bucked and ripped and twisted, but did not shake his mount. The mustang came to a steady trot around the ring, as though its respect had been duly earned. "Open the gate!' Rory yelled. Payat was at the ready and opened it with great haste.

The padre was uncertain about the wisdom of it, but only managed the words, "Do not be long," as the horse and rider blew by and headed into the open meadow.

"Run, boy!" Rory yelled, as he hung on. He tucked down as the horse stretched to a full gallop, pounding the sod with the primal beat of all its instinct. All else fell away as Rory was in the moment: a cocoon of sound and furious energy, of wind rushing and the horse's head bobbing forward like the tip of a spear piercing the air as it pushed through each full cycle of it legs, turning over and over in perfection. He had never been on a horse this fast. And this horse was his. A feeling of awe and pure elation ran through him, his every sense burning bright as night fell around him. He knew he would rise early and tend his horse. And he would ride him every day.

25

Boothe liked Two Rock, mostly because he was relieved to be clear of Dumas and the surrounding country. There were other things to like, too. The town was small, but had a nice little hotel with a dining room that served good food. And the adjacent Snakebite Saloon had atmosphere, card games, and five whores, all of whom looked good to Boothe, especially Monique. Perhaps the best part, though, was that Boothe hadn't spotted a lawman. There was a hoosegow that was not much bigger than a privy, but no marshal or sheriff's office that he could tell. And there were no bulletin boards with "wanted" posters. Boothe puzzled about who showed up if the law got trampled, but decided against asking. There was a stage that passed through on Tuesdays. And there were enough regulars and other passersby to make it a lively place.

Boothe and his three remaining men were making another night of it at the Snakebite when Rupert walked in. His cards were no good, so Boothe threw them on the table. "Fold," he said, then collected his money and headed for the bar where Rupert was draining a shot of rye. The rest of the crew was upstairs with the whores.

"Let's take a walk," Rupert said. The two men headed outside into the cool evening and walked to the end of the street where Rupert stopped, confident that they were beyond earshot of anyone. He lit a cigar and took a slow pull as he casually glanced around.

"What's the job?" Boothe asked.

Rupert let the smoke drift out slowly, some of it coming from his nose. "There's a ranch about ten miles southeast...the Sky W. Owned by a man, name of Sam Winds. He's young...early twenties I'd guess. Brown hair, hazel eyes. Six foot, hundred eighty pounds maybe...strong...and he's smart. Rides an appaloosa...black with white spots. He has a real pretty wife."

Boothe perked up a bit. "That so?"

"Yeah. No kids that I saw. Their place backs up to a river. Big place. Log house with the 'Sky W Ranch' sign out front. Two barns, corrals. There's a bunkhouse about a half mile east...five or six hands likely, but I'm not sure on that." Rupert pulled out an envelope. "Here's a drawing of the whole layout...directions too. There's another cabin on a creek about a mile west. It's part of the spread. Fresh built. An old man and some kids. They called him Padre. The kids must be orphans, because they sure aren't natural brothers and sisters."

Boothe had been looking at the contents of the envelope when the words registered. His head snapped up like he'd hit the end of the hangman's noose. "Padre and orphan kids?"

"Yeah, five that I saw. Couple of white boys, Chinese girl, and two others...Mexican or Indian. The oldest wasn't more than thirteen or so."

"You say their place was new?"

Rupert was surprised at the feverish tone of Boothe's questions. "Yeah...that mean something to you?" Rupert asked, his curiosity suddenly piqued.

Boothe stood silent for a moment, deciding whether he should tell Rupert about the witnesses at Clint Smith's place. "Maybe," he finally said. "We heard tell that a padre and some orphans were livin' at the Smith place the day we hit it. Could be they seen somethin'."

"Could be? What the hell are you talking about? How could they see it if you didn't see them?"

"They was stayin' in a shed, a piece beyond Smith's place. The boys checked it when we got there but no one was around. There was a hillside next to Smith's place...lot a trees. Could be they was up there. We rode it good...came up empty."

Rupert rubbed his jaw like he had an uncomfortable itch. "Hell, they probably already moved on if it's the same group that's out at the Sky W."

Boothe decided against letting Rupert know anymore. "Yeah, that might be the skinny of it," he casually replied as his mind raced ahead. He put the padre and kids first on his list, no matter what the job was. *But what if they showed up in town and recognize me and my crew?* he thought. He considered it in a fraction of a second, deciding that he would deal with them immediately. Rupert interrupted his thought.

"I've got a place for you and your boys to stay till this is over...a few miles north and stowed away nice and private."

Boothe suddenly considered a hideout to be a good idea now that this padre was in the area. "Good, so what's the job?"

"Your end will be everybody on that ranch, except Winds...and that padre and kids, too...now."

"What about Winds?"

'I've got another man here for that."

"He the same man that took down Clint Smith?"

"Yeah. He'll be here in another day or so. It might time you two met. This one's the biggest yet. It's going to take good planning...and timing. You won't be able to ride in and start blasting like you did at Smith's place. Too many men…and salty I'm guessing. They'll need to disappear with no bodies and no witnesses…just like always."

"Why don't you put this other dude on my crew? I lost two men at Smith's place. I could use another gun if Winds has half a dozen men."

"No. He works alone. He has his own methods."

Boothe scowled. "He won't work at all if I kill 'im."

"Don't talk stupid! This job's going to be hard. We need the best we can get…and he's the best," Rupert scowled, knowing that Lucius wouldn't figure prominently in the plan, but wanting to keep his best gunman employed in any way he could.

"Hell, you can give me whatever you're payin' him, and I'll kill 'em all. Only timin' needed there is my own."

Rupert looked at Boothe, unsure of him. "Nope, he's coming. There's money enough."

"What's my end?"

"Three thousand for you alone; plus I'll double your other men's regular fee. And, I've got ten more men coming for this job.

"Ten?"

"Yeah, you'll need them. Good men I'm told. They'll know you're the boss…take their orders from you."

"Why will they do that?"

"Because they want to get paid, and following your orders is part of the deal."

Boothe liked it. It was his biggest payday by a long shot. "I'll play it however you want. And I'll have the rest of my advance now."

Rupert pulled a wad of cash from his coat and peeled off the money. "No mistakes on this one. Use the time till the rest of them get here to scout it out…figure your play."

"I'll do that."

"Evenin' boys," Sammy said as he walked into the bunkhouse. They were stretched around the front room in chairs and on the settee, their attention on Knuckles who was reading from The Brothers Grimm. They all turned and looked at Sammy. Knuckles stopped reading and looked up from the book like the Blessed Sacrament had been interrupted. "Spur that chop wagon and get on with it. I wanna hear it, too!" Sammy declared, and then pulled his makings to twist a smoke.

"It's damn near over now," Knuckles replied.

"Well, ain't the best of it usually at the last? Read on, Skookum, and quit holdin' up the show."

"What's a Skookum?" Knuckles asked suspiciously.

"That's a story onto its own. 'Bout a beast of a man, runnin' around in the woods up in the Northwest...stealin' salmon out of fishermen's nets. Ferocious he is."

"Sounds like Knuckles," said Roasty. "Kin for sure."

Knuckles looked perplexed, unsure of a compliment or an insult.

"Back to Clever Gretel or I'm startin' a cardgame," Jasper announced, exasperated at the delay.

"All right!" Knuckles replied defensively. He looked down at the book, squinting in the lamplight to find his place. "Gretel took the roasted chicken and quickly feasted on it, finding it to be succulent and delicious. When she had finished, she thought, *Oh my! I have eaten half the dinner of my master and his guest.* She went back to the cellar and took yet another hearty draught. Upon returning, she looked lovingly at the second roasted chicken and said, 'Where one has gone, the other must surely follow,' and she feasted on it."

Knuckles had barely gotten out the last of the sentence before breaking into riotous laughter. "Where one has gone, the other must surely follow!" he said again, laughing and gasping for air.

"She sounds like kin to Knuckles, too. Sister, maybe," Bill said.

Porter shook his head. "Must be if she can eat like that."

"I hope she can fight like Knuckles 'cause there's gonna be hell to pay when her master gets home," Jasper opined.

Sammy exhaled a drag of his smoke. "Maybe...maybe not. Maybe this story ain't named Clever Gretel for nothin'."

"Well, they sure coulda named it Hungry Gretel," Matt chuckled.

"Starvin' Gretel is more like it," Roasty chimed. "Two whole chickens? She'll crap like a prize bull."

"Could be her ass is the size of a prize bull's," Matt said seriously.

"Her crap'll be purple. She's been drinkin' wine through this whole story so far. A draught here, a draught there...then a few more draughts," Porter said. "She's gotta be drunk as hell. Drunken Gretel."

"What the hell happens next?" Ben asked.

Knuckles took up his place again and managed to finish the story uninterrupted, recounting how Gretel had told the dinner guest that her master meant to cut off his ears and kill him, whereby he instantly fled. Then she went and told her master that the dinner guest had run off with the chickens. The story ended with the master chasing the guest down the road with a knife shouting "Just one, just one!" meaning he wanted just one of the chickens for himself. But the dinner guest believed he meant just one of his ears, so he ran fast and hard into the night.

"Ain't she the false one," Jasper said at the conclusion.

"Yep, sure was clever," Porter agreed.

"You already had your supper, Sammy?" Knuckles asked.

"No. On my way home right now."

"Might be nothin' left by now. Jenny might tell you the ole pooch Chester ran off with it."

26

Sammy's eyes came open and stared into the blackness. Silhouettes within the room began to form as his eyes adjusted. It was all so comfortable: the bed, the room, the house, and Jenny's breath on his shoulder as she slept. The house creaked and groaned in the stillness, and he could hear the faint, soothing roll of the river a stone's throw behind the house. It was an hour before daybreak and he had slept well. But now, in the quiet darkness, his mind began to turn over about his encounter with Lionel Doan, and his offer to buy the Sky W. Uneasiness drifted through Sammy as he considered Doan's words, and the thought of the happenstance meeting with the two prospectors just weeks before. Something was amiss.

The front porch creaked from the weight on it. Sammy listened intently for a moment more, then slid quietly from the bed and grabbed his forty-four from its holster. Like a cat, he moved silently through the house to the front window. From the edge of the glass, he peered out into the night and saw the shape on the porch. Sammy moved to the door and slid the bolt back easily. The shape on the front porch heard the noise and turned as Sammy opened the door a crack and spoke in a low voice, "Get gone bear. Go on...get gone." The three hundred pound black bear stood easy on all fours, swinging his head slowly side to side. "Go on now. Go see Roasty down yonder. Maybe he's got somethin' for you. There's nothin' here but grief. Go on…get now!" The bear looked for a moment to where the mysterious voice was coming from, and then ambled casually down the porch steps and on into the meadow.

Twenty minutes later, Sammy kissed her gently on the cheek. She stirred in the darkness. "It's early," she sleepily said.

"Yeah, I'm goin' to the Twin T. Go back to sleep."

"I'll get up and make you breakfast."

"No, I'll eat over there. Go back to sleep."

"Are you sure?"

"Yes, ma'am." He leaned down and kissed her once more. "That bear was back again. When you're outside, you wear that holster I gave you."

"All right."

"I'll be home by noon," he said, and then he was gone.

Sammy rode most of the twelve miles to the Twin T before light, under a sky that was clear, moonless, and riddled with stars. He could see well enough in the open, keeping to an easy gallop. Through the trees, he slowed to a trot, letting Dobe lead, but he could have done it blindfolded. Dobe certainly knew the way.

The summer morning was temperate, the darkness waning as Sammy closed out the last mile. Lucilla was frying bacon when Sammy walked in. He glanced at the cuckoo, it read 5:05. Once more, he broke into the song she'd heard many times before. *"Lu, Lu, Lu, Lucilla, muy bonita, por favor comida."*

She turned and blushed as she always had. "You still crazy, Sammy. *Buenos dias.*" Her voice exuded her love and care.

Her hair was gray now, and her body was stout and without curves. She was dressed in a colorful but simple smock.

Sammy hugged her. "*Buenos dias*, Lucilla." He grabbed a cup and poured himself some coffee. "Jacqueline? Raquel?

"Jacqueline is no feeling well. She is in bed. Raquel is visiting her daughter in Albuquerque. Mister Homer is eating…" She nodded to the dining room. "You want breakfast?"

"I sure do…before the rest of the crowd shows." Sammy glanced at the mountain of bacon and hotcakes that stood in a warming pan. "Looks like you've more'n enough…like always," he said as he headed for the dining room.

"I thought I heard voices out there." Homer sunnily offered as Sammy entered. "Good morning to you. How's married life?"

"It's grand, Mister Taylor! Better'n I ever thought possible."

Homer chuckled. "Well, just remember, on the other side of every mountain is a valley. You'll have to hold those reins steady."

"Yeah, I know. But I'm partial to the mountains."

"Aren't we all? What brings you here this early?"

"I wanted to talk to you and Reuben."

"Your timing is impeccable," Homer replied as Reuben entered the room.

"My young man, Sammy!" Reuben cheerfully boomed. "How's your beautiful bride?"

"She's just fine, sir."

Reuben sat down and pushed the head of the brass turtle that sat on the table, emitting a ring. "Good! How's your herd doing?" he queried, turning his eyes directly to Sammy's.

"We calved three hundred and thirty or so—near even split on bulls and cows. Only lost six."

"You're a going concern now," Homer opined.

"That's a fact—a great start! We'll be buying beef from you before it's all over," Reuben added.

Lucilla entered the room with a platter of cups, food, and coffee. She placed plates in front of Reuben and Sammy and poured coffee for Reuben. "Thank you, my dear Lucilla," Reuben said with deep sincerity. Lucilla nodded and disappeared back into the kitchen.

Sammy wanted to get to it before anyone else showed up. "A man showed at my place yesterday offering to buy me out...on behalf of an outfit called Westgate Railroad."

Both men's eyes immediately fell on Sammy. "What!" Reuben declared, his tone half angry. "What was his name?"

"Lionel Doan...what he said."

Homer's face contracted in thought, the crow's feet at the corner of his eyes becoming prominent. "I've never heard of Westgate Railroad or Lionel Doan. It doesn't mean they're not real, but I haven't heard a word about any railroad plans in these parts."

"We would have caught wind of something like that," Reuben said. "Hell, they're just now working on line linking Santa Fe and Albuquerque...and we're a long ways from either of those. I don't see why track would come through here. High country...and from where to where? Maybe La Jara or Stratford over to Albuquerque or Santa Fe, but not through this country. Doesn't make sense."

"That's just what I thought, too," Sammy agreed. "Doan said the West was fillin' up and they wanted to be ready when demand got ripe."

Homer frowned. "Demand will ripen a lot of other places that don't have tracks long before it ripens here." He turned contemplative again. "It sure stands to reason that a railroad interested in your land would want our land, too...damn near regardless of what direction they were laying track." Homer looked Sammy in the eye. "What did you tell the man?"

"He offered twelve thousand. I told him my land's not for sale...at any price. Then he said the government is helping railroads procure land by eminent domain. Said if the government took it, they'd only pay a fraction of what he was offering."

Reuben slapped the table. "That's hog slop! He's just looking to buffalo you. And I sure as hell doubt he represents any railroad."

"I think you're right about that, brother," Homer said. "This whole thing rings hollow."

"There's somethin' else," Sammy added. "I didn't think much of it at the time, but now it's got me wonderin'. About a month ago, I ran two prospectors off...up on the north end at Juney River...a Chinaman and another fella. The Chinaman had quite a kit...bottles and beakers and such. The other man was panning... ran his mouth like he was in charge, but I had a feelin' the Chinaman was the brains of the outfit. This whole deal could be more than coincidence."

Homer frowned. "Oh...I don't know about that being any more than coincidence. Lot of prospectors through here over the years. We always remind them they're on private property."

"It adds up like shit through a sieve!" Reuben declared. I don't know if those two Things are connected, but this whole railroad talk blows false."

"How'd it end up with this man Doan?" Homer asked.

"He wanted to know if it was my final word on the matter. Then he mounted up and headed toward the cutoff.

"What'd he look like?" Reuben asked.

"Forties...medium build and height...dressed nice, grey wool suit, black hat. Had a grey beard...just the chin...brown eyes I recall. Ridin' a fine lookin' chestnut...a stallion."

Both brothers sat quiet for a moment, considering the information. Homer spoke with deadly seriousness. "I fear there could be a move against you, Sammy. Men make their own law out here. Sheriff Ritter in La Jara and Hardy in Stratford have all they can handle just keeping peace in their towns. Don't even have a lawman in Two Rock. Just a couple of locals who lock up drunk troublemakers if they have to. I've got a feeling this man Doan may have his own outfit ready to do whatever he tells them to."

"If that were so, why do you suppose he even bothered with an offer?" Sammy asked.

"You have a deed that's recorded," Homer replied. "A buyout's the easiest. It costs money hiring guns, and they can get killed for their trouble. You have your own outfit...and they're all good men who ride for the brand. This kind of thing happens from time to time. Back in '56, about a year before you came to us, we had our own war right here on the T. Johnny Wehrman...a rich man, hired his own outfit of guns...mostly Mexicans...near thirty of 'em. They came to kill our whole outfit and take our ranch and cattle. We lost six men and had to hire more guns of our own. It was a fortnight and twenty of theirs dead before it ended."

"What made 'em quit?" Sammy asked, dumbfounded. "A man like that might have just hired more guns."

"Well, he might have, but brother Reuben here found out about Johnny being the money man and where he was holed up. Paid him a visit in the night and put a bullet in his head."

Reuben frowned. "A necessary act it was. A dead man can't pay. When the money dries up, so does the gang. As

Homer said, there's no law out here to help you. A man out here makes his own law."

Sammy shook his head. "Why do you suppose he didn't just buy his own land?"

"He should have," Reuben answered. "Through a representative, he tried to buy us out, but we weren't having any of it. He knew our land had the best water in all the territory. And statehood was strongly in the wind at the time. He thought he'd make a killing. Just didn't figure it'd be his own. Of course, statehood didn't come to pass then, but now these years later, the talk is that it's imminent again."

"You think gold could be what Doan's after?" Sammy asked.

"Could be, but it seems unlikely," Homer replied. "We've been here since we were young men, and we've seen color and pulled some nuggets, but nothing more came of it when we dug or panned for it. On the other hand, our sixty thousand acres occupies the most prime position against the continental divide in the territory. We own and control a hell of a lot of water. When statehood comes, our land and yours will eventually be worth more than we can imagine. Whatever Doan's real intentions, I'm pretty damn sure this isn't about laying track."

Reuben's face turned hard and his tone stern. "You and your boys keep your eyes open and your noses in the wind. Avoid traveling alone. You better talk to the padre, too. If anything sniffs bad, send someone with word and we'll bring the whole outfit."

Sammy's eyebrows raised "Well, okay then. Talkin' to you two didn't exactly put my mind at ease. More or less some of the same thoughts I had."

Homer nodded. "Sorry to agree with your thinking. I'll ask around about this Doan fellow...send a few wires out, too. I wish they'd hurry the hell up and get a line strung to La Jara.

Have to go clear to Stratford or Cuba to post a wire." Homer lit his pipe and let out a long, aromatic stream of smoke. "Here's a piece of good news though."

"I'd like to hear it," Sammy earnestly said.

"Buck Thornton will be in court down in Santa Fe today…on behalf of Margaret. He's certain she'll end up with Claire Studdard's property."

Sammy's face registered satisfaction. "That sure sounds fine. Blaine wants Margaret to have it. He'll likely move on when he knows there's a little security for her and Claire's baby, little Robert."

"She deserves it. Living up to a dying woman's wishes and taking her baby is quite a remarkable thing…particularly for a gal so young with no family or property.

She's a rare young gal," Homer concluded. "How old is she? Eighteen?"

"Just turned," Sammy replied.

27

Blaine watched her holding baby Robert as she sat in a rocker by the window, the last rays of the setting sun playing across her hair, casting her face in a half-light that quite suddenly struck Blaine of her beauty like a thunderbolt of revelation. It rolled over and through him, this consideration of all that she was—loveliness with poise and charm and a simple eloquence imbued with strength of spirit and tenacity. To this moment, he had always naturally thought of her as a girl, she being only sixteen at the time of their meeting, and he being caught in the slowly simmering attraction to Claire who was his own age and who had so cared for him as he recovered from the bullet that nearly took his leg. But Claire had died, and he and Margaret had lived on at Claire's house, bound by Claire's dying requests of them that neither denied. Instead, they had supported Claire's last moments with promises and assurances, even if the sum of which in Blaine's mind was only to provide a last comfort to the woman he had fallen in love with. He didn't know if he could live up to the obligation of his words; he only knew he felt honor-bound to speak them.

Margaret had no doubts. She and Claire had shared the burden of months of captivity and horrors at the hands of renegade Apaches. Their bond was devoutly infinite, and Margaret had taken on baby Robert and her promise to Claire as her life's new mission and purpose. Blaine knew it, and his own commitment was bolstered by Margaret's stoic resolve. So they had stayed on together at Claire's house, Blaine residing in a converted tack and tool room off the barn, and Margaret and baby Robert occupying the rather large, three-bedroom house.

Blaine had refused her offer of a bedroom in the house, and she said no more of it. He had quickly transformed the barn room to comfortable living quarters with a plank floor, a window, and a stove that did well in the coldest of winter. And he built his own privy and managed a bathing tub in the corner of his room, as much to his own modesty as to the consideration of hers. When he wasn't working at the wagon shop in town, he hunted, cut wood, tended to other chores, and stocked other provisional supplies for Margaret and himself. They took their morning and evening meals together in the house, but otherwise were both busy and had spent little time together in the six months since Claire had died.

Margaret used some of the gold Sammy had taken from the dead renegade Apaches to enroll in the teacher training school. She took baby Robert with her each day, cradled in a bassinette on the floorboard of the buggy as she traveled the short distance into Santa Fe. The school had a nanny that cared for baby Robert and the other four children of women in training. It was five hours of school that included a forty-five-minute lunch break, during which time the mothers sat with their children for their meal. It presented Margaret, who was the youngest of them, an intimate group of acquaintances with which she shared the camaraderie of motherhood and the challenge of their teacher training.

As a child, Margaret had been an exceptional student in her years of elementary and secondary education, which ended with the eighth grade. There had been few public schools in the territory, and she had been grateful for the opportunity. She had applied herself with unyielding determination and was gifted with innate ability that produced a disciplined and curious intellect.

Now, these years later, she approached her teacher training with the full gravity of life firmly upon her, giving her a clarity and maturity that translated to pure fire of the heart. She spent hours each night in study and contributed fervently while in class, always intensely thoughtful and analytical in discussing educational theory and its practical application. Her insights impressed her classmates and instructor, and it clearly demonstrated her dedication and suitability to the profession. She was the school's top student, though its youngest member.

Sometimes late at night, after finishing her study, she wept, overwhelmed by her circumstances and fearful of what the future held. What would she do when Claire's property was auctioned off, and what would happen when Blaine left, as she was sure he eventually would? Her despair ran deep in the quiet solitude of late evening and she would sob and pray until sleep finally came. But in the morning, she always awakened with renewed spirit, mindful of her faith and her blessings, and of baby Robert and their chance together.

It had been just two hours before that Buck Thornton had stopped by to tell them the good news: his petition to the court on Margaret's behalf had been successful, and the deed to Claire's property had been duly recorded with Margaret's name as the new owner. She and Blaine had been jubilant. They toasted with whiskey and danced as Blaine hummed a lively trail tune and whirled Margaret around in a Dosey Doe, his feet lacking much talent for it, but spurred on by the happiness of the moment.

Now, he sat with his cup of coffee, watching in wonderment as she rocked baby Robert to sleep, the quiet of the room leading both their thoughts in what the happy news really meant.

She rose slowly with the sleeping baby and carried him to her bedroom where she gently placed him in his crib and tucked the blanket to him. Then she returned to the parlor and sat on the settee across from Blaine. With a somber expression, she looked at him and considered that the moment had arrived. She spoke slowly with measured tone. "We have not talked about it," she began, "but we both know that our time together here was brought about by our love for Claire and the obligation of our promise to look after baby Robert. She asked me to be his mother. I will. I hold that promise sacred and will honor it to my death. She asked you to look after us, and though it seemed you two had fallen in love, you were not her husband or baby Robert's father. I do not believe she expected you to be tied to us. How could she? You and I are not husband and wife. I believe she merely hoped you would help us along if and when we needed it. You have honored her and her request. I have the house now...and..." Tears filled Margaret's eyes as she fought for self-control. "And you do not need to feel beholding to me. I know you have thought about going...about your own life. I owe you my life, Blaine. You do not owe me anymore of yours."

Blaine sat stunned for a moment. He had known that a conversation along these lines would take place at some point. But he hadn't imagined it would be right now, just after experiencing these sudden deep feelings for her. Feelings that had been taking root all along, but that he hadn't accepted, wouldn't accept. He'd always planned on leaving. Some days he'd looked forward to it. Now, he knew that the girl before him was all woman. The six years of age difference between them meant nothing anymore. He was certain of his feelings. He looked at her as he tried to collect himself. She looked at him in silence.

After a long moment, he stood up and walked over to the settee, then sat down next to her and took her hand in his. "I reckon I feel quite the fool," he said softly. She searched his face but said nothing. "We've spent a year together...last six months alone. Didn't think about us...what with all that happened and the way things played out." Blaine shook his head slowly at the realization of it. "I feel different now, Margie."

"What do you mean, Blaine?"

"Well, I mean that I don't want to leave you...unless you tell me to go."

"I thought you wanted to go?" she replied, her bewilderment giving way to the hope in her eyes.

"I won't say leavin' hasn't been in the back of my mind, rattlin' around like a thing unsettled...somethin' I couldn't make sense of for all the time here. But it's clear as blue sky now."

"What is, Blaine?"

He squeezed her hand and looked at her with the conviction of life itself. "I love you, Margie. I don't know how or when or why. I just know I do. I don't mean to give offense...if my talk is too bold." Margaret's face became slightly flush with a blank expression. Blaine was suddenly quite uncertain. "If you want me to leave, I'll go. I'll do whatever you want."

Her transfixed eyes clicked alive with comprehension of his last sentence. She pulled her hand from his and slapped him, the reverberant sound of it startling her as to how hard she had hit him. She was unfazed. "I want you to kiss me!" she declared.

Blaine's eyes widened. "Yes, ma'am," he replied with happy obedience. He took her in his arms and pulled her to him, their lips meeting softly at first, but then becoming more passionate as the heat of it overwhelmed them, like a moment they realized had been postponed far too long, the delay heightening the eventual passion of it. Seconds hung in time, flaming like dry tinder needing to be consumed before yielding. Their mouths lingered and moved sensually in discovery of all that there was to their first kiss. Finally, they came apart, their eyes meeting with an afterglow of bliss. "Does this mean I don't have to go?" Blaine asked.

She smiled. "Did you mean what you just told me? You love me?"

"Course I meant it! A man don't throw such a statement around lightly...unless he's a liar and a cheat. And I'm not either one."

"Well, then, you can stay if you are of a mind to."

"How 'bout if I'm of a mind of marrying you...havin' a herd of brothers and sisters for baby Robert, and makin' a good life for ourselves...Lord willin'."

"You can stay then, too," she demurely replied.

He kissed her again.

28

Lightning flashed in the blackness, silently illuminating the night from far away. The strikes were massive with light that sparkled in shading and intensity, making the night sky look as a sheer curtain behind which gunpowder burned. Then, after the long silence, the low rumble would begin, rolling out and over the land in a long drama that stampeded on in a thundering echo until it cleared the horizon and finally yielded back to stillness.

Sammy lay awake, watching the room flash with light as the distant storm owned the night. Jenny slept peacefully beside him, the faraway thunder playing faintly in their bedroom as a serenade to the safety and comfort of their home. But the storm was only the slightest diversion to Sammy's thoughts as he turned over his conversation with Homer and Reuben. Now, a new consideration crept into his mind. Could the killings the padre had witnessed somehow be related? *The Dumas area was a long way north, perhaps a hundred miles,* he thought. He quickly dismissed any connection as highly unlikely, though a twinge of doubt remained.

Earlier that evening, he'd gone to the bunkhouse and talked to his men about the supposed railroad man and the suspicions that he and the Taylor brothers held. "Keep a sharp eye and your guns handy," he'd told them. They'd talked about what to look for and what to do at the sign of possible trouble.

"We got more'n enough cartridges for a war if it comes to that. Still, maybe we oughta pick up more next time to town," Roasty had offered.

"Yeah, that's a good thought," Sammy had agreed. "La Jara's got a much better inventory than Two Rock. Start workin' reloads, too"

"Nice to know the boys from the T are there if a need comes," Knuckles said. "I reckon the way it plays out will decide who might ride for help if we need."

"No tellin' how somethin' might shake out," Sammy had replied. "It'll have to be decided on the spot. No sense in gettin' too worked up about any of this yet. Just keep your wits about you...and your guns, too."

The words and thoughts whirled around in his head as the room lit weirdly and the thunder reverberated from far away. Was there something he was missing? Did he need a better plan for his crew in the event of trouble? And what about Jenny? She was alone much of the day. He hadn't told her of his conversation with the Taylors or his own outfit, not wanting to worry her. Now, he would tell her. Perhaps he would take her with him while he worked, at least for a time. She was good with a pistol and a rifle, but what if she was caught alone? The hair on his neck stood up at the thought of it. He was worried, and his worry brought a rising anger. Tomorrow he would go and speak with the padre also.

Jing Lu was flying, gliding in and out of the clouds with the grace and ease of the other birds that kept their distance from this oddity, a child sharing the sky with them. She gazed down on the land far below, her awe and wonder overflowing with the sensation of flight and the serenity that enveloped her. The warmth of the moment was particularly noticeable in one ear, which felt like warm honey was being poured in it. But there was something else, a sensation that the depth of her slumber had merely blended into the experience. Now, it became more than her dream could tolerate, and her eyes came open. The dog was licking at her ear as if a piece of chicken liver was lodged in it. "Chester!" she uttered in an exasperated whisper.

The room lit from the silent flash through the window, the promise of thunder taking its dear time to arrive, but only in a muted rumble that revealed the great distance of it. With the flash, the dog had burrowed harder against her side and attempted another run at her ear. "It is all right, Chester," she whispered soothingly as she petted the dog.

She and the other children slept in the three new bunk beds that Knuckles and Matt had brought just a day earlier. Camille was above her, and Payat, Tobias, and Rory were along the opposite wall. Rory's bed butted against the end of Tobias's and Payat's. He had taken the upper bed, leaving the lower one empty. Jing Lu wondered if another brother or sister might someday sleep in it.

Another flash of lightning played in the room and Chester once again nuzzled more firmly against her. She petted him again. "Stay," she whispered as she began to crawl out of bed. "There is nothing to be afraid of. The storm is very far away." Chester watched as she stood up from the bed and walked to the window. Her eyes fell on the sliver of moon high above in the clear night sky. She looked to the east where stars were no longer visible, obscured by shapeless thunderheads hanging ominously like a great black wall at the end of the earth. *That was where the storm most certainly was,* she thought. A cannonade of thunder softly pierced the silence and rolled on in the distance. She glanced to the yard below, cast in darkness, then turned her eyes back to the east, patiently waiting for the next flash to come and reveal the heart of the storm.

As she watched, the brilliance of a strike suddenly erupted from the veil beyond, giving shape and context to the far-off clouds as the spider-web lightning split the night. Goosebumps instantly sprang, and her breath caught in her chest. From the corner of her eye, she saw it and immediately turned her gaze to the yard below. But the lightning had ceased and darkness returned. A shiver went up her back as she struggled to determine what she'd seen. Then another flash came as she was looking directly at the spot of her suspicion.

He lit like an apparition of the night, a man upon a still horse looking up at the window where she stood, his eyes glaring menacingly as her eyes, seemingly locked with his. In an instant, he was gone, swallowed by the returning darkness. She tried to yell but her chest and throat had contracted in a knot of fear. Only a weird grunt came forth as she stepped back quickly from the window and tripped over Chester who had quietly assumed a spot just behind her. The dog gave a short yelp as she tumbled over him to the floor. The fall suspended her fear enough that she managed a yell of her own. "Ahhhh!" she let out.

"What's goin on!?" Rory exclaimed. "Who is that?"

"It is me, Jing Lu. I saw a man!" she said, making no effort to be quiet any more, but the other children slept on.

"What man? Where?"

"Outside."

"I can't even see you!" Rory said, his eyes unadjusted to the darkness. "Are you dreaming? Were you having a dream? Where are you?"

"I am here on the floor. I fell over Chester."

Just then a flash of lightning lit the room. "Oh, there you are," Rory said as he climbed down from the upper bunk. He walked to where she stood several feet back from the window.

"I saw a man on a horse…by the garden. He looked right at me!"

Rory went past her to the window and stood to the side of it, peering around the edge to the ground below. "I can't see nothin'," he whispered.

"I saw him when the lightning flashed."

The darkness suddenly gave way with another strike from the distant storm. Rory's eyes widened as he took in all that he could for the brief instant. "I don't see any man or horse."

They heard the stairs creak from the weight of someone coming up them. Jing Lu quickly moved to Rory's side and the two of them moved from the window to the dark corner. The footsteps continued up the stairs at an even pace. Jing Lu crowded in behind Rory who stood frozen, his eyes glued to the door. "Stay here!" he suddenly whispered. Through the darkness, he nimbly darted to where he knew the chest of drawers was, bumping them slightly as he arrived. He ran his hand along the wall above, quickly finding what he sought, and pulling the hanging sheath from its hook. Rory drew the six-inch knife from its sheath just as the door slowly opened and the light from the padre's lamp spilled into the room.

The padre stood in the doorway looking at Rory who held a knife and Jing Lu in the far corner at the other end of the room. "I heard a bump and then a yell. Is everything all right?"

"I tripped over Chester, Padre…just after I saw a man outside in the yard," Jing Lu replied.

"What man?" The padre's attention suddenly fixed on the knife. "Why are you holding that knife, Rory?"

Rory put the knife back in its sheath. "Well, Jing Lu said she saw a man out the window. And then we heard you coming up the stairs…only we didn't know it was you."

"What did you see, Jing Lu?" the padre asked.

Jing Lu crossed the room toward the padre as Payat sat up in his bed and began rubbing his eyes. Payat said nothing, and Camille and Tobias remained fast asleep. "I was looking out the window at the lightning, and I saw a man sitting on a horse in the yard. He was looking up at me."

"Are you sure you were awake? Perhaps it was a dream and you were sleepwalking."

"No, Padre. Chester was licking my ear and woke me up. I saw him, Padre. He was real!" Jing Lu said emphatically, her bottom lip trembling as tears came to her eyes.

The padre recognized the depth of her fear. He pulled her to him with his free arm and held her. "I believe you, Jing Lu. It is all right now." She put her arms around his waist and hugged him. "Do you remember anything about this man? Have you ever seen him before?" the padre gently asked.

"No, I have never seen him before. He had a beard I think. I think he was a bad man."

"A bad man? Why do you think that, child?"

"He was looking at me with a scary face. His eyes looked mean."

"Oh, I see."

"He wasn't there anymore when I looked, Padre," Rory offered.

"Do you remember anything about his horse?" the padre asked.

Jing Lu looked up into his eyes. "I think he was black...all black."

The padre stiffened. "Good...all right then. You all go back to bed now. It is late. I'll have a look around."

"I'll go with you, Padre," Rory quickly said.

"No, no. You stay with your brothers and sisters." The padre paused for a moment, considering a thought. "Light the lamp there and come downstairs with me for a moment, son."

187

He looked down into Jing Lu's eyes. "It is all right Jing Lu. Get back in your bed with Chester. Rory will be right back."

Rory followed the padre down the stairs and over to a shelf where the forty-four revolver resided in its holster. The padre set his lamp down and took the pistol from the shelf, handing it to Rory. "Take this to your room and keep it close...perhaps under your pillow."

Rory looked at the padre, trying to read his face. "Do you think that was a bad man, Padre? Like Jing Lu said?"

"I think we will hail caution," the padre calmly replied. "I don't know why a stranger would be out here in the middle of the night unless he had need of something. But he has not knocked on our door."

"It's the horse ain't it? She said she thought it was all black."

The padre looked at his son, once more appreciating how little escaped him. He patted Rory on the shoulder. "Even if Jing Lu was correct in her recollection, there are many black horses in the world," the padre said.

"Not all black," Rory quickly replied. "All black are pretty rare. You said the leader of the men at Mister Smith's place rode a pure black horse."

"Your imagination is getting the best of you now," the padre replied with impatience creeping into his tone.

"That must be why you gave me the pistol," came Rory's quick retort.

"Rory! Do not be impertinent! Now go to bed!"

"Yes, sir," Rory replied compliantly, not understanding what he'd just been accused of, but knowing he'd been disrespectful with his sarcasm.

As he began up the stairs, the padre's voice came once more with a softened but direct tone. "Keep the pistola close."

"Yes, sir."

The padre waited till the boy had returned to his room, then he lifted the Winchester from the wall rack. A quick glance to the door confirmed it was bolted. He turned off the lamp and moved slowly through the dark to the window, surveying what he could from his vantage point. There were no unusual shapes in the darkness. A moment later, a flash that lit the night offered confirmation that nothing was there, at least of what he could see.

The padre took up position in a chair that was away from the window and near the stairs. He turned the chair so it faced directly at the front door. In the darkness, he sat with the rifle across his lap, watching and listening intently as the lightning continued to stab the night and the thunder called faintly like drums of warning. Somewhere in the long space of it, he dozed off. When he awoke, all was quiet and dark. The storm had left. He stood stiffly from the chair and moved to his bedroom where he laid the rifle next to him in the bed and hunkered in to sleep away what was left of the night.

29

"Come on with me today. See what the Sky W's workin' up."

Jenny was surprised at the request, but thought he'd been out of sorts since he climbed out of bed, which she noted was at least fifteen minutes later than he usually did. She looked at him and knew he hadn't slept well. He nursed his second cup of coffee nonchalantly and had offered the statement as casually as an observance of nice weather. He hadn't eaten half of his pancakes, another sure sign that something was bothering him.

"Well, that does sound quite inviting, Mister Winds. But if what the Sky W is workin' up includes me in the workin', there's more than enough right here to keep me working all the hours of the day."

"No...we sure don't need any extra help. I just meant it might be nice to get out of your regular routine for a while. You can just watch."

"What's wrong, Sammy? Is it the visit from that railroad man, Mister Doan?"

He took another sip of coffee and abandoned any further pretense of deception. She knew him too well and was much too smart. And she needed to know. "I don't want you here alone…at least till we know what the truth is about all this," he said. "Homer and Reuben think Doan's all false, too. Bad intentions might try to be played out. That's why I went to the T yesterday…to tell 'em about it and see if their thinking would fall the same way as mine. It did. I don't want you to worry, Jenny. I just don't want you here alone till I know."

"All right," she said understandingly. "But there is much for me to do right here every day. I know there are more things you want to get done with our home…and around the yard. Perhaps you could stay home some more…until you get this settled. Your men know their jobs, and you've said there's more than enough help for the current size of your operation."

"Missus Winds, you are the thinking one," he replied, nodding in recognition of it being a valid idea. "Sure, Jenny. I'll spend more time home for a while. Of course, I do need to get around…line the boys out, check on the herd. A man who doesn't hold a sharp eye to his business may not have a business at all after a time."

She smiled coyly. "Such a thought might hold true for a man's wife, too."

He grabbed her arm, playfully pulling her from her chair till she landed on his lap where he wrapped his arms around her and held her close. "Don't you ever worry about me losin' a sharp eye for you. It just ain't possible." Their mouths closed the distance together until their lips met in a full, passionate kiss.

Jenny visited with Jing Lu and Camille while Sammy talked with the padre out by the garden.

"Last night?" Sammy asked incredulously upon hearing that Jing Lu had seen a man out the window.

"Yes, but from what she described, I do not think it was the man calling himself Mister Doan. She said the man she saw had a beard and rode a black horse. But there is no certainty of that. Her view of him came with a flash of lightning…so it was but a glimpse."

Sammy's head cocked slightly, remembering what the padre had told him about the men's horses when he'd witnessed the killings. "A black horse?" Sammy asked, surprised. It was just the night before that Sammy had considered and dismissed a possible connection of Doan and what the padre and children had fled from. "Pure black?" he asked again.

"She said the horse was all black, but she may have imagined it. She knew that one of the men at Mister Smith's rode a black horse. I told the children about what the horses looked like after we got away…especially the black horse, because I remembered it best. I thought they should know in the event they ever saw something. It may have stuck in her mind," the padre surmised. "Rory said he saw nothing when he looked."

"He told you that?" Sammy asked, looking for an opening of doubt.

"Yes."

"Was he lookin' at the same time she was?"

The padre paused in thought for a moment. "I do not think so. Jing Lu said she woke up because the dog was licking her ear. She said she fell over the dog when she backed away from the window. That is what woke me. It is likely to be when Rory woke also."

Sammy looked up to the window and wondered. Looking back to the padre's face, he got the feeling the padre believed what Jing Lu had seen. "I have something for you," Sammy said, and walked the few steps to where Dobe stood. The padre's eyes widened when Sammy pulled two Colt Navy .36-caliber revolvers and several boxes of cartridges from his saddlebags. "You keep these guns. Keep 'em and the others you have in different places around the house…where you can get to 'em fast. And don't go anywhere unarmed…not even for a walk. Your kids, too. All right?"

The padre nodded his affirmation.

"Now, let's load 'em up, and we'll have some shootin' instruction for you and the kids."

"Right now?" the padre asked as he struggled to cradle the heap of iron and boxes that Sammy had abruptly handed to him.

"The sun's shinin'. Seems like a good time," Sammy replied, as he loosened a rifle that was tied to the outside of his rifle scabbard. "Here's a Henry, too. Fires like a Winchester, but no wood grip on the barrel. So, if you rapid fire, you'll be holdin' some hot iron. Course, that's better'n receivin' hot lead."

The padre shot him a wry look. "A perverted twist of 'It is more blessed to give than to receive'?"

"No, I didn't have Jesus' words in mind. But come to think of it, there's nothin' perverted about that notion when someone's lookin' to take your life. It's lonely country out here. You want your kids to have every chance against what may come, be it man or beast."

"Yes, certainly," the padre agreed. "Very well…let the shooting instruction begin. But you should know that Rory is already proficient with firearms. He is quite a good shot."

"Good. Now it's time to get the rest of you shootin' straight. It'll help with keepin' meat on your table, too."

From the woods a half mile away, Boothe Haney held the spyglass to his eye and watched with interest as the shooting lesson took place. It was his first look at the padre and orphans who had plagued his mind for too long. *Just some kids,* he thought, *and young at that.* The red-headed boy was the only one with any size on him at all.

He pegged the padre as the old man whose clothes and hat looked nothing like that of a cattleman. But who was the other younger man who most certainly looked like a cowboy? Sam Winds maybe or one of the other hands of the Sky W. Boothe noted the young, dark-haired woman who stood close by. He decided the man must be Sam Winds, and the woman was his wife. He also decided that the gun practice now taking place was no coincidence.

Boothe turned and walked deeper into the woods to where his horse was tethered. He'd seen the layout of the Sky W now—where the ranch house and the bunkhouse were in relation to the cabin of the padre and orphans. Gunshots fired at any of the locations would be heard at the others. Boothe thought about Rupert Crowder's commandment that no bodies or evidence of the murders could be left behind. He had some more planning to do. Right then, he decided he'd lay low for a bit and wait for the additional men that Crowder was sending him. Boothe wondered of Crowder's other man, the hotshot who had gunned Clint Smith. Where in hell was he? Boothe mounted up and put his horse to a walk in the direction of the hideout.

Twenty miles away, Lucius Hammond was riding up the main street of La Jara, heading for the Buckskin Hotel where he would pick up the posting from Rupert that would let him know where they would meet. Then he would find out what the job was.

30

The days went by with everyone a little on edge and always watchful, but all was calm for the next fortnight. Sammy spent most of his time working at home while the hands built fence and tended to the herd and other ranch chores. When Sammy did get out and around, he took Jenny with him. They took the wagon to La Jara once and picked up supplies, including much more ammunition, but heard nothing about strangers hanging around town or anything out of the ordinary. It was much the same story with some of his boys who'd been to Two Rock. They'd asked around about the man named Doan or any other strangers, but nobody noted anything unusual or remembered Doan. Both towns had a fair amount of trail traffic, so it was common that people came and went.

The padre did as Sammy suggested and had the children practice shooting each morning after breakfast for several days. Rory, Payat, and Tobias had constructed a man-size board target from leftover lumber, painting a body on it and a face that Payat had artistically been able to make look quite sinister.

Even Camille, who was the youngest and smallest, quickly became comfortable with the Colt Navy .36-revolver, being able to cock it quickly and hit the target almost half the time from fifty feet. The boys preferred the .44-caliber revolver. It was significantly bigger and heavier than the Colt Navy, which gave them a certain air of superiority in gun handling. "It is too heavy," Jing Lu said when Payat offered it to her during a morning practice. "And it looks like it kicks very hard."

Payat nodded. "Yes, it is man's gun."

"Well, you are just a boy," she quipped, detecting a slight.

"Yes, but I shoot like man."

"Well, I shoot like a woman, because that's what I am going to be," Camille said from several feet away on the other side of Payat where she was the next up to shoot. She took careful aim at the target and squeezed off the shot which hit and splintered the wood just below the sinister eye of the painted face. She raised one eyebrow with an expression of prowess and glanced around, wanting to acknowledge anyone who had seen the shot. Payat nodded silently.

Tobias gawked at the target with surprise. "Good shot, Camille! But I bet you weren't aiming for his face."

"Yes, I was! I was aiming right where the bullet hit!"

Jing Lu was casually swinging her arm by her side holding the other Colt Navy. The nonchalance of them all suddenly became of concern to Rory. "Pay attention to the way you're handlin' those guns and where people are standin' when you get ready to shoot!" he barked. "This ain't child's play!"

The padre stood some distance behind the group, confident in letting Rory conduct the immediate supervision. He was lightly charmed and encouraged by Rory's stern tone and insistence on discipline. Jing Lu was not. "You are just repeating some of the same instructions Mister Winds already gave us," she said. "We have heard it before."

Rory's face turned as red as his hair. "Well, you'll hear it now! And I reckon you'll hear it again! You'll hear it till you hear it in your sleep!" His anger took them all by surprise, especially Jing Lu whose words had rung with challenge and had prompted the harshest retort she had ever received from her brother. She stood speechless, looking as if she might cry. She didn't.

"Rory is right," the padre calmly said. "His manner is strict and tough because an accident with a firearm is unforgiving. You must always be alert and aware. You can never become complacent about it."

All the children looked at the padre, but Camille spoke first. "What does that mean...complacent?"

"It means becoming too much at ease about something...unworried about it any longer. You cannot become complacent standing closely behind a horse because what might happen?"

"Ahh," Tobias immediately chimed with understanding. "If you're not watching out, you might get the crap kicked out of you... and sometimes even if you are watching. Old Roca sure got me once."

A few giggles broke out. The padre frowned momentarily at the boy's choice of words then broke with the slightest smile. "Yes. The larger lesson is that a gun can do much worse than kick the crap out of you or someone else if you are not always paying close attention to the way you handle it. Understand?"

"Yes, Padre," came the chorus of replies.

The horse analogy had brought a thought to Jing Lu's mind, and she felt like changing the subject and the mood. "Have you named your horse yet, Rory?" she innocently asked.

Rory's face, which was a picture of seriousness, remained that way a moment longer before yielding. "Yep, sure have. I call him Dusty."

"Dusty?" Camille asked. "Why Dusty?"

Rory smiled. "'Cause that's all anybody tryin' to keep up with me is gonna get...dusty!"

31

Sammy stopped and turned to the horse he was leading. "Whoa boy," came his easy command. They'd arrived on the south side of the ranch house where the other dead fall logs were. He'd spent all morning pulling them from nearby forest, and now he had a dozen logs that ranged in length from twenty to forty feet. "That's enough to wear me out sawing and splitting the rest of the day." he said to the big roan as if he expected it to agree. He unhitched the final log and pulled the harness and tack from the horse, then watched as the animal sauntered off through the trees toward the river where the water was cold and the shade inviting.

Sammy was halfway through sawing the first log into two-foot sections when he spotted the boy approaching on a mule. It was a good excuse to stop for a few minutes. He wiped the sweat from his brow and walked to the porch where he pulled the olla from its shady spot and took a long drink of the cool water. "Buenos dias, Hector!" Sammy called as the boy grew closer.

"Good afternoon, Mister Winds!" Hector called back, enthusiastically.

Sammy glanced at the position of the sun, judging the boy to be right. It was no longer morning, making it a little later than the time he usually arrived each week. Hector was fourteen now and had been making a Saturday mail delivery for three years to a handful of rural customers that included the Twin T Ranch, and for the last six months, the Sky W Ranch, too. His customers preferred his service to that of picking up their own mail in La Jara after the Friday stage carrying the mail went through. It made it fairly simple for his customers. If Hector didn't show up at your place on Saturday, there was no mail for you. But he always showed up at the Twin T and the Sky W because there was always mail for somebody at each place.

At two bits per recipient, Hector made a handsome day's wages of between three and six dollars for his Saturday route. But he earned his money. It usually took him twelve hours, during which he traveled nearly fifty miles. He had come up with the rural delivery idea on his own, was steadfastly reliable, and had the unwavering trust of his customers who had signed permission slips for Hector to collect their mail from the town postmaster. After realizing how well Hector did with his route, a few Johnny-come-latelys tried to undercut him and steal his customers without success. Hector was too well-liked and respected. And he never missed his route unless the mail stage hadn't made La Jara. Summers were pleasant, but winters were cold, during which he started and finished his route in the dark.

The boy with black hair and dark eyes wore a gun belt with a .32-caliber revolver that he was reported to be a good shot with. He jumped down from the mule, his slight frame landing almost without noise like a cat. "I have a letter for you, Mister Winds…and also a note," he said, quickly pulling the mail from his saddlebag and sorting through it.

"Hello, Hector. Do you have mail for me?" Jenny called from the open door. Jing Lu and Camille squeezed by her on either side and walked out onto the porch to see this boy who brought the mail. They had come for crocheting lessons, which Jenny had offered and the girls had eagerly accepted.

"Yes, Missus Winds. It is here like always," he replied.

Jenny's mother wrote to her every week, as did Jenny to her. It took several weeks in delivery to and from Albuquerque, but the letters always read fresh and were looked forward to by each.

Camille suddenly bolted down the steps. "I will get it for you," she said, as she hurried over to where Hector was handing Sammy his letter and the note for him. Jing Lu was quickly on Camille's heals, not wanting to miss the meeting. Sammy made the introductions as the girls looked inquisitively at the boy.

"I am very happy to make both your acquaintances," Hector said formally as he removed his tall domed, wide brimmed hat, revealing all of his sheened black hair that was plastered in sweat across his forehead.

"It is nice to meet you, Hector," Jing Lu said.

Camille stood a moment longer, trying to be discreet in her staring as she fully took in the boy's features. She knew they were of the same people. His skin was smooth and dark like hers, and she felt the connection. "Yes, it is," she finally stated declaratively, like a verdict had been reached. "It is nice to meet you on this beautiful, sunny day. Please give me the letter for Misses Winds now."

He handed it to her then knelt down closer to her to give her the important information. "She usually will have a letter for me to take also. Go and get it for me please."

"Oh…" Camille said. "I will get it." She turned and trotted back up onto the porch where Jenny stood with the outgoing letter. A moment later, she returned to Hector with her outstretched arm, holding the letter for him to take.

"*Muchas gracias,* Camille. Maybe I will be bringing you or Jing Lu a letter sometime."

Jing Lu lifted up on to her tiptoes for a brief instant, the thought of receiving a letter exciting her right into the air. "That would be a wonderful thing," she said with a broad smile.

Camille frowned. "Who would write a letter to us?" she asked, looking at Jing Lu.

Sammy looked at the girls, their faces abruptly longer at the sadness in such a question. "Why, you are just young girls new to the area. You will meet people and make new friends. And one day, a friend will send you a letter," he said, as if it was a fact that might as well be etched in stone.

"I think that is right," Hector added. "And we are friends now, too. I will see you again sometime, but I must go now. I have far to travel."

"Would you like something to eat or drink before you go," Jenny asked from the porch. "I have fresh baked bread and beef."

"Thank you, no, Missus Winds. I have just had my noon meal, and I have plenty of water with me. I will go now."

They said their good-byes, and then Hector was gone as quickly as he had appeared.

Sammy was eating the fresh bread and beef while Jenny continued her guidance with the girls, each of them becoming defter with the movement of the crochet hooks as they worked their patterns. He finished a bite and looked at the letter and note on the table. Jenny had not opened her letter yet, but had simply gone back to her crochet instruction with the girls. Sammy decided it wasn't rude to read his mail with the girls just across the room. He took another bite of bread, then retrieved the note and opened it, his eyes immediately drawn to the stationary heading—"Sherriff of La Jara, Greg Ritter." It was dated "Friday August 10," and read, "Sam—I have business here and cannot leave town but must talk to you about an important matter concerning one of your men. Please come right away."

He looked across the room at Jenny as she was showing the girls how to end a row. His eyes went back to the note as he considered the handwriting and signature. He'd seen the sheriff's writing and signature before. He couldn't recall the writing, but remembered the long slash of the S and R on the signature, "Sheriff Ritter." The signature looked exactly as he recalled, and he'd seen the sheriff's stationary before, too. His eyes returned to Jenny across the room. She was looking directly at him now. He smiled, but her expression remained piercing, searching. He put the note aside and picked up the letter, examining once again the post mark of "Santa Fe" and the writing on the envelope. He knew who it was from. Sammy eagerly opened the envelope and unfolded the paper. The date was nearly a month old. He began reading the one-page letter, its limited content reminding Sammy of Blaine's inclination for brevity.

Jenny's curiosity overcame her discretion. If he was going to read his mail in front of company, she was going to know who it was from. "What have you received, Mister Winds?" she coyly asked.

Sammy's expression was animated. "It's from Santa Fe...a letter from Ole Blaine Corker! Says he's got some big news to tell us. Says he's got business in La Jara and he'll be there Saturday, August tenth.

"Why that's today," Jenny said, surprised.

"It surely is. Wants to know if I can meet him. He's stayin' at the Buckskin. Says Margie won't be with him. Says if I can't make it into town, he'll come by here on his way back Sunday."

"His way back to Santa Fe? Wouldn't that be a long ways out of his way?" Jenny asked rhetorically.

"Yep," Sammy replied as he considered it. "Wonder what the big news is?"

"We already know about Margaret getting Claire's house...for quite some time now," Jenny said. They both fell silent as each thought about the possible news, considering that Blaine was still living in Santa Fe and what that meant.

"Maybe Miss Margaret and Mister Blaine are going to have their own baby," Jing Lu said, her tone tentative, not knowing if suggesting such a thing was unfitting. "Maybe they got married."

"Oooohhh! Jing Lu is right, I think," Camille blurted out before any reaction from Sammy or Jenny could be aired.

"Girls, that is quite presumptuous," Jenny said with a tone of shock.

Sammy laughed and hooted and hooted and laughed. "Could be you girls are right," he finally said after he'd calmed down enough to speak.

"Are you going to go see him, Mister Winds?" Jenny asked.

Sammy wanted to say "yes." He wanted to know what Sheriff Ritter had to say about one of his hands; something important enough to ask him to come right away. It was odd, but he was certain that the note was of Greg Ritter's hand. And he wanted to see Blaine and hear of the news, whatever it was. He looked at Jenny. She and the girls were looking at him, waiting. "No, I don't reckon I will. Blaine said he'll come by here tomorrow."

"Well, Mister Winds, I will be just fine for a night. You do remember Raquel is coming and spending the night tonight?"

"That was tonight?" Sammy asked, remembering it was, and surprised at his absentmindedness.

"Yes. She's going to show the girls how to dye fabric later this afternoon, and she's attending Mass at their place tomorrow. Others will be there, too. Padre Tomas is gaining a flock."

Sammy knew that the story was out on the padre. The locals didn't concern themselves with why he had left the church. He had been a priest, and he had taken the orphans as his own children. He was a good man. There was only the Lutheran church in La Jara and nothing in Two Rock. For local Catholics, it was a long trip to the mission in Cuba. When Jose Hernandez had come and asked the padre if he said Mass for the children on Sundays, the answer was "yes," so Jose asked if he could bring his family for the service. The padre explained that he had left the church because he had taken a wife, but Jose was not deterred, so the padre extended the invitation of worship.

As the weeks went by, more people began to show up, and there were nearly a dozen now in addition to the children. The padre performed the services outside with his small congregation seated on logs. He wondered what might happen when the weather turned colder. There was certainly enough space in the main room of their home, but what if more came? He was pleased by such a potential predicament, and his children enjoyed the chance to meet new people and make friends with the children who came with their parents.

"I'm glad to hear it," Sammy said. "Padre should have a flock."

"Miss Jenny, could we stay the night here, too," Jing Lu asked hopefully.

"Oh, yes, could we?" Camille instantly followed.

Jenny looked to Sammy with doubt, but he had already decided that he wasn't going to be the one to say "no." "That's all right by me," he quickly pronounced.

The girls began fidgeting with excitement. "Padre would have to give permission," Jenny said.

Jing Lu stood up quickly. "We can go ask him right now. We will run home and back. It will not take long."

Sammy stood up. "No. I'll hitch the buggy and we'll all go," he said, heading for the door.

"Wait here for a moment," Jenny told the girls. Then she followed Sammy out the door, taking his arm as they walked to the barn. "Why don't you go to town and see Blaine?"

"I don't want to leave you alone...especially overnight."

"I won't be alone with Raquel, and maybe the girls, too."

Sammy stopped and looked at her. "They ain't exactly gun hands."

"We can all shoot...even the girls. They told me they have had lots of practice lately." She looked at him in thought. "What was the other piece of mail you got?" she asked.

"A note from Sheriff Ritter sayin' he had somethin' to tell me about one of my men."

Jenny looked surprised. "Who?"

"He didn't say. Smart though...in the event someone else read it. Asked me to come see him."

"You should go, Sammy."

He nodded. "I'll get there...in time."

Jenny looked at him, an expression of determination and resolve on her face. "I love you, Sammy. I'm your wife and I'll make our home wherever you want. But if we are to live out here, then don't ask me to live in fear. Don't ask me to alter our doings because of something unknown. I'll not cower for this."

Her stark words struck him. "I don't want you to cower. But I don't know what we might be up against. There's bad men in this world...types that would kill us for a lot less than we have. I can't say this railroad deal is the bad ones conspirin' against us...but, I don't know, it's not, neither. It takes time to

205

hear back on the inquiries we've made." He put his hands gently on her shoulders and let his eyes burrow deep into hers. "No, we won't cower for anybody or anything, but if a sky looks like it's holdin' a storm, it's best to heed the observance. You're the most important thing in the world to me...so I'm a might overprotective."

She hugged him. "I understand," she said. "Still, you should find out what Sheriff Ritter has to tell you."

"Yeah, I know," Sammy said with concern. "They're all good men. I sure don't know what he has to say, but I'll go find out. I can be back later tonight."

Jenny smiled. "Don't you be foolish. Come back in the morning...and make sure you see Blaine, too. I want to hear all about his big news. Now just hitch the rig and I will take the girls to ask permission. You should get going. It's three hours to La Jara."

"I'll go with you to the padre's before I go. He might need something from town. And I'll have Roasty drop by this evenin' to check up."

"Yes, Mister Winds."

32

"I'm guessin' there's a few mamas and calves down in that arroyo yonder. You wanna see if you can get 'em back up this way?"

"Why, sure, Mister Ben," Rory replied, excited by the challenge. At Sammy's suggestion, the padre had allowed Rory to work the afternoons with the Sky W hands. Sammy thought it would be good for the boy to start learning cattle and the knowhow of the work. The padre had agreed.

Tobias and Payat were jealous of it, but Sammy told them they, too, could help when the herd got bigger and they got a little older. "You'll both get your chance...another year or so," he had said. "For now, though, it's just Rory."

Their jealousy quickly turned to admiration as each understood it as a rite of passage that could happen to them, too. And Mister Winds had told them it would happen. Just the thought of working with the crew and being one of the Sky W hands was the biggest thing either of them could imagine. They would be boys still, but working as men do, alongside other men who knew their business. And soon, they would know their business, and be respected as men who did man's work. Both the boys adopted a new seriousness about all that they did, as if a new course had been set for them. And they would hold the rudder steady to stay on course for their destiny.

Rory had been helping Matt, Ben, Knuckles, and Jasper in setting posts and stringing wire, but had most wanted to do some riding and work the cattle from horseback. "You want me to get 'em back to that bunch down below there?" Rory asked.

"Yep," Ben replied. "They get separated like that and get down in that arroyo, the coyotes are more likely to get 'em. Nothin' down there anyway but rough country. They ain't the smartest animals. You'll figure that out soon enough. Just get around to the other side of the way you wanna move 'em and come up easy. If it turns out you need help, come on back and get me."

"I'll get 'em back here," Rory replied. He mounted up and galloped off.

Jasper pulled out his tobacco and bit off a plug. He chewed it hard for a few moments then let go with a stream of juice. "Think he'll have any trouble?"

Ben looked out to where Rory was growing smaller by the second as his dust trail drifted to the breeze. "Don't know. He can ride, and that mustang can cut. I reckon he'll figure it out in time."

"Might not be this time," Jasper said, then let fly with some more juice.

"He's a game one. Won't wanna ask for help till his horse quits on 'im. Even then he may walk 'em back. I reckon if those cows are there, he'll get 'em moved over here."

Jasper picked up his shovel and stepped off the distance to the spot for the next post hole. "You think we'll ever finish building fence on this ranch?" he asked as he began digging.

Ben looked back down the line to where Knuckles and Matt were stringing wire several hundred yards away. "No," he flatly replied.

A half mile later, Rory made his way down into the arroyo and loped along, following the path of it as it turned back and forth, winding through narrow and then wider areas, alternating from a rocky floor to sand bars flanked by green willows where underground springs surfaced to feed the growth. He saw the fresh prints in the sand. There were many of them. He could read the smaller, less indented steps of the calves and wondered why the mothers wandered down into such an area. A few bleached out bones of cattle, deer, and others were scattered about as Rory rode on along the meandering course, waiting to catch sight of the cattle.

The buckboard rolled up to where Ben and Jasper were some twenty feet apart, each digging a hole for the next posts. Matt sat next to Knuckles who reined the horse to a stop. "Whoa, Monique."

Jasper looked up. "Did you just call that horse Monique?"

Knuckles look amused. "Yeah."

"Ain't that the beautiful whore's name over at Two Rock?"

"Yeah. 'Cept I reckon I don't ever say whoa to her. I ain't ever looking for her to stop."

"Well, it's likely she just can't hardly wait for you, too," Jasper replied.

"She don't have to wait longer'n a minute I'm bettin'," Ben said.

Knuckles's look of lightness held steady. "You two knothole humpin' greenhorns are speakin' from your own shortcomings, I'm sure."

"Did you send the boy hunting for strays?" Matt asked.

"Yep. Might as well find out what he can do," Ben replied.

"Think he oughta ride alone...what with being on the lookout and all?"

Ben shrugged. "Hell, he's just yonder in the arroyo. Packin' a Winchester, and that mustang can sure as hell run. Besides,

209

ain't nobody seen nothin' out of place since we been lookin'...weeks now."

"That's a fact," Knuckles agreed. "The other fact is we're calling it a day."

Ben looked at the sky. The long summer day was beginning its stretch toward evening, though much light remained. "Got tomorrow off. You going to see Monique?"

"Naw," Knuckles said. "We're headed to La Jara tonight. Heard Lupe's Cantina has two new gals nice as Monique."

Jasper swatted at the air like he'd heard it all. "Hell, there ain't two whores nice as Monique anywhere in the territory."

"He just don't want to see her is all," Ben opined. "Then he'd have to pay her the month's wages he owes her."

"She don't run credit for nobody. None of them whores in Two Rock do," Matt said.

Jasper was suddenly curious. "Does any of 'em at Lupe's run credit?"

"A few used to...for some of the longtime hands."

"I'm sort of a long-timer," Jasper said. "Wonder if..."

"You ain't gettin' credit and you ain't gettin' there first," Knuckles announced as he snapped the reins and started the wagon rolling.

"You boys quitting now?" Matt asked from the rolling wagon.

"Nope, not till Rory's back," Ben replied.

"*Adios, muchachos,*" Knuckles called from the wagon as he and Matt headed off.

Jasper yelled after them, "I got cash! Reckon I'll go ta Two Rock...see Monique! Steal her heart so's you won't be able to buy her no more!"

Several moments passed before he heard Knuckles call a faint reply into the rising wind. "You couldn't steal a piece of licorice from a deaf and blind, one-legged store clerk!"

Jasper shook his head. "I don't cotton to licorice," he said under his breath and went back to digging his post hole. "How much longer we workin' today?" he asked of Ben as he made slow progress on the flinty hole.

"We'll set these two and then go get the kid if he's not back."

"I'm for that," Jasper agreed.

They worked on in silence, sweating from the heat of the day and the difficulty of the ground, which had become rockier, and required hard swings with the picks each had. Ten minutes later, they set the posts in the holes and filled in around them, tamping and stomping to firm them up as much as they would. "Let's go round up that boy so we can commence with some Saturday night mud stompin'," Jasper finally said.

They stowed the tools in a canvas sack and were collecting their horses when the weird shriek from the north carried across the plain to them. In unison they turned and squinted in the direction of it. "What in the hell is that?" Jasper exclaimed, stunned by what he was looking at.

The high-pitched scream was deliberate and clear. "Help me!"

A quarter mile away near the edge of the forest, a woman perilously hung on to her horse at a full gallop. In close chase behind her rode a lone Indian with paint on his face. She tried to turn her mount in the direction of Ben and Jasper, but was then flanked by the Indian who yipped several times, and her mount turned back toward the forest. "Help me!" came her frantic plea once again.

"We gotta help that gal!" Ben said, grabbing his saddle horn and jumping up into his saddle without ever touching a stirrup. "Come on!" he yelled to Jasper, who was equally fast at mounting and following Ben's lead.

They broke to a gallop in pursuit of the woman and the chasing Indian who were riding parallel with the tree line again. Jasper was right behind and to the side of Ben. He instinctively touched his holster and felt the revolver, then gave a quick glance to his rifle scabbard for reassurance, seeing his rifle in its proper place. Jasper saw Ben pull his rifle, and was suddenly aware of the pounding in his chest as his heart rate shot up in response to the adrenaline that was coursing through him. He decided not to pull his own rifle yet, fearing he might drop it. Instead, he swung his head from side to side, letting his eyes scan around them, thinking he might, at any moment, see more Indians as he tried to make sense of what was happening. *Why would one Indian be chasing one woman on Sky W land?* he wondered in confusion, as his horse pounded the sod.

Ben let go of the reins and tried to sight his rifle on the Indian, who was two hundred yards ahead. The woman was also in the line of sight and Ben could not begin to hold his rifle near steady as his horse galloped furiously. He shoved his rifle back down into the scabbard. "Hyaaah! Git now!" he yelled to his horse as he tucked in for speed.

Ahead of them, the woman suddenly turned where the trees gave way in a distinctive V shape toward the inner forest like a directional gateway. The Indian followed but seemed not to be gaining ground on her. Jasper hoped the Indian might break off his chase, knowing that the two cowboys were bearing down on him. He did not. The Indian followed her into the natural funnel path as Jasper and Ben spurred their horses on for all they had, closing the distance with each passing second. Jasper caught a last glimpse of the woman who wore a full-length dress and bonnet, just before she vanished into the forest where the V came to an end. The Indian disappeared a second later, and then it was just he and Ben galloping toward the mix of ponderosa pine and aspen, the V closing in on them like the mouth of a great beast about to swallow.

They raced into the forest. The trees gave way in a blur, with enough spacing for them to continue at a slower gallop as they caught glimpses of the woman and Indian ahead. Then they came into full view as the trees parted in a natural corridor. *Why didn't the woman just stop?* Jasper wondered. All at once, she slowed abruptly, and the Indian came alongside her horse and grabbed her reins, bringing them both to a stop. Ben and Jasper were within a hundred feet and slowing when the woman and Indian both dismounted quickly and stood behind their horses. In his peripheral vision, Jasper caught sight of something out of place. Many saddled horses stood tethered to trees a hundred feet or so off to his side. Then he saw Ben falling from his horse with an arrow through his neck just as he felt the arrow pierce his shoulder, then another and another, taking him through the chest. Jasper fell from his horse and hit the ground, horrified by what had befallen him and his friend, Ben. His eyes strained to focus as he began trying to reach for his gun, but his right arm was pinned beneath him and he struggled to draw breath. He knew he was dying. He gasped for air as the woman pulled the bonnet from her head and shook her hair out. The men who approached with crossbows were white men. The fear of it all melted from him, and, in the blink of an eye, Jasper embarked on eternity.

"Get their guns and check 'em for money," Boothe said. "Then get 'em buried quick, and make sure there ain't no trace of a grave."

One of the new men spoke up. "That's a nice hat that one was wearing. I'll have it."

Boothe snapped around. "You ain't takin' nothin'! It gets buried with 'im."

The man looked at Boothe with a blank expression and remained silent. Andy, an original member of Boothe's gang, handed the new man a shovel. "Start digging," he said.

"Crom," Boothe called to one of his men, "take their horses and move out. Follow that compass heading I showed you and you won't cross any open ground till you're long clear of here. When you get to that bull rock with the chimney, head east to the lookout point."

"I know the way there," Crom replied."

Boothe nodded. "All right. Keep a sharp eye on the place when you get there. We won't be long behind. The rest of them hands are miles east...save for that boy. Not sure where he rode off to...headed south. We'll take care of him and that padre soon enough. Get goin'."

33

R ory rounded the bend and saw the seven calves and eight cows fifty yards ahead, eating grass near a pool of water. Several of the cows stopped and looked up at him as he rode up a mild bank, leaving the arroyo and their sight. Two minutes later, he eased back down into the arroyo on the far side of them and began walking his horse toward them. They turned and began moving the other direction. "That's it. Just follow the road you beefsteaks."

The afternoon had grown long with the sun low in the sky when Rory managed to get the cows out of the arroyo near where he had originally entered. It had taken some doing. When he came alongside their flank in hopes of turning them up an easy slope to exit the arroyo, a few turned and headed back where they had just come from. But his horse could cut quickly and Rory worked out the tactics from side to side, utilizing the cows' natural instinct to want to stay together.

He drove the cattle slowly across the plain back to where the crew had been fencing and was surprised to find nobody around. So he continued on, driving the cows another half mile back to the herd. He estimated that he hadn't been gone more than an hour. But maybe he had. His thoughts turned to worry of having taken too long. Would they be mad at him? It seemed odd that Ben had not come to find him and that none of them were anywhere to be seen.

Rory looked to the west and saw the bottoms of the clouds swept with orange, signaling the end of day and the approaching twilight. It was three to four miles to get back home. If he took the long way, he could stretch out even more and get home near dark, or just after. Time on Dusty was all he wanted. Take the long way, he would. "Heeyah!" he yelled to the open space and took off like a canon shot, putting his horse to a full gallop.

Porter and Bill walked into the bunkhouse just before dark. "Howdy, Roasty," Bill chimed. "Is that molasses stew I smell?"

"And cinnamon biscuits," Roasty replied from an easy chair in the corner where he had his jug of shine and was fashioning a carving from a loaf-size piece of wood.

"Good. I'm hungrier'n a mule team that just crossed the Rockies."

"Whatcha carving this time?" Bill asked.

"Well, I'm havin' a go at a railroad locomotive engine…like this drawing here," Roasty replied, holding up a picture.

You're gonna carve that from just looking at that picture?"

"It's more'n I had when I carved that little bear."

"Yeah, but it looks like a whole lot more detail for a locomotive than a bear."

"It is. That's why I have the picture."

Porter was loading his plate with stew and biscuits. "Yeah, that bear you did was good. Painted 'im up real nice, too. Where's he now?"

"I sold him to Agapito's."

"Yeah? Santero paid you for it?"

"Traded. Gave me a two-pound bag of smoke tobacco...rolling papers, too. Said he'd give me cash for this if it turns out nice."

"Hell, Roasty, maybe I should chop it up. We can't be losing you to Agapito's when you become the great carver of the West."

"Well, I suppose you'll have to talk to Sammy about uppin' my wages."

"Where's the rest of the boys?" Bill asked.

Roasty kept his eyes on his work and spoke as he carved without looking up. "Knuckles and Matt lit out for La Jara maybe two hours ago. Haven't seen Ben or Jasper yet... but come to think of it, Knuckles said Jasper was talkin' about goin' to Two Rock to steal Monique's heart."

"Monique, the whore?" Porter asked. "He won't be stealing nothin' from her...and it ain't her heart she's sellin'."

"That's a fact," Roasty chuckled. "You boys headed out tonight?"

"Not me," Bill replied.

"Me neither. Too late a start," Porter said. "But if you wanna share that shine, I reckon we could get a card game goin'."

"Hell, you can help yourself. I got two gallons of it."

Bill and Porter looked at each other like they'd just heard about buried treasure.

"Don't get too happy. You can only help yourself to what I have out...and there ain't no chance of you finding my cache."

"Well, maybe you'd be willin' to bet some of that cache in cards," Bill said.

Roasty stopped carving and looked up. "Long as you got something to stake that, I care to take," he said, and laughed like he was sure of the outcome. It was a known fact that where cards were concerned, Roasty usually came out ahead at the end of the night.

"The boss been by? Maybe he'll wanna have a go at it, too," Porter speculated.

"Nope. He went to La Jara earlier…be back in the morning. Asked me to look in on Miss Jenny. I just got back from checkin' on them."

"Them?"

"Yep. Raquel came over from the T to spend the night with her. Little Jing Lu and Camille are stayin' over, too. I reckon Jenny and Raquel will be learnin' those young gals up on some things."

Bill looked thoughtful. "That's good. Tough for those girls with no mama…way out here. They'll need a little womanly help along the way."

"Maybe they could spend some time with you," Porter said flatly.

Roasty choked on the swig he had just taken from his jug, and spit it out.

The evening star was just becoming visible in the darkening blue of twilight as Sammy rode up the main street of La Jara, taking in the sights and sounds of the bustling little town. He glanced at Doc Payton's office and winced at the memory of spending two weeks in the upstairs bedroom, barely alive for the first few days after being shot and stabbed by the outlaw Lonny the Kid. But Sammy had wrestled the knife away and killed the outlaw. Now, he was rich for his trouble.

He looked at the bench on the boardwalk just outside the doctor's door and recalled sitting there as Lundy fetched the wagon to take him back to the Twin T to finish his convalescence. It was while he waited for Lundy that Jenny had come and told him how she had prayed for him. And she had hugged him and asked him to call on her after he had recovered. The memory of it was sweet and vivid in his mind.

There was no one at the sheriff's office. The door was locked. Sammy considered finding Blaine and catching the sheriff first thing in the morning, but quickly abandoned the thought and put Dobe to a lope heading out the other end of town. He needed to know what the note was all about. A mile out, he turned up the trail and saw the cabin in the distance. There was light in the window. As Sammy reined up and began to dismount, he called out, "Hello, the cabin! Sammy Winds here!"

He heard the bolt slide back and watched from the hitching rail as the door opened. The woman stepped out onto the porch. "Why, hello, Sammy."

Both of them were clearly visible to each other as the night was not yet fully dark.

"Hello, Missus Ritter, it's nice to see you."

"And you, too. Although I'm sure you are not here to see me."

"No, ma'am. Is your husband home?"

"No, he's out to Cavendish Hollow on business. He should be back in several hours. Is everything all right?"

Fine, ma'am. I just want to have a word about a note he sent me. Would it be all right if I stopped back by tonight…say about ten? I'll only need a few minutes."

"Are you staying in town tonight?" she asked.

"Yes, ma'am. I'll be at the Buckskin."

"He'll be going back to town for a bit when he returns. I can tell him to come see you if you prefer."

"That would be fine. I'll leave a note on his office door lest he stops in town first."

They talked for several more minutes, mostly about Jenny whom Missus Ritter knew very well and was exceptionally fond of. Sammy grew anxious to go. "Well, I'm off to see Blaine Corker. He's in town tonight."

"Oh...yes," she said, suddenly recalling the name and the well-known story of what Blaine and Sammy had been through together on their journey to Denver over a year earlier. "Please give Mister Corker our best, and please say 'hello' to Jenny for me."

"I'll do it," Sammy replied, and then he quickly mounted up and headed back to town.

34

R ory had run his horse hard for most of the way home. He had ridden a circuitous path, swinging west and north, and finally east, amid stretches of open meadow, across two streams and a river, through patches of forest, and along ridge lines of buttes, all of which he had come to know well during the weeks that he and his horse Dusty had become well acquainted. With the last of daylight being squeezed to the west, he walked his horse the final mile toward home, coming through stands of aspen and birch, feathered in like long swirls of ribbon amongst the ponderosa and spruce. "That sure was a good ride, boy," he said to Dusty, whose head bobbed easy from side to side on its thick, muscular neck, well lathered with sweat. "I don't know how I got so lucky as to have you for a horse, but I sure am."

Rory caught sight of them just as the first glimpse of his home showed from across the meadow. The men were ahead and to his right, still in the thick of the trees, sitting and eating biscuits and jerky, mostly facing toward the open meadow as if keeping watch, their horses tethered nearby. One man stood at the edge of the trees holding a spyglass that was trained on the cabin across the meadow, Rory's home.

A wave of fear swept over him as a cool breeze sifted through the trees, rustling them like a warning to the haunt of evil at hand. His horse stopped at the boy's unnatural stiffening and tug to the reins. Rory's eyes did not blink and his chest did not expand with breath. He sat frozen knowing what he was looking at, even though the remaining light offered only a muddy view of them. But he could see the pure black horse and something else that brought goose bumps like pebbles. There, tethered to a tree, were Ben and Jasper's horses. Rory could not see any of the men's faces, but he knew that Ben and Jasper were not among them. *Something bad must have happened to them if these men had their horses,* he thought. And he knew that these men were likely here to kill him and his family. He had to warn them.

Like the gentleness of a caress, Rory pulled the reins softly to his right, his eyes fixed on the men, hoping that none would look his way and spot him as his horse began to turn. He was certain he resided in the peripheral vision of some of them, and that any sudden movement would be detected. It would only take one of them turning their head in his general direction. The breeze gusted a little more, again rustling the trees and providing audible cover just as Dusty stepped on a stick. It cracked loudly. Rory prepared to spur his horse to a run, but he saw that none had heard it and his nerve held as he slowly pivoted his horse in a half turn and began a gradual retreat in an angle away from them that he figured provided the best cover. He craned his neck around to watch them, ready to gallop at the first sign that they'd seen him. But they did not, and he rode easily away into denser forest, looking back every few seconds to make sure they weren't coming.

Once he had backtracked what he thought was a safe distance, he put Dusty to a lope, riding another few minutes southeast through the trees until he came to Red Creek, across which the forest died out. He stopped there and eased up to the edge of the meadow. From his vantage point, Rory could look across the meadow to the forest where he knew the men were waiting and watching. Rory sat his horse, watching and trying to determine the best thing to do. The fear was deep in. He shuddered and wanted to ride far away, but his sense of what would happen if he didn't warn Padre and his brothers and sisters terrified him more. He would have to cross at least a quarter mile of open ground to get home. It was about the same distance to the house for the bad men as it was for him, the only difference being the angle of approach: they would come straight across to the front of the house, and Rory would make his approach from the side. If he made a break for it, would they break for him? The thought of it scared him. It would be fully dark in just a few more minutes, he thought, and then he could make it home unseen. But maybe that was all they were waiting for, too—darkness. He bowed his head for a moment and said his prayer, his decision already made. "Please, God, give me courage...and give Dusty speed. "Heeyaah! Go, boy!" Rory called in a soft yell as he spurred his horse to a gallop. Against the backdrop of twilight, the silhouette of horse and rider streaked toward the cabin like a presaging ghost.

The man with the spyglass called to Boothe, "Hey, someone's ridin' to that cabin...hell bent, too."

Half of the men were already riding out of camp as Boothe walked over to where the man was watching and took the glass from him, putting it to his eye and straining to see through the falling darkness. "Likely that boy," Boothe said as he watched, trying to pick out something of the horse or rider to confirm his speculation. "Yeah, that's him," Boothed stated confidently as he took the glass away from his eye and frowned in thought, *Why in hell's he comin' from that direction?* He dismissed his own question as quickly as smoke in the wind. "They're all home now."

From the tuck he was in, Rory sighted between Dusty's ears as if he were aiming a rifle, his eyes fixed to the backside of the cabin where he knew he'd be out of their sight. He held the reins steady to it in a pounding gallop, not slowing until he arrived, and then he reined hard and was beginning his dismount as Dusty was skidding to a stop. Rory hit the ground with both feet and moved quickly, tying Dusty to a cottonwood and running to the back wall of the cabin where he jumped for the window that was high on the wall. His fingers caught the ledge and he pulled up and fixed his forearm and elbow upon it, using his free hand to slide open the window.

The padre's startled voice came from inside the room. "What is that? Who is there?"

"It's me, Padre," Rory said, out of breath just as he tumbled to the floor next to the table where they took their meals.

The padre hurried over to him, his simmering concern about the boy's lateness being swept away by the question of his chosen entrance. "Why are you coming through the window? Is something wrong? Where have you been so late?" came the padre's rapid questions, laced with the tone of admonition. Then he saw the worry on the boy's face.

"Padre, there are men watching us...straight across the meadow from the front...in the woods. I reckon they're comin' for us!"

"Why would..." the padre barely got two words out before Rory abruptly cut him off.

"Padre, listen! I saw the black horse. One of the men rides him. And they had Mister Ben's and Mister Jasper's horses with them, only Mister Ben and Mister Jasper ain't there. I was workin' with them earlier when Mister Ben sent me to fetch some strays...and when I came back, they were gone!"

"How many men?" the padre asked, suddenly recognizing the possible mortality of the moment. "Less than five? More than five?"Rory looked panicked at trying to recollect a number. The padre turned his palms toward the ground and pushed gently against nothing.

Rory understood. He took a deep breath and his eyes came steady. "More than ten…maybe twice that! Padre, shouldn't we go? Where is everybody? We should go now! Dusty's right out back!"

The padre put his hands on Rory's shoulders. "Do they know that you saw them?"

"No, or they woulda been here already!"

"Yes," the padre said, nodding. "We will leave. Go upstairs and get your brothers…but do not run! Your sisters are with Missus Winds at the Sky W. When you come down, stay under the front window. And bring the pistol that is up there."

Rory walked for the stairs like the floor was on fire, and then he quickly vanished up them.

With his heart beating in his throat, the padre walked unhurriedly across the room to the far wall where he collected the Colt .36-caliber revolvers that Sammy had given him. He stuffed them in his waist and filled his pockets with cartridges. Then he walked back to the rear window in the dining area where he was securely out of sight of the front window. Seconds later, the boys came down the stairs, with Rory holding a rope bridle rig in his hand. They got down on their stomachs and crawled speedily across the floor, Rory's .44-caliber clunking on the wood floor from the holster he wore as they made their way to where the padre waited. The boys rose and stood next to him. Rory looked into the padre's worried old eyes. They were clear and sharp in thought, but heavy with grief and ringed by deeply weathered skin that hung in layers like the geologic formations of his ages.

225

Rory spoke with desperation, "Dusty can't ride us all. I gotta get Roca, too. He's in the side corral...they won't see me."

The padre looked pained at it but understood that the boy was right. "Yes, all right," he quickly replied, then gave his instruction, "Out this window we go now!"

They climbed out into the blackness that was full, with only a waif of light from the window casting upon the ground where the boys landed nimbly and the padre stumbled after letting go and dropping the remaining distance to the ground. The night was moonless and cloudless, with stars sparkling like diamonds on black sand. The Milky Way showed as a long wake, with its creamy sheen running a stripe through the sky as the trail of infinity. They stood still for a moment, listening for anything, but there was only the wind, steady and cool, erasing even the sound of the nearby creek. They moved over to the tree where Dusty was tethered.

"You boys will all ride together on Dusty, and I will ride Roca. We will go to Mister Winds's ranch," the padre said. He pulled one of the pistols from his waistband. "Take this Payat. You have two pistolas now and the rifle. Do not hesitate to shoot if these men come upon us."

"I'll be back right back," Rory said, and he vanished to the direction of the side corral where the old horse, Roca, was. The other horse Sammy had given them was to the front side of the cabin. Rory knew he couldn't risk it.

The padre suddenly had a sick feeling that they should not wait another second, but should immediately begin running for the creek where the trees were a cloak, and they would be away from the house. Then in the darkness, he thought, they could move on foot to the Sky W ranch house a mile away. They could collect the women and head for the hands' bunkhouse only another half mile beyond. He knew that Sammy was gone, but surely some of the men would be at the bunkhouse. "Get up on the horse now so that we are ready to go when your brother returns," he whispered to Payat and Tobias. The boys mounted up with Tobias in front.

They waited in the blackness, the seconds seeming an eternity as the boys sat atop the horse with the padre standing next to them. The padre kept his eyes moving, scanning side to side and straining to detect any movement. He saw the deformity of darkness to the opposite end of the cabin, away from where Rory had gone. Two shapes moving slowly around the backside of the cabin. They were on foot. He knew it was not Rory and the horse. "Go now!" the padre implored to the boys in a desperate whisper as he slapped Dusty on the rump, sending the mustang to a leap of movement. Tobias reined the horse toward the creek bridge as the animal broke to a run.

The padre pulled the pistol from his waistband and scrambled to get behind the cottonwood just as he heard the tension release of the crossbows. One arrow struck the tree and the other took the padre through the upper chest just below the collarbone. The force of it knocked him to the ground, his pistol coming loose from his hand as he landed hard on the moist earth. He swung his arm out frantically in search of the gun, but his hand shook uncontrollably from the damage the arrow had inflicted. He saw them coming at him as they were rearming their weapons. "Run, Rory!" he yelled with as much force as he could manage, knowing his son must be near. The dark forms quickly became more distinctive as men who were taking aim with rearmed crossbows. The padre thought he caught the glint of their eyes in the final moment.

The drone of the wind was split by the report of the .44-caliber, thunderous as the announcement of the boy who had taken the measure of his target with deadly intent. Rory was already cocking again as one of the men launched backward like he'd been yanked with a rope, the bullet having hit him center-chest, fragments of it ripping through both lungs before the core of the slug exited his back, leaving a gaping, ragged hole. The second man pulled the trigger of his crossbow, hastily aimed where the barrel flame had just come from, but he waited not to see the outcome. With crossbow in hand, he had turned to run back from whence he'd come when the second shot boomed out, missing the man but prompting him to run a zigzag course away in the darkness.

The men who had taken up position on the front side of the house froze when the shots rang out from the backside. Their decoy, the slight woman about to seek help, was at the front door but had not yet knocked on it. Boothe knew it had gone wrong. "Somebody must be goin' out the back!" he yelled to the men at the other position on the front side. "Get back there! We're goin' in the front!"

Rory had reached the padre who was sitting up and scouring the ground with his good hand in search of the pistol. "They're all around us!" Rory exclaimed.

"The pistola...I dropped it!"

"I have it!" Rory said, having instantly come upon it. He shoved it in his waist and then moved behind the padre, grabbing under his arms to lift him to his feet. Rory felt the arrow head poking him in the chest as he helped the padre up, realizing to his horror that his father had an arrow sticking all the way through him. "This way," Rory said as he helped the padre along, heading directly for the thick trees just steps away. The padre hung on to his son as they descended the grade down toward the creek, moving diagonally away from the cabin and in the opposite direction of the creek bridge. Rory knew the terrain well. They heard bits of the chaos behind; men shouting into a wind that muted quickly, concealing the noise of Rory and the padre as they moved through the trees, over the ground strewn with rocks, sticks, and blotches of ground juniper and potentilla.

Boothe and his men only found emptiness in the house when they breached it. His other men had found only the dead partner in the backyard. Thinly contained rage was borne on Boothe's face as he listened to the one who escaped Rory's .44-caliber tell of what had happened at the back. The man was sure of three things: a horse galloped away with someone on it, he had hit someone else with his crossbow, and a third party had opened up from close range with a large caliber.

"Get the goddamn horses!" Boothe screamed into the night. They'd tied their mounts in a small stand a hundred yards out and had approached on foot. "Sure as hell they made for that ranch!...if some ain't hid along that river! Find 'em!" Boothe howled. The men began running for their horses.

The padre's breathing was ragged, but he kept moving with Rory's grasp, stumbling often and fighting to stay upright. The upper part of his shirt was quickly soaking with blood that ran freely at both points of the protruding arrow. He felt light-headed. "I must rest soon," he said with great labor.

"A little more, Padre," Rory said, firming his grip on the padre's torso. "We can cross the water easy up here. I know some bushes on the other side we can hide in."

The padre didn't expend energy with an answer other than a grunt. He gave his last measure as they reached the creek and began their crossing at a spot that was wide but only a foot deep. The bottom was rocky and slick. Halfway across, the padre slipped badly and pitched sideways taking Rory with him into the black, cold water. The padre's head went fully under as he landed on his shoulder near the arrow causing a spike of pain to shoot through his body such that he involuntarily gulped and swallowed a mouthful of water. Rory quickly got to his feet and checked that he still had the guns. He reached down to lift the padre who had raised his head above the water and was violently coughing, the spasms racking him with pain.

"Help me, Padre!" Rory said in his exertion to lift his father who was consumed with hacking and was not of any assistance. The boy could not do it alone. "C'mon, Padre, get up!" Rory pleaded in a grunt as he lifted again, the arrowhead jabbing him once more as he lifted the padre under his armpits from behind. The padre tensed his body and worked his legs, coming again to his feet.

They completed the crossing with the padre coughing and hacking all the while. After working their way down the other bank they came to the bushes Rory sought. "In here, Padre," he said helping his father down to his knees. Into the bushes they crawled on hands and knees, reaching an open spot where they could sit under the canopy of limbs and leaves.

The padre shivered from his wet clothes and his loss of blood. "I must lie down," he weakly said. Then he grabbed the arrow with both hands at his chest and pulled down with all the strength he could summon. The arrow snapped off near the entry point. "Pull it through from the other side, son!"

Rory moved behind his father and grabbed the six-inch exposed shaft. He pulled gently at first, hoping it would move easily. It did not. "It's stuck good. I'm gonna have to yank hard, Padre."

"Do it! Pull it out! It must come out!"

"All right...here goes," came Rory's determined reply. From his seated position he bent his knees and put his feet on his father's back, then pushed with his feet as he pulled on the shaft.

"Aaahhhhhh!" the padre cried out as the arrow began moving slowly through the chest muscle and the bone of the scapula. Rory continued pulling, the bottom flange of the arrowhead cutting into his palm but securing his grip until the shaft pulled through. The padre rolled onto his side in exhaustion, and then onto his back where the sense of sweet relief overcame the momentous pain. He lay for a moment, shivering and panting until his breathing began slowing toward normal. Rory sat beside him.

The padre could see only the shape of his son's face, reaching up to touch the boy's cheek. "Good, son...good. Your brothers are out there somewhere...on your horse. I pray they will make it to the ranch safely."

"No one chased 'em straight out," Rory said. "I saw that much."

"What of the horse? Where is Roca?"

"I had 'im with me till I had to shoot. Then I reckon he spooked. Didn't see him again after...but there wasn't time to be lookin'. I saw the men comin' toward the front. They were sneakin' up on foot. They couldn't chase Payat and Tobias like that."

"No, but they will be soon looking," the padre replied, his voice raspy and worried. "After time, you will have to leave me and find help."

"I'm not leavin'!"

"My best chance to live is if you will find help...and, if I die here tonight, then leave me to God." He paused for a moment to catch his breath again."No, do not leave now. It is too dangerous. But after some time..."

"You'll go with me when I leave!" Rory said resolutely, his eyes filling with tears that the padre could not see in the darkness.

"I cannot. I am too weak. I would slow you."

"Then I'll get a horse and wagon and take you to where the help is."

"Perhaps you will," the padre replied as he felt Rory's tears run to his hand that was upon his son's cheek. "Do not worry of me, Rory. I have lived a long, blessed life. Whatever comes of tonight, I am with God as you are. But you must do what is necessary for your safety, and for the safety of your brothers and sisters. You are the eldest. They need you."

"We *all* need you, Padre!"

"I will always be with you... always. Now, help me take off this shirt. I am cold from its wetness and I want to close my eyes and rest."

Rory helped his father remove his shirt, and then he removed his own. He too was cold. They lay together in an embrace for the warmth, rubbing each other's backs, the padre able to use only one of his hands. The padre was soon asleep. Rory continued rubbing his father's back and came to think that his father's bleeding had slowed.

35

Tobias and Payat had simply hung on when Dusty bolted, hoping the horse knew its way in the dark. Tobias held the reins in his hands which were clamped on the pommel, Payat behind him with his hands clutching Tobias's belt. They heard the shots behind them, not knowing who was shooting at what, but each boy felt a surge of fear when the reports cut the night.

It seemed the horse knew right where to go as the mustang slowed to a lope near the bridge, taking its own lead of the loose reins and turning onto it. The horse loped over the thirty-foot wood plank bridge, then immediately broke to a gallop across the easy, rising plain, with the gentle ridge a half mile ahead. At the top of the rise, they would be able to see the distant lights of the Sky W ranch house and the bunkhouse beyond.

As they approached the crest, the horse slowed and became skittish, neighing at the scent of something on the wind. Then it was there, the large, dark form that rose in awareness of the intrusion on its feeding. The four-hundred-pound bear stood and growled; its roar bellowing over the stiff wind. It abruptly dropped to all fours and charged them.

Tobias reined over as Payat yelled, "Go other way!" The mustang turned at a right angle and leapt ahead with neither boy bothering to look back, only fighting to stay on as the horse accelerated like a shot. Again, they trusted the horse, the darkness yielding little clue about where they were going, except away from the bear. The stars above offered scant help with visibility. Ahead, they could see the shape of the stand of trees as the horse slowed to a walk. "He's tired," Tobias said. "He was all lathered when we first got on him. Rory surely was runnin' him hard."

"We can hide in trees. Dusty can rest," Payat offered.

"Yeah, all right. I can't tell nothin' from nowhere."

It had been a wonderful afternoon for Jing Lu and Camille, spending hours with Jenny and Raquel, learning the secrets of making dye and how to apply it, and all the while hearing stories and talking as mothers and daughters might. Then they'd had a delicious supper of shepherd's pie followed by honey-drizzled sopapillas that Raquel made for dessert. Both dishes were a first time event for the girls who carefully watched the preparation. Jing Lu also took notes so she and Camille could surprise their father and brothers with the culinary delights.

It was not long after nightfall that Jing Lu excused herself to go to the privy, which was only a few steps outside the back door of the kitchen.

Jenny and Raquel were still cleaning up. "It's dark and the wind is blowing. There are chamber pots in your room if you prefer," Jenny said to her, wanting to present another option for Jing Lu.

"Thank you, Miss Jenny, but I will go out. I remember from using it earlier today."

"All right, dear. I can go with you."

"I will go with her," Camille said. "I gotta go, too."

"You *have* to go, too," Jenny said gently.

"I know it. That's why I said so," Camille replied, obliviously innocent.

"All right, girls, take that table lamp with you. There's a hook on the back of the door to hang it on. Remember the wind and make sure you clasp the door again when you leave."

"Yes, ma'am," Jing Lu replied.

Camille retrieved the lamp from the table and followed her older sister out the back door. "They are such sweet girls," Raquel said as she hung a pan above the cookstove.

Boothe had sent eight men to the Sky W to get Missus Winds, and then ambush whoever was at the bunkhouse, knowing that the Sky W crew was already two hands short, and that Sammy Winds was supposed to be gone. He wanted the woman alive. One man was to bring the woman back to the hideout, while the others laid in wait on those in the bunkhouse. Boothe had heard that Missus Winds was beautiful. Why not enjoy her before he disposed of her. He didn't share with his men that pleasuring himself was his only reason for wanting the woman alive, although they suspected as much.

Boothe's men had just arrived and were preparing to take up positions when the girls came out the door and headed for the privy. The men were not far from the door where the girls came out. They quickly backed up a step to avoid being in the light of the lamp Camille carried. The girls never saw them as they walked quickly toward the privy twenty feet away in the opposite direction. "Who's that?" one man asked in a whisper after the girls had entered the privy together. "I thought just the woman was supposed to be here. They was little girls."

"Well, the timin' don't get any better," Crom said. "I reckon that back door ain't bolted and whoever else is in there will be expectin' those girls shortly. Shumer, you get around

235

front. Reid, you and Barney take those girls when they come outta that shitter. We're goin' in the back right now."

"We supposed ta kill those girls now?" Reid asked.

"I reckon not," Crom replied. "Boothe wants that woman alive. We'll take 'em all alive. Let's move."

Crom gently turned the handle and pushed an inch. The door was unbolted. He had his pistol drawn as he slowly opened the door with two other men right behind him.

"Girls?" Jenny called out. She could not see the door from where she was working but suddenly heard the wind louder and felt the immediate draft. When no answer came, she turned to walk to the door. Her heart caught in her throat. "Aaahh!" she screamed. They were in the kitchen, swarthy and dirty with eyes that were malicious. Two of them kept moving silently toward the front room, while Crom stood with his pistol trained on her, his sadistic smile revealing brownish teeth that were chipped and broken.

Raquel was in the front room returning placemats to the bureau when she heard Jenny cry out. Raquel grabbed the scattergun from the rack above the bureau and turned toward the kitchen with the gun raised. The arrow took her just above the heart as she pulled the trigger, her aim having jolted upward when the arrow hit. In the close quarters, the blast was deafening. Most of the shot ripped the timber beam above the two men's heads.

Crom's attention on Jenny was broken, his eyes shifting instantly from Jenny to the doorway leading to the front room. Jenny quickly moved for the pistol on the shelf just beyond arm's reach. She grabbed it as Crom took two quick steps to her and swung hard with his pistol-filled hand, hitting her near the temple with a blow that knocked her unconscious. She collapsed and lay bleeding on the kitchen floor.

"That fat *puta* shot me!" the man with the crossbow yelled as blood ran from his head where a few errant pellets were now imbedded.

"She might do it again," the other man said as he walked over to where Raquel was lying on the floor mortally wounded but not yet dead. She had pulled the scattergun to her and was attempting to aim when the man kicked it from her hands and shot her point blank in the face.

The man who guarded the front against the escape beat on the door, having looked in the window and seen the others in control. "How loud was them shots out here?" the man with the crossbow asked immediately when he opened the door to his partner.

"Wind's blowin' hard...we're downwind of that bunkhouse. They didn't hear nothin'. Weren't even loud out here," he replied confidently. Both men looked toward the tiny light of the bunkhouse a half mile away.

The two men came in the back door with Jing Lu and Camille who looked with horror at Jenny on the floor, blood pooled by her head. Having heard the gunshots, they thought she was dead.

Crom issued the orders quickly. "Tie 'em up and gag 'em. Put 'em on one of those cowboys' horses...and her on the other," he said, nodding toward Jenny. "And get that dead one the hell outta here! The two of you's gonna have to take 'em back now."

"What dead one?" Shumer asked.

"The dead Mex woman in the next room," Crom replied.

"Whata we do with her? We ain't got no horse for her."

"Tie 'er and drag 'er behind you. Figure it out. Just get 'er clear of here. And clean up the blood, too."

36

"Give me a shot of that Tequila," Lucius said as he eyed the label that he recognized, something that rarely occurred with the bars he frequented. He'd had it once before and remembered liking it. The bartender gave him a glass and poured the golden-hued liquid that Lucius promptly drank, savoring the warmth that descended over his emptiness, a void he had long since given the vaguest thought to. "Another," he said, looking to dissolve his irritation.

He'd waited all afternoon at the trail near town where Sammy Winds was supposed to have come by. Rupert had said he would, nearly guaranteeing it. After all, Rupert had employed his own abilities as a master forger to forge the note on the sheriff's own stationary and had seen to it that the Mexican boy, Hector, had it for his Saturday mail rounds. So, Rupert had told Lucius that Sammy Winds would come, and Lucius had waited along the trail, knowing only a general description of Winds, and that the young cowboy rode an appaloosa with salt and pepper spotting.

"His wife might be with him, but I'm guessing not," Rupert had said. "She's dark haired and a real beauty."

Lucius's reply had been swift. "I won't shoot a woman. I'll take her to Boothe's hideout if she's with him."

But no one had come down the trail. Lucius figured Winds might have known a shortcut and taken it. Unbeknownst to Lucius, he was right and Sammy had passed within a half mile of where he waited. So Lucius had finally headed back to La Jara, not long before Knuckles and Matt happened along on their way to town for some Saturday night entertainment.

"That's fine Tequila," Lucius vacantly commented as the barkeep filled his shot glass again.

"Is the best. You want I should leave the bottle, señor?"

Lucius considered it for a moment. He planned to take a look around town after a while and see if he could find Winds and finish this business tonight. "Nooo," he replied in a slow, southern drawl, and then drained the glass again. "But you can fill it one more time, and then I'll maybe have a go at one of these peach tarts."

The bartender looked confused at the reference, then understood as he saw Lucius giving serious appraisal to one of the working girls in the room. "Yes, señor, the tarts here at Lupe's are the sweetest of peachy."

At the back of the room, the card game had six chairs, currently filled with men who kept looking to see if the particular girl they wanted had become available yet. As it turned out, most of the young night's patrons had heard about the two new voluptuous whores at Lupe's West End Cantina, and had come for their own sampling. So the turnover was rather slow as the men waited, drank, and played poker. The other four working girls were miffed that the new girls were getting most of the action. Lucius had no such proclivities that would be cause for delay. He nodded to one he liked, and she came right over. "How about a naked Dosey Doe 'round my ole south pole," he said, rolling the words out like soft silk.

She raised an eyebrow. "Sure, mister, it'll cost you a dollar."

"If you're good, I'll give ya five, but I'm short on time so let's get to it."

She took his hand and began leading Lucius away, giving the other girls a glance like she'd just hit the mother lode. They looked at Lucius and wondered what the possible excitement could be about.

"Amigo!" Blaine called out across the lobby of the Buckskin Hotel. Sammy saw his friend at the tiny bar against the far wall, sitting on a barstool with a cigar in his hand and a drink before him, his posture puffed and regal like he owned the place.

"Hey, hombre," Sammy said, extending his hand to his friend as he arrived. Their handshake was as if they were trying to squeeze blood from each other. "How's the sage of Santa Fe? You ain't gettin' no weaker buildin' wagons, I see," Sammy said, pulling his hand back and flexing it in jest to see if it was still working.

"Well, you ain't lookin' any fatter being a land and cattle baron, with a wife who can cook with the best. You must be doin' too much of your own work."

"Yeah, well it keeps the spirit strong and the books right," Sammy replied.

"I have no doubt of that," Blaine said as he pulled a cigar from his shirt pocket and handed it to Sammy. "Barkeep, set this man up with whiskey...your best!" Blaine called.

"Must be a celebration. You gettin' hitched up with Margaret?"

Blaine shot him a look. "How in hell did you know that?" he said accusingly, his thunder taken.

"A blind man could see it when you two were here for the wedding. Everybody but you had a hunch about it."

Yeah, well, I'm usually the last to know on most things. But I know now! We're gettin' married! I sure enough love her."

"You picked a grand one. She's a fine, fine woman." Sammy held up the glass the barkeep had just poured for him. "Here's to you and Margaret. May your love keep all your trails sunny."

"Thanks, Sammy," Blaine said appreciatively. "We're gettin' married October twenty first at the San Miguel Church in Santa Fe. I sure hope you and Jenny can come."

"We'll be there."

They clinked glasses and downed the drinks.

"Say, that's only two months from now."

"Yeah, well, that ain't even the end of the big news."

"Yeah?" Sammy asked, waiting.

Blaine took a long pull on his cigar and let the smoke drift out slowly.

"You gonna spill it wagon master or do I have to kick it out of you?"

Blaine smiled like he'd swallowed a cat. "The school in Cuba wants Margie to come be the teacher. She ain't even done with her own schoolin' yet, but they heard she was the best there and wanted her 'fore she's even graduated. And I got a job offer at the Climbin' Tree Ranch there. Met with 'em yesterday. We'll be neighbors! Sort of."

"Well, scald the turkeys and bolt the doors! That's a fine piece of news!" Sammy exclaimed then lit his cigar. "When are you two love birds movin' this way?"

"The end of the year. Already got a good offer on Margie's place in Santa Fe. She's not sad to let it go," Blaine said, pausing in recollection of all that had happened there and of when Claire was alive. "It was Claire's home...that's how

241

Margie thinks of it. Now that we're together, she wants a fresh start. Me too."

"I can understand that," Sammy said. "So you're going to cowboy again?"

"Yep. Of all the things I done, can't say there's any line of work I enjoyed more. Course, there's lots I ain't tried. But I reckon I won't ever be openin' that whore house."

"Nope. Looks like that notion died in that cave. I imagine you got the better bargain now. The Climbin' Tree's a good outfit. Good men."

"Sure seemed that way...what I saw. Say, you hungry? Whadaya say to a bottle of whiskey and a big steak? I'm buyin'."

"I say that steak won't have much time on the plate the way my stomach's yippin'. Not too much of the bottle, though. I'll be talkin' to Sheriff Ritter soon, and I want my wits about me."

"Tonight?"

"Yep."

"You got trouble?"

"I'll tell you about it over that steak."

37

It was a brief, tawdry interlude between Lucius and the whore. Once it was over, Lucius was quick to begin his exit from the room if for no other reason than the overwhelming scent of cheap perfume, which grew more intolerable by the minute, giving him a headache and prompting the thought that it had permeated his clothes and skin and might be as hard to remove as skunk spray.

She liked him, mostly because he had paid big and acted like a high roller, though he certainly didn't look the part. But money was always the persuader, and she had been persuaded. She took notice of his haste and became curious. "What's your hurry? That was real fine, mister…especially the five dollars. You could have a drink and another go if you want. There's a bottle right in that drawer. Won't cost you nothin' more."

Lucius pulled his second boot on and stood up, looking at her with a frown. "You're a pretty one, but I'd rather have my nose in a goat's ass than smell another minute of this room."

"I knew it!" she said with anger. "That crazy Lulabelle sprays it all over when she works in here. Some kind of eau de toilette. She about paints the walls with it…thinks it dainty."

"Dainty as pig shit," Lucius said, and promptly left.

He stopped at the bar for one more drink before starting his search for Sammy Winds. At the poker table, it was getting louder as the imbibed spirits worked their wonders. Lucius was drinking his shot when he heard it. "Damn! The big cheese of the Sky W wins again!"

Lucius turned quickly from the bar and looked to the poker table where a man with his back to him was raking in the pot. Lucius strolled casually to the front window and looked to see if an appaloosa was tied out front. His own horse and one other were the only horses out front, and the other wasn't an appaloosa. *Most men coming to town for the night would tie up or stable their mount at the livery,* he thought. And it made sense to Lucius that a known married man wouldn't tie up in front of the only whore house in town.

Lucius walked casually back to the poker table where one chair was vacant. He went into his act. "Anybody saving this chair?" he meekly asked.

"Savin' it for the next loser. "You'll do...have a seat," a rough looking character replied. A few of the men laughed.

"I sure hope not," Lucius said and sat down. He looked around the table but was interested in only one man, whom Lucius's eyes lingered on just slightly longer, trying to determine if it was Sam Winds. The man was young and strong looking, weighing a hundred and seventy to a hundred and eighty pounds. That fit. Rupert had also described Winds as nearly six feet tall with sandy colored hair and hazel eyes. Although the cowboy wore a hat, the coloring of his sideburns and eyes looked about right to Lucius. He couldn't get a fix on his height, but his upper torso looked to be that of a tall man. Lucius figured it was Winds. Even if it wasn't, the man was certainly one of the Sky W hands and they were all targeted. He could only have one showdown in town and then he'd have to move on. If he was wrong about it being Winds, he'd have to catch up with him somewhere else. Or maybe he'd just take a discounted payment on the remainder owed him and move on. He looked around again, considering if any of the other five men were also Sky W hands.

The man next to Lucius turned his head toward him and sniffed the air. "Smells like you took a bath in it."

Lucius shook his head. "Stay out of the second room down on the right," he said then put his stake on the table. A man began dealing the cards. Lucius decided he'd play to win right from the start, and then look for any opening to bait the man.

After Lucius won the first two hands, one of the men quickly left as the whore he'd been waiting for showed herself to be available. Lucius feared his target might be the next to leave. He had just won a good pot in which they were the only two left in the final betting. Lucius decided to press the issue. "Looks like the stink of that room is some good luck stink. But somebody here's got some cowboy stink on 'im. I can smell that cow shit over anything," he said, as unwittingly as he could manage.

"Are you dumb, mister?" Matt asked.

With a moronic expression on his face, Lucius gazed at Matt. "No, I don't reckon so, but I got a real good sense of smell. Folks back home always said so."

"Did them same folks tell you you're dumb as a post?" Matt continued.

The other men at the table seemed to be enjoying the exchange, curious about where it might go. Lucius was now confident that none of the others were cowboys. After the slightest pause for effect, Lucius replied, "No, none of 'em said that, but they mighta said tryin' to beat three of a kind with two pair is dumber than a post." Lucius chortled to himself like it was an inside joke.

Matt looked at Lucius with a befuddled look. "How 'bout you just shut the hell up, mister."

Lucius nodded, "I didn't mean to give offense…it's just that cow shit smell on you was all."

Matt took a deep breath. "You're smellin' cow shit 'cause your head's stuck up your ass. And if I hear another word about it, I'm gonna split your head open."

Lucius's face went blank and betrayed his dead eyes as he stood up. "I don't abide by insults and threats. Get up and draw. You can pull first."

The other men pushed their chairs back from the table, and then one by one stood and backed away. "Please señors! No gunfight here!" the bartender implored.

Matt was still sitting in his chair across from where Lucius stood facing him. "No worry here, Lupe," Matt said, surprised at the sudden turn of events and not taking his eyes off Lucius. "We don't need any gunplay. If this big talker wants a fight, we'll step outside and slug it out."

"No, we won't," Lucius replied. "Where I come from we settle questions of insulted honor with our guns. You're wearing one, and you just threatened me."

"Look here you dumb bastard, you did the first of the insultin' with your talk of somebody smellin' of cow shit. Now, you want to commence with gunplay 'cause your feelin's got ruffled? Where I come from, we save our guns for more worryin' situations. But if you want a fight, I'd be plum happy to kick your ass up and down the street."

Lucius looked at Matt with contempt. "I won't stay in the same room with a gutless, honorless, shit-covered worm," he said as he began walking for the door. Then just as he was exiting, he threw out his last bait, saying, "Your mama must be one of the jizz bags workin' in back. I expect every woman in your family line's nothin' but a whore." Then he walked outside into the cool evening.

"You son of a bitch!" Matt yelled, jumping out of his chair and storming after him. Lucius was already in the street when Matt pushed through the door and yelled at him from the boardwalk, "You're gonna answer for it now!"

The light from the open door and front window cast across the boardwalk and out onto the dirt street where Lucius stood visible in it, waiting. "Draw, yellowbelly!" Lucius commanded. Matt's draw was fast and smooth as he descended the final step onto the dirt, stumbling slightly from a misstep as the flame from Lucius's gun leapt twice like bolts of lightning with booming reports. The bullets knocked Matt backwards where he collapsed onto the steps, dropping his gun that had never fired.

Lucius walked to his horse and mounted up as men poured out the door of the cantina. "You saw it!" Lucius yelled. "I was trying to leave! He came after me! Drew on me! You saw it!" He spurred his horse and was gone in an instant.

The men closed in around Matt. Knuckles suddenly came out the door onto the boardwalk, having emerged from his romp with the new whore. He had heard the shots fired. "What happened?" he asked, panicked. "Matt!" he exclaimed, recognizing the cowboy sprawled across the steps with the men around him. Knuckles crowded in and kneeled next to his friend. "Matt, can you hear me?" he asked, seeing the blood-soaked shirt and the cowboy's eyes half open.

"I hear you," Matt replied. "I guess I'm shot."

Knuckles looked closely. "Get back!" he yelled at the other men. "You're blockin' the light!" The men quickly backed away a few feet. Knuckles looked closely again. "Looks like you're hit near the shoulder...twice. Long way from your heart, but we gotta get you to the doc. You'll be all right, Matt.

Just stay tough." Knuckles scooped the cowboy up in his arms and began trotting off down the street toward the town.

"You need some help?" one of the men yelled, amazed at the strength and power that Knuckles was displaying.

"Might need some!" Knuckles yelled, as he moved off into the darkness. "I'm headed for Doc Payton's!"

38

Several of Boothe's men had ridden along the banks of Red Creek, winding their way up and down and back and forth through the trees and bushes in a search for anybody hiding. But in vain it was. The darkness was beyond what their eyes could adjust to, and they had no familiarity with the terrain, having to yell loudly to each other over the wind to keep track of one another. Even their horses quickly grew skittish.

"There ain't nothin' here! Even if there was I couldn't see it if I tripped over it!" one of the men yelled within minutes of starting their search. The others quickly agreed and they set out to rejoin Boothe and the remaining men who had taken the search in the direction of the Sky W ranch house. From their hiding place, Rory and the padre had heard some of the shouting but never heard a horseman nearby.

Boothe and his men had seen nothing but the feeding bear as they rode to the Sky W ranch house. "What the hell?" Boothe exclaimed when they arrived and Crom told of finding two young girls and a Mexican woman in addition to Missus Winds at the ranch house. "Looks like were only short a padre and three boys," he said, suddenly realizing the upside. "You sent that other woman and them girls back alive with two men?"

Crom shrugged. "You said you wanted the woman alive, but she's all we was supposed to find here. Just figured you might want the others alive, too. Shumer killed the Mex when she threw down with a shotgun."

"I don't want nobody alive other than his wife," Boothe declared as he stared at the light in the distance from the bunkhouse. "Nobody's seen that padre and boys make for that bunkhouse?"

"We was occupied when we got here, but ain't seen nothin' since we been watching steady."

"Naw, they ain't there," Boothe decided. "It'd be buzzin' like a beehive if they'd a made it. They're still hidin' somewhere. Might show up here yet."

The men who'd been searching Red Creek arrived and sat their mounts in front of the Sky W porch where Boothe and Crom, and the rest of the men stood. "We didn't find any of 'em," one of the men said.

"You sure as hell didn't spend much time looking," Boothe fired back.

"It's black as pitch at that creek. Can't see nothin' and there's trees and bushes everywhere. We rode it good as we could."

Boothe knew the truth of the man's assessment. "Well, we got the little girls now, so we're only huntin' the padre and three boys," he said. "All right, you boys go back and stake out that padre's cabin. Kill anybody that shows up there. Just make sure it ain't one of our own. Use the signal whistle when you're movin' around."

Boothe turned toward his most trusted man. "Crom, I'm leavin' you my men. Leave two of 'em here in case that padre shows. Take the rest and get in position on that bunkhouse.

Could be as many as five or six hands in there. I reckon not...but could be. Some could have blown to town. Your best play's to use Gina. Have her say her wagon turned over nearby and her man's got a broke leg...bad. That oughta bring 'em all out. Once they're outside, open up on 'em before they can scatter. There's seven of you. That oughta be enough. I'll keep looking for that damn padre. "

The full moon rose over the eastern foothills, illuminating the landscape to the movements of the night. "Look at that," Tobias said to Payat as it became visible to them, the silver orb rising like hope as the wind began to calm in the presence of it.

"It is good sign. We can go to ranch. There is light enough," Payat said. "Dusty has good rest enough."

"What about the men?" Tobias asked nervously.

"They are gone, maybe. We watch close...ride away fast if we see them."

The boys walked the horse out of the trees and stood for a moment, carefully scanning the open ground before them and listening. The wind had died to a light breeze. They heard and saw nothing. Dusty whinnied slightly as they mounted up. "Give me rifle," Payat said, sitting behind Tobias. Tobias pulled the Winchester from the scabbard and handed it back to Payat who gripped it firmly, and resolutely said, "Ready." With the moon like a guiding beacon, they headed east at a trot.

Rory became more aware of the sound of the creek as the wind died and the padre slept. He knew that the moon was probably up, but he couldn't see it through the dense bush canopy that enveloped them. *The moon had been full the night before and would be so again tonight,* he thought. He guessed that the wind dying coincided with the moon rising. He had seen such things before and paid attention to how a sunrise or sunset, or full moon rising could bring the wind, or bring it to an end. His sense of nature's mystery was strong, spurring his curiosity and contemplation, and developing in him a keen eye for detail and a penchant for speculation. Now, he speculated about the condition of his father and how long he could survive. His breathing was uneven and labored as Rory ran his hands over the padre's back that had grown colder, a slow trickle of blood continuing to ooze from the entry and exit holes.

Rory quite suddenly decided that his father would die if he didn't get him help. He couldn't wait an hour more or even minutes. "Padre," he whispered in his ear.

The padre grunted, "Yes, son," he answered, his voice raspy and quaking.

"I'm going now to get us a horse...or help...whatever I can find. I won't be gone long. I promise. Here's a pistol," Rory said, placing the pistol in his father's hand. "I got my own with me. I'll call out to you when I come back so you know it's me."

"Good," came the feeble reply. "Go with God."

Rory quickly crawled on his hands and knees through the bush until he exited. He stood and once again felt his holster for the .44-caliber, knowing from the weight that it was there but touching it just the same. The moonlight crept through the trees and danced off the peaks and swirls of the fast moving water. Rory looked carefully all about him and then broke to a run, his feet carrying his lean body nimbly over the uneven ground, instantly adjusting to the terrain with each step. He picked his crossing and skipped through the water, then skirted along the other bank, varying his speed from a trot to a run as the terrain came at him.

The cabin came into view. Rory slowed to a walk and moved cautiously from tree to tree as he worked his way closer. When he came to the edge of the trees where only open space to the cabin remained, he stopped and listened, looking at the rear window of the cabin that he and his father and brothers had escaped through not long before. The lamps were still lit inside. He feared for his brothers, not knowing where they were, and said a prayer for their safety as he watched and listened a moment more. All was quiet, and the yard was bathed in the dim gray of moonlight.

Rory put his hand to his gun and made for the corner of the cabin, running on the balls of his feet almost silently. He peeked around the corner and then moved along the side of the cabin up to the front corner, sneaking a look at the front porch. Chester was curled up by the front door that stood open. The dog's eyes caught sight of Rory and his tail began a slow thump, but he remained by the door, seemingly curious about Rory's cautious demeanor. The old horse, Roca, stood outside of the front corral, comforted in being near the roan that was corralled. Roca still wore the rope bridle rig that Rory had slipped on earlier.

Rory bear-crawled across the porch to a spot just under the corner of the front window, then brought his head up slow and easy to get a look inside. The room was empty. He looked back around the yard again, letting his eyes linger on the meadow beyond. He saw nothing, so he pulled his pistol and moved quickly into the house where, within seconds, he had retrieved his coat and the padre's, too, along with a canteen and some cloth for fashioning bandages and a few stick matches that he stuck in his coat pocket. Rory put both coats on, his fathers over his own, then tried to think of what else was essential to bring, but abandoned the thought as he imagined he was taking too long and would be caught any second.

Out the door and into the night, the boy sped with the dog following him. He had already decided against the wagon, knowing that it would be best for his father but worst if they were spotted and had to make a run for it. He ran across the yard to the lean-to and grabbed a saddle and bridle, then scampered to the corral where he threw the saddle on the roan, not bothering with the cinch straps, but instead rigging the bridle and leading the horse out of the corral. "C'mon, Roca," he whispered to the other horse as he grabbed the lead rope.

He was leading the two horses across the yard when he heard the clacking on the planks of the creek bridge, the unmistakable sound of running horses. Riders were coming. His heart pounded and his skin tingled with a surge of adrenaline as he pulled the lead ropes to get clear of the yard before they appeared. He moved to the far side of the cabin and stopped, waiting for the riders to enter the yard from the other end. Then, he could move across the backyard to the trees and on down to the creek. *But what if they rode across the backyard and came around this side of the cabin?* he thought in a panic. The horses stood easy in the dark with the dog next to them. Rory listened, straining to hear above his own fright. Then he heard the sound of hooves pounding the earth as they grew closer. Which way would they come? The natural path would bring them from the other side, but what if they deviated or decided to split and come from both sides? Rory realized he was trembling. He put his free hand on his gun and braced for it. Chester started a low growl. "Sshh!" Rory pleaded to him. The dog silenced.

Then they were there in the yard, having come from the other side. He could hear them dismounting. Rory began moving through the backyard toward the creek as the voices rang out. "We gotta tie our horses out in the damn woods again?"

"Hell no. I'm not runnin' for my horse if I need 'im."

"Hey, weren't there a horse in that corral before?"

"There sure in hell was! Looks like somebody's been here."

Rory prayed the horses didn't whinny as he led them across the last bit of open space and into the trees with Chester silently following.

39

"I'll be right back," Sammy said to Blaine who was finishing the last of his steak. Sammy walked briskly across the lobby to meet Sheriff Ritter who had entered the hotel and was walking toward him.

"Good evenin', Sammy," the big man with graying hair and a long mustache said, extending his hand to shake Sammy's.

"Evenin', Sheriff."

Sheriff Ritter could sense the anxiety in Sammy's stiff deliverance of the greeting, and he could see the worry in the young cowboy's eyes. "Saw your note on my door. What can I do for you?"

"Why don't we step over here," Sammy said, as he walked to the corner of the lobby to be out of possible earshot of anyone.

The sheriff followed, his curiosity piqued. "Somethin' wrong?" he asked, when they stopped.

Sammy's face registered slight confusion. "Well, that's what I'm here to find out. I got your note saying you wanted to see me right away about one of my men."

Sheriff Ritter looked puzzled. "What note? I did not send you a note."

Sammy's face went blank as he absorbed the words and what they meant. "You did not send me a note?" he asked, disbelieving. A sick feeling rolled through him and his heart began to race.

"Sheriff!" the man who entered the hotel lobby exclaimed. "There's been a shooting at Lupe's Cantina!"

The sheriff's eyes stayed fixed on Sammy's face, taken by the shock he could see in it as it turned ghostly white.

The man who brought the news of the shooting arrived where the sheriff and Sammy stood. "Did you hear me, Sheriff?

Without another word, Sammy broke to a run for the door. Blaine saw it and knew something was terribly wrong. He ran after him. "Where ya going?" he yelled to him, as he chased after Sammy out of the hotel and up the center of the street.

"Trouble, Blaine!" Sammy yelled, without stopping.

"Well, I'm with ya!"

Sammy ran into Parker Livery at the end of the street. "Jed! Jed!" he shouted.

The proprietor shuffled out of his room wiping his face. "A man can't even finish his supper."

"Jed! I need my horse. Would you saddle 'im quick! I have to do something...I'll be right back."

Jed Parker didn't bother with any objections or questions. He could see the stress and panic in Sammy. "I'll saddle him up," Jed replied.

Sammy turned to Blaine. "It was a setup! The sheriff never sent me a note! I have to get home!"

"I'm goin' with you."

Sammy nodded as if he just realized he might need some help. "All right, partner...saddle up. I'll be right back," he said, and then he ran out of the livery.

"Yep! We're partners! We been through it before...we'll get through it again!" Blaine called to him as Sammy disappeared.

Sammy ran down a side alley and then up a backstreet where he quickly arrived at the small house with its kept yard and clean appearance. He knocked on the door with urgency. "Hello, it's Sammy Winds!" he called, leaving no doubt of being heard. The boy he sought answered the door. "Hector!" Sammy exclaimed.

"The boy's eyes were large with surprise. "Hello, Mister Winds."

"I must talk to you, Hector."

A voice instantly came from inside. "Que es?"

Hector turned his head back inside. "Es all right, Mama."

"Hector, the note you delivered today...the one with just my name on it. Do you know where it came from? Who gave it to you?"

Hector did not hesitate. "No, Mister Winds. It was there with all the mail when I picked up this morning." Hector saw the deep concern in Sammy's manner, and then he remembered. "There is something else. I do not know if it means anything."

"What, Hector? What else is there?"

"I saw many men, and a woman riding south from the Juney River...near the Sombrero Rock."

"A woman? When?" Sammy asked with panic in his voice.

"Today, after I brought you the mail. Maybe an hour later."

Sammy felt relief at knowing it couldn't have been Jenny, but it lasted only for an instant. "How many men?"

Hector paused. "I am thinking twelve or fifteen. They were riding hard across the open ground...then they slowed and went into the trees. These men were not any of yours. It was a strange thing."

257

"Which side of Sombrero Rock, Hector? East or west? Please, Hector, I have to know."

"It was east...I am sure. Not more than a quarter mile I am thinking."

"Did any of them ride a black horse? A pure black horse?"

"Yes, a man in the front rode such a horse."

"I'm much obliged, Hector. I have to go."

Sammy ran back to the livery where Blaine stood with the saddled horses. "We have to ride 'em for all they're worth," Sammy said, as he and Blaine mounted up. "Ward Sones has plenty of good horses at his place. We'll trade out for fresh mounts there. Ready?"

"Always was...still am," Blaine replied grimly.

"Much obliged, Jed," Sammy said, and then he spurred Dobe.

Jed had no idea what was going on other than something as urgent as life or death. "Good luck, boys!" he yelled as the two men galloped away into the darkness.

40

"I reckon we're going the right way," Tobias said. He and Payat could see well enough with the moonlight, but it didn't look right. He thought that the light of the Sky W ranch house should have been visible to them. But now he was unsure. He didn't think they'd gotten that turned around when the bear chased them, but they had galloped another direction long enough to confuse his sense of where they presently were.

It was a minute later when Payat said, "There!"

Tobias looked off to the side where Payat was pointing. He saw the flicker of light suddenly appear and then disappear again, the stand of trees between them and the light offering only momentary glimpses as they trotted along. "I see it," Tobias said, reining the horse to the direction of it.

They crossed the open space and then slowed to a walk as they meandered through the trees for a hundred feet or so, finally emerging to a clear view of the light they had seen. It was still a ways off. Tobias reined to a stop, and both boys sat staring at it, trying to figure out what they were looking at, knowing it wasn't the Sky W ranch house. Payat recognized it first. "It is bunkhouse," he declared.

Tobias stared a moment more. "You're right. That's it. We're on the other side of it. That's the side where the garden and chicken coop is."

"Sky W is on other side," Payat stated knowingly.

Tobias walked the horse to the side a few more feet and a more distant light came into view beyond the bunkhouse. "Sure enough! There it is. We sure did get turned around."

"We go there?" Payat asked.

"Well, it's the closest. Mister Roasty and the other men can fight good. They got lots of food there, too. I'm hungry."

"We go there," Payat agreed.

The light from the side window shone to them as they approached at a walk, slow and easy from a few hundred yards away. Stillness hung in the air. An owl hooted. Payat gripped the rifle and looked intensely over Tobias's shoulder, his youthful eyes penetrating the night with complete concentration on the bunkhouse and the area around it. As they drew close, Payat saw the movement in front of the cabin, a glint of moonlight on metal that waved in the air, and the forms in the front yard concealing themselves behind stationary objects. There was one by a wagon and another by the privy and others kneeling or standing nearby.

"Stop," Payat whispered into Tobias's ear. Tobias pulled easy on the reins, nearly paralyzed with fright, knowing his brother had whispered because he must have seen something. Dusty pivoted a half turn as Tobias pulled the pistol from his waistband and looked at the yard of the bunkhouse. He saw several of the shadowy figures his brother had seen, realizing whoever it was could just as likely see them, too.

Someone suddenly came from the darkness and walked toward the front of the bunkhouse as Payat and Tobias sat like statues, watching. Then the woman's voice called out with panic as she reached the porch. "Help! Anyone in the cabin...please help me! There's been an accident! Our wagon turned over!"

Inside, Roasty, Bill, and Porter were half drunk and playing cards. "What in creation?" Roasty exclaimed, as he put his cards down and began to get up.

"That's a woman!" Porter said.

"Sounds like trouble," Bill opined, as he and Porter dropped their cards and got up.

Roasty grabbed the lamp from the table and strode quickly to the door, with Bill and Porter right on his heels. He threw the door open and held the lamp out. The woman stepped into the lamp light, just feet from Roasty who had not advanced outside.

Payat leaned forward and whispered again into Tobias's ear. "It is ambush!"

"We gotta warn 'em!" Tobias replied frantically as he cocked his pistol and aimed in the direction of the front yard with the reins tight in his other hand. Payat followed his brother's lead, aiming his rifle the same direction. They fired at the yard, the shots cutting the stillness with explosive reverberation. Dusty jumped, but Tobias held the reins tight as he and Payat quickly re-cocked and fired again. Tobias loosed the reins enough to let Dusty run, turning the horse away from the bunkhouse and galloping off with a few shots whizzing by them.

The men in the yard had panicked when the shots came from their flank, sizzling by close to a few of them. Half of them returned fire in the direction of the shots while the others simply opened up on the cabin, not knowing what was happening. Shots splintered the doorframe next to Roasty's head, and the woman uttered a grunt as she lurched forward toward Roasty. "Jesus Christ!" he exclaimed, dropping his lamp and grabbing the woman, pulling her into the bunkhouse.

Bill slammed and bolted the door while Porter closed and bolted the side window barricade, then raced to the other windows in the bunkhouse and did the same.

Roasty laid the woman down on the floor, realizing she was shot, the blood pooling beneath her and quickly soaking her dress at the right side of her chest where the bullet had exited. In the dim light of the room, she looked up into Roasty's eyes as he knelt beside her. Bill and Porter didn't stray from getting ready; they strapped on their gun belts and began consolidating rifles and ammo to the middle of the room.

"Who are those men?" Roasty asked her, knowing she was dying.

Her face was beginning to register the pallor of death but still held a look of disbelief. "Idiots shot me!" she said with a wheeze.

"You're with them?"

"I was," she replied, unexpectedly aware that her end had come. "They're here to kill you all."

"How many?"

She coughed up bloody foam and sucked for air.

"How many?" Roasty asked more forcefully.

"Seven out front. Lord, help me," she said.

"You're shot bad, ma'am. I reckon he's the only one that could."

She didn't hear his words. Roasty looked at her eyes that had fixed in a lifeless gaze. "She's dead, boys," he said as he stood. He moved quickly to his own gun belt and began strapping it on. "She said there's seven of 'em out there that mean to kill us."

"Them first shots came from the side...a ways off, and they weren't shootin' at us," Bill said. They was shootin' at whoever's out front."

"Damn lucky for us or she would have played us right outside to a turkey shoot," Porter stated.

"Yep," Roasty agreed. "Whatever or whoever it was saved our bacon. No more shootin' now, though, so somebody vamanosed. I don't reckon it was this gang of seven. Likely they're figurin' their next play right now. We better figure our own. What about it?"

"We could stay put," Porter said. "No fire going...can't plug the stovepipe. Don't reckon they could burn us down, neither."

"Why not?" Bill asked dubiously.

"Logs are too big...too green. They sure as hell won't burn with somebody just tryin' to light 'em...not unless they got a few gallons of kerosene...and even so, they wouldn't stay burnin'."

"Yep," Roasty agreed. "It'd take a raging forest fire. But if they had kerosene, they could pour it down the stovepipe, or maybe just get the roof going."

"Then we pick a way to go out, and go out blastin'!" Porter said.

"Hell, if they're watchin' the door and all the windows, can't be more'n one or two of 'em at each," Bill said. "And there ain't no cover for 'em out that back window. With that room dark, I don't reckon they'd even see it comin' open."

Roasty frowned. "Unless someone's waiting up close...waiting to shoot anyone coming out."

"I'll dive out the son of a bitch first," Bill replied, like it would be his honor. "Just stand ready to lay down cover fire if need be."

"Or we could just stay put," Porter repeated. "All the boys'll be back in the morning...Sammy, too. Till then, that crowd outside ain't gettin' in here without us knowin' about it. If that's their play, it'll be them in the turkey shoot."

"That's a fact," Bill granted. "Them window barricades is stout as hell. Take some doin' breakin' through one.

"Enough doin' to be drinkin' coffee waitin' on 'em," Porter declared.

Roasty shook his head to the inescapable fact that finally hit him between the eyes, ashamed that it hadn't occurred to him until now. "We gotta bust out, boys. Miss Jenny and Raquel and those girls are alone just half a mile away. That dead gal said they were here to kill us all. I fear she wasn't referring to just us."

"They mighta already been there," Porter said grimly.

The men looked at each other, sick with the thought of it. "Somebody fired them warnin' shots," Bill said hopefully. "Could have been them. Ain't nobody else on the Sky W, save for the padre and kids."

"That's the crust of it then," Roasty said flatly. "Nobody else around save for women and children...and one old man. "We can't let these coyotes trap us here. I'll not live with it."

Tobias and Payat had escaped unscathed, and nobody had followed. Now, they sat alone in the woods again, knowing that no place on the ranch was likely to be safe.

From where he rode slowly, between the Sky W and the padre's cabin, looking and listening for sign of the padre and his boys, Boothe Haney heard the volley of shots from the direction of the bunkhouse. He thought he'd heard at least a dozen shots in the burst, with no follow up shooting, leading him to believe that the ambush had gone off as planned. He turned his horse toward the bunkhouse and spurred to a lope, anxious to check what happened.

In the bushes, where he had tied on a crude bandage and helped his father put on a coat and prepare to leave, Rory heard the shots carried on the stillness of the night like an omen of where they dare not seek help. His heart ached with what it might mean, and where he knew the shots had come from.

"Where is that coming from?" the padre asked, his voice weak and ragged, and his senses delusional. "Did I hear gunshots?"

"Yes, Padre...comin' from the Sky W."

"Perhaps Mister Winds's cowboys are shooting the bad ones," the padre said hopefully.

"Maybe so," came Rory's hopeful response. "But we're leavin'. We should ride for the Twin T Ranch. I can get us there...I think. It's about ten miles. I been back and forth there a few times now. We can do it with the moonlight."

"What about your brothers? We know not of them."

"They might be with Mister Roasty and the other hands...or they coulda just rode far away and be hiding somewhere. But we gotta go now, Padre."

"Oh, Lord...protect them all," the padre said in a mumble.

"The sooner we get to the Twin T Ranch, the better for you, Padre...and the better for protecting our family. They can send lots of help."

The padre put his hand to Rory's cheek again. "I will try to ride, son, but if I cannot, you must go on and get the help."

"You can make it, Padre. I'll help you get up on Roca, and then you just hang on to that pommel. I'll be with you all the way."

"Yes, son...and I with you."

41

They filled their gun belts and stuffed their pockets with ammo. Roasty, Porter, and Bill had two pistols each, and each had a rifle—Roasty and Porter with Winchesters, and Bill with a shotgun. "What about it?" Roasty asked. "Go out that back window like Bill talked about? He dives out and we cover. Then Porter, then me…the other two covering for the one that's gettin' out?"

"Yeah, I reckon so," Porter agreed. "No cover for 'em out there other'n those cedars…and they're a far piece."

"No cover for us either," Roasty said, "Light a shuck when you hit the ground. We'll make for the barn. If they show thick that way, we might have to revise our route right in the middle of a lead storm."

The men moved quietly to the window at the back of the bunkhouse and took up positions on either side of it. Bill whispered in the darkness. "All right then. When I ease this window open, let's sit a minute…see what happens."

"Yeah, yep," came the two whispered replies.

As silently as he could manage, Bill removed the cross timbers and opened the wood doors covering the window. He held still a moment, listening. He heard nothing but the breathing of Roasty and Porter as his own heart began to beat faster. From a sitting position just underneath the window, he reached up and pushed up on the bottom window tab, the window creaking slightly at the outset of its movement, but then it slid all the way up almost silently. They held still, the cool night air drifting into the room as they listened intently for any sound of movement. A coyote yipped in the distance and was quickly joined by others, the chorus breaking out in full-throated calls skipping forth in a momentary dominance of the night that lasted the better part of a minute.

Each of the men listened, alone with their thoughts of what would likely soon be upon them, the shattering of stillness in an eruption of gunfire. They listened for minutes more, occasionally moving their heads close enough to the window's edge to steal glimpses of the moonlit yard.

Bill nodded his head in the darkness. "I'm goin'," he whispered. He moved several steps back from the window and stood for a moment as Roasty and Porter readied themselves on each side of the window. Holding his shotgun with both hands, Bill took two quick steps and dove out the window, dipping his head and right shoulder as he tucked his body and began his somersault. He landed on the back of his right shoulder and completed the forward roll, coming up to a crouched position on one knee. A figure stepped into view from around the corner of the bunkhouse. Bill was already pulling the trigger as the man was extending his pistol in a quick aim. The shotgun blast hit the man mid-torso, ripping him backwards with a fatal blow that shredded his shirt. Bill dashed to flatten himself against the back wall of the bunkhouse as another man stepped around from the opposite corner and fired at him. The bullet hit him in the shoulder but did not stop Bill's fluid swing of his shotgun, its barrel belching flame with the blast that found its mark from less than twenty feet, snapping the man's head back where most of the shot had hit.

"Hell's on fire!" Roasty proclaimed, as he dove out the window and rolled on his side with his rifle at the ready. Porter bailed through the window directly after him. Both men came quickly to their feet as no more shooters were immediately present. "Bill, you all right?" Roasty asked, noting that his friend was leaning unnaturally against the wall.

"I'm shot...my shoulder. I'm okay."

"You sure as hell killed those two," Porter said, hastily looking around and then reaching for the scattergun that Bill held loosely. "I'll reload it for you."

"Quick now," came Roasty's urgent whispered command. "We gotta move!"

Porter cracked the breach and flipped out the spent cartridges, instantly reloading the side-by-side barrels and snapping the gun closed. "Here you go. You okay to keep at it?"

"Yeah, damn it!" came Bill's impatient reply. "Let's go!"

As they started moving along the wall toward the north corner of the cabin, the shots came from behind them. Porter and Roasty both groaned with the impact of the bullets but remained upright as two more men appeared in front of them. Bill had wheeled on the men to their rear and fired one barrel after the other as Porter and Roasty opened up on the men in front of them who were simultaneously firing. Bill dropped the empty shotgun, pulling his pistols and turning back the other way to fire on Porter and Roasty's targets. The air was filled with hot lead and smoke as Bill, Porter, and Roasty fired and cocked and fired and cocked, and fired with lethal speed and grim resolve, standing tough in the momentary hail of bullets.

The two men in front of them collapsed and lay motionless. Porter staggered a step and went down to one knee. Bill teetered and fell against the bunkhouse wall but remained on his feet. Roasty saw another head pop out from around the corner in front of them. He fired at it. Bill and Porter followed suit and fired, too.

"Come on," Roasty said hoarsely to Porter as he grabbed him and pulled him to his feet. He walked him back the few steps to the open window and pushed him through it as Bill kept firing at the corner where the man had peeked a moment earlier. Bill backpedaled as he fired till he reached the window. "Get in there!" Roasty said as he stood to the side and fired again, covering for Bill as he crawled through the window. Roasty dived through after him, then jumped to his feet and shut the barricade doors and reset the cross timbers.

Roasty moved to where he knew matches and a lamp were. He lit the lamp and then stepped in close to where Porter and Bill were on the floor, shocked at the amount of blood he saw. "I reckon I did nothin' more than get us all shot up," Roasty said, the regret heavy in his voice.

"You had it right, Roasty...we had to try," Porter said.

"Try, hell!" Bill said with a grunt. "There's six of 'em worse off than us. Dead as shit, I'm guessin'. We whittled that bunch down to one or two."

"You killed four of 'em yourself," Porter said with amazement. "Some shootin' that was."

"Not much to it with that scattergun," Bill said dismissively. He took stock of himself, looking at his shoulder where he was shot, then at his leg and his side where he had also been hit. Bill looked at Porter who was bleeding profusely from the side of his head, and also from his right arm and upper chest near his collarbone. "Are you hit?" Bill asked Roasty.

"Shot in the ass is all, I reckon," Roasty replied as he gave himself the once over to make sure that was all. "I have to get the bleeding stopped on you boys. I'll be right back...gonna get a fire going."

"What if they block up that stovepipe?" Porter asked

"Have to risk it," Roasty replied. "I have to get an iron heating and water boiling. If we hear somebody on the roof, we'll put lead through it the best we can."

"Whadaya gonna do with a hot iron?" Porter asked.

"Well, we can try sewing those holes shut...or we can put the heat to 'em, but we have to get the bleeding stopped, Roasty said, "so might as well have all options available. We have plenty of cloth for bandages. Now get your belts off...we'll get tourniquets going on that arm and leg right now."

Roasty helped them remove their belts, and then strapped one on high on Bill's thigh and one high on Porter's arm. "Aaahhh!" Porter yelled as Roasty wrapped the belt tight around his arm twice and fastened it. "That son of a bitch hurts like the devil. I'll be needin' some of that shine."

"Me too," Bill immediately followed.

"Got plenty of it," Roasty reassured them. "Can you boys get to the front room? It'll be the easiest place to work."

"We'll get there," Porter replied.

Roasty limped badly from the room and down the hall to the front room where he quickly loaded the fire box and started the fire. Then he returned to the back room where Bill and Porter remained.

"We're restin' up," Bill quipped, noting the consternation on Roasty's face.

"You can do your resting in the other room," Roasty replied as he lifted Bill from the floor and hoisted his arm around the back of his neck. "Be right back, Porter," Roasty said as he and Bill began hobbling together from the room. A minute later, Roasty limped back into the room where Porter was unsteadily getting to his feet on his own. Roasty grabbed him as he wavered

"Hey, Roasty, are my brains comin' out a hole in my head? 'Cause I sure am bleedin' from it."

"You sure are," Roasty said as he closely inspected the wound in the dim light.

There was a furrow about two inches long and a quarter inch wide where the hair was gone and the blood flowed freely. "Looks like a bullet just skimmed along your head! No hole I reckon. Come on, let's get a wrap on it," Roasty said, limping along with his arm around Porter who remained unsteady on his feet.

Outside, Boothe and Crom had moved from man to man checking to see who might be alive. They were all dead. Boothe had arrived at the bunkhouse just when the shootout in the rear had commenced. He and Crom had stayed in the front in case anyone tried to get out that way. Crom had finally moved to the rear where he had peeked around the corner and nearly had his head shot off. Now Boothe stood surveying the scene, his anger momentarily in check with the loss of men and the demonstrated ferocity of the men he meant to kill. He'd lost seven men now, and the only of his prey that he knew were dead for sure were the two cowboys they had ambushed earlier and a Mexican woman. His mind turned to the extra money for him and whoever was left at the end of the job.

"There was only three of 'em?" Boothe asked Crom, disbelieving.

"That's all I saw. I'm guessin' that's all there was. We'd a known if there were others. Those three had to be shot up pretty bad. They were in a crossfire. Looks like they went right back in the window they must'a come out of."

Boothe considered it a moment more. "Damn salty trio in there," he remarked casually. "I'll cut their guts out before this is over."

Boothe and Crom spent the next fifteen minutes loading and tying the dead men onto their horses and rigging a lead from horse to horse. "Take 'em and head for the hideout," Boothe told Crom. "Those ones inside will likely be dead by morning. If not, we'll finish 'em then. I'm going to see about the others…then I'll be back at the hideout after a while."

Crom headed off at a trot leading the procession of horses and corpses. Boothe went to the barn and chased out all the horses, then went to the corral and did the same. He mounted up and suddenly felt his anger swell; it was all being drawn out too long. He yelled at the cabin, "You're all dead men in there! You hear me!…dead!"

Bill was sitting on the floor, his back resting against the settee as he watched Roasty work on Porter. He had just taken a slug of shine when Boothe's words rang out. Bill's face contorted with rage. "Go hump a goat in hell you shit eatin' coward! The front door's open! Come on in and we'll fix you up like we did the rest of your sorry-ass outfit!"

In the darkness, Boothe's brow furrowed. *There was no quit in this group,* he thought. He hoped they'd bleed out by morning. Boothe put his horse to a trot in the direction of the Sky W. When he arrived, he gave the staccato whistle that was the signal of friendly approach. The two men appeared from the darkness and walked over to where Boothe stayed mounted on his horse.

"We heard a hell of a lot of shooting over there…two different times" one of the men said, hoping for news of what had happened.

"Yeah, they put some holes in those cowboys," Boothe said, not caring to explain that six of their own had been gunned down. He came right to the point of his visit. "Nobody's showed up here?"

"Ain't seen nothin'," the man replied.

"Well, we got some loose ends we'll have to take care of tomorrow...if that padre and kids don't show up some time tonight," Boothe said. "You two stay put. I'll be back in the morning with the rest of the boys."

"Suits us," the man said. "Plenty of food here...saves us some saddle time, too."

"All right then, keep your eyes open for that padre. Barney and Frank will be at that padre's cabin keeping watch."

Nobody heard the yells from the bunkhouse as Roasty put the fired iron to the skin of Bill and Porter, searing the bullet holes to stop the bleeding. Then Bill did likewise to the bullet that had taken Roasty in the left cheek of his buttocks. They each had howled from the pain, taking several slugs of the shine to temper it. Roasty threw a blanket over the dead woman, then collected some pillows and two old piss pots and took up position on one of the settees, lying on his side. Porter was on the other settee, and Bill stretched out in a large leather chair that had an ottoman. They knew it would be a long night.

42

"Ward! Ward Sones! It's Sammy Winds!" Sammy yelled, as he and Blaine galloped into the yard of Sammy's longtime acquaintance.

Ward Sones opened the door of his small cabin with a whiskey bottle in his hand and stepped out. "You here for the prayer meetin'? he yelled, dryly.

Sammy and Blaine promptly dismounted and began undoing the cinch straps on their saddles. "I got bad trouble, Ward," Sammy said, as he kept working. "We need two good horses...strong and fast! I need your help...you have to help me...can you help me, Ward?"

Even mildly drunk, Ward recognized the desperation in Sammy's words and actions. "Sure, sure I can help," he blurted out, then put down his bottle and walked out to where Sammy and Blaine had pulled their saddles. "What kind of trouble, Sammy?"

"I don't have time to explain right now. My wife, Jenny, is in danger and I have to get there as fast as I can," Sammy said, as he and Blaine began walking quickly toward the large corral where a dozen horses stood easy.

Ward glanced at the horses Sammy and Blaine had ridden in on. "Your horses are sure 'nough played out," he said, quickly following the men to the corral. "I'll put you boys on the best I got...two pepper sauce, three-year-old Morgans. Run all day long, I reckon they could. Sure get you home in under an hour from here,"

Ward opened the corral gate. "Bring your bridles...you can saddle 'em outside." He quickly cut out the two intended, and Sammy and Blaine rigged them and led them out of the corral. The horses were fifteen hands tall and heavily muscled. "You need another man?" Ward asked, as Sammy and Blaine began saddling their fresh mounts.

Sammy paused. "I appreciate the offer, Ward. I'd be most obliged if you could hotfoot it to the Twin T and shake out all the help you can find. Tell 'em to come quick and be loaded for bear."

"I'll do it. You boys ride. I'll get your horses put up...then I'll be on the way directly."

"It's good to see you again, Mister Sones," Blaine said as he swung up into the saddle. Ward looked up at Blaine, unsure of who he was. Blaine reminded him: "I'm Blaine Corker...I used to work on the T."

"Well, hell yes, Blaine. Good to see you, too. My eyes ain't so good anymore, and my mind comes forgetful. But I ain't forgot you two handlin' trouble together before... 'bout a year or two back as I recollect."

"Yes, sir," Blaine replied.

"We're goin', Ward," Sammy said. "I'm deeply obliged for the horses."

Ward shook his head then nodded in the direction of Sammy's ranch. "Get to it! I'll ride for the T."

With light spurs and a flinch in the saddle, Sammy's horse broke to a run like the last chance of life, battering the sod in quad beats, the rhythm of the pattern increasing in speed as the horse warmed and found its nature, stretching out to the length of the long meadow under the full moon. Blaine was close behind.

From thirty feet back in the woods, Payat and Tobias looked to the open ground beyond the edge of the trees. They heard the second round of shooting from the bunkhouse not long after they themselves had begun the first round.

"I reckon the Sky W ranchmen are shooting back now," Tobias ventured, after the long string of pops cracked through the air.

Payat was about to agree with him when his attention was caught by the movement. He held his hand to the side in a warning gesture as he stepped softly to the side of a tree for a clearer view. He saw the riders moving along at a fast walk, one of them sagging in posture with the other one close alongside. Tobias saw them, too.

Then, Payat noticed the quick little shadow, its legs moving in a blur that carried the body in perfect pace behind the horses. "That is Chester!" he whispered excitedly to Tobias, who stared in growing recognition of the dog, and of the gait of the old horse they knew so well.

"That's Roca!" Tobias said. "It must be Padre and Rory!"

Payat cupped his hands and gave an owl hoot that he knew Rory would recognize.

Rory was stunned when he heard it. He pulled back easy on the reins and reached over to stop Roca. The padre's head came up slightly. "Why do we stop?" he asked.

"I thought I heard Payat's hoot," Rory answered in a whisper as he listened intently. The hoot came again from the woods to their left. "That's Payat!" Rory whispered.

Rory cupped his hands and made the sound of an elk bugle in the direction that the hoot had come from. Payat knew Rory's bugle well, too.

"It's them!" Tobias said. He and Payat hurriedly mounted up and trotted out of the woods and into the open, breaking to a cantor and swiftly closing the gap to where the padre and Rory watched with caution and awe.

"My boys!" the padre said with joy brimming in his heart and an overwhelming sense of relief. "My boys! Are you all right? Is anyone injured?"

"We're all right," Tobias answered. There were bad men at the bunkhouse, but we saw 'em and got off some shots to warn Mister Roasty and the others. Then there was a lot of shootin'."

"We heard it, too," Rory said. "Hope the Sky W boys are givin' 'em hell."

Payat looked at the Padre who was slumped. "Padre, you hurt?"

"Yeah, he's hurt," Rory quickly answered.

The padre lifted his head higher and momentarily sat a little more upright. "I am all right boys...now that I see you again."

"He needs doctor help and we need to get movin' right now, so let's quit talkin' and start ridin'," Rory said with impatient fear. "We're ridin' for the Twin T Ranch. I can get us there. Let's go."

"We are happy to see you Padre and brother," Payat said as they started moving.

"Yes, son, our hearts are warmed. Now, you boys do whatever Rory tells you to, understand?"

"Yes, Padre," came their replies.

"We should go a little faster for a while," the padre said, then he kicked Roca just enough that the horse broke to an easy lope. Rory was happy of it and swiftly came abreast of the padre who grasped the pommel and fought to keep upright in the new rhythm of Roca's gait. The padre found it to be much less of a pounding than the trot, but felt more likely to be pitched off at the greater speed, especially if the horse misstepped at all. He grasped the pommel tightly with his left hand and rested his useless right hand upon it.

Rory hoped he could recall the way to the Twin T Ranch. He had only made the round-trip ride once with Jasper, but recalled the direction and landmarks that Mister Jasper had spoken of during their journey. Now, Rory kept the party heading directly south, remembering that the buffalo hump hill was where he and Mister Jasper had turned to the east down the long valley. He just had to find the hill. *It would be at least several miles,* he thought.

"We have to head directly south till we see a bald hill shaped like a buffalo's hump," Rory said, just loudly enough to be heard, figuring all of them looking had to be a good thing.

"How are we going to know we're heading directly south?" Tobias whispered loudly in reply.

"Just keep the moon in line of your left shoulder," Rory said.

Tobias and Payat both looked at the whitish silver orb, large in the sky, its presence casting the light of ghosts. It had already climbed high. "She's been going up fast," Tobias replied. "How we gonna keep it on our left shoulder when it gets up over our heads?"

"See that circle of stars in front of us...low in the sky? Just keep headin' right at them," Rory said, confidently.

"We ride where you go," Payat said, then added, "We look for buffalo hump hill."

"Good, boys, good," the padre raggedly chimed in.

43

W ard had been right about the horses being pepper sauce. Sammy realized they could really top out as they streaked through the night. He and Blaine took the open spaces at a dead run, then slowed through woods and down hills, giving the horses brief rest before running them full-on again. Their urgency across the night sparked small herds of deer and antelope into stampedes of flight as Sammy and Blaine came galloping over hill and dale.

With wind in his face and his horse running in a full stretch, Sammy pulled the rifle from its scabbard, instantly snapping his hand forward into the cocking gate of it and then flipping his forearm and hand forward, creating the full slide of the mechanism that brought the bullet forth into the chamber before the breech closed with the rifle cocked. Blaine, too, drew his rifle when they cleared the horizon of the incline and suddenly saw the riders ahead, a quarter mile away and riding cross-face to them.

"Heyah!" Sammy called, spurring his horse to top speed and riding directly at the riders, his Winchester held at waist level aimed at them. Blaine was just off his right flank. As they galloped toward the riders, Sammy yelled at them, "Sammy Winds here! Who are you? Speak up or I'll shoot now!"

A glint of recognition hit him just as the voice called out in reply. "It's Rory and Padre and Tobias and Payat!"

Sammy saw the dog Chester, too, and let his rifle muzzle come down as he and Blaine closed the last hundred feet in a gallop, coming to an abrupt halt when they reached the small party that had stopped.

The padre immediately spoke up in a weak, wavering voice. "Sammy...there are bad men at your ranch. They tried to take us at our cabin, and there was much shooting where your men live...the bunkhouse."

"Me and Payat fired warning shots at the bunkhouse...so your men knew they were comin'," Tobias instantly followed.

"What about Jenny and the girls? What about my ranch house?" Sammy asked, his voice filled with worry.

"We do not know," the padre said.

"It was the man with the black horse," Rory spoke up. "He had a lot of men with him...and they had Mister Jasper and Mister Ben's horses, but they was gone. The bad ones came to our cabin. We got out, but Padre got shot with an arrow, and I reckon I killed one of 'em. We been hidin' ever since. Never heard anything from your ranch house, but there was shootin' at the bunkhouse. There's a few bad ones at our cabin right now...waitin' for us to come back, I reckon."

Sammy moved his horse alongside the padre's. He could see the old man was nearly all in, fighting to stay upright in the saddle with eyes that were only half open. "Where did the arrow hit, Padre?"

"Here," the padre replied, moving his left hand to the spot on his upper right chest.

"I got the arrow out," Rory said, "but the head went through his back, too. He bled a lot. I got some cloth tied on for a bandage."

The padre spoke up, "Do not worry of me. Go and do what you must do. Find your wife...and my girls. God goes with you."

"Where were you bound for?" Sammy asked.

"I figured the Twin T would be best for Padre," Rory answered.

Sammy paused, considering if the padre could remain in the saddle that long. "Do you know how to get there?" he asked Rory. "It's more southeast of here."

"I rode with Mister Jasper once, and went once in the wagon when Padre drove us to your wedding. The time I rode with Mister Jasper, we went south until the buffalo hump hill, then headed east down the valley."

Sammy had never heard the hill that Rory referred to called buffalo hump before, but he knew well of what the boy spoke. "That'll work. It ain't the fastest way, but it'll be the easiest to follow." Sammy pointed ahead. "Keep to the left of that little butte up there, then come south again and you'll see your buffalo hump...about two miles more, then straight east down the valley for another three miles." He paused for a moment and scanned their horses. "Doesn't look like you have any water."

"No," Rory replied.

Sammy unstrung his canteen. "Are you thirsty, Padre?"

"Yes, I would like some."

"Drink your fill...it's full," Sammy said, as he leaned over and helped steady the heavy canteen at the padre's lips. The padre held his left hand to the canteen, tipping it and drinking fully before he stopped and breathed hard.

"Thank you," the padre said, winded.

Sammy tossed the canteen to Rory. "Take it. If it turns out Padre can't stay in the saddle that long, get him down and build a fire. You have any matches?"

"Yes, sir. Got a hatchet, too, in Dusty's saddlebag."

"Good. If you have to stop, get a fire goin' and check his wounds to see if they're bleedin' again. If they are, you have to pack the holes with cloth."

"I got something for that," Blaine said, reaching into his saddle bag. "Pour this on the wounds...cayenne pepper. Works good for stoppin' bleeding." Blaine tossed the package to Rory.

"Yes, sir...I'll use it if we have need. Thank you, Mister Blaine."

"Looks like you're well armed," Sammy said. "Stay along the route we just talked about. If you don't make the Twin T, we'll know where to come lookin'."

"If we have to stop, one of us will keep going to the Twin T for sure...so we can get help for Padre and for you," Rory said.

"That's a good plan. There's already a man on the way there to get help for us. You just take care of Padre."

"He has already saved my life once tonight," said the padre. "Go now and help those in need."

Sammy nodded at the padre and the boys. Then he and Blaine were off in a gallop.

44

J enny and the girls sat together on the floor in the corner of
the dimly lit room, their wrists tied in front of them. One
of the men had wanted to tie their wrists behind their
backs but was overridden by the other who argued they could
not make good time back to the hideaway if they could not at
least hold on to the pommel.

"They'll be gettin' thrown on their heads every half mile. I
don't wanna have to keep reloading 'em," the man had said, as
if he were talking about freight.

The ride had been tough anyway. Now, Jenny looked at
Jing Lu and Camille with all the calmness she could bring
forth. They looked back at her, their young faces blistered in
terror-stricken expressions, Jenny before them, her blood
having dried caked on the side of her face and thickly stained
on the shoulder and chest of her dress. Nevertheless, she was
alive, and Jing Lu and Camille had both been astonished and
revived of hope when she had regained consciousness and
opened her eyes back at the Sky W. But that was hours before.
Their innocent hope had slowly given way with their arrival at
this lost hideaway, the room squalid with body odor and
alcohol, old spittoon juice, and spoiled food. The two men at
the table drank and played cards, frequently glaring at them,

but mostly looking at Jenny, making crude remarks to one another and laughing cruelly.

The girls were as a tonic to Jenny, giving her the only chance of any composure. She would be strong for them. *Thank God for them,* she thought. Otherwise, she knew she would be whimpering in despair and horror. Her eyes cast upon the girls, drawing strength from her last purpose as she sought to deliver prospect and courage. Her own naivety sold the promise through her eyes, the innocence and belief of her own faith. Jing Lu and Camille fixed on her calm, soothing gaze, clinging to her to stay afloat with hope.

Jenny spoke in the lowest of whispers. "Our men are looking for us right now," she said confidently, knowing it was only a possibility.

"Shut up over there!" came the command from the table.

Jenny sat calmly, fighting to imagine a way to escape, some ploy that might work. Nothing seemed possible to her with her wrists tied. How could she manage it? She again let her eyes drift as inconspicuously as she could manage, taking in anything nearby that could cut rope or be used as a weapon. Nothing nearby gave her hope of it. There were shelves, a stove, and a counter that looked to be used for food preparation across the room from where they sat. She was sure that there must be a knife there, but could see nothing from her position on the floor. And she hadn't had the presence of mind to quickly look at everything possible when they had been led in. Her fear had overwhelmed all, but now her clarity was driven by it. She had to get a better look around.

"I have to use the privy," she said matter-of-factly in an easy tone.

The men looked at her and then at each other. "You ain't going outside," one of them said as he stood and retrieved a spittoon. He brought it over to where they sat and tossed it to the floor in front of them. The half full vessel splashed out some of its contents when it landed and nearly tipped over.

"Use that," he said.

"I cannot do so with my hands tied," she quietly replied.

"Well, then go ahead and do so what you *can* do with your hands tied...'cause that's the way they're staying," the man said, abruptly returning to the table.

The other man at the table leaned forward with piqued interest and a straight face that belied his perversions and rising heat. "We sure won't mind watchin'," he uttered slimily with anticipation that made her skin crawl.

Jenny rolled to her side and then onto her knees and stood up. Her eyes took in the rest of the room, seeing two knives on the far counter and the top of a hanging stove tool that she imagined could maim or kill. She quickly averted her eyes and used her foot to slide the spittoon to just beneath her. "Girls, would you please stand in front of me to give me privacy," she said.

"They don't get to stand in front of you," the slimy one said.

Jenny's face turned from tranquil to burning contempt. "What kind of pigs are you."

"What kind of pig you like?" the slimy one asked.

She caught herself, realizing her error in stridence. "The kind that grants civility...please," she said, submissively.

"Come on, let's play this hand," the other man said.

The slimy one looked back to his partner. "Civility? Don't know what that means, but I'll grant it one time," he said, turning his attention back to the card game.

"All right, girls, you may stand up in front of me," Jenny said softly to them. The girls got awkwardly to their feet and stood shoulder to shoulder in front of Jenny who inched her dress up with her fingers, then managed to pull her underwear to the side as she squatted. The slimy one looked over, moving his head about to see what he could see as he listened. Jing Lu and Camille avoided his eyes, looking down until Jenny had completed her need and arranged herself before scooting the spittoon away from them.

"I wanna have a go at her," the slimy one said with feverish certainty in his voice. "Take her in the other room and do it all. Whadaya say? We'll rope them little girls together to a chair and take her in the next room."

The other man looked at him. "Like to myself but that wouldn't be a good move. You're new to this show. I know Boothe. He'd kill you if you took her first."

"He don't have to know."

"He'd know.

"I don't fear any man."

"You want to get paid? Soon as you get the rest of your money, you can go dip it all you want."

"Not like that one. She's fine as I ever seen. Maybe after Boothe's had her, he'll sell her. I'd pay him a good price."

"I would, too."

The staccato whistling of two low notes, two high notes, and two medium notes, cut sharply from outside. "Somebody's here," the slimy one said.

A moment later, Crom walked through the door. "Boothe ain't far behind me," he said, as he sat down at the table and poured himself a drink. "We lost a man at that padre's cabin and six more at that bunkhouse."

"Six!" both men exclaimed simultaneously. Jenny's heart leapt with hope as she absorbed the news from where she and the girls silently sat.

Crom drained the drink and poured himself another. "Yep, it was some throw down shootin'. Our boys came out on the short end of it. Looked like Gina got shot, too...but one'a them boys pulled her into the cabin, so don't know on her. The other seven of 'em's piled out back here in the woods a ways if you need some new boots. Might be a bit bloody, though."

"I reckon you killed all them cowboys, huh?"

"Nope…not that we know yet. Sure put some holes in 'em but they made it back inside. Might be dead by mornin' but we got some more work to do. We ain't found that damn padre or kids, neither."

This time it was Jing Lu and Camille who felt the pangs of joy and hope, knowing their father and brothers were alive. They would be searching for them, both girls thought.

Crom lit a smoke. "You boys might want to catch a few hours sleep. "We'll be ridin' back at first light. Finish the job. The rest of our men are staked out over there…waiting on that padre or any other of them ranch hands."

"What about them?" the other man said, nodding in the direction of Jenny and the girls.

Crom exhaled a drag. "You might as well tie that woman to the bed in the other room. That's where Boothe's going to want her.

The slimy one suddenly turned thoughtful. "We get the extra money them dead ones woulda got…right?"

"You get some," Crom replied.

"Damn! That's too bad them boys bought it," the slimy one said, with a cruel laugh.

Crom looked at him. "Yeah, you never know who might be next."

45

Sammy and Blaine were about two miles away from the Sky W ranch house when Sammy slowed his horse to a walk. Blaine slowed beside him. "I know we're close," Blaine stated in a low voice. "Rory talked about a couple of men waiting at the padre's cabin...but we're goin' to your place first, ain't we?"

"Yeah," Sammy replied grimly, his response making him sick with fear of what he might find. His guilt at being duped into leaving his wife ate at him, scorching his being like acidic evil. He trembled with worry and burned with anger. "We'll come up easy through the trees on the east...tie up a ways behind the barn and work our way in on foot...then split up by the barn. You work your way over to the toolshed. That'll give you a look at the front. I'll go in the back door and work through to the front. If you hear shootin', come runnin'. I'll do the same. You okay with it?"

"Yeah, all but the toolshed. You didn't say if you wanted me to get near the front door if I don't see no one. And if there's men to the front side, you want me to just open up...or what?"

Sammy thought for an instant. "No, we don't know who might be there. Might be some of my men. We have to know before we shoot. And don't forget about Jenny. She can shoot...and Raquel from the T is there, and little Jing Lu and Camille, too. If you see a woman or a kid, you best tell 'em you're Blaine and I'm with you.

"Will do. Any men to the front, I'll have a rifle trained on. You comin' out the front door?"

"Yeah...or shootin' my way out. We'll play it like it's dealt."

They paced back up to a gallop and rode on for several more minutes before they saw the small, dim light in the distance. Sammy knew it was after midnight and there would normally be no lamps burning at this hour. Across the open meadow toward the woods to the west of the ranch house, they rode, knowing they were visible in the moonlight, and intensely watching around them for anything. Moments later, they were in the cloak of the woods where they slowly weaved their way closer until Sammy held up his hand and they stopped. Both men listened in the stillness for a moment before dismounting and tying their horses. Then they moved like phantoms through the darkness, silently coming to the barn where they moved from corner to corner, and looked beyond only to see nothing unusual. But they couldn't see it all from where they were; the front porch and window were not in a line of sight

"Ready?" Sammy whispered.

Blaine nodded and then took off across the open ground toward the cover of the toolshed.

Sammy trotted on his toes across the side yard to the kitchen window and looked inside. The blackness of it was broken only by a lamp that burned dimly from the dining room beyond. He could tell nothing. With his rifle cocked and his pistol holstered, he quickly moved to the backside of his cabin where he stood at the back door a moment, listening to the river a hundred feet away and appraising every detail of what he could see. The privy door stood open. It shouldn't have been. Then he detected the movement and saw the two horses tied in the thick of the trees nearby. His heart began to race with fear of what it meant. What of his wife, his love, Jenny? Then his anguish soared as he prepared to go in the door and discovered that it was already slightly ajar. He pushed it slowly open and crept into the dark kitchen looking to the doorway of the dining room from which the light came. He saw the stain on the kitchen floor, but the room was too dark to know what it was. The smell of burnt gunpowder became stronger as he moved silently to the doorway of the next room.

The dining room table came into view, a lone lamp sitting on it. Beyond, Sammy saw that his shotgun was gone from the rack, and that the floor area in front of it had been wiped partially clean of blood, though quite a bit remained smeared into the grain of the planking. His horror at seeing it turned his heart cold and his care to that of the reaper. Sammy rounded the corner to the sitting area where little light reached. In the darker part of the room, the man sat on the settee, his head hanging back and turned to the side, drool running from the downward corner of his mouth as he slept. With his gun trained on the man, Sammy stepped mutely to the stove, retrieving the fireplace poker in his free hand. He took a quick glance through the front window where he saw Blaine standing in the dirt in front of the porch, his rifle pointed toward the far corner where the rockers were. Sammy couldn't see who Blaine aimed at. He didn't care. He knew that whoever it was didn't belong.

He stepped quietly in front of the sleeping man, and then raised the poker that he held mid-shank like a knife from his fist. Sammy plunged straight down with brute force, driving the iron tip into the man's upper thigh, piercing the tissue and muscle before slamming the femur bone where it stopped and was then withdrawn as fast as it had been stabbed.

The involuntary high-pitched scream broke the silence as the man came awake in a nightmare that he dreadfully realized was no dream.

"Hold it right there!" came Blaine's command from outside; the man he spoke to had awakened in a panic upon hearing the scream of his partner inside.

Sammy held his rifle pointed at the face of the stranger on the settee. He held the bloody poker in his other hand as he trembled with rage. "Where is my wife?"

The man held his leg and looked up at Sammy, his face contorted in a mixture of pain, fear, and hate. "We got her. If you ever want to see her alive again..."

Sammy instantly swung the poker, hitting the man on the side of the head and knocking him out. He slumped to the side.

"You're not bleedin' on my wife's furniture," Sammy said, as he threw down the poker. He grabbed the man by the front of his shirt, jerking him off the couch and dragging him one-handed across the floor to the front door. Sammy opened the door and dragged the man to the far end of the porch where Blaine held a rifle on the other man. Sammy pulled the unconscious man up and sat him in the rocker next to the other man.

"What'd he say? Where's Jenny and the others?" Blaine asked.

Sammy put his rifle down and then stepped off the porch and pulled the axe from the log-splitting stump it was stuck in. He stepped back up on the porch holding the axe in both hands. His words were deliberate and dispassionate.

"He said they took her."

"Who? Who took her?" Blaine queried.

"His partners...or whoever he's workin' for," Sammy replied, looking at the man sitting in the other rocker. The man's eyes were big and wide open with fear as he looked at Sammy, then quickly looked away. "Whose blood is that on the floor inside?" Sammy asked him.

The man looked off nervously into the night. "I don't know what you're talking about," he replied.

"I'm talkin' about the blood that was wiped up in the dining room...a lot of it," Sammy said, his voice quavering slightly, afraid of the answer.

"I don't know about any blood."

Sammy swung the axe in a high arc, the leaden gray metal of the head moving in a blur with the slightest glint as it hurtled downward and struck at the bone of the ankle, nearly severing the man's boot in two. The man's scream rang through the night like the calling of doom, followed by lingering wailing as he tried to endure the pain and comprehend that his right foot was now attached more by boot leather than by skin or bone.

"Catch your breath there now," Sammy flatly suggested, "'cause I'm only going to ask you one more time. Whose blood is that inside?"

The man gasped for air. "It was a Mex woman."

Sammy froze for a moment. "Raquel," he reverently said in a whisper to himself. "What happened to her?" he suddenly spoke up, with grim anger rising in him.

"She drew down on one of our men with a shotgun. He had to shoot her."

"Is she dead?" Sammy asked.

"Yeah."

Sammy swung the axe again, burying the head of it deep in the man's chest. The man grunted with the impact of it, then his body convulsed several times before his head fell forward and he moved no more.

"Jesus Christ!" Blaine exclaimed, shocked at what he'd just seen. "I guess you had nothin' more to say to him."

"No, I didn't."

Blaine nodded. "Yep, the poor son of a bitch took up the wrong line of work."

Sammy pulled the axe from the dead man's chest. Then he stepped to the other chair and slapped the unconscious man several times until his eyes opened. It took the man several moments to gain his focus and recall where he was and what had happened. The man looked at Sammy holding the axe, and the muzzle of Blaine's rifle pointed at his throbbing head. Then he looked to his left and saw his partner dead in the chair next to him.

"Where are the little girls that were with my wife?" Sammy asked him.

"They're with her. We got 'em. You're going to kill me, ain't you?"

"Are they all right?" Sammy asked, ignoring his question.

"They was when they left here," the man replied nervously.

"Where are they now?"

The man looked at his pants soaked with blood, the pain in his leg excruciating. The poker had struck an artery. "If I tell you, will you let me live?"

"There are slow, horrible ways to die, mister. You're about to find out unless you talk."

"All right," the man compliantly said. "They're at a place maybe two hours west and north of here."

"How many men in your outfit?"

"A dozen or so."

"Is there a woman ridin' with your bunch?

"Yeah."

"You workin' for a man named Lionel Doan?"

The man's face registered no recognition. "Don't know anyone of that name...I swear. I work for a man named Boothe...and I ain't known him but for a few weeks."

"What's his horse?"

"A black Irish...stallion."

"Why are you two still here at my place? How come you didn't go with the rest of 'em?"

The man paused a moment, unsure of his words. "Boothe wants the man and kids that live a ways over. Figured they might show up here."

"Wants 'em for what?" Sammy asked calmly.

"Don't know. We was just supposed to bring 'em."

"The padre? Sammy asked.

"Yeah, yeah...that's what he called him...the padre."

Sammy stepped back a step and drew his pistol. Cold fear came over the man's face. "You said I wouldn't die if I talked. I'll show you where the hideout is if you let me go when you see it!"

"I said you wouldn't die slow and horrible. You picked your trail, mister. It ends here."

In final desperation, the man reached for his pistol. Sammy shot him between the eyes.

46

"**M**aybe you shoulda let that feller show us where that hideout is," Blaine said.

Sammy lit the smoke he'd just rolled and took a deep drag, needing it, the tobacco giving him a moment of soothing respite from his current insanity. He exhaled and spoke, "He wouldn't have made it…would have bled out on the way. Besides, I know where to look. Hector saw their outfit ridin' south up by the Juney at Sombrero Rock during his route today."

Blaine considered it, then nodded at the most recent corpse in a chair, "Reckon the stiff here told straight…that surely is north and west. There ain't no trails anywhere near there. A dozen horses oughta leave tracks a plenty. Can't find tracks in the dark, though."

"It'll be first light by the time we get there."

"It don't take that long," Blaine said doubtingly.

Sammy took another deep drag and threw the cigarette down. He grabbed one of the dead men and dragged him from the chair, off the porch to the dirt in front, speaking as he did so. "Have to go to the bunkhouse first and see about the boys. They might know somethin' we need to know."

Blaine followed Sammy's lead and pulled the other dead man from the chair. "Owner wants you the hell off his porch," Blaine said to the lifeless body as he dragged it next to the other corpse and flopped it on the dirt.

"I'll be right back," Sammy said, bounding up onto the front porch. He went into the house and quickly checked the rest of it. His eyes lingered on their bedroom, he and Jenny's inner sanctum, their most private retreat. The emptiness of it shook him, bringing another wave of rage, fear, and urgency. Moments later, he and Blaine were mounted up and riding toward the bunkhouse.

The padre was slumping badly to the side in his saddle when Rory reined alongside just in time to keep him from falling. "Whoa," Rory said, grabbing the padre's reins and bringing Roca to a halt just as the padre toppled onto Rory's leg, unconscious. Rory grabbed the Padre by his coat and hung on as he kept his horse pushed up tight against Roca. "We gotta get him down. I can't do it like this," Rory called. "Tobias, you and Payat get down and get ready to catch him...hurry!"

The boys jumped off their horse and quickly squeezed in between the padre's horse and Rory's. "Watch out you don't get squished!" Rory urged. "Here he comes!"

Rory slowly reined his horse away and held on to the padre's coat as long as he could before the weight overcame his strength and he let go. Tobias and Payat broke the fall with their extended arms as the padre and the boys went to the ground in a heap. The dog joined the pile of them.

Rory dismounted and brought the canteen to where the padre laid on the ground, the boys sitting beside him with Payat cradling the padre's head. Rory knelt down with the open canteen and put it near the padre's lips. "Padre? Padre, can you hear me?" Rory prompted. There was no response.

"He is cold," Payat said, as he felt his father's forehead and cheeks.

Rory pulled open the padre's coat and put his ear to his chest in search of a heartbeat. Panic and grief came over him as he heard nothing. He moved his head from spot to spot, and then he heard it faintly. "He's alive!" Rory pronounced with relief. He put his fingers to the padre's wound that was fresh with blood. "That bandage ain't on there and he's been bleeding more!" Rory reached in his pocket and pulled out the package of cayenne pepper that Blaine had given him. "Let's see if this works like Mister Blaine said." Rory began pulling his father's coat off. "Got to get the hole in his back, too," he said. Rory poured the powder liberally on both holes, then for good measure packed cloth in each wound, too, as Sammy Winds had told him.

"Are we close to the Twin T?" Tobias asked.

Rory stood up and carefully looked to the south. "We're real close. A mile...two at the most. I can go and get help...get a wagon. Or you can go...both of you, and I'll stay."

"We stay, you go," Payat replied.

"All right, get a fire going next to him and rub his arms and legs to warm him up. Should be some makings in those trees right there. I'll leave you the matches and the hatchet. Here's the canteen."

The padre suddenly spoke, "Where are we? What happened?"

"You fell asleep, Padre," Rory replied.

"I am sorry. Go on boys...leave me here."

"I'm going to the Twin T Ranch for help. I'll come back with a wagon...you won't have to ride anymore, Padre. Payat and Tobias will stay with you."

"Good. That is good. Go with God."

"Rest now, Padre...and drink some water," Rory replied.

Tobias nodded. "We'll look after him. Just hurry up."

"I won't be long," Rory said, swinging up into the saddle on Dusty. He was happy to be on his own horse once more. And as if the horse was pleased to have his master upon him, Dusty galloped to the south like being catapulted by the night itself.

"It's Sammy and Blaine Corker!" Sammy yelled, as they reined up in front of the bunkhouse. The horses that Boothe had chased from the corral and barn earlier had returned and were milling around the yard, a few of them coming close as the two men tied their horses to the hitching rail.

The front door opened. Roasty stood framed in the faint light of the opening with a revolver in his hand and a dazed look on his face. "Blaine Corker you say?"

"Yeah, Roasty…right here, and Sammy too."

Sammy strode quickly to the door. "You all right?" Sammy asked, seeing Roasty weaving a little as he stood.

"I been better."

"Where's the rest of the boys?"

"Bill and Porter are inside…shot up bad. The rest of the boys are in town, I reckon." Roasty turned and limped badly back into the bunkhouse with Sammy and Blaine on his heels.

"You're shot," Sammy said, watching Roasty's limp and seeing the blood thick on the back of his pants.

"In the ass," Roasty replied. "Ain't nothin' next to Bill and Porter."

"Ah, hell," Sammy said, upon seeing Bill and Porter. Whether they were asleep or unconscious, Sammy couldn't tell, but he could see they were both badly wounded. Their faces were pale.

"Put a hot iron to the bullet holes to get the bleeding slowed, 'cept they'd already bled a hell of a lot," Roasty said.

"Who's that?" Blaine asked, looking at the covered body on the floor.

"Damn woman who was laying the trap. Knocked on the door claimin' there'd been an accident...said her wagon rolled over and her men folk were hurt. Some men were in the yard just waitin' to ambush us. Somebody fired on 'em just before we walked outside...warned us. Then her crowd opened up on us and hit her. I pulled her in and we got the door and window shutters closed. Before she died, she said they were here to kill us all. We ended up going out the back window...trying to get to your place and see about Jenny and Raquel and the girls. That's when we got shot to hell. Killed six of 'em though. Bill killed four of 'em his self.

"You boys killed six of them?" Sammy asked, stunned with surprise.

"We surely did."

"That's half their outfit," Sammy said, appraising new numbers in his head. "They just lost two more at my place...but others already took Jenny and the girls to a hideout. They killed Raquel."

"Yellow devil bastards!" Roasty exclaimed.

"Yeah...well, I'm forever obliged you boys tried to get there. You'll be interested to know it was young Tobias and Payat that fired on them to warn you."

"You don't say," Roasty said, with a faint smile. "Those brave little hombres saved our hides. They surely did. Are they all right?"

"Yeah, they're with Padre, headed for the T. We got fresh horses at Ward Sones's and sent him to T for help. Should be on the way by now." Sammy thought for a moment. "Did you see Jasper and Ben after work today?"

"No. Knuckles and Matt said they likely headed for Two Rock. They said Jasper was talkin' 'bout getting delightful with

Monique, the whore. Then Knuckles and Matt rode for La Jara...'bout 5:00 it was. Talk of some new whores over to Lupe's."

Roasty was weakening from standing. He hobbled over and sat down gingerly on the settee, rolling up on his left hip and cheek. "Hot damn this smarts!" came his pained declaration as he tried to settle in. "Why do you ask about Jasper and Ben?"

Worry came over Sammy's face. "Rory said he saw these men earlier tonight. Said they had Jasper and Ben's horses. No sign of them, though."

"Oh, no, no, no, no!" Roasty replied in anguish.

"Yeah...I pray not," Sammy added.

"These boys look in awful bad shape," Blaine said. He was examining Bill more closely. "It looks like Bill's shot three times. Porter, too...three times!"

Bill's eyes opened and took in the room. "Hey, Blaine...Sammy. Good to see you two," he said weakly with a hoarse voice. "Aaahhhh!" he yelled as he shifted positions. "Where's the shine? I need some shine!"

"Me too," Porter said, having just opened his eyes. "And some water...please!"

"Right there on the counter," Roasty said.

Sammy grabbed the jug of shine and the water pitcher, and then he and Blaine each took a vessel and administered to the three men who took good pulls of each liquid. When they were done, Sammy pulled Blaine aside and spoke quietly. "They need Doc Payton right now. Bill and Porter might die. I don't know how many bullets are in 'em, but they need to come out if they can...and those wounds need to be cleaned and tended. Doc's the best there is, and he's got his own hospital right there...nurse and beds.

Blaine nodded his head. "Those boys are poorly. They'll drink themselves to death on shine before they beat the pain. They need some laudanum. I *know* that works."

Sammy looked Blaine in the eye. "I want you to take 'em, Blaine. We'll rig a wagon with bedding in the back."

"Right now?"

"It's their best chance."

"What about your chances goin' alone? You'll have to wait on help from the T."

"I ain't waitin' on nothin'," Sammy said flatly.

47

It was one-thirty in the morning when Rupert exhaled the smoke of his cigar and considered the news that Boothe had just delivered to him; the job was not finished. "You better damn well finish it soon," Rupert told him, then added, "I'm leaving in a day. If you want your money while I'm still here, you better finish before then. Otherwise, you'll have to pick it up in Chama."

"Chama!" Boothe retorted angrily. "I'm not riding all the way up there."

"Then perhaps you should go finish the job instead of standing here."

Boothe wanted to slap the smugness off Rupert's face, but the two men Boothe had never seen before stood close to Rupert. "You'll need men around you all the time if you leave without payin' me. And I want what's still owed to the dead ones."

"You'll get it all when the job's done."

Boothe gritted his teeth and growled under his breath like an animal. "Give me these two to finish the job. We're gettin' shorthanded."

"No...but I'll see what I can do about sending you another man."

Boothe scratched at his beard. "All right. We're going back in the morning, so you better see about it quick. You'll send him to the hideout? How's he gonna know how to get there?"

"He'll get there," Rupert confidently replied.

It wasn't long after Boothe left that the knock came at the door. "See who it is," Rupert said to his men. From where he was seated on a cowhide chair, Rupert could see it was Lucius when the door was opened. Lucius said nothing and simply stared at the two men who stood before him. "Let him in," Rupert ordered.

Lucius walked slowly across the room and stood in front of Rupert, looking down at him. "Who are they?" Lucius asked easily.

"My assistants. Sit down," Rupert said, indicating the other comfortable looking chair perpendicular to his. "Would you like a drink?"

"No. What I'd like is to talk business. What about them?" Lucius asked, nodding toward the two men.

"Don't worry about them. Did you kill Winds?

"Maybe."

"What do you mean maybe?" Rupert instantly fired back.

Lucius looked at Rupert with calm disdain. "Didn't kill him on that trail you said he'd come along on. He never showed. I was in a cantina in La Jara later. There was a poker game going. Had my back to it when I heard a man at the table say, 'The Sky W big cheese wins again.' I saw who he was talking about, so I played for him. He fit the physical particulars you told me. If it wasn't Winds, it was one of his men."

Rupert's eyes narrowed and his mind began to turn over. He knew Winds had left his ranch. One of his assistants had spied on the ranch and confirmed it. If Winds got to town and talked to the sheriff about the note, Winds would know it was a setup. "You staked out that trail all afternoon...where I showed you?" he suddenly asked

"I wasn't where you showed me...wasn't the best spot. Picked a better place close by...was there till damn near dark."

Rupert's face lost color. "I suppose he could have his own way to town, but it seems sure he would be on the trail that close to town."

"He wasn't."

"You say you were in a cantina later?"

"Lupe's, I think it was called. Good tequila and pretty whores."

Rupert shook his head. "Whores? That wasn't Winds then. His wife is beautiful.

"So?"

"So, I'm goddamn sure it wasn't Winds."

"Maybe he was just there for the card game," Lucius offered.

"I don't think so."

Lucius leaned forward in his chair. "I'm looking to be gone. You can pay me half since we don't know."

"Well, hell! That's the point! We don't know! I have to know! You have to stay and kill Winds if it wasn't him."

Lucius frowned. "I killed a man. I made it look like self-defense, but I sure as hell can't go back to that town. I need to be gone. If it wasn't him, have your other boys kill him."

"You won't have to go back to town. If Winds is alive, he'll be back at his ranch. The other men I have on this didn't finish the job yet. They're going back to his ranch in the morning. Throw in with them and we can finish it all up in one swoop."

"I don't throw in with anybody."

"They're shorthanded...lost some men."

"It ain't my concern."

Rupert looked hard at Lucius. "If you want the rest of your money, it'll be your concern."

Lucius's eyes fell dull like the pall of death. He stood slowly and pivoted slightly so he could see both of Rupert's assistants, as well as Rupert. The assistants quite suddenly looked concerned about what might happen next as Lucius flexed his gun hand several times and widened his stance a bit. Lucius looked straight ahead between where Rupert sat and his men stood. He spoke like a judge passing sentence. "If you all want to keep breathin', Rupert here is going to pay me what he owes me. Since we don't know about Winds, I'll settle for half. If that don't suit you, then draw."

"No, no, no! Rupert immediately wailed, holding his hands up to his men. They both had placed their hands to their guns, ready for what may come. "He'll kill you," Rupert said, with the certainty of a commandment.

One of the men suddenly puffed up in offended posture of being doubted in the outcome of gunplay. The other man knew the truth of it, having been present in Dumas the night that Lucius shot Clint Smith. He'd never seen such speed. "Forget about tryin' it, kid," he said to his partner.

"I need you to see this one through, Lucius!" Rupert pleadingly declared. "You boys go outside," Rupert ordered. His men promptly left. Rupert's eyes met Lucius's dead gaze. His tone of capitulation was thick. "I'll give you the thousand I owe you for Winds, and two thousand more if you throw in with Boothe when they go back."

A glint of life entered Lucius's eyes. "Two thousand more?"

"That's right."

"I want all three thousand right now. And one day is all I'm workin'…get Winds or not."

Rupert shot him a look of surprise. "You're changing our regular payment terms. It's always been half before, half after."

Lucius looked at Rupert like he was stupid. He smiled faintly as he spoke. "See, that's the beauty of working only one day, whether I get Winds or not. Half before, half after, don't even apply."

Rupert knew there was nothing more to be said. He also knew Lucius had a strong southern sense of honor that would bind him to his word, and his word would mean that Winds would die if Lucius came across him. "All right then, you help kill off others, too, if need be."

"I'll ride in with your other crew and kill any man I come across there...but I won't be taking orders. I'll be looking for Winds."

"Take that up with Boothe."

"I will. Now, I'll have that drink you offered and my money."

48

S ammy rode to the northwest, his route naturally taking
him near the padre's cabin. He saw the faint light of it
and felt his anger descend upon him like a fog that
blinded him from anything else. It was an irrepressible thirst,
this vengeance that needed satiation as much as his lungs
needed air. He did not worry of it, the iron grip that crushed
any distinction of good or evil, right or wrong, heaven or hell,
life or death. His will, would be done, and it was no longer of
his control. Sammy reined his horse toward the cabin.

He did not cross the plank bridge at Red Creek, but instead
crossed silently down through the trees, walking his horse
through the water and climbing easily up the opposite bank and
slope to the plateau on which the cabin stood. He tied his horse
in the trees behind the cabin and silently moved in a wide arc
around to a view of the front of it. Two saddled horses were in
the front corral, but there were no men on the porch and
nothing to be told from the light that escaped the front window.

As he prepared to head for the front door, he saw the glow
of the cigarette as someone took a drag of it in the darkness
close to the cabin, not more than fifty feet from where Sammy
was. Sammy wondered if the man had heard him, concluding
that the man wouldn't be smoking a cigarette if he had. With a
pistol in one hand and a knife in the other, Sammy moved
stealthily toward the man who sat in a chair amongst a small

cluster of aspen trees, facing the cabin so he might view anyone who showed at the front door. As Sammy drew close, the man finally heard him approaching and turned to look. Sammy cocked his pistol and spoke softly, "Is Boothe inside?"

The man realized someone had the drop on him. He didn't make a move for his gun, reassured slightly at the nature of the question and the mention of Boothe's name. "Is that you, Reid?"

"No. It's Yordun. Where's Boothe now?"

"He's back at the place. Yordun you say?"

"Yeah, who's inside?"

"Barney," the man replied, not sure of who he was talking to. "Why you got that gun on me?"

"Because you're done," Sammy replied as he stepped quickly forward and swung the knife from his side, plunging it into the side of the man's neck. The man rolled from the chair and hit the ground where he flopped around like a fish out of water before he stilled.

Sammy walked quickly and quietly up to the front door where he stood up against the wall to the side of it. "Barney, come quick! We got 'im! We got that padre!" Sammy yelled.

Barney came out of his doze on the divan in a slight panic, mumbling, "What?"

"Quick, Barney! I got the padre!" came the call again.

Barney rose quickly and drew his pistol as he moved to the front door and opened it. "Where you at, Frank?" he called out as he stepped outside onto the porch.

"The name is Winds," Sammy replied, pulling the trigger of his .44-caliber revolver, pointed at Barney's head from five feet away. The booming report cut through the night and was heard by Blaine as he drove the wagon with Roasty, Bill, and Porter lain out in back.

"Sounds like Sammy found someone else he was done talkin' to," Blaine quipped.

Sammy rolled the dead man off the porch then quickly checked the house. Moments later, he was mounted up and riding northwest again.

Boothe was tired and mad, his whole plan having turned to a fiasco. He wanted it to be over so he could drink as much as he wanted, and do as he wanted for as long as he wanted with the lovely Missus Winds. He didn't bother with the identifying whistle as he rode up on the hideout with its several tents to the side. "It's me goddamn it!" he hollered, like everybody better understand it. He tied up and strode inside.

The two men were still playing cards, with a bottle of whiskey and two glasses between them on the table. It was the first thing Boothe saw. "Stop drinkin' till this job's over!" Boothe ordered. "We'll be leavin' in a couple of hours. Better be ready to ride," he said with the tone of a deadly threat. "Where's Crom?"

"Sleepin'…in there," one of the men replied, nodding toward another room. "The woman's in your room."

"Yeah, we tied her to the bed. Figured that's where you'd want her," the slimy one added, his greasy perversion dripping in his tone.

In the flash of an instant, Boothe pulled his knife and put it to the man's throat. "Did you touch her?"

The slimy one suddenly feared that Boothe's carnivorous demeanor might end his life any second. "Only tyin' her to the bed!" he said, panicked.

"That's all he did, boss," the other man said.

Boothe pulled his knife back. His eyes finally swung far left to the corner where Jing Lu and Camille sat huddled together. He glared at them a moment then walked to the counter and cut a hunk of meat off a large slab of roasted beef.

He wiped his knife off on his pant leg and returned it to it sheath as he walked to his room, opening the door and closing it behind him.

Jenny was tied spread-eagle to the bedposts, her eyes betraying her fear as the beast of a man stood at the foot of the bed, eating the hunk of meat, his lips smacking loudly as he grunted with the effort of it. He leaned forward and lifted her long dress at the hem, peering up underneath at her legs and panties. "Ohhh," he cooed through a mouthful of chewed meat. "You're a real flower of love, ain't you?"

"You should fear for anything that gets too close to my bite," Jenny stated, as convincingly as she could.

Boothe raise his head and looked at her. "You won't bite long. I'll have a gun at your head or a knife at your throat. If you're good to me, you'll live. Stay alive like the regular help. If you're not, I'll cut you from head to toe."

Jenny said nothing.

Boothe dropped her dress and walked to the mattress in the corner of the room. He took off his hat and gun belt, then lay out on it and devoured the rest of the meat. "Keep quiet now!" Boothe commanded when he had finished eating, putting his hat over his eyes to sleep. "Get some rest...you'll need it."

49

The padre's eyes opened to the soft light of the room and a woman's face looking down at him. He was delusional, thinking for a moment that perhaps he was dead and the woman was an angel. Then, for the briefest instant, he imagined it was his departed wife, Estella, and his heart bounded with joy at their reunion. But the ache of his wounds caught him and cleared his mind enough to know that he was still alive. The woman's lips were moving. He did not hear the words. "What? What is that you say?" he mumbled, unaware if his words had come out intelligibly.

She leaned in closer. "Padre, do you hear me? It is Jacqueline. You are at the Twin T Ranch...safe. Your boys are here, too, sleeping in the big bed right over there."

The padre's head turned on the pillow, looking in the direction she had indicated. He saw the bed but could not distinguish who was in it. "Rory, Payat...Tobias?" he asked, increasingly aware as he said their names.

"Yes, Padre, they are safe. And many of our men have gone to the Sky W Ranch to help. Reuben Taylor is leading them."

"Good. God bless them...that is good," the padre feebly replied. "They must find Jing Lu and Camille...and Missus

311

Winds and the one named Raquel," he said, as he began to cough and suck for air from the exertion of his words.

"Yes, Padre, they know who they are looking for. You have lost much blood. You need to rest and eat and drink. Do you think you could eat some soup now?"

"I will try."

"Good. I will be right back," she said, and then she was suddenly gone.

The padre became aware of the warm, comfortable bed he was in, and that he was dressed in a fresh nightshirt. As the pain of his injuries began to rise in sweeping throbs, he dismissed it and began to pray.

The night was long of misery when Boothe awakened an hour later, his bout of sleep fitful with his lingering obligation. Nevertheless, he felt the needed rejuvenation of rest and was freshly bloodthirsty. He would see to it now, this killing that remained unfinished at the Sky W Ranch. But first, he would see to the woman.

Boothe got up from the mattress he had slept on and walked to the bed where Jenny was tied. She slept as he leered at her, the heat of it overcoming him. He would have her now. There was time enough. He began to undo his pants with one hand as he reached out with his other and began rubbing her breasts.

Jenny came awake in a panic. "Nooooo!" she screamed at him as she began thrashing her body wildly about.

He slapped her viciously across the face. "Shut up or I'll kill you now!" he yelled, then pulled his knife and held it to her throat.

"Boss!" came the call from the other room.

Boothe recognized Crom's voice and the urgency in it. "What?" he yelled back, distressed at the timing.

"There's a man here...says he was sent and you'd be expecting him."

Boothe looked at Jenny, his heat still burning. "Yeah, that's right," Boothe shouted in reply. "Tell him to wait...I'll be out after a while."

The visitor's voice rang out, "It don't sound like that woman cares for you, so why not haul your ass out here now?"

Boothe pondered the words a moment before his eyes began to bug out and his face deepened in color. He was in full rage by the time he reached the bedroom door, throwing it open and storming into the other room like hell come calling.

Lucius saw no gun on him but instantly knew Boothe meant to do him harm. He spoke as Boothe crossed the room toward him. "If you mean to lay hand on me or cut me with your knife, I'll kill you first."

Boothe was already close upon him when the bore of Lucius's revolver stared him down between the eyes, appearing instantly as if a magician had produced it from air. Boothe stopped in his tracks, frozen in the certainty that he'd die right there if he moved anymore. They'd never met, but Boothe instantly knew who it must be. "Heard about you...knew you were on this job. I pondered if he'd send you when he promised one man," Boothe said, suddenly curious.

"Back up big man or I'll ventilate you in just a second more," Lucius offered graciously.

Boothe nodded as he backed up several steps. Crom and the two men at the table remained still; all were initially curious about what they would witness when Boothe arrived at the man who had told him to haul his ass out there. But now, the man had a gun in Boothe's face, and Boothe's mortal respect for the man's talents was on display.

"All right, mister. You wanted me out here. You got something to say?" Boothe asked, disaffected.

313

Lucius holstered his gun to the amazement of them all. "Be riding in with you. I'm here for Winds. I'll be another gun if we run into others there, but I ain't part of your crew, so don't bother tellin' me to do anything. When do we leave?"

Boothe relaxed and walked toward the counter where the roasted beef was. "Soon...half hour or so," he said, as he cut himself some meat. "I figured you were supposed to get Winds last night, seeing as he wasn't home when we called at his ranch. You didn't get him?"

Lucius ignored the question. "Is this all the men you have?" he asked.

"Four more staked out there right now," Boothe replied, then stuffed his mouth with a bite. Boothe chewed the meat and stared at Lucius. He would kill this gunslinger when the job was done, he decided. He began walking back to the room where Jenny was. "I'll be out when it's time to go. If you don't want to hear the screaming so bad, wait outside."

"What about them?" Crom asked.

Boothe stopped at the bedroom door, turning around to look. "Who?"

"Them there," Crom replied, nodding at Jing Lu and Camille.

"Kill them now," Boothe answered.

"Me?"

"Yeah, you. You're the one that ordered them here. Kill them now.

"Why don't you have these two here do it? They've had an easy night of it. I ain't even eaten yet," Crom replied, speaking of the slimy one and the other man at the table.

Boothe squinted slightly. "All right...you two do it. Get rid of them. Do it now!" he sternly ordered, and then went into his bedroom and slammed the door.

"You heard 'im," Crom said as he walked to the counter where the roasted beef and other food provisions were. "Get it done." Then he directed his words to Lucius as he cut meat for himself. "There's food here if you want. We'll leave when Boothe says."

The slimy one abruptly jumped to his feet and strode toward Jing Lu and Camille.

Camille's throat constricted and was unable to make sound. Instead, she shuddered uncontrollably as an ascending, tonal pitch began in Jing Lu's throat and rose fully up and beyond her lips in a shriek of terror.

The slimy one reached down and yanked Jing Lu up by her neck, wrapping his arm around her head and clamping his hand over her mouth. From the other room, Jenny screamed, "Don't you hurt them! Nooo! Don't touch them!"

"I told you to shut up!" Boothe yelled. The echo of a brutal slap followed straightaway.

"Get the other one!" the slimy one called to the other man, who was finally up from the table and moving quickly toward Camille. He grabbed her at the neck of her dress and pulled her to him. With Jing Lu and Camille squirming desperately, the two men crushed their resistance in their grips and headed for the front door.

From a dead part of him came the calling of light, seeping in on him in the defining moment of what he would end as. Lucius was still by the door as they approached. "Hold it!" he yelled. "Let 'em go."

The two men stopped and held tight on the girls. "Like hell we will. We don't take orders from you," the slimy one said.

"You do now. They got nothin' to do with nothin'. They're kids. You two women are nothin' but maggot-covered shit even thinkin' about it. Let 'em go."

"Boothe!" the slimy one yelled at the top of his lungs.

"You're lookin' to die, mister," Crom said from where he stood at the counter, his guns strapped on.

Lucius nodded. "I been lookin' a long time. Why don't you see if you can help?"

Boothe opened the bedroom door and stepped out into the far side of the room, wearing no gun belt. "What goes on here?" he bellowed, knowing it was some kind of showdown.

Crom ignored Boothe's question and positioned himself to draw. "Turn them girls loose boys. We'll all gun on him."

"Is that what we should do boss? Let 'em go and gun on him?" the slimy one asked, turning his head slightly toward Boothe, but never taking his eyes from Lucius.

Boothe began backing into the bedroom as he replied, "Shoot that little runt dead!"

The two men released their grips on Jing Lu and Camille who quickly ran for the corner they'd been pulled from.

"Now!" Crom yelled an instant after he had begun his draw. The other two men flashed for their guns, both confident in three against one.

It was like a webbed lightning strike when the reaper called, the three shots nearly indistinguishable of each other in one rolling boom of flame and smoke. Crom collapsed first, followed by the slimy one, and then the other man—from right to left, like a line of dominoes. Crom had been taken through the heart and was dead. The other two were regaining their purpose when Lucius shot each of them again.

"Did you get him?" Boothe yelled, from the bedroom.

"Your boys are on the ferry crossin' the river. If you want to try your luck, come on out...otherwise, I'm leavin'. You can finish the job with the men you have left at that ranch."

Boothe was stunned at the news, knowing better than to step out into the next room. He would catch up with this man another time. "Go on then, and get out!" Boothe yelled back.

Lucius looked at Jing Lu and Camille. "You kids get over here," he said.

They did not move.

"C'mon...it's all right. You're goin' home," he coaxed, barely above a whisper.

Jing Lu and Camille came slowly to him.

"I'll cut these ropes off you now," Lucius said, before pulling his knife so as not to frighten them. He cut the ropes from their wrists, and then quickly led the girls outside. "Is one of these horses yours?" he asked.

"No," Jing Lu replied.

"Then it won't matter which one. Do you want to ride double or separate?"

"Double," Camille immediately answered. "But what about Missus Winds? She's in there. Please help her...please!"

"Yes! She is the nicest lady! That man will hurt her! You could save her!" Jing Lu pleaded.

"That's Missus Winds in there? The wife of Sam Winds?" he asked, suddenly knowing Boothe would kill her."

"Yes," Jing Lu replied.

Lucius thought a moment. He had his money and had already blown the deal wide open with the killing of Boothe's men. His association with Rupert Crowder was burnt. Why not free the woman. He didn't abide by anyone who would kill women and children. *There wasn't a scintilla of honor in Boothe's outfit, or in Rupert,* he thought. "All right...up you go," Lucius said, lifting the girls up one at a time onto the horse. "I'll get her. If anything goes wrong, you kick this horse and ride out of here."

"But we do not know which way to go," Jing Lu said.

"You just kick the horse and ride. It won't matter which way."

317

The shot rang out from the front door of the cabin where Boothe stood with his rifle aimed. Lucius was falling as Jing Lu kicked the horse, which broke to a run into nearby trees. Boothe stepped farther out and fired at them as they vanished. He walked over to where Lucius lay on his back with his arms outstretched and his eyes open, fixed on the night sky that would soon come light. There was no movement from Lucius.

"You ain't such a blur of speed now, are you gunslinger?" Boothe held the rifle to Lucius's face and reached down, undoing Lucius's gunbelt, and then pulling it free. "I'll tell Rupert about your disposition…how I had to kill you. Give 'im your gun to prove it. Shoot Winds myself and take your pay, too."

"I can't move," Lucius finally said.

Boothe pulled his knife and slowly cut a deep gash across Lucius's belly as Lucius said nothing and did not move. Boothe flashed a sadistic smile. "Shot you in the back. Must'a hit the part that makes your arms and legs work," he said then looked up at the sky. The faintest trace of dawn was upon it. He knew he should have already been headed back to the Winds ranch. His men would be waiting.

"Kill me," Lucius said.

"No. You just lie there and think about what crossing Boothe Haney got you. If you're still alive when I get back, you can ask me again…after I get some time with the woman. I might be more agreeable then. Enjoy the morning."

50

All was still when Sammy heard Boothe shoot Lucius. The rifle shot was faint in the distance. He was already north of Sombrero Rock and had stopped for a moment to water his horse. The animal was well played from the unrelenting pace of the ride. "Thank you, Lord," Sammy said, realizing he would not have heard it had he been riding at the time. He fixed the direction of it in his mind and figured the distance at no more than two miles, then gave the horse a minute more before remounting and loping off.

The moon was gone. Morning hung in the graying light above while the land below was still gripped in darkness. Sammy prayed as he rode on, angst heavy on him as he thought of the gunshot he'd heard. He did not want to contemplate it, but could not push it from his mind. He wanted only to be consumed with holding the correct course as he rode up an easy slope of open ground and cleared the rise. Then the plain leveled and the first light of dawn spread over it, giving sight across the half mile of meadow with the trees beyond.

The lone rider was headed toward him, the legs of his horse only half visible through the ground fog that lifted from the heavy dew of the grass. Sammy spurred his horse to a full gallop and leaned into it, working his horse for all the speed it had. The approaching rider was on a black horse. A calm rage welled up in Sammy as he closed the distance between them like a comet across the sky.

"Who is it?" Boothe yelled out, thinking it must be one of his men bringing news. Maybe they'd gotten the padre and his boys. Maybe it was all over already, he hoped. It was the last hundred feet between them before Boothe understood he did not know the man.

Sammy saw the black horse slowing and the man drawing his pistol. Sammy tucked low and spurred his horse again, holding it to the course of his vengeance. He did not hear the shot that missed him just before his horse slammed into the black horse, sending Boothe hurtling from his saddle to the ground where he landed on his back, the impact knocking the air from his lungs and the gun from his hand. Sammy sprung down from his horse and came upon Boothe who had rolled over to his hands and knees and was gasping for breath. Boothe began reaching for his pistol a few feet away when Sammy stepped quickly and swung his right leg, kicking Boothe across his mouth with a blow that knocked Boothe's front teeth out and sent him sprawling.

"Where's my wife and the little girls?" Sammy asked, as he drew and cocked his pistol.

Boothe regained his breath and quickly stood up with his mouth pouring blood that dripped from his beard. "I don't know your wife...or any little girls," came his mumbled reply, heavy with contempt.

Sammy fired, hitting Boothe in the left thigh. Boothe howled his pain into the still morning air.

"Where's my wife!" Sammy shouted, his patience at an end. He fired again, hitting Boothe in the other leg.

Boothe stumbled and collapsed, grunting and snorting with the knowledge he was finished. "She's a dead, goddamn whore! Go to hell with her!" Boothe yelled.

Sammy's breath caught in his chest, followed by a sob. "No!" he cried.

He hung his head and shook for a moment, feeling sick to his stomach. Then his head came up and his eyes fixed on Boothe. He walked quickly to him as Boothe pulled his knife. Sammy's gun hand came up firing. The knife flew from Boothe's grip as half of his hand went with it. Boothe screamed.

Sammy leaned down over him. "Go to hell, you say? Let me show you how to get there." He walked quickly to his horse and got his rope, then tied a noose at one end. He walked back to where Boothe lay and pulled his revolver once again, shooting Boothe through each shoulder joint, making his arms useless. Boothe was in shock and fading quickly from his loss of blood, but was aware enough to feel the noose go around his neck and see the remaining fifty feet coiled near his body. Sammy walked Boothe's black stallion over to where Boothe lay, and then cinched the horse's saddle straps tighter before tying the other end of the rope to the saddle pommel. "So long, shitbucket," Sammy said quietly. He slapped the big black on the rump and yelled, "Heeyahh!" The horse bolted to a dead run and the coiled rope quickly fed out behind it till there was no more. Boothe's body jerked violently as the noose took him at the neck with a snap, and off he went.

Sammy remounted and rode in the line that Boothe had come from, being able to see the tracks in the ever increasing light of the morning. He had not gone far before he caught sight of them from his peripheral vision. Jing Lu and Camille were at the edge of the woods. They had heard the shooting and then seen him coming from the direction of it. They knew it was him but hesitated briefly, not recognizing the horse he rode. When he was closer, no doubt remained and Jing Lu rode forward with Camille's urging. Sammy turned toward them and galloped as he waved his hat and yelled, "Jing Lu! Camille! It's me...Sammy!"

"He reined up to them and immediately asked, "Where's Jenny?"

"She is still there...at the cabin we were at!" Jing Lu blurted, frantically.

"Is she alive?" Sammy asked, his heart in his throat.

"I think so. I think she was alive when we got away."

"There was a rifle shot a little while back," Sammy said. "Do you know what that was?"

"The man that helped us get away got shot by the leader of the bad men. He was going to get Miss Jenny free, too. But then he got shot," Jing Lu hurriedly replied.

"A man helped you?" Sammy asked, surprised.

"Yes, he did!" Camille exclaimed, wanting to be heard, too.

"And he killed all the other bad men there...save for the leader," Jing Lu immediately added.

Hope rose in Sammy's soul. "Take me there now," he said.

Jing Lu looked around, confused. "It is not far from here but I am not sure of the way."

"Follow me," Sammy said, then spurred his horse back toward the line that Boothe had come from.

The sun graced along the treetops as the clear sky became blue of its presence.

"That's him. That's the man that helped us," Jing Lu said, as they finally came upon the cabin where Lucius lay close by in the dirt on his back, his arms outstretched in the position he had fallen.

Sammy glanced at the man, but his mission was singular in purpose as he jumped down from his horse and bounded toward the door of the cabin with his pistol at the ready.

"Mister!" Lucius called weakly to him from his stationary position. Sammy stopped for an instant and looked back, having thought the man was dead. He hadn't moved.

"In time," Sammy replied, and he immediately continued on into the cabin, its door standing open. Three dead men littered the floor, their guns next to them where they had fallen. Great trepidation weighted each step across the room to the closed door of the bedroom. He threw it open. "Oh, God in heaven," he said in a low whisper to himself. She was there, tied to the bed, dried blood matted in her hair and stained upon her dress. Her face was badly bruised and swollen, and her eyes were closed. She had fought in vain against the ropes, her wrists and ankles bleeding and raw of it.

Through the tears that filled his eyes, he saw her breast move as she drew breath. He felt saved in the moment and quickly cut the ropes that bound her, carefully straightening her legs and putting her arms to her side. Then he sat on the bed next to her and touched her face gently. "Jenny...Jenny," he softly called. "Jenny, I'm here. Jenny...open your eyes...please!"

Her eyes opened halfway, unknowing of what was real, the trauma of her experience having brought unconsciousness in escape of the horror. But then she saw him, and her eyes suddenly gleamed of life and hope. "Sammy! Is it you...my darling?"

She reached for him and winced at the pain in her shoulders, then recognized she was still in the cabin of her nightmare. "The man with the beard! He might come back!" she worriedly said.

"He's dead. They're all dead. You're safe now."

She took a slow and deep breath. "Oh, Sammy," she cried. "I love you so much. I want you to know that their leader, Boothe, meant to rape me, but never found the right moment. Thanks be to God. I am all right, husband."

Sammy hugged her and kissed her face. "Yes, thanks be to God."

Jing Lu and Camille appeared at the doorway of the bedroom. "Hello, Miss Jenny," Camille said with great joy in her voice.

Jenny's eyes turned to the door. "Oh, girls! You're safe!" she cried out to them.

They ran to the bed and fell gently upon her.

"You stay with her, girls. Bring the water pitcher from the other room," Sammy said. "I need to see about the man out front for a moment." Jenny's eyes anxiously searched his, unsure. "I'll only be a minute," he said.

Sammy kneeled next to Lucius whose eyes were half open. He could tell that the man was in bad shape. "Who are you, mister?"

"The name is Lucius Hammond. Water, please. I can't move."

Sammy fetched a canteen and poured water in Lucius's mouth, speaking as he did so, "I'm much obliged to you, Mister Hammond, for helpin' those girls and tryin' to help my wife."

Lucius finally turned his head away from the canteen having had his fill. "Don't be. I was here to kill you...but only you."

"Sammy's eyes narrowed. "Why?"

"I'm a hired gun."

"For Lionel Doan?"

Lucius showed a faint smile. "His real name is Rupert Crowder, I reckon. Didn't know he was in the business of killing women and children, too. That put me sideways of the other crew on this." Lucius paused, sucking for air, then continued, "I don't reckon Rupert will quit on you. He'll keep coming. You can find him at a cabin 'bout three miles due west of Two Rock. There's a burned out wagon to the side of it. He's leaving tomorrow." Lucius coughed and gasped for more air. "I'd be obliged if you'd shoot me. I would do it myself but I can't move anything but my head now. Sinned a lot in my life; never planned it that way. Just happened all of itself. Lost my way somewhere. You look to be a young man, Winds. Take care you don't lose your way. Now, I'm askin' you…shoot me. I don't want to lie here dwindling. I got better than three thousand dollars in my pocket. Shoot me and take the money."

Sammy stood up. He realized the man was paralyzed and might lay there for hours before dying. "All right," Sammy agreed. "I believe you found your way again when you helped those girls. I'll dig you a grave and we'll pray for you."

"Obliged," Lucius said.

"Looks like that eagle over there is waitin' to carry you home, Lucius."

Lucius turned his eyes away from Sammy, looking in the direction of where Sammy had looked. He saw the majestic bird floating to the west on the morning breeze. Sammy pulled the trigger.

51

Sammy dug the grave in a clearing where wildflowers grew. They prayed for Lucius and then left, returning to the Sky W before noon. The stop was brief.

"We're goin' on to the Twin T where you'll all stay for now. I have to be gone for a bit…finish this business," Sammy stated as fact. Jenny protested to no avail while Sammy rigged a wagon for their travel. They reached the Twin T mid-afternoon, where the reunion of Jing Lu and Camille with their brothers and father was sweet salvation for them all.

"I just received word yesterday on Westgate Railroad and Lionel Doan," Reuben Taylor said to his brother, Homer, and Sammy as they met in the den of the enormous Twin T ranch house. "It's a paper phantom…a subsidiary of other subsidiaries that all web together with no master entity and no real corporate officers…just fictional names, with the exception of a few real ones that turned out to be dead people. The whole of it seems to be nothing more than an untraceable front for somebody's dealings…all from back East."

Homer shook his head. "It's traceable," he said with venom in his voice. "But on the more pressing front, Sammy, I just spoke with J.P. who returned from La Jara. Your boys are all alive, although Doc Payton says it will be touch and go for Bill and Porter for a few days. Matt's there, too. Seems he got in a gunfight with a stranger at Lupe's Cantina and took two bullets. They're all shot up bad but they're in good hands with Doc. Knuckles and Blaine are with them keeping watch."

"Any word on Jasper and Ben?" Sammy asked.

"No," Reuben replied. "We found Raquel's body in the woods near your place," he said, his voice quavering. "We'll bury her here tomorrow with a proper service. Jacqueline and Lucilla are devastated."

Sammy nodded his head, unable to speak. Jacqueline, Raquel, and Lucilla had all helped raise him. He put his hat on and walked for the door.

"Sammy?" Homer said, confused at his sudden departure.

The young cowboy turned at the door. "I'll be gone a little while. I appreciate you looking after Jenny and Padre and the kids."

"Jacqueline and Lucilla will see that they're well cared for," Homer replied, realizing there was no stopping Sammy from whatever he had on his mind.

"Some of the boys and I will ride with you," Reuben said, grabbing his hat.

"No," came Sammy's flat reply, and he promptly left.

Rupert's assistants were gone, sent to check on what had happened. Boothe had never showed for the rest of his money, and Rupert had no idea of the status of the job. Now, he was more than nervous about it and had told his assistants of another meeting place a day's ride to the north if he should be gone when they returned. His assistants had been gone no more than an hour when Rupert decided to fly the coop. He hastily packed his things and walked out the front door of the cabin into the fading daylight. *Not so bad to camp a night somewhere,* he thought. Better than waiting around for an unexpected surprise, which is what he thought likely as an ever increasing sense of foreboding overcame him in the form of stark fear. He quickly saddled his fine chestnut stallion and arranged his saddlebags. Then he felt a sense of relief as he rode out at a gallop.

The wind in his face was welcome, but quite suddenly carried the unexpected sound of something else. He looked over his shoulder to see a horseman behind him closing the distance in a fierce gallop. In the frozen moment of shock, he recognized it was Sammy Winds. Rupert put the spurs to his horse and rode in flight of the reckoning. Then he felt the lasso fall over him an instant before he was yanked from his saddle, flying straight backwards from it and landing brutally hard, the force of it breaking his tailbone. He didn't bother trying to pull his pistol as Winds was already upon him with a drawn revolver before he had regained his senses. "Don't kill me!" Rupert pleaded. "I have money…lots of money! It's yours!"

"Who do you work for Mister Rupert Crowder? We both know it's not Westgate Railroad…don't we?"

Rupert was shocked that Winds used his real name, knowing he'd been sold out. "I can't tell you anything."

"I'll kill you if you don't."

Rupert looked down and paused a moment. Then he heard Sammy's gun cock.

"His name is Lambmorton…Sheldon Lambmorton," Rupert said, defeated.

"Did you say Lambmorton?" Sammy asked, unsure of Rupert's mumbling.

"Yes."

"Where do I find him?"

"He moves around."

"Where is he right now?"

Rupert's eyes met Sammy's. "Taos...but you must understand...he will not relent unless I arrange it. I'm the only one that can save you!"

"I got an idea. I'm the only one that can save me," Sammy said, then he pulled the trigger. Sammy found seven thousand dollars in Rupert's saddlebags. A moment later, he was riding north.

Two nights later, Sheldon Lambmorton smoked a fine cigar and sipped his expensive brandy, having just finished a delightful meal of succulent pork, sweet potatoes, fried okra, and apple pie. The dishes were still on his desk. He preferred to take his meals in the privacy of his office where he could eat like the hog he was, ravishing the triple portions in a manner he had grown very comfortably accustomed to. He burped loudly and enjoyed another sip of brandy, wondering of the lateness of the maidservant to collect the dishes.

The reserved knock came at the door. "Come," he said with the authoritative tone of a king.

Lambmorton was looking to the beautiful wall clock near the window when the door opened. "Mister Lambmorton?" came the question from a voice foreign to him.

Lambmorton's head turned quickly to see Sammy walking toward him. "Who are you? How did you get in here?" Lambmorton queried with impatient, unrestrained arrogance.

"Why, I knocked on the door, and you said, 'Come,'" Sammy replied with a tinge of sarcasm. "I am here on behalf of Rupert Crowder who wished me to relay an important message concerning the dissolution of his latest endeavor."

Lambmorton squirmed slightly in his chair, suddenly wary of the discrepancy between the cowboy-like appearance of the man and the manner in which he spoke. He cleared his throat. "What is the message, Mister...?"

"Mister Winds...Sammy Winds," Sammy replied as he drew his .44 in a blaze of speed and pointed it at Lambmorton's head. "The message is that your scheming days are over. Now, fat man, tell me who you work for." The beads of sweat appeared instantly on Lambmorton's forehead as recognition of the cowboy's name came to him. Sammy stepped around behind Lambmorton's desk to where he sat, noticing from his new proximity that the safe behind Lambmorton's desk was slightly ajar. He switched the gun to his left hand and pulled out his knife, putting it to Lambmorton's throat. "I asked you a question. Who do you work for? Who's behind Westgate Railroad and the rest of this charade?"

"I don't know what you're talking about. I work for no one."

"What's in the safe?"

Lambmorton panicked, realizing it wasn't locked. "There is no money in it," he answered calmly, knowing the truth of his statement.

"That's not what I'm interested in."

Lambmorton supposed that the man could be reasoned with. He was a cowboy after all, nothing more, and certainly nothing like the killers who he knew. This man was not brusque and made no threats. *Winds was out of his depth*, Lambmorton thought. He decided to imply harm to scare him off. "See, here, Mister Winds. My power is beyond your understanding. Take my advice and leave here now...lest you may end up dead."

"You've already tried that," Sammy replied, and he drove the knife into Lambmorton's throat to the hilt, then pulled it out and stabbed him directly in the heart. Sammy moved quickly to the door and locked it, then removed papers from the safe and Lambmorton's desk, stuffing them into an office satchel before he slipped out the window and dropped into the darkness of the alley below. Then he was gone.

Autumn leaves of gold and red drifted on the breeze of changing seasons as the distinguished gentleman walked to his coach near the Potomac River. "Good afternoon, Senator," the curb attendant said with dignified respect, as he nodded his head in a slight bow and opened the coach door for the gentleman. Senator Wilkinson boarded and promptly rapped his gold-headed cane on the floorboard, signaling the driver to depart.

"Home, Marcus," he called.

"Yes, sir," came the obedient reply.

As the coach rolled along the avenue, the richest gentleman of the United States Senate pondered the last few telegrams that had come from Lambmorton. They were not in code and had simple statements, the first being "All is well," and the next two reporting, "Everything moving along as planned." Of course, the senator knew that all could not be well, but he knew not that his own identity had been disclosed in receiving them.

The papers from Lambmorton's safe had included coded telegrams showing the origin of them to be from the State Street Telegraph Office in Washington D.C. with a respondent's name of Mister Steven Byrne. Also pulled from Lambmorton's desk was an outbound telegram of code that consisted of letters and numbers, addressed to Mister Byrne at the State Street Telegraph Office, with the notation "For pick up."

Having been raised in New York City, the Taylor brothers had contacts back East and quickly moved to have the Washington telegraph office staked out. It was not many days before an older man of modest dress showed up. "Telegram for Mister Byrne?" he asked at the window, only to be overheard. But the stake out man was unable to keep up with the elaborate delivery method that ensued, and so it was on the third pick up that enough people were in place to follow the route of the telegram, eventually uncovering who the true recipient was.

The coach had been in route for half an hour, rolling into a rural and posh neighborhood of mansions, when the older man on horseback wearing a long cape rode up alongside of the carriage and peered in. "Good day, Senator Wilkinson," he said.

The senator was mildly startled at the sudden appearance of the horseman trotting along just outside his carriage window, but quickly noted the stranger was finely dressed and well mounted, and very mature at sixty years or so. "Good afternoon to you, sir," the senator replied.

"Have you recently heard what has been said about killing a snake?" the stranger asked.

The senator was dubious about what the man had just said to him. "Pardon me?" he answered.

"No, I'm afraid I won't. They say you must cut the head off to kill the snake," Reuben Taylor replied, as he pulled the short-barrel shotgun from beneath his cape. He aimed at the senator's head and fired.

The carriage driver was reaching to retrieve the revolver he carried when Reuben fired the second barrel, disintegrating the reins well in front of the driver's hands and scaring the two percherons to a wild gallop. Reuben turned away from the runaway carriage and quickly dropped the shotgun and undid his cape. He galloped several miles to where he had posted another horse, and then rode calmly away on his new mount.

52

He kissed her and held her, and she held him, ever thankful of their blessings this first Thanksgiving at their home. He placed his hand on her stomach. "What will we name him?" Sammy asked.

"What will we name her?" Jenny answered.

Sammy laughed and she laughed with him, happy of her husband's joy and her own. He had been heavy of heart the past three months, his soul troubled of his actions to save her life and end the threat against the Sky W and those who lived there. He kissed her again. "I love you, Missus Winds."

"I love you more, Mister Winds. Now go and be with our guests. I'll never get these pies finished if you stay here any longer. I'll be out in a few minutes."

"Yes, ma'am," he said, and headed for the door.

The afternoon was warm of the Indian summer that had visited on the land for several days. Matt, Knuckles, Porter, Bill, and Roasty sat around a table on the far end of the porch, engaged in a lively game of dominoes. Rory, Jing Lu, Payat, Tobias, and Camille ran in the meadow with Chester the dog, playing a kick ball game. The padre sat in a rocking chair reading a book, but looking up at the action in the meadow or

333

at the domino table every time the sound of exuberance graced the air.

Sammy sat down next to the padre and rolled a smoke. "How are you feeling, Padre?" he asked.

"Very well, Sammy," he replied, smiling. "I have something to tell you. I recently received a letter from the Blessed Sacrament Orphanage in Santa Fe asking if it would be possible for us to accept two more children, a seven-year-old boy named Fernando, and a nine-year-old girl named Rebecca. They are simply overfull there. I have written back to tell them we would be delighted. They will arrive in several weeks, escorted by a Señor Diego. My children are very excited."

"That's great news, Padre. How did they know to contact you?"

"Miss Margaret is acquainted with them and spoke of us to them."

"You know, now that you mention it, I believe I met Señor Diego at Blaine and Margaret's wedding in Santa Fe last month. I'm sorry you were not well enough then to attend. You would have met Señor Diego yourself."

"Yes, I should have liked that very much."

Sammy took a drag of his cigarette and let the smoke drift out. "You know, Blaine and Margaret will be living much closer to us soon. They both took jobs in Cuba. Movin' there the first part of next year."

The padre suddenly had a sly look on his face. "Sammy, you know how you said I should use the money you recently gave me to build a little chapel and perhaps a small schoolhouse...?"

Sammy looked at him, waiting, as he exhaled another drag. "Yeah...? I remember. That ten thousand I lifted off those crooks will build all that and do much, much more. And now that you've got more kids coming, you better start makin' plans for that school…and a proper teacher, too. For that matter, you better start plannin' that chapel, too. I counted eighteen heads last Sunday."

"Well," the padre chuckled, "as it happens, I have written to Miss Margaret asking if she would consider becoming the teacher here. We will have eight children soon, and perhaps more before too long. I offered her thirty dollars a month and ten acres of our land."

Sammy's eyes widened as a smile crept onto his face. "Well? What did she say?"

"She has happily accepted on the condition that it met with your approval, though she will not come until next summer as she has promised the school in Cuba that she would remain with them through the term."

"She doesn't need my approval, but I'm happy she's comin'!" Sammy chimed. "Blaine will be lookin' for work, too, and he's a good hand. I could use another man." Sammy's face quickly lost its momentary joy, and he bowed his head, melancholy with the remembrance of Jasper and Ben. They'd never found their bodies but were sure the two cowhands were dead.

The padre knew his pain. "Sammy…how are *you* getting along?"

"Oh, I'm gettin' along fine," he answered, with little conviction. He paused a moment, then looked at the padre, his eyes moist. "I've got more blessings than I could have ever imagined. But killin' all the men I have throws a heavy shadow. I'd do it all again to protect the people I love, but that doesn't make it go away."

"I understand. I pray for you always, and I know that God loves you."

"Thank you, Padre."

The padre reached out and put his hand on Sammy's shoulder. "Oh, and one more piece of news. I have decided to name the enclave of our home and the soon to be school and chapel. It will be named 'Redemption'."

"Redemption?" Sammy asked.

"Yes," the padre replied knowingly. "All of ours," he said, sweeping his arm to indicate the children and Sammy's men. Then he looked at Sammy with his soft, old eyes. "And most certainly yours, too."

Sammy smiled as he looked out across the meadow. And the children played.

About the Author

Harvey Goodman grew up in Los Angeles and attended the University of Colorado where he studied history and developed a love for western literature and the great outdoors. He visited and worked in some of the West's remotest locations during his years running an oilfield vessel-buildings outfit. Mr. Goodman went on to teach history and coach football, eventually becoming a high school principal, and superintendent of schools.

In his youth, Mr. Goodman excelled as an athlete, being named the MVP of the University of Colorado football team his senior year. He was drafted by the St. Louis Football Cardinals and played in thirty-two NFL games, including the 1976 season for the Denver Broncos. Harvey and his wife, Gabrielle, have three sons and three grandchildren. Harvey and Gabrielle live near Westcliffe, Colorado.